We hope you enjoy this book. Please return or renew it by the due date.

You can renew it at www.norfolk.gov.uk/libraries o by using our free library app.

Otherwise you can phone 0344 800 8020 - please have your library card and PIN ready.

You can sign up for email reminders too.

6/23

FELIX FRANCIS

HANDS DOWN

A DICK FRANCIS NOVEL

**SIMON &
SCHUSTER**

London · New York · Sydney · Toronto · New Delhi

First published in Great Britain by Simon & Schuster UK Ltd, 2022

This paperback edition published 2023

Copyright © Felix Francis, 2022

The right of Felix Francis to be identified as author
of this work has been asserted in accordance with the
Copyright, Designs and Patents Act, 1988.

1 3 5 7 9 10 8 6 4 2

Simon & Schuster UK Ltd
1st Floor
222 Gray's Inn Road
London WC1X 8HB

Simon & Schuster Australia, Sydney
Simon & Schuster India, New Delhi

www.simonandschuster.co.uk
www.simonandschuster.com.au
www.simonandschuster.co.in

A CIP catalogue record for this book is available from the British Library

Paperback ISBN: 978-1-4711-9668-3
eBook ISBN: 978-1-4711-9667-6

Typeset by Palimpsest Book Production Ltd, Falkirk, Stirlingshire
Printed and Bound in the UK using 100% Renewable
Electricity at CPI Group (UK) Ltd

MIX
Paper | Supporting
responsible forestry
FSC
www.fsc.org
FSC® C171272

My thanks go to
Ben Haslam, Middleham racehorse trainer,
David 'Shippy' Ellis, jockeys' agent.

And, as always with my love,
to Debbie.

1

'Sid, it's over.'

'What's over?'

'Our marriage.'

I stared at Marina.

'What on earth do you mean?'

'What I say. There are three of us in this relationship and it's too crowded. So I'm leaving.'

'But I love you.'

'Not as much as you love that!'

Marina pointed at my left hand.

I say 'my left hand' but the reality is that it is someone else's, or at least it was before it was surgically attached to my own forearm below the elbow.

'Don't be ridiculous.'

'I'm not,' she said. 'Ever since that *thing* arrived, I've been shunted down the pecking order and I've had enough. Over the last few years, I've tried my best to love it, but every time you reach out for me with it, I still feel I'm being touched up by a complete stranger, and it makes me shudder.'

I was stunned. What was she talking about? My new left hand was now fully part of me. It might have once been part of someone else but it was now totally mine, and it was a fully integrated part of my own body.

Only then did I spot the suitcase standing behind her.

'You mean you're leaving right now?'

She nodded, choking back tears.

'Darling, please . . .' I took a step towards her, arms outstretched.

'Don't!' She put up her hand, palm facing me, and I stopped. 'I've made my decision. I have to get away. At least for a bit.'

To my ears that sounded a tad more promising than 'it's over'.

'Where are you going?'

'To my parents. My dad's not very well and Mamma could do with some help.' Marina's parents lived in Fryslân, a northern province of the Netherlands.

Both of us knew it was a valid reason for her to go, but also that it was not the main reason.

'What about Saskia?' I asked.

Saskia, or Sassy as she was known, was our nine-year-old daughter.

'I'm taking her with me. I've booked a flight from Heathrow. I'll pick Sassy up from school on the way. I've packed her things.' She pointed down at the suitcase. 'I called Mrs Squire. She said it was okay. There's only a few days left of term anyway.' Mrs Squire was the head teacher of the school in the next village. 'I didn't go into the details. I just said I had to go and look after my father.'

I wasn't sure I liked the idea of Saskia being taken out of the country, but what could I do? Forcing Marina to leave her here with me would be worse. It would mean having to explain too much to her, and to everyone else.

'How long for?' I asked, maybe not wanting to hear the answer.

'I don't know. I'm due some leave from work. A while, certainly.' She paused. 'Then we'll see.'

'Please don't go.' I was now also choking back tears.

'I have to.'

Through the window I could see a white taxi sweep into our driveway.

'At least let me take you to the airport.'

'No, Sid,' Marina said. 'It's better this way. I'll tell Sassy you're busy.'

'Why don't I follow you to the school? To say goodbye.'

'No, Sid,' she said again, more firmly this time. 'I'll call you when we get to Fryslân.'

She then wheeled her suitcase out to the taxi, climbed in and disappeared through the gateway without so much as a backward glance.

I stood there for quite some time staring down the road, perhaps forlornly hoping she would turn the taxi round and come back. But, of course, she didn't.

Had I seen this coming?

I knew things hadn't been perfect between us for the past few months.

When Saskia had turned nine last August, and with no likelihood of a second child on the horizon, Marina had gone back to working four days a week in the Cancer Research UK laboratories in Lincoln's Inn, staying over with a colleague in London on Monday, Tuesday and Wednesday nights and only taking the train out of town to our home near Banbury on Thursday evenings.

I hadn't been very keen on the arrangement and that was putting it mildly. I'd argued that Saskia needed her mother at home every night, to say nothing of how much I needed her too. But Marina was totally committed to her work in trying to develop a single blood test to detect multiple cancers. 'The world has needs too,' she would say. 'Hence, you and Sassy will simply have to share me.'

And she wasn't being arrogant or conceited. She was a major player in an international team of molecular chemists sequencing floating fragments of methylated DNA in the blood as an indicator of a whole range of different cancers, and long before there were any physical symptoms. 'Early detection is the magic key to successful treatment,' she would often say. 'One day, not so far away now, everyone will take a simple blood test and then, if it's positive, swallow an appropriate pill to empower the person's own immune system to kill off those particular cancer cells before they can do any damage. It's the Holy Grail.'

But being separated from her for half of every week had certainly put a strain on our relationship. I'd still thought we would get through it okay, and all would be fine. I had no idea it had got so bad that she would leave me.

I looked down at my left hand.

Was it really to blame?

My real left hand, the one I'd been born with, had been severely injured in a racing fall, so much so that it had totally ceased to function. The fall itself had been easy enough – I had simply rolled off my falling mount onto the turf. It had been the horse jumping the fence behind me that had done the damage. In order to save a few pence, the trainer had fitted it with old racing plates, the lightweight aluminium horseshoes used only in races. The edge of one shoe had been worn down so much that it had become as sharp as a razor, and it had landed slap bang onto my outstretched palm, severing muscles, bones and tendons so badly that a team of plastic surgeons had been unable to rebuild it.

Indeed, they had wanted to amputate my hand there and then but I had insisted they sew everything together as best they could, in the expectation I would regain some use of it over time. But that had been a forlorn hope and my race-riding days were suddenly over for good.

However, the final *coup de grâce* for my by then useless limb had come a couple of years later as a result of the less-than-delicate handiwork of a sadistic villain. He had been trying to compel me to tell him the whereabouts of some incriminating photographic negatives, the location of which I would rather have kept a secret. With his considerable strength, plus the use of an iron poker, he had totally destroyed the surgeons' former repair job and, this time, the medics had had no choice but to remove my hand altogether.

For many years after that, I had been fitted with a fibreglass, steel and plastic myoelectric hand that, while being very sophisticated and top of the range, was no proper substitute for real flesh. Electrical impulses in my forearm could make the prosthetic wrist rotate and the thumb and fingers move, but there had been no sensations involved and hence I could just as easily let a wine glass slip out of my grasp as crush it into a thousand fragments.

When I'd been selected as a possible recipient of a hand transplant, I'd jumped at the opportunity and, for the most part, my new hand had been a life-changing revelation.

But was it now more life-changing than I had expected, or wanted?

Was this new hand of mine really that of an alien being, capable of causing my wife to shudder from its touch? Or was there something more, some compelling other reason? Was my hand simply the excuse?

I'd had my new hand for almost three years.

In many ways I had been fortunate to be offered it. I'd been asked to be part of a research project to start hand transplants in the UK, after some successes with the treatment in France and the United States. But, since my operation, it was now being offered only to those with a double hand amputation.

According to my surgeon, it was something to do with the risk-benefit ratio. There was not only the immediate risk to life of non-essential major surgery, there was also the risk – and the cost – of lifelong anti-rejection medication, something that reduces the patient's immune response, making them more susceptible to possible life-threatening infections such as sepsis and Covid-19, or even simple pneumonia and flu.

The medical number crunchers had decided that the benefit

from gaining a second hand, if you already had one, was not worth the risks. I'm not sure I agreed with them but, so far, I have been happily free of any infection worse than the common cold.

I have seen film of some people born without arms, many of whom can do amazing things using their feet – there is even a professional concert soloist who plays the French horn using the toes on his left foot to control the valves – but there are so many actions that need two hands – actions that most of us take for granted.

You can certainly eat one-handed but you can't cut up your steak. Shoes can go on one-handed but the laces won't get tied. You can hold scissors in one hand, but who holds the thing you are cutting? And as for knotting a tie, zipping up the front of a waterproof jacket, uncorking a bottle of wine or playing the violin, forget it. Even drawing a straight line on paper with a pencil and ruler is bimanual.

Although I had never been able to play the violin, I could now do all the other things once again. Indeed, the day I could tie my own shoelaces, twenty months after my transplant, was the day I realized that my post-surgery physiotherapy was complete.

But was it really worth it?

Did the risk-benefit calculation take into account the fact that one's wife might leave you because she felt she was being touched up by a stranger?

The phone in my pocket rang.

I grabbed at it, thinking it might be Marina having second thoughts, but I didn't recognize the number displayed on the screen.

I answered it anyway.

'Is that Sid Halley?' asked a voice in a rather squeaky northern accent.

'Who wants to know?' I responded in my usual bland manner to cold callers.

'Ah, Sid, it is you. I'd know your voice anywhere.'

'Who is this?' I asked.

'It's Gary. Gary Bremner.'

A name from my past. We had once been jockeys together. Fierce competitors rather than really firm friends.

'Hi, Gary. Long time no see.'

'Too long.' He paused. 'Look, Sid, the thing is, I need your help. I've been watching you ever since . . . well, you know why.'

I did know why. Gary had been riding the horse that had destroyed my hand, but it hadn't been his fault, and we both also knew that.

'So I'm well aware you do that investigating stuff.'

'I used to,' I said, correcting him. 'I'm retired from all that now.'

After the disastrous encounter with the over-sharpened horseshoe had destroyed my racing career, I had spent many years earning a living as a private investigator, first at a London detective agency called Hunt Radnor Associates, and then as a freelance. But that was all in the past.

'Look, Sid, I'm worried,' Gary said, ignoring me. 'Someone's threatening me.'

'Threatening you? How?'

'I can't talk about it over the phone but, to be honest, Sid, I'm shit-scared.'

His voice quivered.

Jump jockeys are a breed apart from the norm. Almost every day, sometimes six or more times, they take their lives in their hands sitting atop half a ton of racehorse galloping at thirty miles per hour over huge obstacles. When the horses fall, as they invariably do at some stage, the jockeys tend to break things – collarbones in particular. If they don't have the courage to get back up on the next horse in the next race, they might as well quit there and then.

In his youth, Gary had been a jockey for more than ten years – never quite the champion but always fairly near the top of the list. He wasn't short of courage but here he was with his voice trembling with fear.

'Can you come and see me?' he said in a rush, his voice now a tone higher.

Gary was a trainer at Middleham in Yorkshire, two hundred miles away.

'Sorry, mate. No way. Like I told you, I'm retired from investigating. Anyway, I have to be at home for family reasons.'

'Come on, Sid. I need to see you. Just to get some advice.'

I sighed. 'Okay. But, if you won't talk on the phone, you'll have to come here.'

'I can't.'

'Why not?'

'I can't leave the yard. I need to be here to look after the horses.'

I thought it was a poor excuse. He could surely leave his horses for a day if he really wanted to. His stable staff could tend to them.

'In that case, Gary,' I said. 'I can't help you.'

There was a little whimper from the other end of the line.

'Please, Sid,' he pleaded.

How could I tell him that I had my problems too? The last thing I wanted was to be two hundred miles away if Marina and Saskia came back.

'No. Not at the moment.'

He hung up abruptly, without even saying goodbye.

I stood staring into space, wondering what that was all about, when the phone suddenly rang again in my hand.

'Look, Gary—'

'Who's Gary?' asked a different voice, one I recognized.

'Oh, hello, Charles. I'm sorry about that, I thought you were someone else.'

'Clearly,' he said. 'Are you okay?'

'Yes. Why?'

'Marina just called me.'

'Oh.'

'Do you fancy a tot of whisky?'

'What? Now? It's not even midday.'

'The sun will be over the yardarm somewhere. I thought you might need one.'

'What did she tell you?'

'Not much. Just that she's gone home to her mother. And she's worried about you.'

That was something, I suppose.

'Come on over. I have a new bottle of single malt for you to try.'

10

I didn't really feel like going. Getting drunk on single malt whisky was hardly going to make things any better in the long run.

'Do I have to come and collect you?' Charles asked in a mock stern tone.

'No, Charles. You do not.' I sighed. 'Okay. Give me about half an hour. I'll come on my bike.'

'Good. I'll be waiting.'

2

Just over an hour later, I rode my aged Raleigh the two miles over the hill to Charles's house at Aynsford, all the while worried that I wouldn't be at home if Marina returned.

But she wouldn't return.

By now she and Saskia would be at Heathrow, waiting for their flight to Amsterdam.

I felt wretched. How could it have come to this?

'I was beginning to think you weren't coming,' Charles said, meeting me at his front door, glass in hand.

'I nearly didn't.'

'But it was an order.'

Charles Roland, retired Royal Naval admiral, was well used to giving orders, and he expected them to be carried out.

My ex-father-in-law from a former marriage to his daughter, he was my muse, my best friend and my mentor, and now, it seemed, also my commanding officer. In his mid-eighties, he had finally started to slow down a bit, not least due to the unwanted attentions of a particularly nasty former Northern Irish terrorist who had fractured his skull while trying unsuccessfully to beat some information out of him.

I followed him across the hallway into his drawing room where he handed me a cut-glass tumbler containing at least three fingers of malt whisky.

'From Dalwhinnie, in the Highlands,' he said, lowering himself into his favourite armchair with his own glass. 'One of my favourites.' He took a sip. 'Now, tell me what's going on.'

'I wish I knew.'

'Is there anyone else?'

I looked across the room at him. The same question had, of course, crossed my mind.

'I don't think so but . . . I don't know. I didn't even see that she was so unhappy with me until it was too late.'

'Is it too late?'

I could feel the emotion building up in me again, with tears welling in my eyes. I turned away. In spite of not being a blood relation, Charles was the nearest I had ever had to a father, my biological one having carelessly fallen to his death from a ladder eight months before I was born. But even Charles would have had difficulty coping with a surrogate son in tears. All those years in the Navy had taught him to keep his upper lip very stiff, and he would expect the same from me.

I gathered myself and turned back.

'I hope it's not too late.'

'What did she say?'

Part of me thought that it was none of his business but, I

suppose, it was. With Marina's family living across the water in Fryslân, Charles had become a surrogate father not only to me but also to her, plus a much-loved honorary grandfather to Saskia. Indeed, just before she'd been born, we had moved out of London to the house in West Oxfordshire just so we could be near him.

'She said I loved my new hand more than I loved her.'

'And do you?'

'Of course not. They're different things. But she said that, whenever I touch her with it, she shudders with revulsion.'

'Oh dear.'

It certainly was *oh dear*.

I slumped down into the armchair facing Charles and took a large swig of the Dalwhinnie malt, enjoying, as always, that first searing heat in the throat as the alcohol descended.

I loved my wife more than anything else in the whole world, with the possible exception of my daughter. But I also adored having two hands again. It made me feel whole and normal after so many years as an oddity – someone who hadn't even been able to join in applause.

Okay, I had to admit the hand wasn't perfect.

For the transplant to occur in the first place the team at Queen Mary's Hospital in Roehampton had had to find a left hand that matched not just my blood group but also the size, colour and hair patterns of my right. Whereas they had done their best, it wasn't like plugging in a new light bulb that matched exactly the one that had blown. There were differences, not least in my skin, where there was an obvious zigzag join in my arm between the real me and the newcomer.

It had taken fifteen hours of surgery to splice everything together. First the two forearm bones were joined with stainless-steel plates at just the right length. Next twenty-three separate tendons needed to be attached with the correct tension balance back to front to allow the hand to operate – too tight at the back and the hand wouldn't close, too tight at the front and it would be a permanently useless clawed fist. Then the multitude of nerves had to be joined, with no convenient colour-coding to show which had to be connected to which. And finally all the blood vessels, arteries and veins, right down to the capillaries, some of them less than half a millimetre across, were sewn together under a microscope using thread much finer than a human hair. Only then could the skin be finally closed. And all of it done at an icy temperature to keep the hand 'fresh'.

One doesn't realize how the human hand does far more than allow you to stick two fingers up at the motorist that cuts you off at a roundabout or indicate that you are 'okay' by touching your thumb to your index finger. A hand has the grasp and strength to swing on a trapeze or to brandish a sword, but also the precision of touch to pick up a stray needle or play Scott Joplin ragtime on the piano. It can be an organ of sight, reading Braille for the blind, and what would sex be without a sensual touch?

Except that Marina hadn't found my touch sensual, at least not with that left hand. Quite the reverse.

I had known that she didn't much like looking at the scars, lumps and bumps on my forearm so I had taken to wearing a thin tubular flesh-coloured bandage, even to bed.

In spite of the surgeon's best efforts, the skin tones were not an exact match, with my new wrist and hand somewhat paler than further up my arm. It was a mixture of strange sensations – the hand felt and behaved like my own, but it didn't quite look the part.

I had to admit that I might have been insensitive to how the differences in appearance may have affected the way Marina regarded it.

Each potential transplant recipient undergoes a series of intense psychological tests to discover if they are a suitable candidate. The whole series of probing questions is designed to reveal any potential future emotional problems. Perhaps they should also submit the patient's partner to the same examination.

'So what are you going to do now?' Charles asked, bringing me back to the present.

'What can I do?' I asked.

'Well, you could go after her to Holland and beg, but I'm not sure it would work, especially if there *is* someone else.'

'It wouldn't work either way.'

Marina was nothing if not stubborn. She would do things only when she was ready, and not because someone else was telling her to. It had been one of the traits that had attracted me to her in the first place, not least because I was exactly the same. But it had caused a few fireworks when we both wanted to do the complete opposite to the other.

Did I really think there was someone else?

Being away in London for three nights every week would certainly have given her the opportunity. Was I even sure that

Sam, the colleague she stayed with, was a Samantha, as she had assured me, and not a Samuel?

What had she said before she left? *There are three of us in this relationship and it's too crowded.* But hadn't she meant that my new hand was the third one, not some other lover?

'So what then?' Charles asked.

'What do you suggest?' I took another hefty gulp of my whisky.

'Well, I wouldn't just sit there on my arse getting drunk and feeling sorry for myself.'

I laughed. 'That's rich. It was your idea for me to come here for a drink in the first place. Indeed, you told me it was an order.'

'To get you here, yes,' he said. 'So that we could devise a strategy and form a detailed plan to defeat the enemy.'

He was clearly getting carried away with memories of past sea battles.

'But Marina is not the enemy,' I pointed out.

'An unknown lover might be.'

Good point, I thought . . . but was attacking another man she loved more than me, if he even existed, the best way to get my wife back? Hardly.

I sat glumly looking at the bottom of my empty glass.

'Marina will do what Marina wants to do,' I said profoundly. 'I simply have to make life with Sid Halley in it more attractive than life without him.'

'And how do you propose to do that?' Charles asked, standing up to pour more Scotch into both our glasses.

'I'm not sure yet. I need to speak to her first to find out what I'm up against.'

Charles nodded, as if agreeing the strategy. Detailed planning would have to wait for the intelligence to be collected.

In the meantime, I continued to sit on my arse, get drunk and feel sorry for myself.

At six o'clock, I cycled a meandering path back over the hill to my house in the village of Nutwell as the late March light was beginning to fail. Only two more days, I thought, and the clocks would go forward and the longer evenings would be here.

Spring had arrived. A time for renewal and rebirth. But would it be a renewal of my marriage or a rebirth of living alone?

'You could always stay the night,' Charles had said as I unsteadily applied cycle clips to my trousers. 'Did you know you can get fined a thousand pounds for being drunk and disorderly in control of a bicycle?'

'I'm sure I'll be okay.' At least, I hoped so.

'I could open another bottle if you like. I have a particularly fine single malt from the Island of Jura.'

All those nights spent in ships' wardrooms had clearly given Charles hollow legs.

'I think I've had enough already, don't you? And anyway, I have to get back to feed the dog.'

And the dog was waiting for me just inside the back door, hungry as always, and not just a little cross that it was well past her usual supper time.

'Good girl, Rosie,' I said, patting her red head. 'Supper time now.'

I went into the kitchen and was suddenly struck by how empty and lonely the place felt. At this time on a normal Friday evening, all the lights would be on, music would play loudly from the built-in speaker system as Marina prepared dinner on the Aga hot-plates, and Saskia would be sitting at the breakfast bar, either reading a book or playing games on her tablet.

But not on this particular Friday.

Today it was all dark and quiet in the kitchen because Marina and Saskia were both in the Netherlands on their way to Fryslân, and who knew when, or even if, they would ever come back.

I turned on the lights, put my hands up over my eyes and leaned down, resting my elbows on the worktop.

What should I do?

Only when Rosie nudged my leg did I realize I still hadn't fed her.

I measured out some dog biscuits from the tin under the stairs and added some of her usual wet food on top, mixing it all together in her bowl with a fork.

'Here you are, Rosie,' I said, putting the bowl on the floor.

Dogs are so unquestioning as long as they're fed. There were no histrionics about where Marina had gone and why, or where was Saskia, although Rosie would normally follow her around the house wherever she went, even to bed.

I wondered if all dogs were as loyal to their owners. Maybe it was just a matter of loving the person that feeds them – except that Saskia never did feed Rosie, it had always somehow been a job for either Marina or me, mostly me.

And dogs, it seemed, were far more accepting of change than human beings. When I'd arrived home from hospital with a new hand, Rosie had given it a couple of quick sniffs and then embraced it without question – if it was attached to me, then that was fine by her, even if it did look a little strange and, no doubt, smelled a bit different too.

I looked at my watch, which, even after the transplant, I continued to wear on my right wrist.

Quarter to seven here, quarter to eight in the Netherlands.

If Marina and Saskia had caught the three o'clock British Airways flight from Heathrow to Amsterdam, as we usually did when visiting her parents, they should soon be at the family home, depending on delays due to immigration, customs or heavy traffic on the motorway going north.

I made myself a strong coffee and tried to sober up a bit. It wouldn't do to be slurring my words if and when Marina called.

My phone rang and I grabbed at it, but it wasn't Marina.

'Hello, Sid,' said a mumbling, squeaky, northern voice.

Gary Bremner.

He too had been drinking, and by the sound of him, he'd had far more than I.

'Hello, Gary,' I said with slight irritation. 'What do you want?'

'I want you, mate,' he slurred. 'Come and sort out my life.'

'I told you to come down here and we would talk.'

'I can't.'

'Why not?' My irritation was rising. I didn't want to miss a call from Marina because I was talking to a drunken Yorkshireman.

'I daren't leave the horses.'

'Why not?' I repeated.

'Because someone will bloody kill them, that's why not.'

He was getting quite agitated.

'Why would anyone do that?' I asked in as civil a tone as I could muster.

'Because they said they would.'

'Who did?'

'If I knew that I wouldn't need the great Sid Halley to find out, now would I? I have to stand guard all the time.'

And being drunk, I thought, wouldn't necessarily add to the horses' security.

'Why don't you call the police?'

'I did, but they told me to eff off, or words to that effect. Said I was making the whole thing up. But I'm not.'

'Did you explain about the threats?'

'Course I did. But they'd been over the phone, hadn't they. No evidence, they said. But it's true. Come on, Sid. I bloody need you here.'

'I'm sorry, Gary. I can't at the moment.'

'Don't you believe me either?'

'It's not that. I just can't leave my home at the moment. Can't your stable staff guard the horses while you come down here?'

'Don't make me laugh.' But he did. 'I don't trust any of those buggers.'

My phone buzzed in my hand, indicating that there was another call waiting.

'Sorry, Gary. I have to go now, but why don't we speak again in the morning, when you've sobered up.'

I disconnected his call and took the other, but that wasn't from Marina either.

'Just wanted to check you got home okay and hadn't fallen off your bike.'

I sighed.

'Thank you, Charles. Yes, I'm home, safe and sound. I'm just waiting now for Marina to call, that's if she does. I think it would be better to let her call me rather than the other way round. I really don't want to annoy her.'

'I'm sure she'll call you,' Charles said, but he didn't sound too convincing.

And she didn't.

I had a restless night alone in the marital bed, waking often and having difficulty each time getting back to sleep. Finally, at half past five, I went downstairs to make myself a coffee.

Rosie was lying on her bed beside the Aga. She opened one eye and watched me, but wisely decided it was far too early to actually get up.

In spite of having passed the vernal equinox, the mornings were still cold and I relished being able to warm both my hands on my coffee cup.

Sensation had been the last thing to return to my new left hand and, one afternoon in my first post-transplant winter, I had suffered from chilblains on my new fingers simply because I hadn't realized they were getting so cold. My surgeon wasn't very happy with me but at least the lack of feeling meant that I hadn't suffered from the pain and itching as a result.

For no particular reason, I flicked on the television in the kitchen to watch the early-morning news and I was stunned by the top story — a racehorse stable fire in Middleham, North Yorkshire, had killed a number of horses.

A reporter in a bright red anorak was shown at the scene, standing in front of several fire engines, their blue lights still flashing brightly in the early-morning twilight. 'According to one eyewitness,' he said into camera, 'the fire broke out shortly after midnight in a barn used to store hay. Many of the horses have been saved but I am informed by the senior police officer present that there have sadly been some equine fatalities. The police are also seriously concerned about the whereabouts of the trainer who was last seen re-entering the burning building in a further attempt to lead his horses to safety. The cause of the fire is, as yet, unknown. Now back to the studio.'

The reporter hadn't mentioned the name of the trainer but I knew who it would be.

Gary Bremner.

I daren't leave the horses . . . because someone will bloody kill them . . .

And, it seemed, they might have killed him too.

3

Marina finally called me just after seven-thirty, my time.

'Are you awake?'

'Of course I am, I've been up since half past five. I couldn't sleep.'

'Oh.' If anything, she seemed disappointed, although I couldn't think why.

'How about you? Did you sleep well?' I asked.

'Not particularly. Sassy insisted on sleeping in my bed.'

I smiled. When Saskia insisted on something there was nothing you could do to deflect her.

'Lucky Sassy.'

'Stop it, Sid.'

'Stop what? You're my wife and I love you. And I want you home.'

'I told you . . .' She tailed off.

'Told me what? That my new hand revolts you? So what do I have to do to get you back, have it cut off again?'

'Don't be silly.'

'I'm not being silly.' I paused. 'I want you back. You are more important to me than anything. Just tell me what I need to do.'

This was not how I wanted or expected the call to go but my emotions were overriding everything else.

'What's got into you?' she asked.

'Nothing. I'm just upset.'

'I'm sorry.'

'It's not just you,' I said. 'It looks like a friend of mine has been killed.'

'Who?'

I told her about the fire at Gary Bremner's stable in Middleham.

'How dreadful.'

'It's much worse than that. He called me last night asking for my help because someone had threatened to kill his horses.'

'Oh my God, Sid. What did you say to him?'

'He was drunk. I told him to sober up and I'd call him in the morning.' I paused. 'But there's obviously no chance of that now.'

'Are you sure he's dead?'

'It just said on the news that the police were seriously concerned about his whereabouts.'

'Then he might be all right.'

'I doubt it. I've watched every bulletin since I first saw it and they're still saying the same thing.'

'Maybe they're wrong.'

I loved the way she looked on the bright side about most things. I just wished she had the same attitude towards my new hand.

'How's your dad?' I asked, changing the subject.

'Not great. His heart is failing and that makes his breathing difficult. And his feet are bad too.'

'His feet?'

'Yes. Something to do with poor circulation. He's in so much pain that he can hardly stand, poor man.'

'I'm so sorry. How's your mum coping?'

'Pretty well, I think. But she gets so cross with him. I've told her that it's not his fault he's unwell but it doesn't seem to make any difference.'

'People deal with their fears in different ways. She must be terrified she'll lose him.'

'Well, she doesn't show it. She's told me twice already she'll be better off when he's gone.'

'Is that likely?'

'At any time, apparently, and my mum's indifferent attitude towards him is driving me crazy.'

She was clearly upset.

'Do you want me to come over?'

'Oh God, Sid, I don't know what I want.'

Did that sound slightly more promising, or maybe not?

'How's Sassy?' I asked, not wanting to push things again. I'd done that already in this call – and far more than I had initially intended.

'Sassy's fine. As always.'

I wanted to ask if she missed me.

'She's gone out with Mamma to help feed the chickens and collect the eggs.'

I smiled again. That was always her favourite thing to do when staying with her grandparents.

'What did you say to her?'

'Nothing. I just told her we were going to stay with Opa and Oma.'

'Did she ask you why I'm not there?'

'I told her you were busy with work and you might come out later.'

'And will I?'

This time there was a very long pause from the other end of the line.

Into the silence, I couldn't help myself. I asked the question that had been burning a huge hole through my brain for the past twenty hours.

'Is there somebody else?'

'What do you mean?'

I sighed.

'You know exactly what I mean. Are you leaving me for somebody else? Is the hand thing just an excuse?'

'Don't be stupid.'

'I'm not being stupid. You spend half of every week away from me. Are you living as another man's lover during that time?'

'Stop it, Sid. You're being ridiculous.'

'Marina, I need to know.'

'In that case . . . no, there isn't anyone else. There, are you happy now?'

Did I believe her?

I suddenly realized that I should never have asked. Would she have told me even if there were? So was I any the wiser? All I had done was further undermine the trust between us.

'I'm going,' she said, clearly angry, and she abruptly hung up.

I berated myself for being such a fool. I had spent most of the past twenty years investigating people, knowing if and when to ask the right telling questions, but here, with my own wife, I had committed the cardinal sin of exposing my own position without getting anything from her in return.

Marina was right, I had been stupid. Really stupid.

My plan to make life with Sid Halley more attractive than life without him had got off to a very poor start, and it was all my own fault.

I watched the eight o'clock BBC news bulletin.

The fire had been pushed to second place in the headlines by the high-profile resignation of a senior member of the cabinet who had been caught on CCTV kissing his secretary but the reporter in the red anorak was still at the scene in Middleham, which was now bathed in bright spring sunshine. Someone had clearly sent up a drone to give an aerial view, and a team of firemen in yellow helmets could be seen damping down the still-smouldering stable yard.

'Three horses are now known to have died in the fire,' said the reporter over pictures of the collapsed roof, 'and the police are very worried about the racehorse trainer Gary Bremner, who hasn't been seen since the early hours of the morning when he was spotted entering the burning building in a failed attempt to save the horses. A full police investigation of the fire, together with the search for human remains, will begin as soon as the fire brigade confirm that it is safe.'

What should I do?

Did I contact the North Yorkshire Police to tell them that Gary Bremner had called me last night, several hours prior to the fire, and told me that someone had threatened to kill his horses?

But, according to Gary, they would already know that. He told me he'd spoken to them about it but they had accused him of making it all up. I wondered what they would be thinking now.

Perhaps I would wait and see what the fire investigation threw up. However, whether it turned out to be an accident or arson, murder or manslaughter, I resolved that I would leave the investigation of it solely to the police. They wouldn't welcome a private individual sticking his nose in, even though I had solved a few cases in the past after the boys in blue had tried and failed dismally.

I took a cup of coffee and a slice of buttered toast through to my office. Investigating wrongdoing might be my passion, and it had been my sole wage-earner in the past, but nowadays it was my dealings on the world's financial markets that paid the ever-increasing gas bills. In spite of it being a Saturday, there were things I needed to do in the run-up to the end of the tax year on 5 April.

Why was it, I wondered, that the UK tax year was so out of step with the calendar one?

I sat at my desk and sent an email authorising my stockbroker to sell some of my portfolio, utilising my annual Capital Gains Tax allowance, and to use the funds to invest my maximum annual permitted amount in an ISA, a tax-free Individual Savings Account. If I left either until after the tax year ended, it would be too late.

But it took me ages. I wasn't paying proper attention and I had to read carefully through the instruction twice, correcting several errors before I sent it.

My mind kept wandering to the two big topics in my head – Gary Bremner and Marina, especially Marina. They circled in my brain, like a pair of hungry hyenas stalking their prey, attacking my concentration whenever I let down my guard, so much so that I finally abandoned any notion of doing any further useful work. I was far too likely to make a mistake, and mistakes in financial dealings were always expensive.

I went back to the kitchen feeling lonely and miserable.

Saturday mornings were usually a highlight of the week. The house would be alive with activity – Saskia doing her music practice on the piano in the sitting room, while Marina would bake bread or cakes in the kitchen, and Rosie would run back and forward between them like a mad dog, never quite sure whether she wanted to be with Sassy, as was usual, or with Marina in the hope of a dropped titbit she could then consume.

Or maybe Marina would ask some of our neighbours to pop round for a coffee, especially Tim and Paula Gaucin and their daughter Annabel, Sassy's best friend from school.

But none of that was happening today.

Instead, Rosie lay on her bed, looking up at me with a questioning expression, as if asking what had happened to her playmates.

Irish setters in general have an unjustified reputation for being stupid dogs but Rosie clearly realized that something wasn't right. At one point, she came over and leaned against my leg, as if wanting to give me some comfort. Aged eight and a half, she was now getting to be quite an old lady in dog years. We'd had two other red setters in her lifetime, one older, one much younger, but they had both died early and Rosie now seemed content to be alone as the centre of attention.

I wondered if Saskia was missing Rosie more than she was missing me? And what would happen to our lovely dog if I couldn't get my family back together again. Never mind Rosie, I suddenly thought. What would happen to me? I would be fifty in a couple of months. What would I do? Was I too old to start again? Oh, God.

I decided I had to stop feeling sorry for myself. There were worse things that could happen, like dying in a fire.

The thought made me reflect on the death of Thomas Cranmer, first Protestant Archbishop of Canterbury under Henry VIII, who, in spite of signing papers recanting his Protestant faith, was later burned at the stake as a heretic by the Catholic Queen Mary. In his final moments, he declared that Protestantism was the only true religion and he should never have signed the recantations, thrusting what he called his 'unworthy' signing hand first into the flames.

Life, and death, is clearly all about hands. That and religion.

Pushing such morbid images aside, I made a cheese and pickle sandwich for my lunch and marvelled, not for the first time, how wonderful it was to be able to spread butter on a piece of bread using my two hands – one holding the knife and the other the bread. With just one, you could find yourself chasing the bread all the way round the kitchen worktop. I knew. I'd done it hundreds of times.

I looked down at my left hand. It was undoubtedly part of me. Could I ever contemplate having it removed again, even to save my marriage?

I ate my sandwich and turned on the television for the BBC lunchtime news.

The Middleham stable fire had been shunted even further down the running order, mostly because there was nothing new to report – the cause of the fire was, as yet, unknown and there was still no sign of Gary Bremner.

Again I wondered if I should call the North Yorkshire police. Maybe later.

I flicked over to a different channel to watch the racing from Doncaster.

Doncaster on this Saturday in late March, or the first in early April, had traditionally always been the first day of the flat-racing season in Britain; but now, in a world driven by gambling, flat racing takes place throughout the winter months on the 'all-weather' sand tracks. But Doncaster is still the first day of the year when the flat horses race on turf, with the Lincoln Handicap being the feature race, and the TV station was making a big deal of it.

Before the racing started, they included a segment about the fire in Middleham, the glum-faced presenters paying tribute to the ex-jockey turned trainer Gary Bremner, emphasising the fact that it was assumed he had died a hero's death trying to save his horses.

They also named the three horses known to have died, one of which, Kicking Rupert, I'd heard of as it had finished second in the Cheltenham Gold Cup just two weeks previously. A big bold grey, much loved by the racing public, it had been Gary's best horse. Such a waste.

My phone rang and I grabbed it in the hope it would be Marina. It wasn't.

'So now do you believe me?' said a squeaky northern voice.

4

On Sunday morning, having dropped Rosie off at Charles's house, I drove the two hundred miles north to the Yorkshire Dales town of Middleham.

I thought back to the very strange telephone conversation I'd had with Gary Bremner the previous afternoon.

'So now do you believe me?' he'd said.

It was quite a shock but I kept my voice calm.

'The police think you're dead.'

'And it's better for me if they go on thinking that.'

'Why?'

'Because then they might investigate who killed my horses.'

'Surely they'll investigate that anyway, if the fire was arson.'

He'd laughed. 'They won't prove that. We're not dealing with bloody amateurs here. There'll be no incriminating empty petrol can or an open box of firelighters. Someone will have just tossed a burning match or a lit cigarette into the hay store and whoosh, up it goes. You watch. It will be concluded that the fire was accidental

– they'll say that either one of my stupid staff was smoking where he shouldn't have been, or even that the hay spontaneously combusted. It can, you know, if it's not been properly dried.'

I did know. Farmers are always being warned about the fire risk but that was usually in freshly cut hay, not in March.

'So what are you going to do?'

'Lie low for a bit. But I still need you here.'

'Where's here?'

'Never you mind. If you don't know where I am, you can't be accused of withholding the information from the police.'

But should I tell them he was alive? I did know that. And they could probably trace his whereabouts from his phone signal.

'What about the other horses? Those that survived.'

'What about them?'

'Don't you need to look after them?'

He'd laughed again. 'And where do you think I should do that? Have you seen the remains of my yard? They'll all have to go somewhere else – probably already have. My fellow Middleham trainers will have probably been swarming round them all day like bees round a honey pot, trying to poach them for themselves. Especially as they all think I'm dead.'

'But surely you'd get them all back when you reappear.'

There had been a pause.

'I'm not really sure I want them back. Not now.'

'So what do you want?'

'To nail the bastards who did this. Nail them good and proper, preferably to a fence post and then leave them there to rot.'

I thought back to that former Northern Irish terrorist that

Charles and I had had some unfortunate dealings with in the past, a man who'd had a penchant for nailing people to the floor and leaving them there to die of thirst. I shivered just thinking about it.

'Do you have any idea at all who the bastards are?' I asked Gary.

'I'll tell you when you get here.'

'You seem very sure that I'll come.'

'Course you'll come. Don't you want to find out who killed my horses? The Sid Halley I know wouldn't give up this opportunity.'

Maybe I was no longer the Sid Halley he knew.

After my hand injury forced my retirement from the saddle, I'd been employed by the detective agency only because it had a racing-mad owner.

Deep down, I knew that I'd been offered the job more out of pity for a now-crippled former champion jockey rather than in any expectation of me doing any real detecting. However, with the dramatic intervention of Charles Roland, I had been thrown into a situation where I'd had no choice but to investigate and, furthermore, I'd discovered that I had a flair for it.

Jump jockeys are renowned for accepting risks – without taking them they would never win anything – and that was the same attitude I employed in my pursuit of the wrongdoers, with no real concern for my own safety. So much so that, in fact, I had earned a bit of a reputation. In the criminal underworld it became well known that attacking Sid Halley in an attempt to stop him investigating something would be counterproductive – the harder you hit him, the harder he would come after you.

Only with the arrival of Marina in my life had things begun to change, and that was because the criminals had started hitting her instead. Whereas I could bear injuries to my own body – I had got used to those from racing falls – I couldn't stand by and watch my girlfriend having her head split open.

So I had stopped my investigating and spent my time sitting at a desk, risking only my money rather than my own body, and those of my loved ones.

Only once had I come out of this self-imposed isolation, to deal with the Irish terrorist, and then I had immediately returned to my hermit-like existence. It's what Marina had wanted, at least she had said so, loudly and often. She had constantly urged me to quit my investigating for the safety of her and Saskia.

So I had.

But it had obviously made Sid Halley rather a dull boy, and now Marina had left me. Would a return to the risk-taking, swashbuckling, superman-like Sid Halley, the ultimate symbol of truth, justice and hope, be more attractive to her as a mate?

Only one way to find out.

'All right, I'll come,' I'd said, wondering if I was doing the right thing. 'But I make no promises. If I feel that the police are more appropriate to carry out the investigation, we'll leave it to them, okay?'

'Attaboy.'

I could almost hear his smile coming down the line.

'So how do I find you?'

'How well do you know Middleham?'

'Not at all. I went there a couple of times when I was riding but haven't been since.'

'Come to the marketplace and then take the road signposted towards Coverham. About three-quarters of a mile out of town there's a big pond on your right. It's called Pinker's Pond. You can't miss it. I'll meet you there at noon. What sort of car do you drive?'

'A dark-blue Discovery Sport.'

'With that fancy number plate of yours?'

Several years ago, in a moment of madness, Marina had paid a small fortune to buy me the number plate MYS 1D, and had then spaced the letters illegally to read MY S1D.

'How do you know about that?' I asked.

'Like I said before, I keep my eye on you. That plate's too distinctive. Have you got anything else?'

I'd thought of Marina's car sitting unused on the drive.

'My wife has a grey Skoda. That's if I can find the key.'

'Perfect. Come in that. Park it well off the road near the pond and I'll find you. And don't let anyone see you. Wear a disguise of something. We don't want to put the bastards on the alert, now, do we?'

I'd thought he was being rather overdramatic but here I was, at half past eleven, driving Marina's grey Skoda into Middleham wearing dark glasses and with a cap pulled down over my forehead.

I had found the Skoda key thanks to my Christmas present to Marina – a NeverLoseIt tag, a fancy new electronic tracking device designed to help you find your stuff. She was always losing her car keys, indeed we had permanently lost one of them, so I had given her a bright-red leather key ring with the NeverLoseIt tag included, to ensure we didn't lose the other.

On this occasion, she had left the key ring in the top drawer of her dressing table and the NeverLoseIt app had taken me straight there. I'd been worried that it might have shown the key to be in Fryslân but my fears had been unfounded.

I drove the Skoda past the wide Middleham cobbled marketplace, where there was a Sunday market in full swing, with two lines of brightly coloured stalls and lots of people milling around.

I pulled the cap down even further over my eyes.

The previous evening, I had looked up the town on the internet.

After the Norman invasion of 1066, great swathes of land in the area were given by William the Conqueror to his cousin Alan Rufus and the town itself was included in the Domesday Book, the great survey of England in 1086. But it was the building of Middleham Castle at the end of the twelfth century that put the town properly on the map, and it is still dominated by the medieval castle, although the buildings themselves are mostly ruins today, with no roofs.

The castle and the town became a centre for commerce and politics, especially during the lifetime of King Richard III, who spent many of his teenage years living as a guest at Middleham, and he later acquired the castle for himself by marrying the former owner's daughter.

After Richard's defeat and death in 1485, the castle became the property of the victorious Henry Tudor and remained owned by the Crown until it was sold by James I in 1604 but, by this time, the castle fabric was already in decline.

The first reference I could find of Middleham as a centre for racehorse training dated from 1765 and, nowadays, there were so many stables in and around the town that it was sometimes nicknamed the Newmarket of the North.

I drove past the castle and took Coverham Lane out of the town up the hill, past the training gallops on my right to Pinker's Pond, where I pulled well off the road. For good measure, I drove a little way along a dirt track until the Skoda was partly shielded from view by a row of low trees.

There was no sign of Gary.

I waited.

Noon came and went with still no appearance by the elusive Mr Bremner.

At a quarter to one a battered old Ford Escort pulled up some distance behind me. *At last,* I thought . . . but it wasn't Gary Bremner.

I watched in my rear-view mirror as the occupant got out of his car. He turned away from me to relieve himself before then leaning against the car's rear wing and lighting a cigarette.

I sat and waited some more, beginning to regret having left home so early.

I tried Gary's number but without success: *This person's phone is currently unavailable. Please try again later.*

Eventually, the man behind me finished his cigarette, climbed back into the battered Ford and drove away, leaving me once again on my own.

How much longer should I wait?

By half past one I was getting quite impatient. I was also hungry. I decided that I'd wait for another fifteen minutes. If he wasn't here by then, I'd go and have a look at his burned-out stables, then go home. Maybe I'd also talk to the police.

I dozed a little so I didn't actually see Gary arrive, but he was suddenly opening the Skoda's passenger door and getting in quickly next to me.

'About time too,' I said.

'Sorry, Sid. I couldn't get away.'

'From where?'

'My place.'

'I thought you were lying low.'

'I am. I have a sort of summerhouse shed thing up the top of my garden. Hidden by the trees. I slept in there last night.'

'So why couldn't you get away?'

'Because the Old Bill have been searching my house all morning. I couldn't leave or they'd have seen me.'

'Why have they been searching your house?'

'I dunno. Probably looking for me, especially if they've found no trace of me in the remains of the yard.'

'You're crazy. You have to speak to them.'

'Maybe. But later.'

'Do your family know you're alive?'

'I don't have any family. Emma and I divorced years ago.'

I rather wished he hadn't mentioned divorce.

'How about kids?'

'We had two, a boy and a girl, teenagers they were, but they blamed me for the divorce. They went with Emma and said they never wanted to see me again. And they haven't. That was near on ten years ago now.'

'But they must still be worried.'

'Delighted, more like.' He laughed briefly. 'Most of the time we were married, Emma wanted me to drop dead.'

'Why did the children blame you for the divorce?' I asked.

'Because they caught me fucking a stable girl in the hay barn. Went straight off to grass me up to their mother. Stupid of me, really. Sudden impulse. The girl offered and I accepted, but it was no big deal, not until my kids made it one. But I was fed up with the marriage anyway. Happy to get out of it, if the truth be told. It might have been nice to have kept in touch with the kids, mind, but it doesn't bother me, especially after they were so bloody nasty to me at the time. I say good riddance to all of them.'

How sad. The thought of never seeing my darling Saskia again filled me with dread and horror.

Gary turned his head and looked out of the car windows, as if perhaps checking that Emma and his children weren't out there somewhere looking in.

'So what are you going to do now?' I asked him. 'Rebuild the yard?'

'Maybe. Not sure yet.'

'Were you insured?'

'Oh, yeah. Course. Fully covered for the buildings, and for loss of earnings.'

'How about the horses?'

'Not by me. Not my property. That's up to the owners, but I doubt it. Rupert may have been but not the others. Jumpers are notoriously expensive to insure.'

He glanced down at my left hand.

'I heard you got a new mitt,' he said. 'Does it work?'

I lifted it up and twiddled the fingers.

'So am I forgiven now?'

'I never blamed you. It was an accident.'

'And I could have landed on your face.'

Would that have been worse? Possibly not, provided it hadn't killed me, of course.

'So when are you going to speak to the police?' I asked him.

'Not until after I've spoken to you about something.'

'Okay. Here I am. So what is it you want to talk about?'

He shifted in his seat and looked straight at me.

'Sid, someone is making a mockery of racing.'

'In what way?'

'In all sorts of ways and I seem to be the only one who can see it. That's why they torched my stables. To make me toe the line, but I'm not having it. That's why you need to sort it out before they bump me off altogether. You will, won't you?' He was almost begging and he again looked over his shoulder as if checking that no one was on the back seat listening. He was clearly very frightened.

'Come on, Gary,' I said. 'You'll need to give me more than that. For a start you need to tell me who burned your stables and what else they're doing to make a mockery of racing?'

'I don't know who did it.'

'But you must have some idea.'

He shook his head.

I was slightly exasperated and beginning to think that my journey north had been a total waste of time.

'So who are we hiding from, meeting out here in the wilds of Yorkshire? And who are the bastards you spoke about yesterday?'

He looked at me. 'Agents,' he said finally.

I almost laughed.

'What sort of agents? Estate agents? Secret agents? Was it James Bond who set fire to your stables?'

Now I was laughing, but Gary wasn't.

'Bloody jockeys' agents,' he said seriously and with venom.

In my racing days, jockeys who had agents were a rarity, with most of us booking our own rides or relying on 'our' individual trainer to book them for us. Most of the best riders of the day were 'retained' as a one-stable jockey, as I was. My primary job was to ride the horses from that stable. Only if there were none of 'mine' running would I be free to accept rides from other trainers, perhaps when they had two runners in the same contest, or horses running at more than one racecourse on the same day.

The system might have been thought of as haphazard and disorderly but it worked, not least because, back in those days, the jockey only had to be declared to ride just an hour before the race started. Hence, it was not unusual to pick up a 'chance' ride by arriving at a racecourse early and looking out for a trainer in need.

However, since the advent of computerization and the introduction of rider declaration for jump races at least one day beforehand, such chance rides were now rare and usually only happened because of an on-the-day injury to the declared jockey.

With there being about 90 thousand runners in more than 10 thousand races each year in Great Britain, each of which needs a jockey declared at least one day in advance, and often two, it is no wonder that a better system of matching horses with their riders had to be developed. And it was basically invented by the jockeys' agents.

Of the approximately 450 licensed professional jockeys currently riding, almost 80 per cent now have an agent, including all of the top ones.

Usually invisible, a jockeys' agent rarely, if ever, actually goes to the races. He spends his life on the telephone, constantly calling trainers and owners to find out which of their horses are going to run, and then booking his jockeys to ride them.

Entries are normally made by the trainer five or six days ahead of the race, although for some major fixtures this can be much longer – entries for the Epsom Derby, for example, are made some eighteen months beforehand, when the horses are still unraced yearlings, many of whom may not have even yet been named.

Horses can sometimes be entered for multiple races on the same day. The trainer will then look at the other entries for each of those races before deciding which one to declare the horse to run in, to give it the best chance of winning. Then the agents will call the trainer, offering one of their jockeys to ride it. At least that was how the system was meant to work.

'So what is it about jockeys' agents that upsets you?' I asked.

'They're too damned big for their boots.'

'In what way?'

'Telling me how to do my job, and wanting paying for it too. But I won't bloody pay them.'

Perhaps he should have done.

'So one of these agents burned down your stables because you wouldn't pay him?' It sounded a bit extreme.

'And also because I wouldn't let him tell me where and when my horses are to race and whether they are to win or not.'

Now that was far more serious.

'You don't know the half of it,' Gary said. 'There's a turf war going on over who controls British racing, and not just here in Middleham but all over the country. The bastards are trying to manipulate it for their own financial gain, and it's worth millions, maybe tens of millions a year. It's enough to make your hair curl, but no one else seems to realize what's going on except me.'

5

Gary slipped away from the Skoda in the same furtive manner that he had arrived.

'Where's your car?' I asked him.

'At home, but I'm not using that. Everyone knows my car in Middleham. It's a small place.'

'So how did you get here?'

'How do you think? I came on Shanks's pony. But not on the roads, mind. I used a roundabout route on the footpath through Cover Banks.'

'Can I give you a lift back?' I asked.

'Not bloody likely. I wouldn't be seen dead talking to Sid Halley.'

'But you're already dead.'

He laughed. 'So I am.'

'And what are you going to do about that? You can't stay dead forever.'

'I might for a while longer. Let the bastards sweat a bit, thinking they've killed me.'

'And who exactly are the bastards?'

'That's what I'm wanting you to find out, mate. So we can nail them, good and proper.'

And with that he had gone, disappearing into the undergrowth.

I sat there for a while longer, wondering what to do.

Was Gary right or was he being a fantasist? Could it really be the case that someone was trying to manipulate all of British racing for their own greedy ends? And if so, how could I stop them?

I was quite cross that I'd driven all the way up here and still Gary hadn't told me the names of anyone he suspected.

What should I do now? Simply drive the four hours home again?

I thought about anyone else I knew in Middleham.

In all there were about a dozen trainers based in and around the town, and I knew most of them either personally or by reputation. A few, like Gary, were former jockeys, and one of those, Simon Paulson, had been riding in my era, and we'd shared a number of close battles together.

Surely it couldn't do any harm to pay him a visit.

Simon's stables were in the shadow of the ancient castle, the ruins dark and somewhat intimidating under the leaden sky.

I pulled the Skoda into his yard just after two-thirty, when all should have been quiet. I just hoped he hadn't gone to Doncaster, but that was unlikely as Doncaster on this day was flat racing, and he only trained jumpers. And he surely wouldn't have gone all the way to the jump meeting at Ascot, but I was worried that he might be at the one at Carlisle.

He wasn't.

He opened his front door at my second ring, but didn't seem

too pleased to have his Sunday afternoon slumbers disturbed, and especially not by me.

'Hello, Sid,' he said, rubbing sleep from his eyes. 'Long time no see. What brings you all the way up here? Or shouldn't I ask?'

'Just passing through on my way home,' I lied. 'I was up at Kelso races yesterday.'

'I was there too! Had a winner. But I didn't see you.'

'I was in a corporate box all day, keeping out of the rain.' I smiled. 'Yes, well done with Regal Monarch in the Borders Chase.'

I'd just used my phone to check yesterday's Kelso weather and also the racing results on the *Racing Post* website. Regal Monarch had won easily, in a downpour.

'Yeah, did well, didn't he? That was his fifth straight win in a row.'

He stepped out of the door and closed it behind him. Then he glanced down at my left hand, as everyone did. I was well used to it.

'Now what can I do for you?' he asked, looking back up at my face.

'As I was passing, I thought I'd pop in to see how you are. Is Jackie well?'

He stared at me. 'She left me eighteen months ago.'

Now I hadn't been able to find that out on the internet.

'I'm sorry,' I said. And maybe I knew how he felt – or maybe not.

'Yeah, well. I'm not really that sorry,' Simon said. 'She ran off with an accountant from Leeds. He's welcome to her, and her bloody nagging – eat this, don't drink that. Poor sod. I almost feel sorry for him.'

It started to rain.

'Can I come in?' I asked.

'I'd rather not,' he said. 'It's a bit of a mess in there.'

Clearly no one was nagging him to keep the house tidy either.
We both stood there on his doorstep getting wet.

'Is there somewhere else we could talk?' I asked.

He didn't much look like he wanted to talk to me at all but
the rain was getting harder.

'Come into the yard office.'

He led the way across the gravel, past a small horsebox with
SIMON PAULSON RACING painted on the back, and into a large
barn with a line of stalls laid out on each side and a wide walkway
down the middle. Several of the equine occupants of the stalls
put their heads out over the half-doors to check out the human
arrivals.

'Are you full?' I asked.

'Pretty much. I have a few spare boxes round the back. But
always room for one more if you're thinking of buying?'

I laughed. 'No chance of that.'

'Shame.'

'Have you taken any from the Bremner yard?' I asked him
nonchalantly.

He shook his head. 'I hear that all those that survived have
gone to a place up near Leyburn. Though God knows what will
happen to them eventually.'

We walked down the line of stalls, Simon pausing to stroke
the noses of each of the occupants in turn.

'This is Regal Monarch,' he said as we reached the last horse
on the right, a tall liver chestnut with a proud-looking head.
Simon gently pulled at the animal's ears in affection. 'He seems

to have recovered well from yesterday's exertions. Ate up well last night and again this morning, didn't you, old boy?'

The horse raised and lowered its head as if nodding in agreement.

'I plan to step him up a level and go for the Bet365 Gold Cup at Sandown next month, that's if the going is still soft. He likes the mud.'

I wondered if I should ask Simon if it was his idea to enter the horse at Sandown or was someone telling him to.

'Who owns him?' I asked.

'A local chap called Henry Asquith. Inherited pots of money from the old Yorkshire wool trade. Bit of an eccentric. Mad keen on his racing, but also on history. He's chairman of the castle events committee plus he runs some historical re-enactment society. Spends much of his life fighting past battles, you know, in old uniforms with pikes and muskets. Always pestering for me to allow them to use his horses for the cavalry.' He laughed. 'Can you imagine a Thoroughbred as a cavalry horse? It would cause bloody chaos.' He laughed again. 'Needless to say, I tell him that if he takes one of his horses out of my yard for that, it won't be coming back.'

He led me into his stable office, which was hardly tidy itself with the desk covered in piles of papers, each held down by a dirty coffee cup. Among the detritus there was a large computer monitor adorned with yellow Post-it notes stuck all round the edges. I wondered how he managed to enter his horses in any races from this shambles.

He saw me looking at all the clutter.

'Don't worry. My secretary knows where everything is. She's a wizard.'

I think he meant a witch.

Simon had put on quite a lot of weight since I'd last seen him and he now lowered his considerable bulk gently into a filthy-looking armchair in the corner of the office. I, meanwhile, sat down on the witch's swivel chair by the desk and turned it round to face him.

'Now,' Simon said, looking straight at me, 'Why are you here, Sid? And don't give me any more of that "just passing through" claptrap. Is it about Gary's yard being torched?'

'What do you know about it?'

'Me?' He spread his hands. 'Nothing. How could I?'

'So why did you just say that the yard was *torched* rather than the fire being an accident?' It was the same turn of phrase that Gary Bremner had used.

Simon was flustered. 'I never said that.'

'Yes you did, and it was exactly what you meant. So why?'

His unease deepened considerably.

Maybe my trip north to Middleham was not going to be such a waste of time after all.

'Come on, Simon, if you know something about it, tell me, or else you'll have to tell the police.'

'The police?'

'Yes. The police. Just a quick word from me and they'll be round here faster than a Quarter Horse. I'm sure they take arson very seriously in these parts, especially if it results in murder.'

He wasn't so much flustered now as positively frightened. 'I tell you, I don't know anything about it.'

I didn't believe him.

'Have you been threatened?'

'I think it's time you went,' he said, struggling to get himself out of the armchair.

'Simon,' I said quietly, without moving. 'I'm on your side.'

'And which side, pray, is that?'

He stood close, right in front of me, looking down, but I didn't move, other than to lean back in the chair.

'What are you going to do?' I asked. 'Physically throw me out?'

We both knew he was in no condition to do that. I suspected he had lived on a diet of mostly beer, wine, frozen pizzas and takeaways since his wife left him, and they had taken their toll on his fitness as well as his waistline.

He stepped back.

'Speak to me, Simon.'

'Do you think I'm fucking crazy or something? You've seen what they did to Gary Bremner. It's easier just to pay.'

'Pay who?'

He stared at me again. 'Don't you ever give up?'

'No,' I said, staring back. 'Never. Not when the integrity of racing is at stake. So, tell me, who do you pay?'

He sighed. 'All of them.'

'All of who? The agents?'

He nodded silently as if by not actually speaking the word he wasn't really admitting it.

'How?' I asked.

'How what?'

'How do you pay?'

'How do you think? They send me invoices with their bank details.'

I was surprised. Such payments would be so easy to trace.

'What are you actually paying for?'

'Trainers' premium, they call it. Bloody stealing if you ask me.'

'What's a trainers' premium?'

'It's a ruse the agents have dreamed up to make themselves more money. Like all those clever auctioneers who created what they call the "buyer's premium", so they get paid by both the seller and the buyer. It's daylight bloody robbery but they all do it. And it's legal.'

He was right. The big auction houses nowadays charge both commission to the vendor and a premium to the purchaser, sometimes as much as 25 per cent on top of the hammer price. And it does feel like daylight bloody robbery.

'So how does the trainers' premium work?' I asked.

'Agents are meant to be paid only by the jockeys they represent. Most charge ten per cent of all their jockeys' earnings. A jockey's riding fee for a jump race is now about £200 so that's £20 a ride the jockey has to pay to his agent. Plus the same percentage of any prize money he wins. But some of the agents don't feel that's enough, so they are now charging ten per cent of everything to the trainer as well. They claim they are doing us a service by finding jockeys to ride our horses so we should pay them for it. Bloody cheek. We do them a service by running horses for their jockeys to ride in the first place.'

The age-old question of who is doing whom the favour – the seller or the buyer?

'And what if you don't pay?'

'Then you find you can't book a jockey to ride your runners, or at least not one who's any good. Or worse, your declared jockey simply doesn't turn up, or else has a nasty attack of tummy ache just before the race, leaving you completely in the lurch.'

'But then he wouldn't get paid his fee. Surely it's in his best interest to ride?'

Simon emitted a hollow laugh. 'It is solely in a jockey's best interest to do exactly what his agent tells him to do. Otherwise, he will find himself out of work altogether.'

'But he'd switch agents, surely?'

He shook his head. 'Most of them, the big ones, have all started working as a cartel, at least round here. Cross one and they all stand up in solidarity. Any that won't join the club get forced out altogether. The agents rule the racing roost these days, make no mistake.'

'But every agent has to be licensed by the racing authority. Why don't you complain to them?'

'And have your yard burned down? I don't think so.'

'Is that what they say?'

'Not in so many words, but there is always an implied threat. Gary Bremner was trying to get us all to stand up to them and look what's happened to him.'

'But it must be costing you a fortune.'

'I simply pass it on to the owners. They have to pay for the entries and the riding fees anyway through Weatherbys. I just add the premium to their training-fee invoices. We all do.'

Weatherbys was the private bank that had administered all

payments in British racing since the mid-eighteenth century. Every registered owner, trainer and jockey must have a Weatherbys account and all race entry fees and shares of prize money were automatically deducted or added respectively.

'So it's the unfortunate owners who have to pay?'

'They pay for everything else – race entries, jockeys' fees, transport to the tracks, farriers, even their horses' use of the gallops – they pay for the lot. This is just another cost on top.'

'Don't they complain?'

'Most don't even know it's been added. But no one forces them to own horses. They do it for the love of the sport. And some even make a profit.'

His tone implied that most didn't, especially in jump racing where the prize money was moderate and there were no large stud fees to be earned.

It seemed to me that it was actually the owners who were doing everyone else in racing the favour.

I thought back to my conversation with Gary.

'What else do the jockeys' agents demand?'

'What do you mean?' he asked, but his body language made it quite clear he knew exactly what I meant, and he didn't like it.

'Do you ensure a horse won't win if an agent tells you it must lose?'

'Of course not.'

But it was clear from his demeanour that he did.

I obviously had much to do.

6

By the time I collected Rosie from Charles's place at eight o'clock, she was more than hungry and somewhat angry that her supper had been so delayed.

'Mrs Cross did give her some biscuits,' Charles said, 'but she didn't seem to like them very much.'

'Dog biscuits?' I asked.

'No. Digestives, I think.'

'I hope they weren't chocolate ones. Chocolate is poisonous for dogs.'

Charles looked worried and scuttled off to find out from his housekeeper.

Rosie didn't look like she'd been poisoned as she jumped up at me.

'Plain digestives,' Charles said with relief, returning to the hallway.

'They still contain too much salt,' I said. 'But it's my fault. I didn't expect to be back so late. I'll get her home now for her usual food.'

'Any news from Marina?' Charles asked as I was getting Rosie into the Skoda.

'Not since yesterday morning. I tried to call her on my way south but she didn't pick up.'

Charles pursed his lips. 'I'm so sorry. Is there anything I can do?'

'I don't think so.'

'I'm sure she'll come back.' But he didn't sound sure.

'I don't know,' I said. 'Marina can be very determined. And she won't want to lose face by simply deciding she was wrong to have gone in the first place.'

'Then you had better damn well get yourself over to Holland and fetch her back, or else.'

Charles had always been a keen advocate of gunboat diplomacy.

In truth, I had considered the same thing but decided to bide my time.

It would be hugely counterproductive to arrive unannounced, demanding that Marina come home at the very moment her father was dying. Better to leave it for a while, to see how the old man's condition developed, and to wait until Saskia was homesick for her friends and Marina was thoroughly fed up with her mother's apparent indifference to widowhood.

'I'll give her some more time,' I said, getting into the car.

'Don't leave it too long,' Charles advised through the open window. 'You don't want her getting used to being back there.'

'She won't want to stay there very long. She is far too keen on her job with Cancer Research UK to give that up.'

Even if she gives me up, I thought miserably.

'Come again soon,' Charles said. 'I have plenty more single malt in the cellar and it's in danger of outliving me.' He laughed but we both knew it was true. His health had declined appreciably in the three years since our run-in with the terrorist and his previously ramrod-straight back was definitely now showing a bit of a stoop.

He waved me away and I drove the two miles back to Nutwell, and to a cold, empty house.

I fed Rosie, who wolfed down her food quickly, as if fearful I might take it away again. But she wasn't the only one who was hungry. I had managed to grab a mediocre ham sandwich at a motorway services on my way south but, apart from that, I'd had nothing to eat all day.

I searched the dark recesses of the fridge but there was precious little to be found. In the end, I simply made myself some scrambled eggs on toast and washed them down with a large glass of red wine. Nice, but hardly glamorous.

I poured myself another glass of wine and thought about what I'd heard earlier. And what I should do about it.

The simple answer was to go to the racing authorities and tell them exactly what was going on, but Simon Paulson had made it perfectly clear to me that he would deny ever telling me anything. And, as he had maintained, the trainers' premium, just like an auctioneer's buyers' premium, was not illegal and I could find nothing in the Rules of Racing that outlawed it either.

Indeed, whereas valet fees are fixed and automatically deducted from a jockey's riding fee by Weatherbys, the rules state quite clearly that an agent's fee is negotiated solely between the jockey and the agent, and payment of such fees is not the business of the authority. And at no place in the rules does it maintain that any agent is forbidden from also charging a fee to the trainer.

However, what I found infinitely more disturbing was Gary Bremner's assertion that the agents were also directing where and when trainers should run their horses, and whether they would then win or not. That was clearly a serious breach of racing's integrity regulations, which could undermine the trust in the sport that is essential for the gambling industry, something that racing depends on for its lifeblood.

But I had no evidence other than the rantings of a man who everyone else believed had been consumed by fire.

I decided that, before I went to the authorities, I would need to find greater corroboration of what Gary had said than just my inferences from Simon Paulson's body language.

I turned on the television to watch the ten o'clock news. The bulletin was dominated by the fallout from the cabinet resignation, with leaders of the opposition parties calling for the Prime Minister to step down as well, amid accusations of cronyism and sleaze. Only right at the end was there a brief mention of the fire in Middleham, with no indication of any human remains being found, or not. Hence, I assumed that Gary Bremner was still lying low and the Old Bill hadn't found him yet in his garden hideaway.

My phone rang and I reached for it, again hoping it was Marina. It wasn't.

'I told you to ensure no one in Middleham saw you,' said an angry squeaky northern voice – one I was getting quite used to.

'No one did.'

'Then how do I know you went to see Simon Paulson after I left you?'

'So how do you?' I asked with surprise.

I had donned the sunglasses and cap again while driving through the town to and from Simon's yard, even though wearing sunglasses to drive on such a dull and miserable day was probably more suspicious than anything.

'Because you were seen there.'

'Who by?'

'I don't know, but someone saw you,' he said 'It's all over social media that Sid Halley was snooping round Middleham this afternoon.'

'The police will trace you if you keep using your phone.'

'No chance. I took the SIM card out.'

'So how are you calling me?'

'It still connects to the internet. I'm using Wi-Fi calling. And I'm logged on to the free guest Wi-Fi from the pub at the back of my garden.'

'I bet they can still trace it.'

'I don't think so, because I've turned all the tracing apps off.'

I wasn't so sure, but did I care? He'd have to show himself sometime. But I was far more concerned about the fact that my presence in Middleham this afternoon was now being advertised on social media. Had Simon Paulson told someone? I thought it most unlikely, but who knows what people do when they are stressed, and Simon had clearly been stressed.

As hard as I'd pushed him, he hadn't admitted to me that a

third party was directing where and when his horses ran. In fact, he had said almost nothing else other than to implore me not to tell anyone about me going to see him. Hence, I believed that it must have been someone different who had seen me. But how?

Simon's stable yard was off the main road behind the seventeenth-century Black Swan Inn. Even its postal address was Back Street.

I tried to remember if anyone had been on the road as I turned in but, even then, I had still been wearing my crude disguise. I'd only removed it as I walked over to Simon's front door.

What had I then been able to see? I scoured my mental image.

The castle. Mysterious and forbidding, it towered over Simon's yard.

Back in the early 1480s, Richard, Duke of Gloucester, king of the castle and also of the rest of England, would have easily been able to look down into Simon's stable yard from the high battlements – except, of course, the yard hadn't been built then.

I reached for my laptop on the kitchen counter and looked up the castle on Wikipedia. Sure enough, it told me that there is a viewing platform high in the turret on the south-east corner, right above the yard. Anyone there would have been easily able to watch as Simon and I walked across from his house to the barn. And I reckoned someone must have, someone who had recognized me, and that someone had then posted the fact on social media. But who? And why?

To be honest, I was a little worried about Simon. He had almost begged me to leave and to tell no one of my visit.

'It would put me in great danger if certain people knew I'd been talking to Sid Halley,' he had said.

'Which certain people are those?' I'd asked, but he resolutely wouldn't say. Instead he had simply ushered me back to my car, then quickly disappeared into his messy house, closing the door firmly behind him.

But now those 'certain people' would surely know.

Did I phone and warn him?

'So what are you going to do?' Gary asked, bringing me back from my drifting mind.

'What do you suggest?'

'Nail the bastards who burned down my yard. If you won't do it, I'm going to have to go to the BHA myself and tell them – not that they'll believe me. I have form. But they would believe you.'

I wasn't so sure about that.

'It would help if you would tell me the names of these bastards.'

There was a long pause.

'Have you ever heard of a man called Anton Valance?'

'No. Who is he?'

'He's a bastard.'

And with that, Gary abruptly hung up.

I reached again for my laptop and typed 'Anton Valance' into the Google search panel, but the only reference was to a Russian abstract artist and I doubted that Gary was referring to him.

A search for any Anton Valances in the UK online telephone directory also produced no useful results.

Any further searches were interrupted by my telephone ringing again and, this time, it *was* Marina.

'How are things?' I asked in as light a tone as possible.

'OK, I suppose.' She paused. 'Well, actually, they're not. I had to take Pa to the hospital in Leeuwarden this afternoon because his breathing was so laboured.'

'Was he admitted?'

'No. They just gave him some oxygen and an injection to stimulate his heart. He improved a bit so they sent him home again. But the doctors weren't very reassuring. It was as if they can't do anything more for him.'

She was in tears.

'I'm so sorry,' I said, wishing I could take her in my arms for comfort.

'Yeah. Me too.'

'Do you want me to come over? Even if only to look after Sassy?'

'Maybe. If Pa gets worse again. I'll call you.'

Now that sounded more hopeful.

'How about your job?' I asked.

'I'm currently reviewing a paper to get it ready for publication and I can do that here, online. They're not expecting me back in the lab for at least two weeks, maybe three.'

Not so hopeful.

'So what have you been up to today?' she asked.

What did I say?

'Not much really. I went to see a couple of old friends. We were all once jockeys together.'

'That's nice. Where do they live?'

She was only making small talk, so that we didn't have to

discuss the elephant in the corner of our rooms. Should I lie to her?

I decided not to.

'Up in North Yorkshire, in Middleham.'

'Wasn't that where that dreadful fire was?'

'Yup.'

There was a brief pause from her end.

'Was that the reason you went?'

'It certainly was.'

Another pause, longer this time.

'And what did you find out?'

'That the fire is extremely suspicious, and also that somebody is trying to seriously undermine the integrity of British racing.'

Yet another pause.

'Then you had better get on and find out who that somebody is.'

7

That Sunday night, I went up the stairs to bed with mixed emotions.

Marina had just given me the green light to carry on investigating the Middleham fire and the other things, so that was good. But I worried that the major switch in her position was simply because she had no intention of ever coming back to me and so it didn't matter to her one jot what I did.

I squeezed the toothpaste from the tube onto my brush, marvelling at the fact that I could now do it easily after so many years of spreading the red-and-white-striped stuff one-handedly all over the bathroom sink. But had this simple dexterity come at a price I couldn't afford?

I looked down and studied my new hand.

Whatever magic the surgeons had weaved in making it move and feel, it still looked somewhat alien to me too. For a start, it had someone else's fingerprints, and also their DNA. Even though I was told by the doctors that the human body regenerates itself all the time, the new cells take their pattern from the old ones they replace, so the DNA doesn't change.

If my left hand were to be cut by a knife and bleed, the blood spilled would have the Sid Halley genetic structure, while the skin cells that might be deposited on the blade would have that of the original donor.

I smiled at the thought of some poor police forensic officer in the future trying to work out why two sets of DNA had been found at a stabbing crime scene when it was known for sure that only one person was injured. A bit like those locked-room lateral-thinking conundrums.

But having a part of me with someone else's DNA was a bit of a challenge, not least because my immune system tended to view this alien intruder as an enemy, rather than as a friend, and would happily destroy it.

Rejection is what it is called and, even though my conscious brain had warmly welcomed my transplanted hand's arrival, my unconscious physiology never gave up the struggle to rid me of it.

To prevent this, I took a daily cocktail of drugs specifically designed to suppress my natural immune system. While they allowed my new hand to be tolerated by the rest of my body, it had the unfortunate side effect that it made me more vulnerable to infections. A common cold could render me sick and in bed for a week, while flu was to be avoided at all costs.

The trick was to balance the giving of just enough of the drugs to prevent rejection of the transplant, while leaving enough residual protection to ward off infectious diseases.

Covid-19 has been particularly dangerous for donor-organ recipients. In the first year of the recent pandemic, some 40 per cent of unvaccinated transplant patients who developed Covid-19 died from the disease, against a mortality rate of less than 2 per cent of infected people in the population as a whole.

Hence, in the first lockdown, Marina, Sassy and I had shielded, keeping ourselves away from absolutely everyone. Since then, I had been jabbed with all sorts of vaccines, and with regular boosters, to try and stave off infections of any kind and, so far, the balance had been pretty good. But I had to remember to take my medication religiously every night. Even leaving it for one day could result in rejection problems, as I knew only too well.

Early on, just after my transplant, I'd been forced to miss taking my daily pills. We had been on our way back home from a holiday in Australia when our flight was delayed for 24 hours at Singapore by an engine fault.

All the passengers were put up in a hotel but I'd only kept a single dose with me and the delay meant the journey would now take two nights. By the time we arrived in London, when I was finally able to retrieve my medication from our checked baggage, my hand had gone bright red and the skin had begun to itch mercilessly.

Thankfully, the damage had not been permanent and my hand had soon recovered, but the experience taught me an important lesson: make sure I had plenty of back-up doses close to hand. Even Marina had taken to keeping some of my pills in her handbag, just in case.

Clinical rejection of my hand had only been one of my problems after the operation. When I'd first woken after fifteen hours of anaesthesia my mind had been like cotton wool and waves of nausea had swept over me. But I could still remember my surgeon, Harry Bryant, also known as Harry the Hands, standing next to the bed asking me to try and move the fingers on my left hand.

Was he crazy? my muddled brain had thought at the time. *I don't have a left hand.*

Except, of course, I now did, and there it was, right next to my head in a sort of sling, pointing upwards, with my new fingers sticking out above the bandages. I remembered looking at those alien sausage-like appendices, stained yellow by an iodine solution, and wondering if I'd done the right thing.

'Can you move them?' Harry the Hands had asked.

For many years, I'd controlled my prosthesis by sending impulses to the muscles in my arm. The electrical signals had been picked up by sensors on the skin and, over time, I had learned to use those nerve messages to rotate the wrist and open and close the fake fingers. But the stimuli I sent to activate the electric motors weren't the ones I had previously used to control my real fingers, those I'd been born with.

So used was I to this indirect control of my mechanical digits, that I now sent the same message to my arm. Needless to say, the new flesh fingers did not budge one iota.

But Harry had been well ahead of me.

'Open and close the fingers on your right hand.'

I had done that. I hadn't even had to think much about it. My brain had just sent the signals and the fingers moved. Easy-peasy.

'Now do the same to both hands simultaneously.'

Both of us had stared at the new fingertips and there had been just the faintest of twitches, nothing substantial but more than enough to satisfy Harry, who smiled broadly.

'Well done. We must have connected something right, anyway. That will do for now. You need to rest.'

He had then departed but, for several hours after, I had marvelled at the slight movement my new fingers could make whenever I wanted them to. And I still marvelled at it three years later.

Those three years had involved months of physiotherapy stimulating not only the reconnecting of the motor nerves but also the sensory ones, to the point where I could now feel the vast majority of the skin surface, and I could pick up, maybe not a needle, but certainly a coin.

However, the rejection issue remained and I would need to continue taking take my immunosuppressant medications for the rest of my life. So I now swallowed the six tablets I took every night to keep my hand intact and made ready for another night alone in my bed.

My main worry at the moment was that I faced a totally different kind of rejection, one that fancy medicines couldn't prevent.

First thing on Monday morning, I went back to my search for Anton Valance.

I could find no trace of anyone of that name involved in British horse racing.

In desperation, I called Toby Jing, a contact I knew vaguely in the integrity section of the BHA, the British Horseracing Authority, but he wasn't particularly happy to speak to me.

'I've told you before, Sid,' he said. 'I have a duty of confidentiality, so I shouldn't be speaking to you at all and certainly not on my work phone.'

'Come on, Toby,' I implored. 'I only want to know if you've ever heard of someone called Anton Valance.'

'I'm very sorry,' he said, not particularly sounding it. 'You must know that there are now very strict regulations concerning the protection of personal data. The damn General Data Protection Regulations now rule my life. So I can't tell you.'

'Even if it means that the integrity of racing is put at risk?'

'How is it at risk?' he asked with concern.

'I don't know yet. That's why I need to find Anton Valance.'

He sighed loudly down the line. 'Sid, I'm afraid I can't help you. Why don't you try the TBG, the Thoroughbred Business Guide? They list almost everyone involved in racing.'

'I've tried that. He's not in there.'

There was a slight pause.

'Then I'm sorry. My hands are totally tied by GDPR. I would be breaking the law if I said anything to you about any individual without their specific, freely given, plainly worded and unambiguous consent.'

It sounded to me like he'd used that excuse many times previously.

'All right, but just do me one thing,' I asked quickly, before he had a chance to disconnect.

'What's that?' There was a degree of suspicion in his tone, and with good reason.

'There is no need for you to say anything. Then you can't be breaking the law. I'm simply going to ask you a question. If the answer is no, then hang up immediately. Here goes. Is Anton Valance a BHA-registered jockeys' agent?'

There was no sound from the other end.

'Are you still there?' I asked.

'Certainly am,' came the reply.

'Okay,' I said. 'Here's another.'

'What's this? Twenty questions?'

'Yes,' I said. 'And if the answer to any of them is no, you hang up and I lose my turn. So here's question number two.' I worked it out carefully in my head. 'Would you say Mr Valance was *un*trustworthy?' I emphasized the 'un'.

Still no sound.

'Okay,' I said again. 'Question three: Has Valance ever been the subject of a BHA investigation?'

I could hear breathing down the line but nothing else.

'So was there an enquiry held of which there is an official record?'

He hung up.

So what had I learned?

Anton Valance was a registered jockeys' agent in spite of not being listed in the TBG, he was considered untrustworthy by the BHA Integrity Department, had been investigated, but had not been found to have broken the Rules of Racing, at least not sufficiently for there to have been an official enquiry. But I still didn't know how to find him.

I tried Gary Bremner's phone.

This person's phone is currently unavailable. Please try again later.

Where did I go from here?

I tried the Racing Administration website but I needed to enter a password to gain access and, as I was not a BHA-registered person, I didn't have one. Damned GDPR. They made life so much more difficult for us private investigators.

I wondered who I could ask to use their password, even though they would know it was against the racing regulations.

Once upon a time, even after I'd retired from riding, my standing in racing as a four-time former champion jockey had been quite high and most honest people would help me out, as they realized the good I was doing in rooting out the dishonest ones. But it had been a long time now since I was a regular on a racecourse and many of my former contacts had either retired or died.

And it didn't help that, three years previously, I'd been questioned on suspicion of child abuse.

The accusation had been without foundation, and was designed to undermine an investigation I was involved with at the time. I had quickly been released without charge but most people forgot that part, only remembering the widespread reporting of the original arrest after my name had been maliciously leaked to the press by the police.

One of my best racecourse sources of both real information and juicy gossip had been a man called Paddy O'Fitch. He'd been a walking encyclopaedia of racing knowledge, but he had finally drunk himself into an early grave the previous year.

And I could hardly ask Simon Paulson. He'd made it perfectly clear that he didn't want me to contact him again – ever!

Even the nature of racing's hierarchy has changed in recent times.

When I'd first started my investigating, racing had been administered under the direct control of the Jockey Club, a private institution dating back to 1750, which, at the time, had been responsible for all rule and disciplinary matters.

New members of this prestigious organisation, many of them with titles, were elected only by the already existing members, but all of them were steeped in racing, either as owners, trainers or amateur riders, although current and former professional jockeys were, and still are, specifically excluded from the club bearing their name.

In the early twenty-first century, the self-electing and largely aristocratic nature of the Jockey Club was considered inappropriate for the body charged with regulating a modern major industry, and so the governance of racing was passed to an independent institution, the British Horseracing Authority.

However, one of the consequences of this change has been that the new chiefs were often career sports administrators who may have come to racing with little or no prior knowledge of our particular sport.

For me, whereas I had once been able to have a quiet word of warning concerning racing's integrity with a senior member of the Jockey Club, many of whom had owned horses I had ridden, I was seen now as just another face in the crowd, and every communication with the powers that be had to be officially logged.

I thought back to what Sid Halley in his investigating heyday would have done.

Whereas subterfuge and evasion might have paid dividends eventually, a full-frontal attack had usually produced results more quickly.

Hence, I resolved to go back to Middleham the following day, to make myself known in full sight, and to ask some difficult questions of anyone and everyone I could find, and at full volume.

8

The six o'clock television news on Monday evening was dominated by a new development from Middleham, one I found even more disturbing than the news of the fire.

Gary Bremner's body had been found, not burned to a crisp as everyone else had thought, but hanging from a tree in the undergrowth at the bottom of his garden. The bulletin showed the Deputy Chief Constable of North Yorkshire Police being interviewed standing in front of a blue tent erected behind him.

'It would appear,' he said, 'that Mr Bremner did not die in the fire at his stables, as has been widely reported over the last two days. At this time, we are treating the death of Mr Bremner as unexplained.'

The news reporter was then shown on camera stating that the authorities seemed to be treating it as a case of suicide. One of his police informants, he explained, had told him that they had found a note near the body. The reporter speculated that the loss of Gary's training yard, and of his best horse, might have affected his state of mind.

I, meanwhile, believed nothing of the sort.

To me, even at a distance of two hundred miles, it had all the hallmarks of a murder made to look like a suicide. But the note was a problem. I hoped that the North Yorkshire Police would give it to a forensic handwriting specialist to compare it against other things Gary had written.

While I was digesting the unwelcome fact that my primary source in Middleham had just been permanently eliminated, my phone rang. Marina's number showed on my caller ID, so I answered it, wondering what I should say to her, but it wasn't actually her on the line.

'Hello, Daddy,' said a nine-year-old voice.

My heart leaped.

'Hello, Sassy, my darling. Are you having a good time?'

'Not really. Opa isn't very well and so I have to be quiet all the time.'

'I know, but are you being chief nurse?'

'I'm trying to, but everyone seems so sad. Mummy's been crying a lot.'

'Darling, it isn't easy for Mummy with her daddy being so unwell. So just be a good girl and look after her for me.'

'Okay,' she said reluctantly. 'But can I come home soon? I'm missing Rosie and it's Annabel's birthday next week. I just *have* to go to her party. And she's getting her own phone as a birthday present.'

Sassy's sarcastic tone was asking the usual question – why couldn't she have a phone? It was a subject that had been discussed very regularly in our household.

'Everyone else has got one,' she would often whine, even though it wasn't true. Marina and I had decided that, at nine, she was still too young, but we were swimming against the tide as more and more of her classmates now had them, and Saskia felt she was being left behind.

'Pleeeeease, Daddy, can I have a phone?'

'No, darling. Not yet. Annabel is older than you. She'll be ten next week. So you will have to wait a little longer.'

And Marina and I had secretly decided that twelve would be the best age, although I sometimes felt that we had almost no chance of putting off the inevitable until then.

'It's not fair,' Sassy moaned.

Life's not fair, I thought. *Lose a hand, gain a new one and then lose your wife. Not fair at all.*

'Can I speak to Mummy, please?'

Marina came on the line.

'How are things?' I asked.

'Not great. I think it's just a matter of waiting for the inevitable.'

'I'm so sorry.'

'How about you?'

'I'm okay. A bit lonely. I miss you and Sassy.'

There was a long pause from the other end, and then a sigh. 'I'm missing you too.'

That was encouraging.

'Have you found out anything more about the Middleham fire?'

'Well,' I said. 'There have been some happenings that you simply won't believe.'

I told her about Gary Bremner being found dead and the police believing he had committed suicide. She was shocked.

'And do *you* think he killed himself?'

'Not for one second. When I saw him on Sunday he was determined to catch the bastards responsible for killing his horses. There's no way he would have just given up.'

'So what are you going to do about it?'

'What do you suggest?' I asked.

'Do you have a client?'

We both knew what she meant. She was asking if anyone was paying me. When I'd done investigating for a living, having a paying client was essential to fill the coffers.

'Only Gary Bremner, and now he's hardly in any position to pay.'

'How about the BHA?'

'No chance. I'm beginning to think I've become *persona non grata* in those quarters.'

No organisation likes to have its failings exposed, especially not by an outsider, and that is exactly what had happened to the BHA when I'd once revealed that the much-heralded head of their security service was, in fact, a villain.

'So this would be another Sid Halley investigation done only for the good of racing rather than for hard cash?' Her tone was full of irony. We had been here before. 'Why don't you just leave it all to the police and the racing authorities?'

'You know why.' I said it slowly and softly.

And she did. Sid Halley had never been one for leaving important things to anyone else. Maybe it was the self-belief, or perhaps a touch of arrogance, that I could do it better than others.

It was part of my make-up, and delegation of duties had never been one of my strongest attributes. Add to that a burning desire to see wrongs righted in the sport I loved, especially when its very future was at risk, and there was no chance of me giving up just because I wasn't being paid.

'Would what I say make any difference?' Marina asked.

Probably not, I thought, but I would still love to have her blessing, for her to be onside. There had been a time when she had found the whole process exciting. She had even nicknamed me 'Sherlock' for a time when we first got together.

'Are you coming home?' I asked, slightly dodging her own question, but her answer to mine might make a difference to my answer to hers.

She sighed. 'I can't at the moment. Mamma can't cope with Pa on her own and the hospital won't take him.'

What, I wondered, would have happened if she hadn't been there?

'How about Elmo? Can't he help?'

Elmo was Marina's elder brother. He'd lived in New York for many years and rarely came over to this side of the Atlantic. He hadn't even made the trip when his little sister had married me.

'He has too many commitments at work to come at the moment.'

As I had half expected, Marina's brother wasn't prepared to drop everything to come and help his mother. Perhaps he'd make it to his father's funeral, I thought, when I believed he really should be coming now to say goodbye.

'Is that house a suitable place for Sassy to be staying at the moment?'

'Not really. She keeps asking me when Opa will get better. I've tried to tell her gently that he might not, but it's hard. Today she asked me if he was going to go to Heaven like Tilly did.'

Tilly had been an Irish setter we had bought after one of our other dogs had been killed on a road. Very sadly, Tilly then died of bloat and a twisted gut aged only one and a half, and it had taken Saskia a long time to get over the loss. So distressed had she been by Tilly's death that she opposed our plans to buy her another puppy, just in case it happened again.

'She has been asking me if she can go to Annabel's birthday party,' I said.

'I know, I heard. She's been asking me the same thing, all the time, and also about her getting a phone.'

Our little girl was nothing if not determined. Just like her parents.

'When is the party?' I asked.

'A week on Saturday.'

'That's still twelve days away. Let's see how things develop.'

'In what way?' she asked.

'I meant with your dad.'

'Oh, yes, of course. And let's see how other things develop too.'

'Right, we will.' I took a breath. 'But, in the meantime, I plan to be off to Middleham in the morning to make some waves. And I'm going to ask Charles to look after Rosie, in case I'm not back in time to feed her.'

'Okay. But, Sid, please be careful.'

So she did care.

*

Very early on Tuesday morning, having dropped Rosie off at Aynsford, this time with a supply of her usual dog biscuits, I drove my dark-blue Land Rover Discovery, complete with distinctive number plate, MY S1D, north from Oxfordshire to the Yorkshire Dales.

To make some waves, I'd said to Marina. But, given the seriousness of the situation, maybe causing a tsunami might be more fitting. So I had to produce an earthquake.

I drove into Middleham just before nine o'clock in the morning and, as always at this time of day, there were several strings of racehorses either making their way through the town to the exercise gallops, or home again afterwards.

At the top end of the town, near the castle, is the fifteenth-century Swine Cross, a set of double-sided steps surmounted by two large blocks, one of which was once the base for a market cross.

I parked nearby and went and stood on the top of the steps.

As the strings of horses passed, I caused my earthquake.

'My name is Sid Halley,' I shouted at all the riders going by, some of whom may have been licensed jockeys with agents. 'Do any of you know someone called Anton Valance? Tell him I want to speak to him about the death of Gary Bremner.'

If that didn't bring him out into the open, nothing would.

However, the first person to arrive was not Mr Valance but a uniformed policeman in a blue-and-yellow-checked patrol car, which screeched to a halt right in front of me.

'Are you Mr Sid Halley?' the policeman asked up to my lofted position through his open window.

'Indeed I am.'

'Then please come down off there. That's a protected historic monument, not a soapbox.'

Did this policeman not know that, back in the Middle Ages, crosses such as this one were used for preaching and making public proclamations, as well as for defining a space of personal sanctuary? Was I not just carrying on a centuries-old tradition, protected from persecution and the law?

However, I decided against arguing the point with this particular officer of the law, and so I came down off the steps.

'Now get in my car,' he said.

'Why?'

'My guv'nor wants to speak to you.'

'Then tell him to come here.'

The policeman looked at me. 'Are you trying to get yourself arrested for causing damage to listed property?'

I got into his car.

'Where are we going?' I asked.

He didn't answer but he soon turned into a driveway. To my right I could see a fire engine with several yellow-helmeted firefighters still moving about in the burned-out remains of a stable yard. We drove past the ugly scene and pulled up some fifty yards further on, in front of what I could only imagine was Gary Bremner's house.

'Round the back,' the policeman said, climbing out.

I followed him down the side of the building and into the rear garden.

The television report had said Gary's body had been found in the undergrowth at the bottom of his garden, but the whole space was overgrown, with the grass looking like it hadn't been cut for many years, probably since his wife and kids departed.

It was strikingly different to the lawns on either side of the driveway at the front, which were immaculate. Clearly, prospective horse owners weren't shown round to this part of the estate.

Standing almost knee-deep among the stinging nettles and dandelions were two men engrossed in conversation. One was wearing a head-to-toe white forensic suit while the other was in black trousers and a blue waterproof jacket. Beyond them in the far left-hand corner was the blue tent I'd seen on the news.

'Wait here,' said the policeman who'd collected me.

I waited while he went to speak to the others and, presently, the man in the blue jacket came over to me.

'Mr Halley, I'm Detective Chief Inspector Williams, North Yorks Police. Thank you for coming to see me.'

'I didn't have much choice in the matter,' I said pointedly, implying I wouldn't be here otherwise. I didn't have any great respect for police officers since they had arrested me on the bogus child-abuse allegations.

But this one ignored the slight.

'I understand that you have been making something of a spectacle of yourself this morning, standing on the Swine Cross in the town centre and shouting randomly at passers-by.'

'No,' I replied. 'Not randomly.'

'So what *have* you been doing?'

'Investigating.'

'Investigating what?' he asked, sticking his chin out towards me.

'Just something. Nothing you need to worry about.'

He wrinkled his nose in displeasure. 'Mr Halley, you should leave all investigating to the police. Do I make myself clear?'

'It's not a police matter,' I said, although it was. 'I am actually looking for someone, and I don't have access to all the data you do. So it seemed logical for me to ask those people who might know where he is, and they were all on horseback. Hence I rose up to their level and had to shout above the sound of the horses' hooves on the road surface. I assure you there was no spectacle.'

'As may be but, nevertheless, there was a complaint of a breach of the peace.'

'Who by?' I asked. 'And why have I then been brought here rather than to a police station? Do detective chief inspectors normally deal with breaches of the peace?'

'You were heard to shout the name Gary Bremner. I am the senior investigating officer in the case of the unexplained death of someone of that name.'

'But, surely,' I said, 'you mean his murder.'

9

Detective Chief Inspector Williams stared at me. 'At the present time, Mr Bremner's death is only being treated as unexplained.'

We were still standing in the overgrown garden of said Mr Bremner's house.

'The news reports imply you lot think it was suicide,' I said in a sceptical tone.

'But you don't?'

'Not for a second. I knew Gary. Have done for decades. He would never kill himself. He had far too much courage.'

'Don't you need courage to kill yourself?' DCI Williams asked, surprised.

'You need far more courage to go on living,' I replied quickly. 'Anyway, why would he?'

'Because he was divorced, estranged from his children, and had now lost his livelihood.'

'Why his livelihood? Stables can be rebuilt.'

'How about his horses that were killed?'

'They weren't his, they belonged to the owners. He just trained them. Horses in yards are always coming and going. Some retire or die, or move to other trainers, and new ones arrive to take their place. And, as for his family, he didn't care much for his ex-wife or his kids anyway.'

'How do you know?'

'He told me.'

'When?'

Ah! What did I say?

If I told him I'd been with Gary on Sunday, or even that I'd spoken to him again on the telephone later that evening, then the detective would have had every right to ask me why I hadn't reported the fact to the police when everyone had believed Gary had perished in the fire during the early hours of Saturday morning.

'Recently,' I said.

'How recently?'

'I spoke to him briefly on Friday afternoon and then again that evening. He called me at my Oxfordshire home on both occasions.'

It was the truth, even if it wasn't the whole truth.

And the police would probably know about those calls by now, I thought, by checking Gary's phone records, at least those calls made when he'd still been using his SIM card. It wasn't called the *Subscriber Identity Module* for nothing.

DCI Williams nodded. So he had known.

'What did you talk about?'

'Various things. Mostly old times. About when we were both riding in races together.'

'What else?'

I'm not sure why I didn't want to tell him about Gary's accusations against jockeys' agents, the threats he'd received, or why he'd been so frightened by them, or the fact that I had known he didn't die in the fire.

Perhaps I was still smarting at having been effectively frogmarched over here from the centre of town. It was not that I didn't trust the police, although that was questionable after the way they had treated me in the past. Or maybe my reticence was due to the Halley arrogance that Marina and I had touched on the previous evening. But did I really think I could do a better job at investigating Gary Bremner's death than this professional investigator?

Maybe not, but my priority was different to his. I was only interested in protecting the good name of British horse racing.

Having newspaper banner headlines describing wrongdoing among BHA-licensed individuals, as would surely happen if I left it to the police, was unlikely to maintain trust in racing as a whole among the betting public. And that trust was essential.

Unlike in the United States, where it is a federal offence to lie to an FBI agent, in the United Kingdom it is not illegal to tell untruths and mislead the police, even though they would like you to think it is. Only if you sign a false sworn statement, or actually lie under oath in court, can you be liable for prosecution for perjury or perverting the course of justice.

'So why do you believe that Gary killed himself?' I asked the detective, dodging his own question. 'Did you actually find a suicide note as the news reports suggest?'

The detective chief inspector pursed his lips in displeasure.

I wondered if it was because I'd asked him the question, or was it perhaps due to the fact that it confirmed he had a mole in his organisation passing on information to the press? I expected the latter.

'And if so,' I went on, 'I hope you've had the handwriting analysed. Because I wouldn't believe it even if I'd seen Gary write it himself.'

'It wasn't handwritten,' said DCI Williams, who was clearly then immediately angry with himself for having said anything at all.

'So where was it?' I asked.

'Typed on his iPhone.'

'But anyone could have keyed that in. You cannot seriously be using that as evidence of suicide. What does the note actually say?'

He stayed silent for a moment, perhaps deciding whether to tell me or not.

'Not much,' he said finally. 'It just said he was sorry but he had lost everything, his stable yard, his wife and his children, and he couldn't go on any longer.'

'But he hadn't lost everything. He still had this house and the stables were fully insured.'

'How do you know that?'

'He told me.'

'So while you two were reminiscing about old times and races you rode in together, he not only told you that he didn't care much for his ex-wife and children, but he also casually slipped into the conversation the fact that his stables were fully insured, and that just one day before they were burned to the ground? Would you call that somewhat suspicious, Mr Halley?'

This whole conversation was getting more awkward by the minute and I was beginning to regret not having told the detective everything in the first place. But I felt I could hardly go back now.

'Why is it suspicious?' I asked.

'Because, if the insurance of his stables was on his mind the day before his stables were destroyed by fire, then I have to ask the question of whether he set them alight himself.'

In truth, after I'd been called by an alive Gary on Saturday afternoon, I had also briefly considered if he had set the fire himself as his way of proving to me that his horses really were in danger, but I had dismissed the notion almost as quickly as I'd thought it. There was no way he would have purposely put his horses at such risk, especially not his star performer, Kicking Rupert, which had died in the blaze.

I shook my head. 'You must be wrong. Why would he do that?'

'To collect the insurance money.' He paused. 'And perhaps the real reason he killed himself is because he couldn't live with the guilt that his little scheme had gone wrong and he'd killed three of the horses, but he didn't want to admit to that in his note.'

We were moving here into the realms of fantasy.

Racehorse trainers are very fond of the horses they train but not to that extent. Thoroughbreds are very delicate creatures, created by centuries of inbreeding in the quest for the ultimate racing machine. They may have strong bodies but they also have very thin legs, designed for speed. Those legs are fragile and every trainer, especially a long-standing jump trainer like Gary, has often experienced the anguish of losing a horse to mortal injury.

The death of a horse, in whatever circumstances, may often be something to cry over, but could it ever be a serious reason for suicide? I thought not, although Richard III, once owner of Middleham Castle down the road, had lost his life due to the lack of a horse to ride after his charger had been killed beneath him at the Battle of Bosworth Field – as William Shakespeare had written in his tragedy, *King Richard the Third*: 'A horse! A horse! My kingdom for a horse!'

'What was used?' I asked.

'For what?'

'To hang him.'

'I can't tell you that.'

So I wasn't the only one withholding information.

'How about his phone?' I asked. 'Have you examined that, other than to read the suicide note?'

'Of course,' the policeman replied with a don't-tell-me-how-to-do-my-job expression. 'And that digital search is ongoing.'

I wondered if, in spite of the SIM being removed, the phone itself would reveal that Gary had made calls to me on Saturday afternoon and Sunday evening. I would soon find out if it did, that was for sure.

'Anything else you need me for?' I asked.

'Not at this time,' the detective replied in true police-speak. 'But I will need your contact details.'

'You already have my phone number. It's on Gary Bremner's phone records.'

He nodded. 'But also I need an address.' He removed a notebook from the pocket of his coat. I gave him my home details and he wrote them down. 'Thames Valley area,' he said, almost under his breath. 'I did two years with them as a traffic cop when I first qualified, before coming north.'

'Why the move?' I asked.

'My wife's from up here. We moved for her to be nearer to her parents.'

My mind drifted to Marina. When her father died, would she want to remain in Fryslân to be nearer to her mother?

'I'll arrange for the constable to take you back to your car, but no more standing on ancient monuments and causing a breach of the peace. Do you understand, Mr Halley?'

'Yes, okay,' I replied, but I actually intended to do a lot more than just make a little noise in the street.

The same policeman took me back to Middleham town centre in the back of his patrol car.

'I wonder where he got the rope?' I asked casually on the way.

'Oh, he didn't use a rope,' the constable replied, lacking the reserve and confidentiality of his chief inspector. 'He hanged himself with his belt.'

Poor Gary, I thought.

But how did anyone hang someone else with a belt if the victim wasn't a willing participant? Human beings are heavy and lifting one high enough to get a suspended belt round the neck was difficult for just one other person, if not totally impossible. Especially if the belt was fairly short, as would have been the case with Gary, because he hadn't put on a huge amount of weight since his riding days.

Did that mean that there had to have been more than one assassin?

But I also knew that some suicides hang themselves without being totally suspended. Serial killer Fred West had killed himself in his prison cell by simply putting a makeshift blanket-strip ligature round his neck, attaching it to a window catchment and sinking to his knees. And the actor and comedian Robin Williams had been found hanging in a seated position with his legs firmly on the floor. He had also used his belt, wedging the far end of it between the door and the frame of his wardrobe.

'Had Mr Bremner been standing on a chair?' I asked, nonchalantly. 'One that he then kicked over?'

The policeman looked at me briefly via his rear-view mirror and, like many people, he couldn't resist telling something that he knew and I didn't.

'He hadn't been standing on anything. He was just slumped face down with the belt tight around his neck. The other end was attached to a tree.'

So Gary could have been strangled first by a third party, who then just hung his body half up by his belt round his neck to make it look like suicide. Surely the police wouldn't be fooled by that. But would they? For my money, they seemed to be giving far too much credence to the existence of the suspect suicide note.

We arrived at my blue Discovery and I extricated myself from the back seat of the constable's car.

'And keep off the Swine Cross,' he ordered.

'I know. Your boss already told me.'

The policeman indicated that I should climb back into my Discovery and drive away. But I decided not to.

'I'm going to visit the castle,' I told him, and I walked off in that direction.

In the fifteenth century, Middleham Castle had been one of the most palatial residences in England but centuries of neglect have left it as just a shell of its former glory – not that the ruins themselves are not still impressive, now under the protection of English Heritage.

I paid my entrance money and spent half an hour wandering around trying to imagine what the place had looked like in its heyday, when grand royal banquets had been prepared in the huge ground-floor kitchen for service in the great hall above.

The massive castle keep, the central stronghold, was thirty-five yards long by twenty-six wide, with its imposing walls still standing to over sixty feet above the surrounding grass apron. That, in turn, had originally been enclosed on all four sides by high outer curtain walls, against which had once been built accommodations, stores, ovens, guardrooms and a chapel. Nowadays, these outer walls remained intact only on the north, west and south sides, having collapsed along half the castle's length on the east.

However, the structure I found most intriguing was the latrine tower set into the centre of the western outer wall, where the several primitive medieval toilet cubicles had once included special chutes to send the human waste out through the wall into the dry moat beyond.

Finally, I took the steep internal stone spiral staircase to the high observation point at the top of the south-east corner of the keep and, sure enough, there was a good view down into Simon Paulson's training yard.

Above me, the sky was darkening with threatening rain clouds so I quickly descended and made my way back to the Discovery.

The policeman had gone but, even so, I decided not to clamber again onto the Swine Cross. Most of the horses were now safely back in their stables anyway, after their morning exertions on the gallops.

I climbed into the vehicle and drove off.

Only as it started to rain and the Land Rover's automatic system turned on the windscreen wipers, did I notice that there was a small piece of yellow paper stuck under the driver's side blade.

I pulled over in at the marketplace to remove it.

The paper was about two inches by one and it had a telephone number scribbled on it in black ink.

I dialled the number. It was answered at the first ring as if someone had been waiting for my call.

'Hello,' said a young male voice.

'I'm Sid Halley,' I said. 'Who is this?'

'You don't need to know that,' came the reply.

'Okay,' I said, 'but why did you want me to call you?'

'I hear that you are looking for Anton Valance?'

'Indeed I am.'

'Why do you want him?'

'You don't need to know that,' I said, echoing his earlier reply to me. 'Not unless you are, indeed, Anton Valance.'

'I am not.'

'So how do I find him?' I asked.

'You don't need to. He'll find you. He knows you're looking for him.'

'How does he know that?'

'Because I told him. I heard you shouting it earlier in the town.'

'So if you've already told him that I'm looking for him, why did you then bother to leave your telephone number under my windscreen wiper?'

There was a slight pause from the other end as if the caller was now sorry he had.

'I just felt I should tell you, that's all.'

'Why?' I asked.

'Look, I don't want to get involved,' he said with obvious concern.

'But you are already involved. You gave me your number.'

'Maybe I shouldn't have done. I was only trying to warn you.'

'Why do I need to be warned?'

'Because Mr Valance is not a very nice man.'

'Well, thank you for the warning but I'm a big boy now,' I said. 'I'm sure I can look after myself.'

'Maybe that's what Gary Bremner also thought,' the young man said, then he hung up.

10

I sat staring at my phone for quite a long while after the man had hung up. If I had his number, surely, even with GDPR and the other privacy regulations, I should be able to find out his name from somewhere.

If he had really wanted to remain anonymous, he had simply to *not* give me his number in the first place. But he had, and he had been trying to warn me. I wondered if my mystery man was up to his neck in trouble but fundamentally on the side of the angels.

What did I do next?

I had dropped Rosie off at Charles's place at Aynsford at a quarter to six this morning and, even though it felt to me like the majority of the day had already passed, the clock on the Discovery's dash stubbornly showed it was only five to eleven. More than an hour, even, to midday.

I checked the horse-racing fixtures app I had on my phone. There were three meetings scheduled for this particular Tuesday:

jumping at Fontwell Park near the South Coast, close to Bognor Regis; an evening floodlit meeting on the all-weather flat track at Wolverhampton; and, finally, an afternoon of jump racing at Catterick Bridge racecourse, just fourteen miles down the road from Middleham, and the first race was due off at 1.50pm.

Perfect.

I decided I would go to the races at Catterick, and make some more waves.

'Hello, Mr Halley,' said the man on the gate to the car park reserved for owners, trainers and jockeys. 'Long time no see.'

I racked my brain to try and remember where I'd seen him before, and what the hell was his name?

'Hello,' I said, failing badly in both departments. 'Please can I come in here?'

'Do you have a pass?' he asked.

'Sorry, no. I forgot it.'

'No problem,' he said. 'Always loved your riding back in the day.' He fleetingly looked over both his shoulders. 'If you promise not to tell, I'll let you in.'

I put a finger to my lips. 'Thanks.'

'And my name's Fred,' he said as I passed him. 'Used to be at Haydock.'

'Thanks, Fred,' I shouted out the window, laughing. He had been so far ahead of me.

There has been horse racing at Catterick since 1783 and it is one of the busiest racecourses in North Yorkshire, with twenty-seven jump and flat meetings spread throughout the year. The first grandstand was built here in 1906 and the same basic structure remains, albeit with considerable modern improvements made within. The old wooden stand roof, with its many gables and painted edge decoration, reminiscent of that used on old railway stations, gives the place a cosy feel and it is no surprise that this course is well renowned for its friendly atmosphere.

I rode at Catterick only twice in my riding career as I was mostly based in the South, but I have happy memories of snatching a last-gasp victory in the North Yorkshire Grand National Chase here on a bitterly cold Thursday in January. Thankfully, the weather on this particular day was considerably warmer and the earlier cloud and rain were giving way to brighter skies and even some watery sunshine.

I parked the car and decided to spend the £15 entry money rather than trying to rely on my old battered jockey's badge, which I had simply kept when I'd retired. At almost fifty, who would I be kidding?

Frankie Dettori may still be racing in his fifties, and Lester Piggott famously rode his last winner in his sixtieth year, but those two, and the other older professional jockeys, tend to ride on the flat where crushing falls week-in week-out are less likely than for their jump-racing counterparts. AP McCoy, champion jump jockey on an unprecedented twenty consecutive occasions, was forty when he finally hung up his racing saddle, and he was considered to be a very senior statesman at the time.

I bought a racecard and studied the horses that would be racing later, taking particular notice of their trainers and declared jockeys. As I had expected, most of the trainers were based in the North with quite a few from Middleham. Indeed, Simon Paulson, the trainer I had been to see on Sunday afternoon, had two runners, one in the first race and another in the fifth.

I don't suppose he, for one, would be pleased to see me.

Tough.

I wandered over towards the weighing room on the end of the grandstand, close to the parade ring. Every trainer and jockey would have to come here at one time or another, the jockeys to change and weigh out for the races, and the trainers to collect their saddles, once weighed, to put on the horses.

The whole place has much changed since my riding days, with a new and larger parade ring, a reconfigured winner's enclosure, and a totally refurbished weighing room with a wide glass frontage so racegoers could actually see the jockeys standing on the scales.

'Nice,' I said to the official at the door, indicating towards the new fancy glass.

'Treated like royalty now, them jockeys are,' he announced with a certain degree of envy detectable in his tone. 'Spanking-new changing rooms with individual power showers, warm-up area, physio room, free café, relaxing area, the lot.'

Not like when I'd started riding, I thought. Back in those days, at some courses, you were lucky if you found an old wooden chair in the changing room to put your day clothes on. The communal showers had been uniformly stark with aged cracked and rust-stained white tiling, while the hot water emanating from them would often only last for the first few races. Refreshments had consisted solely of a drinking-water tap in the gents' loos and a tray of fruitcake squares, universally known as weighing-room cake, put out on a table at the end of the day.

Not that I begrudged the modern jockeys their creature comforts. They put their lives on the line every time they went out to race so why shouldn't they have a comfortable relaxing area and a free café, if and when they got back alive?

It was still nearly an hour and a half until the first race so I leaned on the rail by the new unsaddling area and waited for the participants to arrive.

Just like the trainers, most of the jockeys riding here today were those who worked mainly at the northern English tracks or those in Scotland, and I knew very few of them by sight. It also didn't help that some of the young men riding now hadn't even been born when I'd been forced to retire. The racecard helped a little by having a tiny photograph of each rider printed in it next to the horse they were to ride but, even so, I thought I might have a problem identifying any of them.

When I'd first started riding, jockeys had always travelled to and from the races wearing a suit and tie, to impress their employers – the trainers and the owners. Indeed, the majority of racegoers were also attired in a similar fashion, just like audiences at the London theatres. But, as in so many situations in the twenty-first century, casual and comfortable was now the norm for all, but the jockeys were still fairly easy to spot. For a start, they were generally smaller than the population as a whole, and they mostly carried a holdall slung over their shoulders containing their riding kit, often with their whip sticking out the top.

As the first few early birds started arriving, I stood by the glass door of the weighing room and asked each one in turn if they were represented by Anton Valance. Most just shook their heads and pushed past me into the sanctuary of the changing rooms. One young man, however, stopped and stared at me.

'Weren't you once Sid Halley?' he said.

I smiled. 'I still am.'

'Yeah, of course,' he said with a laugh. 'I just meant—'

'I know. That I was once the *jockey* Sid Halley.'

'The *champion* jockey Sid Halley,' he corrected. 'When I was a boy, my father was always talking about you as being the best ever. So I wanted to be you. Except for . . .'

He tailed off and glanced down at my left hand.

'And now you are being me,' I said, trying to be upbeat and not too conceited.

'I'm not yet the champion,' he said, looking back at my face. 'But I'm doing my best.'

'Well done. I'll look out for you later. What's your name?'

'Peter Minter. But everybody calls me Minty.'

'Well, Minty, how many rides do you have today?'

'Two. One in the first and another in the bumper.'

A bumper was the National Hunt Flat Race, always the last on the card.

'Who booked them for you?' I asked.

'Do you mean the trainers?'

I shook my head. 'No. Who's your agent?'

'Dale Wroxton. From Leeds. He looks after quite a few of us from round here.'

'Not Anton Valance?'

He looked at me quite sharply. 'No.'

'Why not? I hear he's very good.'

'Very good at poaching, you mean.'

'Poaching?'

'He's very good at getting some jocks, especially the younger ones, to switch from whoever acts for them to him. He charges only eight per cent while Dale charges me ten, and some agents even charge twelve.'

Anton Valance could afford to take less from the jockeys, I thought, if he was also charging a 10 per cent trainers' premium.

'Has he tried to poach you?' I asked.

'Several times,' said Minty. 'He works for a company called The Jockeys Stable and they're always leaving leaflets in the jockeys' car park, you know, stuck under the wipers. They also keep sending me emails promising to get me two or three times as many rides, and for all the top trainers. But as my dad always says: "If it sounds too good to be true, it probably is." Anyway, I'm happy with Dale. He knows where I prefer to go and is happy for me to ride for the people I like.'

Good for you, I thought. But it might not make you the champion.

'But the other jockeys,' I said, 'those he does sign, do they seem happy with him?'

'Suppose so. Not my business. You'd better ask them. I have to go now or I'll be late for the first.' And, with that, he disappeared into the changing rooms.

I remained standing there and used my phone to look up The Jockeys Stable on the internet. Sure enough, it was there, but there was still no mention anywhere of someone called Anton Valance.

No wonder I was having so much trouble finding him.

Even on the Companies House website, the name Valance was not listed among the officers of the company, nor among the persons of significant control. My suspicious mind wondered if that was because he preferred to remain in the shadows, like a puppet-master, controlling everyone else with invisible strings.

The next person to arrive was Simon Paulson and, as I had predicted, he wasn't happy to see me. There was a distinct falter in his stride when he realized it was me, but he wasn't alone and, short of veering off at a tangent, he had no choice but to continue towards me.

'Hello, Simon,' I said all cheerily. 'Nice to see you again.'

'Yes, hello, Sid,' he replied somewhat hesitantly. 'It's been a long time.'

Only about forty-eight hours, I thought, but decided not to push the point. Instead I stared at the person Simon was with, a tall man in his mid-seventies, wearing a camel-coloured overcoat, brown leather gloves and a slightly battered brown trilby. Eventually, the message got through.

'Oh yes, sorry,' Simon said, slightly flustered. 'Henry Asquith, this is Sid Halley.'

'Call me Harry,' said the man, holding his gloved right hand out towards me. 'Everyone else does.'

As I shook his hand, his gaze strayed just briefly from my face down to my left side. I suppose I should be used to it by now – but I wasn't.

'Harry is one of my owners,' Simon said in a nervous rush, perhaps remembering that he had already told me about Henry Asquith when I'd visited his yard on Sunday. He was heir to the wool trade and the eccentric battle re-enactment enthusiast. He who wanted to use his racehorses as cavalry chargers.

'Harry has a runner in the first. We're just delivering his colours.'

He held up a set of royal-blue-and-red-halved silks, and a white cap with a red cross.

I looked in the racecard. 'Plantagenet King?'

'That's my boy,' Harry said with obvious pride. 'A sure winner.'

'So it has a real chance?' I asked.

'Always a chance, Sid, always a chance.' Simon said it quickly, with a laugh, and I couldn't read in his demeanour if he thought those particular chances today were good or bad.

I, meanwhile, wondered if the horse would even be running on its merits, to the best of its ability.

11

I found a spot in the old grandstand to watch the first race, a two-mile handicap hurdle of just five runners.

Catterick is a tight, left-handed track of just over nine furlongs round, with a two-furlong chute attached to the far end of the finishing straight. The two-mile start was at the far end of the chute so that the horses jumped three flights of hurdles before passing the winning post for the first time, then had another complete circuit to run with five more flights to the finish.

Unlike flat races, which are almost exclusively started with the horses loaded into a line of special starting stalls, jump races begin with the horses walking or jog-trotting towards a tape. When the starter is satisfied that all are ready, he lowers his flag and releases the tape, usually when the field is still some five or ten paces behind the official start point. Such was the case in this race, with the five coming forward together in a single ragged line.

As the starter dropped his flag, I could see the royal-blue-and-red-halved colours of Plantagenet King being rather slow away compared to the other four, who set off at a tremendous gallop down the hill towards the first flight of hurdles. By the time the five of them passed the grandstand for the first time, Plantagenet King was still in last position, about three or four lengths to the rear of the leader.

As they swung away left-handed to start the final circuit, the horses climbed steeply and, if anything, he fell slightly further behind. By the time they reached the top of the hill, still some seven furlongs from home, he was adrift of the others by a good six lengths.

Catterick has a well-deserved reputation as being a track where it is difficult to make up ground on the opposition. The sharp corners, combined with the fact that it is mostly downhill from the beginning of the back straight all the way to the finish line, mean that frontrunners historically do better here than, say, at Cheltenham or Hexham with their testing final climbs to the winning post.

Based on his previous form, Plantagenet King had started the race as the short-priced bookies' favourite, but I could see, quite early on, that its backers were going to be disappointed.

The jockey did his best, kicking on hard in the final few furlongs and riding a finish for all he was worth, but he had left the horse far too much to do. The damage had been done in the early stages.

He finished second, beaten three-quarters of a length by Peter Minter riding the fifteen-to-one outsider of the five.

I went down from the grandstand and stood by the rail of the winner's enclosure, waiting for the connections of the first three to arrive.

Harry Asquith led his vanquished favourite into the space reserved for the runner-up, his solemn expression in stark contrast to the glee of Peter Minter as he rode into the winner's spot. Minty clearly hadn't been expecting to win and I sceptically wondered if he had been the only jockey not in on the fix, that's if a fix was in fact the case.

I watched as Plantagenet King's jockey slipped down off the horse. He was in deep conversation with Simon Paulson. I couldn't tell if the trainer was reprimanding him for having allowed the others to get too far in front or congratulating him on not winning while giving every appearance of having tried to.

Many of the disgruntled losing punters had also come down to the unsaddling enclosure and some were not at all happy.

'You're a disgrace, Shilstone,' one of them shouted loudly across at him. 'Call yourself a jockey? My old grandmother could have ridden better than that.'

I looked the jockey up in the racecard – Jimmy Shilstone. I'd not heard of him before but he had no weight allowance shown next to his name in the card so he must have ridden at least 75 winners. But this race would not be one of them.

Perhaps I should give him the benefit of the doubt – or perhaps not.

'Well done, Minty,' I called out as Peter Minter hurried past me on his way to weigh in, carrying his saddle on his hip.

He stopped, turned and smiled broadly. 'Thanks, Sid.' He was genuinely pleased by the comment. *Nice kid,* I thought.

Jimmy Shilstone, meanwhile, was not so pleased by my presence.

'Hard luck,' I said, falling into step with him as he too made his way back towards the scales, head down.

'Go away,' he said, without even looking up.

'Who is your agent?' I asked.

This time he did glance up at me. 'And who wants to know?'

'Sid Halley.'

He flinched as if I'd poked him with an electric cattle prod. He may not have recognized my face but he certainly knew my name.

'Fuck off,' he said, more forcibly this time, and he started walking faster.

I stepped in front of him, barring his way in through the weighing-room door. 'Where is Anton Valance?' I hissed. 'Was it him who told you not to win that race, or was it Simon Paulson?'

There was a distinct look of panic in his eyes.

'Don't you care about your riding career?'

'Get out of my way,' he shouted, and the official on the door came to his aid, asking me brusquely to move aside.

'I'll be waiting for you,' I shouted after Shilstone as he rushed into the sanctuary.

I looked in the racecard to see if Jimmy had any more rides today and, sure enough, he had also been declared to ride Simon Paulson's other runner in the fifth race. I reckoned there was no chance of him emerging from the weighing room in the meantime, so I wandered off in search of other prey.

In spite of most of the trainers with runners here being based in the North, a few had made the long trek up from more southerly points. One of those was Clive Beale, who trained in North

Oxfordshire, just a few miles from my house in Nutwell. According to the racecard, he had a runner in the third race called Devil's Own. Even though Clive and I were not close pals ourselves, we had several mutual friends and often saw each other at local Christmas parties and the like. I'd even been to his yard once, when a racing magazine had done a feature on past champion jockeys, and they had wanted some photos of me with horses.

I found him in the hospitality area reserved for the owners and trainers.

Everyone in racing knows that the future of the sport relies on people being prepared to spend their money buying horses, and then also paying for the training of them. Hence the racecourses have realized that their very existence is dependent on looking after the horse owners with complimentary car parking and entry tickets, plus free lunches. The trainers are also feted in the same lordly manner, as it is usually they who choose at which racecourses the horses in their care will run and, who knows, a good lunch and a free glass of wine might make all the difference.

At Catterick the owners and trainers' hospitality areas are in the new Dales Stand, a magnificent two-storey facility built right next to the track and close to the parade ring. The stand also houses the special Winner's Room, where the winning connections are invited to join the racecourse chairman for a celebratory glass of champagne, and a chance to watch a rerun of their victory on television.

Clive was finishing his free lunch in the Wensleydale Room and I blagged my way in to see him, telling the doorman I was his assistant and needed to talk to him about the welfare of our horse.

'Hi, Clive,' I said, sitting down facing him at the same table. 'You're a long way from home.'

'So are you, Sid,' he replied.

He popped the last morsel of steak and kidney pie into his mouth.

'Devil's Own must have a good chance in the third,' I said. 'Otherwise why would you bring him all the way up here?'

'I think he has a very good chance,' he said with a twinkle in his eye. 'But it was actually the owner who insisted I run the horse here rather than at Fontwell. His son is based down the road at Catterick Garrison and he's brought a couple of his army buddies to watch the Devil run. They're downstairs in the owners' bar. Trying to drink it dry, I reckon.'

I laughed. 'Is the owner here too?'

Clive shook his head. 'Never was coming. Lives in Gibraltar. Says it's because it's warmer, but I think it's probably for tax reasons. He owns a kitchen appliance repair company. Made an absolute fortune and now wants to sell up, and there's no Capital Gains Tax in Gib.' He smiled. 'Good news for me, though, because then he'll probably buy more horses.'

I looked in the racecard. The owner of Devil's Own was listed as CWMR Ltd.

'What is CWMR?' I asked. 'It sounds Welsh.'

'That's his company,' Clive said, laughing. 'And it's not Welsh. CWMR stands for Coventry Washing Machine Repair.' He laughed again. 'They even came and fixed my yard washing machine last year, the industrial one I use to wash the horses' rugs. Charged me, mind.'

FELIX FRANCIS

Of course, I thought. You don't make an absolute fortune by giving things away.

I looked again in the racecard. The jockey of Devil's Own was listed as Timothy McKeen.

'Does Timothy McKeen ride for you a lot?' I asked.

'Not really, but he has done so a couple of times. He's not bad.'

'Where's he based?'

'Sheffield, I think. Not sure. He's ridden one or two of mine when I've ventured up north and my regular jocks are otherwise engaged elsewhere. Dave Jenner rides most of mine, that's if he's free, but he's down at Fontwell this afternoon.'

'So how did you book McKeen?' I asked.

'Why? Not thinking of becoming a jockeys' agent, are you?'

'No chance,' I said. 'I was just wondering. The system's changed so much since I was riding.'

'Certainly has. Increasingly the jocks book you rather than the other way round. Or rather their agents do. They call me all the time, first really early in the day to check if I will be declaring, and then again later to book their riders.'

'So who called you to book McKeen?'

'As I said, his agent.'

'Yes, but who is that?' I asked insistently. Maybe a tad too insistently.

Clive looked at me closely across the table. 'What is this, Sid, the Spanish Inquisition?'

I was suddenly worried that Clive, too, had been corrupted, and there was only one way to find out.

'Are you paying a trainers' premium to McKeen's agent for his ride today?'

'No, I'm bloody not. I was asked for one but I refused point-blank.'

'Was that wise?'

He looked slightly worried. 'What do you mean?'

'Has McKeen any other rides here today?'

We both looked through the racecard. Devil's Own was his sole declared ride of the day.

'Is he here yet?' I asked.

'I was assured that he'd be here in good time.'

'Who assured you of that? His agent? The very same man to whom you refused point-blank to pay a trainers' premium? I'd check if I were you. Do you have McKeen's number?'

'I can only contact him through his agent.'

'Then call his agent right now to confirm he's here.'

Clive reached for his phone and dialled, but I could hear it ringing and ringing with no answer. He tried again but with the same result.

'Hopeless,' Clive said. 'He's not picking up.'

'Who is it?' I asked.

'Someone called Anton Valance.'

12

Needless to say, Timothy McKeen never did turn up at Catterick to ride Devil's Own in the third race.

Clive Beale was apoplectic with rage and, when he finally got through to the agent, he was told just that these unfortunate errors very occasionally happen – no apology, no explanation – and that did nothing to assuage his anger.

Fortunately for Clive, I had forewarned him early enough for him to have time to find an alternative rider and to get the stewards' permission for the change, as it was due to circumstances beyond the trainer's control, i.e. the non-arrival of his jockey at the racecourse. This didn't mean, however, that Clive would get away scot-free. He would still be subject to a fine from the authority, as it remained his official responsibility to ensure that the declared rider was present.

In the race itself, to make matters even worse, a fast-finishing Devil's Own was beaten a short head after the replacement jockey mistimed his run for the line, overtaking the eventual winner just a fraction of a second *after* having passed the winning post.

It was all doom and gloom for the owner's son and his well-oiled army mates in the unsaddling enclosure, and Clive could hardly contain himself. He gave the unfortunate jockey a right royal roasting with everyone around able to hear. Certainly, no one anywhere near was left in any doubt that Clive Beale had desperately wanted, and had fully expected, his horse to win.

'What the hell do you think you were doing?' he shouted at the poor lad as he struggled to remove his saddle from the sweating horse. 'You left it far too late. You're a stupid boy.'

At least I was certain that this particular loss was as a result of incompetence rather than from any malicious intent. No jockey of whatever skill level would have been able to purposely engineer a defeat by such a small margin. And, on this occasion, the majority of the crowd seemed quite pleased with the outcome, as it had been the favourite that had undeservedly hung on to win by a whisker.

Eventually the wretched jockey finally managed to undo the girths, pulled his saddle down from the horse's back, and scuttled off towards the refuge of the weighing room with the trainer's sharp reprimands still ringing in his ears.

I intercepted Clive as he made his way back towards the owners and trainers' hospitality area together with the disappointed owner's son and his two army chums.

'Bad luck,' I said to them all.

'That wasn't bad luck,' said one of the young men sourly. 'Just stupidity.'

Clive gathered himself just enough to introduce me.

'I hear you're in the army,' I said.

'Officers in the Royal Lancers,' one of them replied proudly. 'Queen Elizabeths' Own.'

'Lancers?' I said. 'Surely you don't fight with lances?'

'We did once, on horseback, but now we're mechanised,' said another. 'Reconnaissance light tanks. But we're still considered to be cavalry.'

'Death or Glory,' boldly claimed the third loudly, even if his words were slightly slurred.

No glory today in that race, I thought. But, thankfully, no death either.

The trio went on towards the owners' bar, while I managed to steer Clive away for a quiet word.

'So, next time, will you pay the trainers' premium?' I asked him.

He stopped and stared at me. 'No, I bloody won't. Why should I pay anything to some jumped-up bullies who do nothing for racing except bleed it dry? I hate the agents.'

So say all the bosses of every football club too, I thought, but it wasn't going to make them go away from that sport either.

'How could someone have deliberately left me in the lurch like that? We'd all be in a mess if booked jockeys don't turn up when they are supposed to.'

'You should count yourself lucky,' I said. 'They burned down Gary Bremner's stable yard when he wouldn't pay.'

'What!' Clive was truly shocked. 'Is that why he killed himself?'

'That's if he actually did kill himself,' I replied. 'And I have serious doubts about that.'

Clive was shocked again.

'So what are you going to do about it?' he asked.

'Me? Why should I care? You're the trainer. What are *you* going to do?'

'I'll report it to the racing authorities,' he said confidently.

'On what grounds?' I asked. 'The authority has made it quite clear that the financial arrangements concerning a jockey and his agent is nothing to do with them and it should be negotiated directly between the parties without them getting involved.'

'But that surely doesn't include the trainers.'

'I bet it does. And I'm sure that many of the jockeys, maybe all of them, would agree that the trainer should pay some of the agent's fee rather than all of it coming out of their pay.'

'Whose side are you on?'

'Neither side. I'm just stating the facts.'

'But what happened here today was nothing short of blackmail.'

'I agree, and that was appalling.'

So too, I thought, was Gary's claim that the agents did far more than simply charge the trainers a fee – they also directed the running of the horses.

'Was this the first time you've had a run-in with a jockeys' agent?' I asked.

'What do you mean?' Clive responded.

'Have any of them demanded money from you before?'

'Not like this. I was once asked to share the agent's fee with a jockey that everyone knew was hard up as a result of being laid off for months with an injury. I happily did that.'

'Have they ever demanded anything else?'

'Like what?'

'Like where you must run your horses?'

Clive stared at me again. 'Don't be ridiculous.'

'I'm not. That's what I've heard.'

He shook his head. 'You'll be telling me next that the agents also decide who will win.'

I said nothing. I just stood and looked at him.

'Oh my God. You *are* saying that.'

Clive Beale and I watched the fifth race together from the balcony at the front of the owners and trainers' lunch area, and we were paying particular attention to the second of Simon Paulson's runners, Night Shadow, again ridden by Jimmy Shilstone.

I had told Clive of my concerns about the first race and how, in my opinion, Jimmy had purposely not won on Plantagenet King by being far too slow early on, hence giving him too much to do to catch the eventual winner in the closing stages. Clive had watched a rerun of the race using the *Racing Post* app on his phone and, while he was not totally convinced, he did agree that Shilstone had not ridden his best-ever race.

The fifth was a Class 5 Handicap steeplechase over two miles and three furlongs, the start being at the highest point of the course, at the beginning of the back straight. The horses had to complete almost two full circuits and negotiate sixteen fences in total – five down the back and three in the home straight, jumping each of them twice.

Handicaps are races where the better the horse, the more weight it carries, such that, in theory, each of the runners have an equal chance of winning.

Every horse that is qualified to run in handicaps is rated each Tuesday by the official handicapper, calculated on its previous performances. The very best steeplechase horses, like those that compete in the championship races at the big meetings at Cheltenham and Aintree, are usually rated higher than 160 – the great Arkle was rated at 212 – but this particular race was a lowly Class 5 contest, which meant that none of the runners had an official rating of more than 100.

Night Shadow had a rating of 99, which was the highest in the race, and hence he carried the top weight of eleven stone twelve pounds, while the other nine carried one pound less for every one point that their rating was lower. The horse carrying bottom weight was rated at 80, nineteen lower than Night Shadow, so it carried 19lb less weight, at ten-stone-seven.

However, top weight clearly hadn't put off the betting public and Night Shadow went down to the start as the four-to-one favourite.

'It's moved down a class since its last outing,' Clive said to me, checking the horse's form on the *Racing Post* app. 'And I reckon the handicapper has been quite generous.'

So, it appeared, did everyone else, and its price on the bookmakers' boards shortened to seven-to-two before the off.

Unlike in the first, Jimmy Shilstone was ready and eager when the starter dropped his flag, and he led the field of ten into the first fence, although, this time, the pace in the early stages was quite moderate.

Night Shadow popped over the first, landing a length in front of his nearest rival, and by the second he had extended his lead to three lengths. But it was at the next fence that things went horribly wrong – or perfectly right, depending on your point of view.

The middle of the five fences in the back straight is an 'open ditch'.

According to the BHA, there has to be at least one open ditch every mile in a steeplechase, and at Catterick there are two open ditches every complete circuit, easily exceeding the minimum requirement.

An open ditch is basically a plain fence with a ditch dug out in front of it, with a wooden rail up to two feet high set ahead of the ditch. It effectively increases the 'spread' of the fence from at least six feet to eight or more. But, these days, due to the general reduction in fence sizes because of horse-injury concerns, most runners have no problems with them.

Back when I was riding, the actual ditches could be up to six feet wide, making these obstacles ones to really worry about. The Chair, in the Grand National at Aintree, the most famous open ditch in all of horse racing, once needed a mighty leap for a horse to cover its six-foot-wide ditch plus its five-foot-high and four-foot-thick fence in a single bound.

But Catterick isn't Aintree, and the open ditches there are of minimum specification. Notwithstanding that, Night Shadow made a complete hash of it, and I, for one, put the error totally down to the jockey rather than the horse.

For some reason that escaped me, other than to think that he did it on purpose, Jimmy Shilstone asked his mount to put in an extra stride when, to all of us watching, he was already perfectly set for the fence.

Night Shadow didn't like it – he knew what he was doing – but, nevertheless, he complied with the clear request from his rider, shortened and put in an extra stride, which left him far too close to the front rail at take-off. The horse clipped the rail with his front hooves, twisted in mid-air and landed four-square on top of the birch fence, before sprawling onto the turf and sending Jimmy Shilstone somersaulting over his head, much to the obvious dismay of those watching in the grandstand.

'Bloody hell,' Clive said next to me as we saw the horse go down in a flurry of legs, both equine and human. 'That jockey is either bent, or he's a fucking idiot.'

'So now do you believe me?' I asked him, echoing the words Gary Bremner had said to me the previous Saturday.

Over a cup of tea, Clive pleaded with me to do something.

'Like what?' I asked.

'We must go to the authorities.'

Both Simon Paulson's horses had started as favourite and neither of them had won. There was nothing particularly unusual in that. Statistically, only about a third of the favourites in the betting actually win. Bookmakers are so adept at setting their prices that even if you bet only on every odds-on favourite, you would still lose.

As far as I could tell, the racecourse stewards at Catterick had not deemed it necessary to hold an enquiry into the running of either of the two Paulson horses, presumably because they hadn't believed that anything was wrong. It was only because I'd already had my suspicions aroused that I felt sure that both horses had not won on purpose. But why would anyone want *not* to win on purpose?

Anyone can back the winner – indeed, everyone can back every winner. You simply bet on every horse running in a race. Then you would be sure to back the winner.

However, you would still lose money, as the sum of your stakes lost on the losers would always be greater than your winnings from the victor – bad idea.

But, if you knew for certain that the favourite wasn't going to win, especially a short-priced favourite, you could just back all the others and guarantee a positive return – good idea.

And that is what I believed had happened in both those races. It was a fraud on the betting public . . . but proving it would be another matter altogether.

Going to the authorities now, without proof, would surely have no effect other than to simply drive Anton Valance or whoever underground, until they reappeared directing the running of the horses of some other poor trainer. Perhaps I had already done that by announcing I was after him so publicly, and maybe it had simply been too late to change today's arrangements.

'Let me continue digging for a bit first,' I said to Clive. 'To get some more concrete evidence.' As long as I wasn't digging my own grave, I thought.

'Okay, but keep me informed,' he insisted. 'I must get going. Clare and I are meant to be out for dinner tonight, and I should have left here hours ago.'

Clive rushed off towards his car and so I hung around for a bit outside the weighing room, hoping to intercept Jimmy

Shilstone again, but without any success. When I finally asked the official on the front door to try and find him for me, I was informed that he had already left for home via the side door of the jockeys' medical room.

Horse racing is the only sport where the participants are actively pursued by medical teams – ambulances, doctors and vets – together with several other vehicles, along a special emergency-service road adjacent to the track. One vehicle contains crews whose job is to set up screens around any injured horse or rider, and at some courses there is even another for the designated 'loose-horse catcher'.

Shilstone must have been brought back to the medical room in another of those following vehicles, specifically the one assigned to pick up any fallen jockeys, at least those who didn't need the services of the ambulance.

When I had started riding, there had been no such luxuries for jockeys, not even a chasing ambulance.

During my first season as a professional jockey, I could remember falling at the final fence down the back straight at Chepstow in the last race on a chilly, damp November afternoon. The racecourse at Chepstow is almost two miles round and is particularly long and thin, such that the distance from that fence back to the weighing room is the best part of a mile.

In spite of it being an easy fall with no resultant injury, I had decided to remain down on the turf, writhing as if in agony, in the hope and expectation that the fence attendant would use his white flag to summon the racecourse ambulance, which could then give me a lift all the way back to the changing room. However,

I made the serious mistake of jumping up to my feet as the ambulance approached. When the driver saw that, in fact, I was unharmed by the fall, he immediately turned his vehicle round and drove away again, consigning me to a long, cold, wet trudge.

Having failed to doorstep Jimmy Shilstone, I went in search of Simon Paulson, but he too had slipped away, probably to avoid speaking to me.

Time for me to go too, I thought. As it was, I'd be back at Aynsford later than I had hoped. I had better call Charles to remind him to feed Rosie, and this time not with digestive biscuits.

I walked out to my car during the running of the seventh and last race, the bumper, but if I thought I could get away from Catterick that easily, I was very much mistaken.

13

There were two large men in black balaclavas waiting for me beside my car and they were both wielding baseball bats.

Oh Christ, I thought, *not again.*

'Halley,' one of them shouted, 'we want a word with you.'

Well, that was as may be, but I didn't particularly want a word with them.

On the last occasion I'd encountered men with baseball bats and ill intent, I'd only just escaped with my kneecaps intact and, that time, I'd had a ready-made club in the form of a myoelectric false hand on my left arm to help. Now I'd swapped that for a soft and flabby transplant, which would be about as much use in a fight as a feather duster.

Hadn't they heard of the Sid Halley reputation that beating him up wouldn't stop him? Perhaps they had but, nevertheless, were determined to prove it wrong. Maybe with good reason. It was a long while now since anyone had tried it and my aging body was screaming to my brain to just turn and run.

I looked around for some support but the car park was deserted. The early departures had already left and those remaining were all watching the last race. Even Fred the gateman had long gone. I was on my own.

One of the men swung his baseball bat and smashed the driver's-side window of my Discovery into thousands of little pieces.

Damn them. I instantly became very angry. Hitting me was one thing, but damaging my car was quite another.

Instead of doing the sensible thing of turning and running, I advanced on the two men.

'What the hell do you want?' I shouted at them.

Just for a second they seemed somewhat taken aback by my aggression, glancing at each other through the eyeholes of their balaclavas. Sadly, their composure returned pretty quickly and they moved apart to be on either side of me.

'What do you want?' I shouted again.

'We have a message for you,' said the one on my left.

'Who from?'

'Never you mind,' the man replied.

'So what is this message?'

I feared the message was going to be purely physical rather than verbal, but I was wrong.

'Piss off back south and don't come back,' said the man. 'Or else.'

I turned slightly towards him while keeping the other one in my peripheral vision. 'Or else what?' I demanded belligerently.

'Or else you might get hurt.'

'I'm not frightened of you,' I said calmly, although I was. 'And you can tell Anton Valance to stuff his message up his arse. Do you hear?'

Not much of their faces were visible through the eye and mouth holes of their balaclavas but it was enough for me to know that they were not fazed one jot by my use of the Valance name. They knew exactly who he was, and that he was the one who had sent the message.

Both men raised their baseball bats and advanced menacingly, and I wondered if turning and running might have been the better option after all.

'You asked for it,' said the one on my left, swinging his bat at my head.

I dodged that one but his mate was also swinging and he caught me a glancing blow across my shoulders as I ducked.

I was in trouble, deep trouble.

'Help!' I shouted at the top of my voice, but without much hope, as I could hear the racing commentary rising to a crescendo as the bumper neared its finish.

'Help!' I shouted again and, to my great relief, and much surprise, help did arrive – and in the form of the cavalry.

Three supremely fit, if rather inebriated, young army officers dived straight into the fray, knocking both my assailants off their feet. The two men jumped up but they were now confronted not by one person but by four. For a few seconds, the six of us faced each other in a tableau that strangely reminded me of stories of the shoot-out at the OK Corral. But, on this occasion, thankfully, no one drew a gun.

Instead the two in balaclavas wisely decided that the odds were no longer stacked in their favour so they turned and ran, one of them even leaving behind his baseball bat.

'Thank you,' I said with feeling to the three young men.

'No problem, Sid,' one of them replied. 'But what did they want?'

'My car keys,' I said, reckoning that their real purpose would require too much explanation. 'They already broke my window.' I gestured towards the Discovery and the pile of glass fragments lying on the grass next to it.

'Bloody hooligans. Someone should lock them up.'

I agreed. 'And throw away the key.'

We all laughed. Tension eased.

'Can I offer you a lift?' I asked.

'Thank you, but we have our own car,' replied one of them.

'You're surely not thinking of driving,' I said. Each of them was at least three sheets to the wind, maybe as many as five.

He laughed. 'Not likely. We have a driver to take us back to base.' He indicated towards a Jaguar saloon parked just beyond my Discovery, with someone now getting out of it. The driver must have seen the whole confrontation between the masked men and me, but he had remained safely in his vehicle throughout. I couldn't blame him. Only fearless army officers are prepared to get themselves involved to save others.

The three of them weaved their merry way across to the Jaguar and were driven away. I suddenly felt quite exposed without them, so I quickly picked up the discarded baseball bat, chucked it onto the back seat of the Discovery, climbed in and also drove away, setting my nose south towards Oxfordshire, cursing the fact that the driver's door window was missing and I was in for a long, noisy and cold journey home.

But, notwithstanding that broken window and the huge fright I had experienced in the car park, I felt that overall it had been a successful day.

I had not only found out exactly how Gary Bremner had died, but the arrival of two balaclava-clad thugs at Catterick to deliver me a message, or worse, had confirmed that Gary had been right – the very future of British racing was at risk.

Marina called as I was on the M1 south of Nottingham. I answered on my hands-free system.

'How are things?' I asked.

'Not great. Pa's breathing was worse again in the night. I called the doctor this morning but there's nothing more he can do. We are obviously nearing the end game. I just wish it would happen soon for all our sakes, his too. It's no way to live.'

She was crying.

I blinked away tears from my own eyes. I hated to hear my darling in so much pain.

'How's Sassy?'

'Sad. But she's being a great distraction for Mamma. She's now given all the chickens individual names and she goes and chats to them when the atmosphere gets too bad in the house.'

I smiled. Typical Sassy. All the many teddy bears and dolls in her bedroom had their own different name, and she never forgot or mixed them up.

'Do you want me to come over?' I asked.

Marina sighed. 'I don't know, Sid.' She sighed again. 'Elmo is coming from New York. I told him that Pa didn't have long and that he'd been asking for him.'

'And had he?'

'Not really, but Mamma has.'

'When does he arrive?'

'He's on the red-eye tonight. He should be here in the morning.'

I knew she hadn't seen her brother for a long time. 'That will be nice for you.'

'Not in these circumstances.'

'I'll leave it for a few days, then,' I said, slightly fishing for a positive response.

'I think that would be best.'

At least it wasn't an outright *no*.

'I've had an interesting day,' I said. 'I went to the races at Catterick.'

'Where's that?'

'In Yorkshire.'

'Oh.'

She knew exactly why I'd been to Yorkshire.

'What's that noise?' Marina asked.

'Wind noise,' I replied. 'I'm driving on the motorway and the driver's door window got broken.'

'How did that happen?'

'You don't want to know,' I said with a laugh. 'I'll drop it into the dealership tomorrow to get it fixed.'

She was silent for quite a long time.

'Are you still there?' I asked.

'Sid, please be careful.'

'Always, my love.'

And I would be careful. I couldn't rely on the cavalry coming to my rescue again.

I'm not sure who was more pleased to see me, Charles or Rosie, when they met me in the hallway at Aynsford.

Rosie barked and wagged her tail, while Charles looked rather haggard.

'Mrs Cross was away today,' he said. 'Her daughter was unwell and she had to look after her two grandsons, so it was just me here. That dog of yours is hard work. When she's inside, she wants to go out, and when I put her out, she immediately wants to come in again. I've had absolutely no peace.'

'I'm sorry,' I said, trying not to laugh. 'Has she been fed?'

'I gave her the dog biscuits you left.'

'What? All of them?' I'd left enough for at least two meals.

'Yes. Was that wrong?'

'No, it's fine.'

No wonder Rosie was happy.

'Do you fancy a snifter?' Charles asked. 'I'm going to have one. I think I've earned it.'

'Go on, then.'

The three of us went into his drawing room and he poured a good deal more than a snifter of whisky into each of two cut-glass tumblers. He handed one to me.

'Our men,' he toasted, taking a large swig.

'Good health,' I replied, doing the same, only with a smaller swig.

Charles and I sat down in the armchairs facing each other, while Rosie curled up on the carpet at my feet and went to sleep.

'I just don't believe it,' Charles said, looking down at her. 'Why didn't she do that for me?'

'I must have a natural way with animals.'

'Don't give me that bullshit,' Charles said, laughing out loud. But then he got more serious. 'Have you heard from Marina?'

'She called me this afternoon. She was in tears. Her father is dying. The doctors say they can do nothing more for him.'

'What a bugger.' He took another large slug of his whisky. 'But it comes to us all in the end. Are you going over there?'

'Marina says not to come at present. Her brother is flying over from New York.'

'But she needs *you*, not her brother.'

Did she?

Did she really want someone who couldn't give up the investigating drug?

I had tried – God, I'd tried – but there was something in me that needed to right the wrongs I found, especially those in the other love of my life – horse racing.

Please don't ever ask me to choose between my wife and my addiction. I craved both.

Christ, how I craved both.

14

In all, I spent a good hour with Charles. Both he and I seemed grateful for the company.

'Fancy another?' he asked, standing over me with his favourite decanter.

'Better not,' I said. 'I have to drive home soon.'

'You could always stay over. Mrs Cross always leaves the bed in the spare room made up.'

'Thanks, Charles. But I'll have to get back.'

I had to take my anti-rejection pills and they were in the bathroom cabinet at home. I should keep some in the car, I thought, just in case.

'As you like.' But he poured himself another generous measure.

'So what have you discovered?' he asked, sitting back down in his armchair.

'What do you mean?'

'Come on, Sid, I know you too well. You didn't drive all the way to Yorkshire twice in three days just for the view. You've been investigating something, so what is it?'

'Have you been watching the television news over the past three days?'

'Of course.'

'The story about a stable fire in Middleham, and then the discovery of the body of the trainer?'

He nodded. 'Suicide.'

'That's what the police think.'

'But you don't?'

'No.'

I told him about Gary Bremner calling me on Friday, the day before the fire, and then again on Saturday after it, when everyone believed he had died in the flames. I described my trip to meet with Gary on Sunday and my subsequent visit to Simon Paulson's yard and our discussion about jockeys' agents and trainers' premiums.

Charles's eyes grew wide with astonishment, and his eyebrows rose closer and closer to his hairline.

'There's more,' I said, and went on to describe my encounter with the detective chief inspector in Gary Bremner's garden after Gary's body had been found, and then my trip to Catterick races and my firm belief that the results of at least two of the races there had been manipulated. I finished by recounting the details of my encounter with the two masked men in the racecourse car park.

By the time I'd finished, Charles was sitting there with his mouth hanging open in disbelief, his glass of whisky undrunk in his hand.

'Does Marina know what you're doing?' he asked eventually.

'She knows some of it,' I replied. 'But please don't tell her about the men with baseball bats.'

'Are you going to report them to the police?'

'What do you think?' I asked sarcastically. 'It would be a total waste of time. No one got hurt, so the police wouldn't do anything, even if they could find them. Anyway, I'm grateful to them.'

'Grateful?'

'Yes, because they have confirmed that what Gary told me is true.'

'So what will you do now?'

It was a good question.

Did I have enough to take to the racing authorities?

Hardly.

So what else did I need?

'I think I might go and see someone.'

'That policeman?' Charles said.

I laughed. 'Maybe I should, but he wasn't who I had in mind.'

'Who then?'

'Jimmy Shilstone.'

'And who is he?'

'The jockey who rode the two losers today at Catterick.'

I drove Rosie back to our dark and lonely home in Nutwell.

Only when I was unlocking my back door did I wonder if it had been sensible to have walked down the unlit path at the side of the house.

My address was hardly a secret and if I could drive up and

down to Yorkshire in a day, so could my assailants from the Catterick racecourse car park.

I suppose I should have been thankful that Marina and Saskia were not here to be targeted. I was only too well aware, from past experience, how certain lowlifes could apply pressure to me by attacking those I loved.

The thought of meeting the balaclava wearers again made me shiver. I was no longer the ultra-fit, fearless crusader I had once been. My many racing falls, and the subsequent injuries, were beginning to catch up with me, with creeping arthritis in some of my joints, especially my ankles.

And my new hand needed protecting.

'Try hard not to damage it,' my surgeon had said to me on the day I'd been discharged from hospital. 'One of the side effects of the anti-rejection drugs might be that all your body tissues bruise more easily. And bruising is particularly dangerous for the transplant itself. The increased blood that sits in a bruise has been known to trigger rejection problems in some patients.'

So, whereas I had once dived into every encounter with my false left hand to the fore, I now shielded the new one, often putting it behind my back so it couldn't get damaged accidentally.

So was I being unrealistic in taking on an individual or organisation prepared to send a couple of thugs with baseball bats to beat me up? Was it ever worth it?

But, equally, could I really stand by and allow something as dear to me as British jump racing to be effectively killed off by greed – greed that transcended fair play and tore up the rule book?

*

Before taking my pills and retiring, I went round the whole house checking that all the doors and windows were firmly shut and bolted, and for good measure I collected the long iron poker from the fireplace in the sitting room and placed it by my bed.

But the night was uneventful other than Rosie barking at a squirrel in the garden at half past six and frightening me rigid.

The rest of Wednesday morning was occupied by me taking the Discovery to the local Land Rover dealership and persuading them to fix the driver's door window while I waited. They tut-tutted about how such a thing could have possibly happened and I didn't enlighten them. But fortunately there was a spare glass of the right dimensions in their parts department and, by lunchtime, I was back on the road in sublime warmth and quiet.

The afternoon was filled with me first catching up on some correspondence from my accountant and then using the *Racing Post* website to study the full videos of recent races, specifically those sent out from Simon Paulson's stable and ridden by Jimmy Shilstone.

They'd been very clever, I thought.

In the past three weeks, Simon Paulson had had eleven runners, not including the two at Catterick the previous day, and seven had been ridden by Jimmy Shilstone. Two of those had been winners and, of the other five, I reckoned that one was a definite fix, and maybe one of the others was also suspicious. But proving it would be nigh-on impossible. Indeed, it was only the look of panic in Jimmy's eyes when I'd confronted him after the first race at Catterick that had made me truly certain that something hadn't been right.

The race I was pretty sure had been fixed was a Class 4 two-

and-a-half-mile handicap chase held at Newcastle during the previous week.

Unlike at Catterick, where the last seven furlongs are mostly downhill, at Newcastle there is a stiff rise from the start of the home straight all the way up to the finish line. Hence, races tend to be run here at a slower pace and often the contests don't get going in earnest until near the end, as everyone is trying to hold something in reserve for that final climb.

Everyone, that was, except Jimmy Shilstone.

The video showed he had set off on the favourite at a tremendous gallop, leading the field by eight lengths or more by the time they passed the winning post on the first circuit. As he turned into the home straight for the second and last time, he had still been leading by two lengths, but his horse soon paid the price for that fast early pace, fading badly over the last four uphill fences in heavy going to finish third, some ten lengths behind the eventual winner.

Shilstone had also had a ride in a later race on the same day, but for a different trainer. It was another handicap steeplechase, this time over two miles, and one reserved for novice chasers – young horses that hadn't won a steeplechase prior to the start of the current season in late April.

I watched that video too.

On that occasion, Jimmy had ridden a completely different style of race, starting slowly and only making his run for victory up the concluding hill. And it had proved successful, with him catching the long-time leader some ten strides from the finish to win easily, with his hands down.

I wondered if the racecourse stewards had questioned him as to why his tactics in the two races had been so different. Probably not. It was only obvious when you watched the two races immediately one after the other as I had just done, rather than separated by an hour and a half, as they had been on the day itself.

It was definitely time to go and visit Jimmy Shilstone, and maybe also Simon Paulson for a second time. But would they talk to me? Or would they run off to tell tales to their puppet master, putting me in greater danger? What could I do that would convince them that the former was the best route?

I looked up Jimmy Shilstone in the *Thoroughbred Business Guide* but his entry didn't give his address, only a telephone number, and I didn't want to give him the chance to hang up on me when I was asking him some pertinent questions. That had to be done face to face, not on the phone.

Next I scanned the *Racing Post* website to see if he had any rides booked, so I could confront him at a racecourse. I discovered that he had nothing for tomorrow but was due to ride at Ayr in Scotland for two days after that. Ayr was almost twice as far away from Oxfordshire as Middleham, at least six hours in the car each way. I decided I'd wait until he was a little closer.

But what about the mystery man who had put his phone number under my windscreen wiper? Where was he? Was visiting him a possibility instead?

I still had the piece of yellow paper. I retrieved it from my pocket and looked at it. It had a mobile number beginning 07 written on it in black ink.

I searched on the internet for any help in finding out whose number it was. There were quite a number of commercial tracking websites, but on closer examination it became obvious that, under the laws of the United Kingdom, they could only track the person from the number if the individual concerned had given their permission and had a certain app installed on their phone.

Dead end.

An easier route seemed to be to simply call the number and ask, but I had tried that before and he'd refused to say, so there was little point in me trying it again. But could someone else?

I reckoned that, if the telephone owner was riding a horse when he heard me shouting from the Swine Cross in Middleham, and he knew Anton Valance well enough to call him, the chances were high that he was a BHA-licensed jockey.

In order to prevent the disclosure of sensitive information to either gamblers or bookmakers, all licensed jockeys riding at any race meeting have not only to register their mobile phones with the authority, but are banned from making or receiving calls, texts or emails during a restricted period beginning half an hour before the advertised time of the first race and finishing when the last race starts, unless under the strict supervision of an official in a designated 'phone zone' within the weighing room. They also have to agree to provide the authority on request with fully itemized billing records for any calls made by their phones during that restricted period.

I called Charles.

'Could you do me a favour?' I asked.

'Depends on what it is,' he replied.

'Can you phone a number for me and pretend, in your most severe Royal Naval voice, to be from the Integrity Department at the British Horseracing Authority?'

'For what reason?'

'I have someone's number but I want to know his name. I think he must be a jockey, and all jockeys have to register their phone numbers with the BHA. So please could you ring the number as the BHA and ask his name.'

'But will he tell me?'

'I don't know. He wouldn't tell me yesterday morning, so probably no, not if you ask him straight out. So I suggest you could ask him for his postcode, as a security question, and for the first line of his address. Then you say that the details he's given you are different to the ones the BHA have on file. Then, sounding confused, you check that it is actually, I don't know, Joe Bloggs you're talking to. He'll say no, of course not, it's . . . and he'll give you his name.'

'Sid, you're a genius.'

'Only if it works.' Which I feared it wouldn't.

'Okay, what's the number.'

I read it out from the piece of yellow paper.

'Right, I'll call you back.'

I sat and stared at my phone as five minutes became ten.

Eventually it rang and I grabbed at it.

'His name is Marcus Capes,' Charles said. 'He's a twenty-year-old conditional jockey employed in Middleham by a trainer called Noel Kline. He lives in digs at 42 Leyburn Road with an elderly widow, Mrs Doris Robinson, and her Siamese cat, Tiddles, and he's trying his best to save up to buy a second-hand car to make getting to the races easier.'

'How on earth did you get all that?'

'I rang the number you gave me and I told him my name was Commander Crichton from the Integrity Department of the BHA and we were running a periodic security check. I did as you suggested with the postcode and the first line of his address, and he coughed up his name, right on cue. Then he simply volunteered the rest. In fact, I could hardly stop him talking.'

'You're amazing,' I said, laughing. 'Thank you.'

'Oh, yes, and there's one more thing. He's represented by an agency called The Jockeys Stable. He told me his contact there is a certain Anton Valance.'

Why was I not surprised?

15.

On Thursday morning I took Rosie with me to Yorkshire.

I had tried to suggest leaving her again with Charles but, as Mrs Cross was still away looking after her grandchildren, he had baulked at the idea.

'I'm very sorry,' he said. 'I simply can't have her again today. She's just so exhausting.'

Rosie, however, was delighted to be coming with me.

Unlike the other Irish setters Marina and I had owned, each of whom had detested going in the car to the point of shaking and vomiting whenever it was suggested, Rosie was in her element, barking loudly at every passing vehicle. I knew I should have put her in the back of the Discovery, behind the special dog grille, but she much preferred being up front with me, her head stuck out the passenger window into the wind.

And, in truth, I loved her company.

I just wish I had trained her better – in particular, to bite anyone wearing a balaclava.

*

Marina had called me on Wednesday evening with the latest update from Fryslân.

Her father had rallied somewhat with the arrival of Elmo from New York, but I wasn't at all sure if Marina had been pleased or disappointed by the development.

'This could go on for weeks,' she'd said in desperation.

'Just relax,' I'd said. 'Make the most of the time he has left to enjoy his company. When he's finally gone, there will be no chance of ever speaking to him again.'

I knew. I still sometimes wished I could tell my own mother things, and she had been dead since I was sixteen. I suppose that feeling never goes away.

Marina had sighed. 'You're right. You're always right. I should make the most of him.'

'Ask him about his childhood,' I'd said. 'And get him to tell you who people are in old family photos. Get Sassy to help you. All that knowledge will die for ever with him unless you write it down.'

It would also give them both something to do, I thought, rather than just moping around the house waiting for his heart to finally pack up.

On this occasion, I hadn't asked her about me going over there to help.

I had things to complete here in the UK first.

42 Leyburn Road was the middle one of three terraced, stone-built cottages set close to the road, about 200 yards down the hill from the centre of Middleham.

I parked MY S1D in the marketplace and, much to Rosie's chagrin, I left her in the back of the Discovery, behind the grille, with all the windows slightly open. For all her usual gentle nature, Rosie was not very fond of cats and I didn't want there to be an ugly scene with Tiddles to distract me from my real purpose.

I had studied the *Racing Post* app, and although there was jump racing only forty miles away down the M1 at Wetherby that afternoon, Noel Kline didn't have any runners and Marcus Capes had not been declared to ride for anyone else. So, with morning exercise well over by noon, the chances were quite reasonable that he would be at home at one o'clock.

I knocked loudly on the front door of number 42 at precisely two minutes past the hour.

It was opened an inch or two by a white-haired old lady wearing slippers.

'Yes?' she snapped through the narrow gap. 'What do you want?'

'Are you Mrs Doris Robinson?'

'Who wants to know?' she replied caustically.

I ignored her question. 'I'm here to see Marcus Capes. Is he in?'

She didn't reply. She just opened the door a bit wider, turned her head and shouted up the stairs. 'Marcus, it's for you.' And then she went back down the hall and disappeared from my sight.

Late the previous evening, I had spent some time on my computer researching young Mr Capes. As Charles had said, he was a conditional jockey employed by trainer Noel Kline.

A 'conditional' is a young, inexperienced jockey just starting out in his or her career. Unlike their more experienced counterparts, who are considered to be self-employed, a conditional is paid directly by the trainer as an employee of the stable.

Marcus Capes had been born in Preston and was now riding in his third season. He had won a total of thirty-eight races, half of them in the present term, putting him joint eighth in the current conditional jockeys' standings. And I knew what he looked like from googling images of him from the internet.

I had also watched video replays of all sixteen of his race rides in the past month. Two of those had been winners and none of the other fourteen had aroused my suspicion that he hadn't won because he wasn't trying. Either he hadn't actually 'stopped' any of those, or else he was very good at it.

From where I was standing just outside the front door, I could see straight up the stairs, and some legs in blue jeans soon appeared on the landing.

'Thanks, Doris,' Marcus shouted, bounding down, two steps at a time. Only when he was near the bottom did he see the face of the person who had come a-calling. He stopped dead.

'Hi, Marcus,' I said. 'Fancy a chat?'

'Not with you.'

'Who with then?' I asked. 'The BHA Integrity Department?'

He looked confused, as well he might.

'Can I come in?' I asked.

'No, you can't. Go away.'

'I assure you I won't be doing that,' I said. 'I will just stand here and tell everyone who passes that I've come to talk to you but you won't let me in.' I looked up and down the road as if selecting who to talk to next. 'In the end, Marcus, you will have to speak to me. The only choice you have is when, and whether the police are also involved.'

'The police?'

'Yes, the police. Especially the ones down the road investigating Gary Bremner's death.'

'But I know nothing about that. I swear to you.' As I'd hoped, he was seriously rattled by my mention of the police.

'In that case you have no reason to worry about talking to me. So can I come in?'

He stuck his head out of the door and looked up and down the road. There was actually no one in sight either way.

'Quickly, then, before someone sees you.'

I stepped past him into the cottage and he closed the door behind me.

'Upstairs.'

We went up to his bedsit on the first floor.

His room was not at all as I had expected. I had imagined that a twenty-year-old young man, probably living away from home for the first time in his life, might have let things slip somewhat in the tidying-up department. But I was totally wrong.

The place was spotless, with a neatly made single bed in the corner behind the door, a clutter-free bedside cabinet, a smart sofa facing a large flat-screen TV fixed to the far wall – on and tuned to the racing channel – a sparkling glass-topped coffee table and, in the corner opposite to the bed and partly hidden behind a curtain, a small kitchenette with a sink, a shelf above holding some crockery, a teapot and two saucepans, and an electric mini-oven, together with integral hob on top. And all of it as neat as a new pin with no discarded dirty socks kicked under the bed, or any lingering washing up waiting in the sink.

And it wasn't because he had been expecting me, that was for sure.

'Delightful,' I said.

He seemed to sense that I was mostly referring to the cleanliness.

'My father was in the army,' he said. 'He spent eight years as a regimental sergeant major. He's obsessed with just two things – horse racing and tidiness – and I suppose they've both rubbed off on me.'

Time for me to dive in. 'So what would your sergeant-major father say if he knew you were intentionally not winning races?'

The colour drained from his face.

'But . . . but that's not true.'

'Isn't it?'

His body language said it was.

He sat down on the arm of the sofa and lowered his head.

'Tell me about Anton Valance.'

'What about him?' he asked, looking up at me.

'Why did you tell me on the phone that he is not a very nice man?'

'Because he's not.'

I felt we weren't getting very far.

'Perhaps you would like to come with me to talk about him to the BHA.'

Marcus pulled a face. He clearly didn't fancy that idea. Like all those involved in racing, he had a deep-rooted fear of the

BHA, and with good reason. The BHA regularly took away people's livelihoods with a single stroke of its unforgiving pen.

The rule of racing in question here was Rule F(37): '. . . a Jockey must, and must be seen to: (a) ask the horse for timely, real and substantial effort to achieve the best possible position, and (b) take all other reasonable and permissible measures throughout the race to ensure the horse is given a full opportunity to achieve the best possible position.'

The BHA doesn't have to prove a breach of its rules beyond a reasonable doubt, as in a criminal court, but only on the balance of probabilities, and the penalties are harsh to discourage potential offenders – disqualification for up to 25 years if it's intentional and for personal gain, or done with the knowledge that the horse has been backed to lose.

And, if the BHA disqualifies you from racing in the United Kingdom, you are automatically disqualified from horse racing everywhere else in the world.

It would end even a young jockey's career, stone dead.

'So what is it about Mr Valance that makes him not a very nice man?' I asked.

Marcus looked up at me again.

'Because he traps you.'

'How?'

He sighed loudly, as if he had the weight of the world on his shoulders.

'"Just the once," he says. And I reckon the nag has no chance anyway. So I say – okay. Who wouldn't for an easy two hundred quid in readies? Worst bloody decision of my life.' He sighed again. 'Not that I rode it any different to how I would have done. I gave it every possible chance just like the rules say I should. It just isn't quick enough to win even if it starts yesterday. Tailed off, we are, when I pull him up before the last two flights.'

'Then you've nothing to worry about,' I said, trying to sound reassuring but not believing it.

He stared up at me. 'Tapes it, doesn't he? Our conversation. With his phone. Even takes a secret video of me counting the notes after he tells me to check that he's given me the right amount. Slimy bastard. Sees me coming a mile off.'

'And now he's blackmailing you?'

He nodded, dropping his head down into his hands.

'How did you get involved with him in the first place?'

'Flattered, wasn't I,' he said miserably. 'Who'd have thought a top agent like him would be interested in me? He calls me last summer after I won a couple of races on the same card for Mr Kline at Hexham. Tells me he thinks I am going places and he wants to act for me. He isn't the only one, mind. Two or three other agents also pitch for me to join them, but he's offering the best terms.'

'Eight per cent instead of ten?'

'That's right. Seems like a good deal. And it was, too, at least for a while.'

'So when did it change?'

'Last October. He rings me and tells me that I'm not to ride a specific horse in a conditional rider's race at Sedgefield that I've already been booked for. I ask him why but all he says is I am not to ask why or to contact the trainer, nor to answer my phone. I just have to not turn up at the races.'

'So what happened?'

'I don't go. I sit in here and watch it on the telly. There's a right hoo-ha, I can tell you. My phone is ringing on and on all afternoon but I don't answer it. Mr Valance tells me that, if I don't do exactly as he says, he'll not book me any rides and he'll make sure I don't have any future in racing.'

He was on the verge of tears but he held it together.

'Then he comes and sees me, all apologetic, like. Says there was a bit of a mix-up with the trainer but now it's all sorted.'

'So it wasn't one of Noel Kline's horses?'

'No. It was one of Simon Paulson's.'

And what was it that Simon had said to me about the trainers' premium?

It's easier just to pay.

He clearly knew from experience what to expect if he didn't.

16

Apart from checking once briefly on Rosie, I spent nearly three hours with Marcus Capes, mostly listening to his pitiful tale of woe, but also watching the afternoon's racing from Wetherby on his television.

He had been an impressionable nineteen-year-old when he had first signed up with Anton Valance and The Jockeys Stable. Sadly, unlike for Peter Minter, the jockey I had spoken to at Catterick, Marcus's father, for all his obsession with tidiness, hadn't told him that if something sounded too good to be true, it probably was.

To start with, it appeared that his decision to join The Jockeys Stable agency had been a wise one, with plenty of rides on good horses for various trainers coming his way, but the events of that afternoon at Sedgefield, when he had failed to appear, had given him a reputation for being unreliable, and most of the extra rides had quickly dried up.

Not, it seemed, that Valance had cared much. Clearly, his

determination to extract a premium from the trainers was more important than the good name of the jockeys he represented.

Marcus told me that Noel Kline had been furious about it and had almost terminated his employment as a result. He'd had to promise that it would never happen again in order to keep his job.

'And has it?' I asked.

'No. Never. Although Valance tried it on again with me just before Christmas. He told me not to turn up for a ride at Doncaster.'

'But you did nevertheless?'

'I would have but the meeting was abandoned early in the morning due to snow. Bloody marvellous, it was.' He laughed.

'And he's never asked you again?'

'Not to miss a ride, no. I told him straight up after that that I wouldn't be doing it again.'

'And what did he say to that?'

'He said I should learn to do as I'm bloody well told. And it's two weeks later that he stitched me up with his damn recording.'

He paused and I encouraged him to go on, but it was clearly hugely embarrassing for him.

'I'm not really bad,' he said, perhaps trying to convince himself as much as me. 'It was just after Christmas and I was really short of cash, desperate even, and he turns up and offers me two hundred quid to make sure I don't win a certain race. But I was riding a total no-hoper in it anyway, so I thought he was crazy. So I take his cash to pay my overdue rent. What harm can it do?' He raises his eyes to the ceiling. 'How stupid am I?'

He paused while we watched the third race from Wetherby, a two-mile Class 4 handicap chase.

'I should be riding in this,' Marcus said forlornly, as the starter dropped his flag.

'How come?'

'I won on Mackerel Fisher at Haydock last September.'

Mackerel Fisher was the short-priced favourite in this race, and he was being ridden by a jockey called Danny Fletcher.

'He ran again the week after my non-appearance at Sedgefield, and I wasn't offered the ride. Not surprising, I suppose. Anyway, he wins again, this time with Danny riding, and he's been riding him ever since.'

Those involved in horse racing could be very unforgiving, and not just the BHA.

Danny and Mackerel Fisher duly won the race, and at a canter.

'He'll be moving up a class next time out, that's for sure,' said Marcus bitterly. 'Maybe two classes. Perhaps even to a listed.'

Listed races were all Class 1, where the purses on offer were serious money.

I was surprised how much it mattered to him.

When I'd started my riding career all those years ago, my fellow jockeys and I had studied the *Sporting Life* newspaper every morning over our breakfasts to note the winners from the day before, to try and decide whether we had a chance in any upcoming races. Nowadays, it was all more instant, with every race available to watch live on the satellite TV channels and replays instantly available on your phone via the internet.

How the world has been changed by technology, I thought,

and almost exclusively for the better. Certainly the probity of British horse racing had been much advanced by the introduction of reliable dope testing, and by the DNA profiling and electronic microchipping at birth of every Thoroughbred foal born worldwide. Gone forever were the bad old days when running a 'ringer', a horse purporting to be one when it was, in fact, another, had been commonplace.

Some may hanker after a perceived former romantic era when racing attracted an array of dodgy characters, many with syringes of 'go-faster' or 'go-slower' juice in their pockets, and everyone over a certain age has a colourful story about 'a friend of a friend' who got away with beating the bookies. But beating the bookies also involved defrauding the betting public, and it was no coincidence that race-going among the young had increased greatly in recent years due to the widespread appreciation that horse racing is honest and fair.

But, it seemed, there was still someone out there who wanted to manipulate the results, and blackmailing susceptible young jockeys, such as Marcus Capes, was his chosen modus operandi.

So what could I do to stop him?

Marcus and I sat in silence for some time, me waiting patiently for him to continue and he probably worrying about what he had already told me.

I needed him not only to trust me, but also to help, and I had to weave a careful path if he was not to cut and run straight to Anton Valance or, worse still, to pack in his whole career.

We watched the next race from Wetherby, a three-mile novice hurdle with six runners. Three miles was just over two complete circuits of the anticlockwise course, so the start was just to the left of the winning post as the camera viewed it from the grandstand.

All the six jumped off at a very sensible steady pace. Three miles was a long way for novices in heavy going, and they also had to jump twelve flights of hurdles, three down the back and three in the home straight on each circuit.

Bucks Fizzy, the three-to-one favourite, took a keen hold early on but was held up to the rear of the field as the sextet completed the first circuit at no great pace. Down the back for the second time, the jockey nudged him along to track closer to the leaders, but the horse jumped badly to the right over the fourth last, and, in spite of the apparent best endeavours of the jockey, he weakened quickly on the turn for home – so much so, in fact, that he became tailed off and was pulled up before the last.

The race was won by a five-to-one shot.

Six minutes of unremarkable racing – yet another favourite had not won, but nothing about the race made me particularly suspicious.

As far as I could tell, the jockey had satisfied Rule F(37) to the letter – he had asked the horse for a timely, real and substantial effort, and had taken all other reasonable and permissible measures to ensure the horse was given the full opportunity to achieve its best possible position.

Bucks Fizzy had simply not been fast enough on this day.

'Another losing favourite,' I said finally into Marcus's silence, perhaps fishing for a response.

'Happens all the time,' he said. 'It's a strange sport, really, from a jockey's point of view. Even the best of us lose far more races than we win. You just have to get used to it.'

It was true. AP McCoy, without question the most successful jump jockey in the history of the sport, won over four thousand races during his riding career but he also lost more than 13 thousand others, with at least a thousand of those ending up with him hitting the turf.

Would Usain Bolt be considered the greatest 100-metre sprinter of all time if he had lost more than three-quarters of the races he had run in? Even the tennis greats, Nadal, Federer and Djokovic, all of them playing in the same era, have each won more than two-thirds of the tournament finals they've played in, to say nothing of their earlier-round victories to get to the final in the first place.

Only in horse racing do even the very best have to get used to losing far more often than they win.

Marcus looked across at me and smiled broadly. 'But there's no feeling on earth like that of winning. Winning is everything. No one ever remembers who comes second – or cares.'

He was so right. I thought back again to my time in the saddle. I'd chased the same dream as him for almost ten years. My attitude then had undoubtedly been 'win or nothing', and I'd been a dreadful loser, blaming myself, the trainer, the ground or the opposition, but never my horse, who I always felt had done its best, even if its best wasn't good enough to win.

'So what happens now?' Marcus asked, bringing us back to the serious matter in hand. 'I'm not going to the BHA if that's what you're after.'

'It's not, at least not for now. My first suggestion is that you change your agent.'

'I've tried that,' he replied. 'But he tells me that the video of me counting the money will be posted on social media if I do.'

'Have you actually seen this video?' I asked.

'Sure have. He showed it to me right here in this room. I'm standing over there by the window,' he pointed, 'counting the wedge. Course, he gives me the two hundred quid in tenners, doesn't he, so it takes me a while to count them.'

'But you could just be counting money that is legitimate, maybe obtained from a cash machine.'

He looked at me. 'Use a bit of common. I don't hardly have twenty quid in my bank account, let alone two hundred. So how do I get twenty ten-pound notes from a cash machine?'

'But it still doesn't prove you have done anything wrong.'

'It does when you add the bloody voice recording to it.'

'So what does that say?'

'It's basically me agreeing to prevent a horse called Second Yellow from winning the two-and-a-half-mile novice hurdle at Catterick on New Year's Day.'

'But isn't Valance's voice on the recording as well?'

'Course not. He's far too fucking clever for that. Edits himself out of it, doesn't he. It's just mine. He even got me to repeat back to him what he wanted me to do just to make sure I got it right. I'm too damn stupid for my own good.'

And too trusting, I thought. Just as he'd trusted that Charles was calling from the BHA the previous evening, in order to get his name and address.

'But the video will still be on his phone,' I said. 'That must prove that he's involved.'

'But it won't be on his phone after he uploads it onto YouTube, and then deletes it, will it? It's all a fucking disaster.'

I wasn't so sure. Deleting things from phones or computers was not as easy as people thought. Devices had a habit of remembering what was done to them, especially if they automatically back up files to the cloud.

'I still think that the video alone doesn't prove you've done anything wrong,' I said, trying to raise his spirits.

'But it doesn't need to prove it,' he said miserably. 'Even if the BHA takes no action against me, Mr Kline and every other trainer will. I'll be instantly out of a job with no prospect of ever getting another one.'

Unfortunately, he was almost certainly correct on both counts.

'Well,' I said. 'In that case we have to prevent Valance from posting the video on social media.'

'And how do we do that, other than by me doing exactly what he wants?'

That was a good question, and one I hadn't yet worked out the answer to.

Marcus stared at me and, once again, he was close to tears. 'Why do you care anyway? It's my problem, not yours. And it's all my own stupid fault.'

I thought for a moment.

'I care, Marcus, on a number of different levels,' I said. 'Firstly, I care passionately about our sport of horse racing, particularly jump racing. Second, I care very much that someone is trying to manipulate the fair running of racing for their own advantage. And third, I care that you are being used as an unwilling pawn in a much bigger chess game, simply because you naively made one silly mistake.

'Valance knew exactly what he was doing. He probably heard that you were short of money and offered you some manna from heaven at a time when you were absolutely starving. Who wouldn't take it, especially as you both knew the horse was a no-hoper anyway? That's why he asked you to stop that particular one. To knock you off your guard. If it had been the favourite, or any other with a decent chance, you'd have probably told him to bugger off.'

He nodded, although I wasn't altogether sure he would have done.

'So don't beat yourself up too much. I intend to defeat this man and I need your help to do it.'

He suddenly looked less willing.

But I wasn't finished. 'I need you to tell me everything he says to you. If he calls and says you are not to turn up at the races or not to win on a certain horse, I need to know about it. Not the following day, but straight away.' I emphasized the point. 'Everything he says, without fail. Do you understand?'

'But why?'

'Because if you don't, you can kiss goodbye to your riding career for good. Even if Valance doesn't ruin it, I will. If I'm to help you keep your jockey's licence and your job, I need to know everything. Do you understand?'

He nodded again, if one can nod and also hold one's head down in shame at the same time.

'Look at me,' I said, slapping him on the arm.

He lifted his head and looked straight into my eyes.

'We will win. Trust me. And that will be a victory worth celebrating.'

But I'm not sure he believed me.

Perhaps I didn't believe it either.

At four o'clock in the afternoon, Marcus had to go and do evening stables at Noel Kline's yard.

By then, I think I had finally convinced him to call me whenever Anton Valance contacted him, but only time would tell if I had been successful.

He was certainly a very unhappy boy. He had foolishly got himself into something that was way over his head and getting out unscathed was going to be difficult, if not impossible.

Rosie, in contrast, was overjoyed to see me when I walked back to the Discovery in the marketplace. With her barking enthusiastically in the back, I climbed in and drove out of the town on the Coverham Lane. After about half a mile, I pulled off the road alongside the gallops on the Low Moor and let her out for a run.

Was it really only four short days since I had come this way in Marina's Skoda to meet secretly with Gary Bremner just slightly further on at Pinker's Pond? It felt like much longer ago than that.

I watched as Rosie ran fast along the edge of the gallops, her nose held low towards the ground as if following the scent of another dog or maybe a rabbit, or even a fox. Over the years, and in spite of my initial hesitancy at having dogs at all, Rosie had given Marina and me so much pleasure. If this marital separation of ours was to be made permanent, we would likely argue just as hard over custody of our dog as over custody of our daughter.

'Oh, God.' The very thought of it made me cry out in anguish.

I stood with my face pointed into the brisk, cold, northerly wind and enjoyed the spectacular views across Wensleydale towards the distant Bolton Castle on the far side, where Mary, Queen of Scots, spent some of her nineteen-year imprisonment prior to being executed in 1587, aged just 44.

Something about that, and also the thought of King Richard III strutting his stuff through the streets of Middleham more than a hundred years earlier, made me take stock of how transient human life can sometimes seem but, equally, how important it remains for every one of us. We may exist for only a fleeting moment in terms of the total length of human history, and for a much shorter period than that in comparison to the age of the hills and dales that were laid out before me, but how we each feel right now continues to be relevant and meaningful.

I wiped tears from my eyes with my sleeve and tried to tell myself they were caused only by the wind.

'Come on, Rosie,' I called out. 'Time for us to go.'

But we didn't go home. Not yet.

Instead, we went to see Simon Paulson.

17

I drove my Discovery into Simon Paulson's yard during the height of evening stables, when his staff were either rushing about with sacks of dirty bedding slung over their shoulders or measuring out feed and carrying buckets of water for their charges.

'Can't you bloody leave me alone?' Simon said bitterly.

'Not a hope,' I replied.

I glanced up at the dark, threatening edifice of Middleham Castle to my right, and wondered if anyone was watching me this time from up high on the viewing platform.

'Why did you tell Anton Valance that I was at Catterick on Tuesday?'

'What do you mean?'

'Two of his heavies were waiting with baseball bats to ambush me in the car park as I left to go home, and they hadn't just turned up by coincidence. Someone tipped them off that I was there.'

'Don't be ridiculous,' he replied, but there was something about his body language that told the real story.

'Two runners, both favourites, and neither of them even came close to winning. They had no chance, did they, Simon? Because you made sure they wouldn't win. I'm surprised the Catterick stewards didn't hold an enquiry.'

I could tell he was frightened, as well he might be.

'You and I need to talk,' I said.

'I'm not talking to you.' He turned to walk away.

'Oh, I think you will, Simon,' I said to his retreating back. 'Either that or you can talk to the Integrity Department of the BHA after I send in a report to them. Or perhaps I'll tell Anton Valance that you have agreed to assist me in arranging his downfall. I'm sure he won't be happy with that. Is your fire insurance up to date?'

He turned back to face me. 'You wouldn't.'

'Try me.'

Rarely had I seen a man's shoulders slump so much in resignation.

'Shall we go to your office?' I asked.

'There's too many people about,' he said, waving a hand at his staff. 'You'd better come into the house.'

The state of it was every bit as bad as he had said, worse even. There were stacks of unwashed plates everywhere, some of them growing a green mould, and the carpet in the living room was almost invisible under a mass of strewn newspapers and empty biscuit wrappers.

He should get together with Marcus Capes, I thought. He could learn a thing or two about being tidy.

Simon shifted one of the piles of papers spread out on the

sofa to give me some room to sit, while he descended into an armchair.

'I told Valance it was a bad idea,' he said, before I even had a chance to ask him my first question.

'What was a bad idea?'

'To send someone to beat you up. He said it would frighten you off, but I knew it wouldn't. I told him that you're not like other people. All it would do would be to make you more determined.'

Simon had been right.

'So you did call him to tell him I was at Catterick?'

'That wasn't why I called him – at least, not exactly.' He looked away from me briefly, then his eyes returned to mine. 'After you confronted Jimmy about his riding in the first, we both felt it was too dangerous to do it again in the fifth, so I called Valance to tell him that Night Shadow would be running on his merits. He went totally ballistic. Claimed they had too much invested on the race and I would be liable for their losses if Night Shadow won. It was then that Jimmy agreed to make the horse fall. But I didn't like it. Not at all.'

I sat there in silence for a few moments, not quite believing or wanting to believe what I was hearing. Making any horse intentionally fall could easily result in unnecessary injury, or even a fatality.

'What is the hold that this man has over you and Jimmy that would make you take such drastic action not to win a lowly Class Five handicap chase?'

He sighed deeply.

'I think I'll retire,' he said. 'Right now. This minute. The BHA can't take away my licence if I haven't got one.'

'They can still warn you off.'

'Warned off' was the old-fashioned term for what is now called *exclusion*. It was originally called 'warned off Newmarket Heath' and it is the ultimate sanction handed out by the racing authorities to miscreants and cheats. It means that not only are they forbidden from entering any racing establishments, including their own stable yards, but they are also banned from associating with any other licensed individual, which includes all owners, trainers, jockeys, vets, farriers and stable staff – indeed, everyone involved in horse racing – on pain of those also losing their own licences.

The racing community is actually very closed, with everyone knowing everybody else, generation on generation, with outsiders rarely admitted. Those *warned off* are even banned from speaking with other licensed members of their own family, and may be forced to move out of their own homes.

Such sanctions are purposefully extreme, to act as a deterrent.

If he was warned off, Simon would not only have to retire from training, he would have to retire from all his friendships, to say nothing of having to leave his house.

'Maybe there's another way,' I said, throwing him a lifeline. 'But you will need to help me.' He didn't look very happy at that prospect. 'And to start with, you must tell me how you got into this godawful mess in the first place.'

He took a little more persuading but, eventually, the whole sorry saga was laid bare.

'My wife, Jackie, apart from always nagging me about my

drinking and eating habits, she also did all the stable books – you know, staff salaries, paying bills, owners' invoices, that sort of stuff. That's how she met the accountant she's run off with. Anyway, after she left, everything went a bit pear-shaped on that front. Still is, if I'm honest. I've been trying to sort out the mess but . . . it seems beyond me sometimes. See, I'm quite good with horses but less so with figures.'

I looked again at the piles of paper on the sofa, some of which I could see were unpaid utility bills with FINAL REMINDER stamped on them in red.

'My secretary took on doing the payroll and paying some of our essential suppliers so we didn't get caught out without staff, food or bedding, but sending out and chasing the owners' invoices sort of fell between the stools.'

'So you basically ran out of money?' I asked.

'Big time. Suddenly last summer I had my bank manager on the blower threatening to shut me down at once and foreclose on the house.'

'So what happened next?'

'I got offered a loan, just to pay off some of the urgent stuff like the bank mortgage payment and the salaries, to tide me over until I received what was owing to me from my owners. I mean, it wasn't as if I didn't have the funds coming in eventually. I wasn't insolvent or anything. In fact, I made a decent profit last year, best in a long time, mostly thanks to Regal Monarch.'

But cash was still the king. Without sufficient cash in the bank you can't pay your staff and your business will fold overnight as they desert you. And Simon's wouldn't have been the first profitable business to go bust from a lack of cash flow, far from it.

'I assume this loan didn't come from your bank.'

'No,' he said. 'It didn't.'

'Please don't tell me you resorted to the loan sharks at some impossibly high interest rate.'

'I actually wish I had. They would have only taken all my money, not rob me of my reputation and self-respect as well.'

'So was this loan made to you by Anton Valance?'

'Not ostensibly, but he organized it.'

'How? I mean, how did he even know you needed a loan in the first place? Did you tell him?'

'Of course not. But I did call all my owners to urge them to please settle their invoices immediately, and also to ask if any of them would consider paying a month or two of their training fees in advance. Doesn't take rocket science for them to work out I was a bit short.'

'Even so, it's quite a big step for a jockeys' agent to find out.'

'I don't know. Maybe I mentioned it to him. He was always calling me. Anyway, by then I didn't care who knew, all I cared about was getting some fresh cash into my account.'

'How much?' I asked.

I could sense that he was reluctant to tell me.

'Come on,' I said. 'How much?'

'Sixty grand.'

That was not too bad, I thought. At least it wasn't a quarter of a million as I'd been half expecting.

'Valance claimed he had a consortium of backers, current and former racehorse owners and such, who didn't like to see people, especially trainers, be forced out of racing due to small downturns, or plain bad luck. He said they were prepared to help by lending me some money as a short-term contingency.

'I thought the terms were pretty high, mind, but they weren't excessive, not hundreds of per cent interest like the bloody loan sharks were offering. Trust me, I'd checked them too. And Valance also said his consortium didn't want any form of surety over the loan, so I suppose I couldn't really complain.'

'Have you paid it back?' I asked.

'Some of it. The trouble is, it keeps growing due to the high interest rate.'

What a complete mess, I thought. Getting into debt can be so easy – people will do anything if they're desperate – but getting out again can be impossible. It's how all loan sharks operated and this consortium, if it even existed, was doing far more harm to trainers than any good that they claimed.

'So what happened next?' I asked.

'Valance called me and said there was another way to pay back the loan.'

What a surprise – not!

'Was that before or after he arranged for Marcus Capes not to turn up to ride your horse at Sedgefield last October?'

He looked across at me sharply. 'How do you know about that?'

'Let's just say I know all sorts of things that would surprise you. So, was it before or after Sedgefield?'

He put his head to one side as if thinking.

'It must have been after.'

'Why do you say that?'

'Because in October, Valance was still trying to squeeze his trainers' premium out of me. That's why he stopped Capes riding at Sedgefield. To teach me a lesson for not paying, even when he knew bloody well that I was already stony-broke. So it had to be after that. November, maybe?'

'What did he offer you to make a horse lose?'

I could tell he didn't want to tell me.

'Come on, Simon,' I said. 'You've told me enough to hang yourself already. What difference would a little more make?'

'Just don't talk to me about hanging.'

No, I thought. Perhaps not a good turn of phrase to use. Not after what had happened to Gary Bremner.

'Okay, I won't, but tell me, what did he offer?'

'He said he'd write off ten grand from the outstanding loan if I agreed for a horse of mine not to win when he told me. Just the once, he said. He promised.' He sighed again. 'I must be bloody stupid, especially as, by then, the fucking loan had increased by more than ten grand in the six months since I'd taken it out due to the interest charges, so he was actually giving me nothing.'

Yes, I thought, Simon had been bloody stupid. Probably more than that. But stupidity doesn't necessarily mean wickedness. And, at least, the ten grand was a much more attractive sum that the paltry two hundred quid Valance had offered Marcus Capes.

'So I decided to do it just the once,' Simon said. 'In fact, I couldn't afford not to. Jimmy Shilstone was also in on the fix – he had his own reasons that I didn't ask about. And it was so easy. The horse Valance wanted us to make certain didn't win had absolutely no chance anyway. It was a cast-iron loser right from the start. We didn't need to do anything special.'

Now where had I heard that before?

I didn't leave Simon Paulson's place until nearly seven o'clock, by which time he had laid bare his soul. And I spent much of the journey back to Oxfordshire going over in my head exactly what he had said.

He had admitted to me that he and Jimmy Shilstone together had made sure that horses of his didn't win on eight separate occasions. After that first one, there had been a gap of a couple of months but, inevitably, Valance then came back for more. The requests were now becoming more frequent, with the latest two being on the same day: those I had witnessed at Catterick on Tuesday.

'But, at ten grand a time, you must have surely paid off the loan by now,' I had said to him encouragingly.

He had looked at me. 'Don't be daft. He didn't offer me ten grand the next time. Only five. And it's been going down ever since. He even told me on Tuesday that I would get no reduction in the loan at all for the latest two. I protested, but he simply said that if I didn't like it I should complain to the BHA. I ask you.'

'So why did you still do it?'

'Because he has me over a fucking barrel, that's why. I still owe about thirty thousand on the loan and he said he would send details of all the horses Jimmy and I had stopped to the BHA unless we continued.'

'And you believed him?'

'I couldn't take the chance not to.'

Anton Valance was very clever, no doubt about it. He lured in his victims like a patient fisherman dangling a juicy worm. He said he only wanted you to do it once, a nice easy task, something that didn't even feel like it was dishonest – the horse had no chance anyway, so what difference did it make? But, having made that first easy step, when you've tasted his bait, he strikes and now has you well and truly hooked, playing you forever at the end of his line until you are too tired to refuse anything he asks for.

So I finally knew for sure what was going on – or, at least, a part of it. Now all I had to do was stop Valance doing it again in the future, and somehow to manage that without the blame for past transgressions falling squarely on his vulnerable victims.

So where did I start?

It was gone ten o'clock by the time I reached home and Rosie was beginning to complain bitterly that it was way past her suppertime.

I was hungry too.

I had stopped briefly at a motorway services to fill the Discovery's fuel tank with diesel – all this toing and froing to Yorkshire was doing dreadful things to its mileage – but, otherwise, I had pushed on through without stopping to fill my own fuel tank.

I yawned as I turned in through the gate. I was glad to be home, even if the place was deserted and in darkness, but how I longed for things to be back as they had been, with a warm welcoming kiss from my wife.

Rosie also seemed glad to be back and she bounded across ahead of me down the side of the house towards the back door. But suddenly, she stopped dead in her tracks and started barking.

The hairs on the back of my neck stood up.

Something wasn't right.

I retreated rapidly back towards the Discovery, calling for Rosie to follow, but she remained rooted to the spot, facing the back door, still barking loudly. Ideally, I would have loved to get back in the car and drive away, but I felt I couldn't leave Rosie, not least because she would have run out onto the road to chase me, and I'd already lost one dog through being hit by traffic.

I used my mobile phone to dial 999.

'Emergency,' said the operator, 'Which service?'

'Police.'

I was put through.

'I wish to report intruders at my property,' I said. 'And they are still here.'

They took the details and promised to send a squad car immediately.

I then turned the Discovery slightly to the left so that its headlights lit up the side of the house before retrieving the baseball bat I had thrown onto the back seat in the Catterick racecourse car park. I would have loved to have had two proper working hands to hold it, but one and a half would have to do.

I went back down the side of the house. Rosie hadn't moved, although her barking had now reduced to a constant menacing growl.

'Come on, where are you?' I shouted as I advanced. 'I've called the police. Now show yourselves.'

Two of them appeared around the corner of the house, both wearing balaclavas. I was sure they were the same pair from Catterick. One of them still held his trusty baseball bat and the other now sported a long pole to replace the bat he had left behind on that last occasion, the one I now held at the ready against him.

Rosie started barking loudly again and the two of them took a step backwards, as if they were both afraid of her. Good girl, I thought.

Emboldened, I shouted at them again. 'Come on then, you bastards.' I swung the baseball bat around in a circle above my head. 'I'm ready for you. Show me what you've got.'

I could hear a distant but fast-approaching police siren, and the men heard it too. Even through their balaclavas, I thought I could detect a moment of panic in their eyes.

They rushed towards me, stepping round Rosie. I swung my bat at the lead one's head but he brushed it aside with his forearm and almost ran straight over me, Jonah Lomu style, such was his determination to get away. Both of them disappeared down the side of the house and out towards the road, leaving me gasping for air on the ground in their wake.

Rosie came over and playfully licked my face. I almost laughed and tickled her tummy. But she was far more interested in getting fed than anything else.

The police arrived with flashing blue lights, a screech of brakes and a shower of gravel on the driveway. There were two of them, in uniform, and they had their Taser stun guns drawn at the ready.

I could do with one of those, I thought – if only they were legal.

'You're too late,' I said to them. 'The intruders knocked me over and ran off when they heard you coming.'

I wondered if a stealthier approach might have been more productive, but my assailants might have beaten me up in the meantime or, even worse, done away with me completely. And it wouldn't have been much comfort for me, if I was already dead, that my killers had been caught red-handed.

On balance, I was happy not to have been beaten up or murdered, even if the two men were still on the loose to have another go in the future.

As the policemen searched my garden, I unlocked the back door and went into the house to give Rosie her much-deserved supper.

Eventually, the two police also came into the house. They had discovered no additional persons lurking in the shadows but they had found something equally disturbing – an abandoned plastic container full of petrol.

Perhaps it was *me* who should have been checking that my fire insurance was up to date.

18

I had a disturbed night. Every bump or creak from the cooling house had me on edge, straining to hear if my unwelcome visitors had returned.

The two policemen had stayed for nearly an hour. Most of the time they had been out in the garden looking unsuccessfully for any other discarded evidence, but they also came into the kitchen to ask me some questions.

Did I know who the men were?

No.

Did I know what they were after?

No.

Did I know of anyone who might want to do me harm?

No.

The answer to the third question, of course, was 'yes', but that would have involved me giving them detailed reasons, and I wasn't yet ready to do that.

But the thought of anyone setting fire to me, or my house, did fill me with terror. Once before I'd had to deal with a man who liked to use fire as a weapon against me and, ultimately, he'd been the one who'd been consumed by it. I remembered that image all too clearly, and it was something I never wanted to see again, let alone experience.

'It was probably just an attempted burglary that you foiled by returning home when you did,' one of the officers had said in a matter-of-fact tone.

'But what about the petrol?'

'Forensic teams are so good these days at finding people's DNA from the slightest drop of sweat or saliva that some burglars will do anything to cover their tracks. And fire destroys DNA. Maybe it was their intention to burn the house down after robbing it.'

In the end, the officers had departed with the petrol container sealed in a plastic bag, promising that it would be tested for fingerprints, to check against the records held on the Police National Database. But their attitude made it clear that I shouldn't raise my hopes very high.

I didn't. I knew that only a meagre 3 per cent of burglaries committed in England and Wales are ever solved to the point of a successful prosecution.

I had asked about the possibility of them providing me with some protection overnight in case the men came back. Sorry, they'd said, they didn't have the manpower.

No manpower to prevent crime, or to solve it.

All they had done was leave me with a crime reference number, even though I wasn't even sure that a crime had actually been committed.

I had been very fortunate. At Catterick, the cavalry had come to my aid and here, without Rosie's wondrous sense of smell, I would have walked straight into their trap. I didn't fancy the men being third time lucky.

I lay awake for much of the night, thinking that it was high time I summoned some reinforcements.

At seven-thirty the next morning, I called Chico Barnes.

Chico and I had first worked together after I'd been forced to retire from race riding. We had both been employed by the Hunt Radnor detective agency and had been sort of thrown together when I'd done him a favour by covering for him at a stake-out, so he could have an assignation of a romantic nature with a 'bird', as he called all women, but with affection not malice.

As a result, I had ended up getting shot in the guts and, at the time, it had been touch and go as to whether I would survive. I knew that Chico had always felt slightly responsible, not that he'd ever let on to me.

'Bugger me. It's Sid Halley,' he said, answering after two rings.

'How do you know?'

'Your number, mate, popped up on my phone. How are you? And how's that fancy new paw of yours doing?'

'It's doing just fine, thank you.'

'How about your gorgeous bird?'

Chico had a soft spot for Marina, something that was reciprocated after he had helped save her life.

'She's also fine,' I replied. 'She's in Holland at the moment helping to look after her dying father.'

'I'm sorry. How about your kid?'

'She's in good order, thanks. Over with her mother at the moment. How about you?'

'Never better, well, except for a touch of bleedin' arthritis in my knees. But, at my age I shouldn't grumble.'

I laughed. No one knew exactly how old Chico Barnes really was. He had been abandoned as a toddler in a pushchair on the steps of Barnes police station, in west London – hence his surname.

Neither of his parents had ever been traced and he had been nicknamed Chico by one of the policemen due to his small size and curly hair – after the diminutive curly-haired Chico, one of the Marx Brothers.

The name had simply stuck, and was now official.

Many years ago, I'd spoken to him about being abandoned, suggesting that, with new DNA techniques, it might now be possible to trace his parents.

'For what?' he'd said. 'As a youngster, I was always very angry with them for discarding me, just as if I'd been a bag of unwanted clothes left at a charity shop. But by the time I was about twenty, I had finally worked that anger out of my system. So why would I want to reignite it again now? So they could beg my forgiveness and I could absolve them of their guilt? Don't make me bleedin' laugh.'

And we had never discussed the matter again.

'Is the arthritis very bad?' I asked.

'Nah, nothing that a few paracetamol don't fix. At least I'm still able to do my job.'

Chico taught PE and judo at a comprehensive school in Tottenham, north London.

'Aren't you on your Easter break?'

'Starts later today. Two whole weeks away from the bleedin' juvenile delinquents. What joy!'

'Do you fancy a holiday job?'

'Doing what?' He sounded wary.

'Bodyguarding.'

'Who's the target?'

'I am.'

'Not upset another bleedin' terrorist, have you?'

'Something similar. What do you say?'

'Are you being serious?'

'Deadly.'

'Please don't use that word. Not after last time.'

'Sorry. But, yes, I'm being perfectly serious. I need you.'

'Do you have a client?' he asked.

'Several.'

'So you're getting paid then?'

'Not exactly.'

'Come on, Sid. How many times do I need to tell yer, you must have a bleedin' client to pick up the tab. All this "pro Bono" stuff is stupid.'

I laughed. He'd pronounced it Bono, like the singer.

'I will pay you, though,' I said. 'If you'll come.'

'How much?'

'How much do you want?'

There was a short pause.

'Come on, you old bugger, you know I'll do it for nothing. Nothing other than a bit of fun, and to spend some time with you. I'll need my keep, mind.'

'It's a deal. When can you start? How about today?'

'Sorry, mate. I'm on a promise for tonight. Nice Swedish bird who fancies me rotten.'

'Can't you put her off?'

'Put her off?' he sounded incredulous. 'You must be bleedin' joking. Not all of us has a nice sexy wife like yours on call for a bit of nookie whenever you want it.'

Little did he know.

'And I've been working hard on this beauty for weeks.'

'Tomorrow then,' I said. 'Early.'

'Okay, unless tonight goes better than expected.'

'And what is expected?' I asked, laughing.

'That's none of your bleedin' business.'

We agreed that he would take the train from London to Banbury the following morning and I would pick him up from there. That was, I thought, if I hadn't been beaten up or burned to death by the two balaclava wearers in the meantime.

For about the fifth time, I went round checking that all the doors and windows of the house were securely locked.

Suddenly, with the arrival of a container full of petrol, I realized this was no longer a game. Sure, those two boneheads had probably been responsible for burning down Gary Bremner's stables and, quite likely, they were also guilty of his murder, but this was me and mine, and that was a different matter altogether.

I called Charles.

'Fancy a coffee?'

'Sure,' he said. 'Where?'

'Here, preferably. If you can.'

'Give me an hour, I'm still in my pyjamas.'

While I waited for him to arrive, I called Marina but it was Saskia who answered her phone.

'Hello, Daddy,' she said excitedly. 'Mummy's in the shower.'

'That's all right, Sassy, my darling. I'd much rather talk to you anyway. How are you?'

'I'm bored,' she said, sounding it, 'and I want to come home.'

'But you always love staying with Opa and Oma.'

'Not this time. I hate it that Opa is sick. And Mummy cries all the time.'

'Darling, Mummy is very sad that Opa is unwell. That's why she cries.'

I wondered if Marina was also crying over the collapse of her marriage.

'Now be a good girl,' I said. 'And look after Mummy for me.'

'Why don't you come here? Then you could look after her yourself.'

I sighed inwardly. 'I will come just as soon as I can. It must be nice having your Uncle Elmo there.'

'I don't really remember him.'

'That's all the more reason for getting to know him now.'

'But I miss Rosie,' she said miserably.

'Rosie misses you as well,' I said. 'But she's being a good girl too. I took her with me yesterday all the way to Yorkshire. She absolutely loved being in the car and you should have seen her running along the moors looking for rabbits. She had a wonderful time.'

For obvious reasons, I didn't also say that she had been barking at masked intruders.

'Will you tell Mummy that I phoned and ask her to call me later.'

'Okay,' she replied gloomily. 'But please can I come home? I've got to go to Annabel's birthday party.'

'That's not for another whole week. I hope you'll be home by then.'

I was trying to sound encouraging but it was breaking my heart to hear my daughter so sad, especially when I couldn't even give her a cuddle to cheer her up.

'Don't forget to tell Mummy.'

'I won't.'

'I love you, my darling.'

'Love you too, Daddy. Bye.'

We disconnected and I sat for a few moments with the phone in my hand, feeling very low. I needed her home, and her mother too, but how could I bring them back to this house when there were men in balaclavas, together with petrol cans, determined to burn it down?

Charles arrived fifty minutes after I'd called him and he was no longer in his pyjamas. In fact, he was wearing smartly pressed grey trousers, a starched white shirt with gold cufflinks, a double-breasted blazer, plus a striped tie and highly polished black shoes.

'Casual would have been fine,' I said, letting him in through the locked back door.

'This is casual,' he said. 'Smart would have been a suit, or uniform.'

You can take an admiral out of the navy, I thought, *but never the navy out of an admiral.*

'Now, what is all this about?' he asked.

'Why does it have to be about anything?'

'You'd never ring me before nine o'clock in the morning for nothing.'

He clearly knew me too well.

'Do you want a coffee?' I asked.

'Black, please, no sugar.'

I used Marina's new-fangled coffee machine to make our drinks, popping in a couple of the foil capsules. I splashed some milk into mine, and then Charles and I sat down at the kitchen table.

'Now,' I said to him. 'I have some things to tell you. You don't have to do anything, I'd rather you didn't, but I would like you to know a few details just in case.'

'In case of what?' he asked seriously.

'In case I become incapacitated, or worse.'

'I see. And is that likely?'

'You know the two men in balaclavas I told you about, the ones who came looking for me in the car park at Catterick?'

He nodded.

'Well, they turned up again here last night.'

I told him how it was only through the good fortune of Rosie's reaction that I had avoided walking into their ambush. I also told him about the police arriving and then finding a container of petrol.

That shocked him.

Both he and I knew what villains with petrol were capable of. The front of his house still bore the physical scars while we carried the mental ones with us every day.

'So what did you tell the police?' he asked.

'Not much. They seem to think it was a potential burglary that I interrupted.'

'But you don't?'

'No.'

'So why didn't you tell the police that?'

'It's complicated.'

'I have all day,' Charles said, leaning back in his chair and crossing his legs. 'And I'm pretty good at complicated.'

I told him about my trip north to see Marcus Capes, and also my second visit to Simon Paulson's yard, and I summarized what they had both told me.

When I was finished, Charles sat silently for a few seconds, drumming his fingers on the table.

'I can't see why you don't just go straight to the racing authorities and tell them what you've found out. Both these men you spoke to have clearly broken racing's rules and surely they deserve to suffer the consequences.'

The Royal Navy, throughout history, had always erred on the side of harsh punishments, rather than forgiveness. Perhaps Charles would also want me to advocate flogging them both with a cat-o'-nine-tails.

I was baffled by his position, and not a little annoyed.

'Come on, Charles, be reasonable. Can't you appreciate that these two men are victims here, rather than true rogues? If I go to the authorities now, the real villain will inevitably walk away unscathed and he would simply coerce more trainers and different jockeys in the future to do his dirty work.'

I don't think Charles was convinced.

'So who is this despicable arch-villain?' he asked sardonically.

'It's a man called Anton Valance but, other than what Marcus and Simon told me yesterday, I have no real evidence against him. And I don't believe either of them would tell the authorities what they've told me anyway. They would simply deny all of it to save their own skin. And what Gary Bremner said to me would quite likely be inadmissible because he's now dead. Any accusations he made might be thrown out as just hearsay. That's why I didn't mention Valance's name to the police. I need far more proof first.'

'And how do you intend to get it?' Charles asked cuttingly.

'I'm not sure yet, but I'm working on it.'

'Why are you telling me this now?'

'So that you can tell the police if anything happens to me.'

'As a result of those two men who came here last night?'

'Yes,' I said. 'Exactly that.' I swallowed, realising what I was saying. 'Tell me, Charles, how is it that evil men are able to recruit heavies to illegally beat people up? I couldn't do that. Could you?'

'What do you mean?'

'Just watch any of the James Bond movies. The bad guys, Ernst Stavro Blofeld or whoever, seem to have a whole army of willing helpers who are prepared to get shot, stabbed, strangled or blown up by 007, and for what? A bit part in destroying the world?'

'But that's only fiction,' Charles said with a dismissive wave. 'It's just made up.'

'I know,' I said. 'But it seems to be true in real life as well, especially if these two goons are anything to go by.'

He waved a hand. 'It seems that some people will do anything for money.'

He was so right, but how much money had the balaclava pair been paid in order to kill Gary Bremner?

And how much more would they need, I wondered, for them to also kill me?

19

Charles remained at my place for the rest of the day and we spent the afternoon in my sitting room watching the racing from Ayr on the television.

'Which is the jockey you want me to watch?' he asked.

'Jimmy Shilstone. He rides a horse called Lateral Flow Test in the second and another called Wit Of Cricket in the fifth.'

'And you think he might be stopping them?'

'I don't know. I just want to wait and see. Neither of the horses is trained by Simon Paulson.'

'Who then?'

'Two different trainers, both from Scotland.'

Ayr is the largest of the five racecourses north of the border and, in my career, I had ridden there quite a few times, notably in five Scottish Grand Nationals, one of which I had won.

Lying just a mile from the sea, close to the outer reaches of the Firth of Clyde, the course has well-draining sandy soil providing excellent underfoot conditions throughout the year for both jump and flat racing. Its oval track is about a mile and a half round with slight undulations along the back, a downhill turn into the home straight, and a gentle rise from there to the winning post.

The second race on today's card was a three-mile novice hurdle although, at this late stage in the jumping season, with only four more weeks to go, the 'novices' in this race were all pretty experienced, with one of them having run as many as seven times over hurdles prior to today.

Jimmy Shilstone's mount was the second favourite at four-to-one and he jumped off in the middle of the pack as the starter dropped his flag.

With two complete circuits of the course to run, and twelve flights of hurdles to negotiate, the early pace was steady, with the field of eight closely bunched as they raced down the back for the first time. Only when they had completed the first loop did the race begin in earnest. Jimmy took his mount to the front as they swung downhill into the home straight for the final time and he jumped clear over the final three obstacles, was never headed, and won by two lengths.

'Well, he obviously didn't stop that one,' Charles said.

He certainly hadn't, and he had ridden a flawless race, judging both the pace and the strides of the horse into the hurdles to perfection. It was in striking contrast to the two races he had ridden at Catterick earlier in the week.

'Not what you were looking for then?' Charles said.

'No,' I agreed, 'but it did show he can do it properly if he wants to.'

In the fifth race, a two-and-a-half-mile handicap chase, Jimmy finished a poor third on a grey that had simply not had the puff to stay close to the front pair on the climb to the finish but, as far as I could tell, it wasn't from any lack of judgement or effort from its jockey.

'Fancy a whisky?' I asked Charles as I turned off the television after the last race.

He looked at his watch.

'That would be lovely.'

'I'm afraid I only have blended Scotch. No single malts.'

'That's all right. I'll just have a small one anyway. I have to drive home.'

'You could always stay the night,' I said, echoing his earlier words to me.

'Would you like me to?' he asked seriously.

Did I? Would it make me feel safer? But was it fair to place Charles in potential danger just because I would feel more comfortable with some company?

'No,' I said. 'I'll be fine. You don't have any overnight stuff anyway.'

Such as your pyjamas, I thought.

'I could always go home now and collect a few things. My shotgun, for instance. *Si vis pacem, para bellum.*'

'What's that?'

'It's Latin. Motto of the Royal Navy. *If you wish for peace, prepare for war.*'

The shotgun was certainly a tempting offer. But I'd been in trouble with the police before for using Charles's shotgun, even if, without it, he and I, plus Marina and Saskia, would have all been murdered.

Eventually, the police had agreed that my use of it was in self-defence and therefore justified under the special circumstances we had encountered, but they hadn't been at all happy and had subsequently tried to revoke Charles's shotgun certificate. But he had successfully argued in the Crown Court on appeal that he still needed it to control vermin.

Could men in balaclavas with baseball bats be considered as vermin?

Definitely.

'What a good idea,' I said.

It would surely be foolhardy to turn down such an offer now, and then find out in the night that I had no defence against unwelcome intruders carrying more petrol. I could hardly ask them to wait patiently in my garden while I completed the four-mile round trip to Aynsford and back to collect it.

What was the old adage our politicians often use to justify the billions of pounds spent on maintaining and updating our country's nuclear weapons?

Better to have them and never use them, than to get rid of them and only find out later that you really needed to keep them after all – as a deterrent, of course.

Perhaps I could also do with a deterrent, and maybe the discharge of a couple of 12-bore shotgun cartridges over balaclava-clad heads would do the trick.

Charles went off to collect his shotgun, his pyjamas and a few other things, while I remained at home with the doors firmly locked. Rosie lay on her bed by the Aga and snoozed. That was a very good sign. She had always been able to hear visitors arriving long before I could, either welcome or unwelcome, and she would bark in excitement that they might provide her with a treat.

Even though it wasn't yet dark outside, I went round the house turning on lights to make the place look more occupied than it really was.

Charles soon returned and he'd brought some ten-year-old Laphroaig with him, along with his other stuff.

'If we need a drink,' he said, giving the bottle to me, 'and I do. We might as well have the best.'

'Not too much, mind. I wouldn't want to be sleeping it off if our friends come back.'

'I also bought a whole box of cartridges,' he said, putting the shotgun down on the kitchen table.

'Let's just hope we don't need any of them.'

I collected two glasses from the cupboard in the dining room and splashed three-quarters of an inch of Laphroaig into each.

'Cheers,' I said, taking a small sip from one.

'A willing foe and sea room,' Charles replied, lifting the glass to his lips.

'Eh?'

'Friday's toast. In the Navy. Sorry. Force of habit.'

'Don't apologize. I'm all for a willing foe if it means he leaves us alone.'

'I'll definitely drink to that.' Charles took another sip. 'Do you have any food? I'm quite hungry. Mrs Cross would have normally left my supper out and I could have collected it just now, but she's still away on grandmother duty.'

He made it sound like a huge inconvenience, which it may well have been. Being a naval officer probably meant you didn't need to cook your own food very often, so he'd probably never learned how to.

I went and looked in the fridge. It was even more empty than last time.

'I could do you an omelette,' I said. 'With some chips and peas.'

'Sounds great.'

I put some frozen oven chips in the Aga, peas in the microwave, and cracked my last five eggs into a bowl. And, I thought, what joy to have two hands to do it with.

I also found some cheese in the fridge door, so we were soon sitting down to a feast of cheese omelettes with all the trimmings, washed down with one of the Isle of Islay's best single malts, followed by two scoops of chocolate-chip-cookie-dough ice cream, Saskia's favourite.

What decadence.

'Have you spoken to Marina?' Charles asked, finally laying down his ice-cream spoon.

'Not today,' I replied. 'But I did speak to Sassy this morning.'

'How is she?'

'She said that she was bored and wanted to come home.'

'That's a good sign.'

But it wasn't a good sign that Marina hadn't called me back. I told myself that it was maybe because Saskia had forgotten to pass on my message. Or perhaps she had, and Marina had just chosen not to call.

I went over to the house phone to check it was still working and hadn't been cut off by the balaclavas. It hadn't. And my mobile was fully charged, with plenty of signal from the new mast installed at the top of the village.

I sighed. 'Marina's very busy looking after her father.'

'Shouldn't he be in hospital?'

'They've tried. Marina took him to their local one, but the doctors sent him home again.'

Charles shook his head and tut-tutted. 'Getting old is certainly not for the faint-hearted. I just hope I pop off in my sleep when no one expects it. I'd hate to be a burden on anyone. There should be a pill we can all take when we've had enough.' He sniffed his whisky. 'Not that I'm ready to go yet, mind. Plenty more of this in my cellar to finish first.' He smiled at me but it was one more of resignation than amusement.

'You've got plenty of years yet,' I said.

'Yes, well, I hope so. But things are beginning to fail, and my old waterworks are a pain. I have to get up so often in the night these days.' He sighed. 'Do you know I've now been retired from the Navy for almost as long as I served? Where have all the years gone?'

'Come on, Charles,' I said. 'Stop being so morbid. What would you like to do? Shall we watch something on TV? Or maybe a film?'

He turned up his nose at my suggestion. 'They all speak so fast in films these days, and mostly in regional accents. I find it so difficult to follow what they're saying.'

My, he must be getting old.

'How about a game then?' I said.

So we played Scrabble and I discovered, to my cost, that he might be old but there was nothing wrong with his brain, and he certainly didn't lack a competitive edge.

Twenty-five years ago, when I'd first met Charles, at a time when he had been horrified by his daughter's choice for a husband, I had beaten him easily in our first ever game of chess because he had underestimated my ability. He had assumed that, because I had left school aged only sixteen with no academic qualifications, I was simple-minded and unable to grasp the strategic nuances of the game.

Perhaps, now, I was guilty of doing the same thing with him, due to his advanced years.

After about an hour and a half of playing, and with two more wee drams of Laphroaig consumed each, we had run out of letters to pick up. I was doing very well, winning easily, when I put down an A and an S on an available P to make a vertical ASP.

'With the double-word score, that's ten points,' I said, feeling quite pleased with myself, but my joy was premature – much too premature.

I had carelessly left the A sticking up near the corner of the board.

'BAIZE,' Charles said triumphantly, putting down his last four tiles around the A. 'That's the Z on a double-letter score, and the whole thing on a triple-word score. So that's two times ten for the Z, plus three for the B and one each for the vowels. Twenty-six, times three for the triple, that's seventy-eight points in total.'

I sat there totally stunned.

'But you don't double the Z score first and then triple it,' I complained.

'Yes, you do.'

We resorted to reading the rules that were stuck to the underside of the box lid and, guess what, he was right.

'Seventy-eight,' he said again, writing it down on the score sheet. He added up. 'That now puts me nineteen points in front, so I win.'

He smiled broadly and clapped his hands.

'All right, all right. Enough,' I said. 'There's no need to rub it in.'

I felt I'd been beaten on the line by a short head, having led all the way from the starting gate. Worse, it was a Devon Loch moment.

'Want another game?' Charles asked.

'No.'

'You're just a bad loser,' he said with a laugh.

'Indeed I am,' I agreed. 'And, because of that, I have no intention of losing to Anton Valance.'

Nor of losing my wife and daughter.

20

I spent most of the night awake, much of it sitting on a chair in front of the Aga in the kitchen, with Charles's loaded shotgun across my knees, while Rosie slept soundly at my feet.

Nobody came.

Charles appeared at seven o'clock, coming into the kitchen wearing his pyjamas and a dressing gown. He yawned loudly, setting me off too.

'Sleep well?' I asked.

'No,' he replied. 'I lay awake for hours on end listening.'

'So did I. I just dozed occasionally.'

'Have you been outside?' he asked.

'I went right round at first light but there's nothing untoward.'

'We should be grateful.'

Grateful was not the word I would have used. Relieved, maybe, but not grateful. I couldn't go on living like this. And I certainly couldn't bring my family back home into these circumstances, that's if Marina ever decided to return. Either way, I needed to get on and sort out Mr Valance and his two cronies, pronto.

Charles went home after a breakfast of toast and marmalade, but with no butter – I really needed to go to my local supermarket.

'Shall I leave you the shotgun and cartridges?' he asked as he was packing his other stuff into his car.

'We would both be breaking the law if you did,' I replied. Maybe we had done so already, as the weapon in question had been in my charge all night anyway, but at least he'd been in the same building.

'So, is that a *yes* or a *no*?'

'Yes,' I said. 'But only if you are happy about it.'

'I'm not happy about it one bit. But I'd be a lot less happy if your house got burned down with you in it.'

Charles was nothing if not pragmatic.

'I promise not to fire it unless it's necessary.'

'I should hope not.'

'And, even if I do,' I said, 'I'll not actually shoot at anyone. It'll just be a deterrent.'

'But deterrents don't work if you're not prepared to use them. Do you remember the Falklands War back in 1982? Who would have thought that Argentina could have been so stupid as to attack Britain, a nuclear power – but they did. But, even then, we didn't use our modern and very expensive nuclear arsenal – of course we didn't – and the Argies knew all along that we wouldn't, so it had no deterrent effect whatsoever.

'However, a single and almost obsolete Vulcan bomber, flying the

8,000-mile round trip from Ascension to the Falkland Islands and back, just to drop a few ineffectual Second World War bombs across the runway at Port Stanley, had far more impact as a deterrent. The Argentine junta believed, quite rightly, that we could, and would, do the same to Buenos Aires, so they kept most of their air force at home to protect their capital city. And that may well have been the difference between us winning and losing that war.'

'So are you telling me, in a roundabout manner, to use your gun to shoot someone?'

'Yes, I am, if you have no alternative. If they know for certain that you won't shoot at them, it's not worth having the gun in the first place. Indeed, it could be more of a liability than a help, especially if it is captured and then used against you. That's what happened to the British Army at Rorke's Drift.'

'Rorke's Drift?'

'During the Anglo-Zulu War in southern Africa. Almost a third of our deaths at Rorke's Drift were due to the Zulus firing our own rifles back at us – rifles that had been either captured from us earlier, or actually ripped from the hands of the defenders themselves as the battle unfolded.'

'How on earth do you know that?' I asked him with incredulity.

'Every officer cadet, in whichever service, has to study prior battles during their basic training to make sure that mistakes made in the past are not repeated in the future. What happened at Rorke's Drift is ultimately why, during the Iraq and Afghanistan Wars, all British infantry weapons were attached to our soldiers with webbing belts so they couldn't simply be pulled away by the enemy and then used against us.'

I was certainly impressed by Charles's encyclopaedic military knowledge – but I still had no intention of shooting anyone with his shotgun, not unless I absolutely had to.

I spent an hour stocking up on food at Tesco before collecting Chico from Banbury railway station at noon.

It had been almost three years since I had seen him and he had spread a little around his waist, plus he had a few more grey flecks among the tight, dark curls on his head, but otherwise he looked just as I'd first seen him all those years ago at Hunt Radnor.

He lobbed his holdall onto the back seat and climbed into the Discovery next to me. I set off back to Nutwell.

'So how was your night with the Swedish beauty?'

'Don't ask.'

'Not as expected then?'

'Have you ever seen *The Crying Game*?'

I looked across at him 'No!'

'Oh, yes. Ingrid, my gorgeous Swedish beauty. Turns out she used to be a bleedin' Ivan.'

'When did you find out?' I asked, trying very hard not to laugh. 'Don't tell me it was only when she took her clothes off.'

'You mean *his* clothes off. Seems she's still legally a bleedin' man. He certainly had everythin' intact down below, just like in the film, even if he does have tits as well. It's all very confusin', I can tell you.'

'My God. What did you do?'

'What do you think I did? I made my excuses and left. Sad,

though. She – he – was really nice about it. We talked for a bit before I went. Poor kid is really troubled. By the end, I felt really sorry for her – him.'

'Will you see her again?'

'I said I might, especially if she had the operation. Seems she'd been thinkin' about havin' it for a quite a while now.'

'What a varied life you lead.'

'You can talk. You're walkin' around with some dead geezer's hand sewn onto your arm. That's bleedin' gruesome for a start.'

Chico clearly had an intuitive way with words.

'How is it, anyway?' he asked.

I took my right hand off the steering wheel and drove along holding the wheel only with my new left one. 'It's totally part of me now. I don't even think about it as being different.'

'So it's better than that fancy electric job you had before?'

'Much better. I can *feel* things with this.'

'Like that bird of yours? Bet she loves it, you now having two hands to stroke her lovely body.'

If only, I thought.

'Chico, behave yourself. She's not here at the moment, anyway.'

'Yeah, you said. Over in Holland with her sick dad. Pity.'

We drove on in silence for a while.

'Tell me,' Chico said eventually, 'who are the bad guys you need me to protect you from?'

'A couple of heavies in balaclavas.'

'Not more Northern Irish terrorists, I hope?'

Chico had also been there when we'd had our troubles from the Irishman in the past.

'No. These two are from Yorkshire, but they're still pretty terrifying.'

As I drove home, I brought him up to speed with the details of my encounters with the two men, first in the car park at Catterick races on Tuesday afternoon, and then again outside my house on Thursday night.

'Not petrol again,' he said. 'Don't people ever learn? You should never ever start fires with petrol. It's far too bleedin' dangerous. It explodes.'

'I'll be sure to tell that to my Yorkshire friends next time they come calling.'

'Did they come back again last night?'

'Nope.' I laughed. 'Nothing exciting happened here either.'

Chico ignored my little joke.

'But I sat up all night with Charles's shotgun on my knees just in case.'

'The admiral?' Chico said. 'How's he doin'?'

'He's fine. I'm sure you'll see him sometime while you're here.'

We arrived at my house in Nutwell and Rosie was as excited to see the new arrival as he was her.

'Amazin' how they remember,' Chico said, tickling Rosie's chin and stroking her head, as her tail wagged enthusiastically further back.

'It's your smell,' I said. 'Dogs never forget a smell.'

'Right then,' Chico said, standing up, welcome over. 'Fill me in with all the gen.'

We sat at the kitchen table drinking cups of coffee as I told him the whole story, right from when Gary Bremner had called me eight days previously.

The only thing I missed out was the real reason Marina had taken Saskia to Holland, that was before she found out how ill her father really was.

'And you don't want to just go to the racing authorities and tell them the whole lot?' he asked when I finished.

'Not yet,' I agreed. 'This man Anton Valance is no fool, far from it. He will have ensured that, if the authorities investigated, he would come out of it squeaky clean, while all his victims would carry the can.'

'He doesn't seem very clever to me,' Chico said. 'Otherwise he'd never have sent a couple of heavies to beat up Sid Halley. Bleedin' stupid, that was. Everyone knows that's the best way to get your arse kicked.'

'That may have once been true, but time passes and people forget. And it doesn't change the fact that Valance will have covered his tracks. You mark my words, if we go to the authorities now, nothing will stick to him and he'll simply be free to entrap new jockeys and trainers to do his dirty work. We need to get something on him that will stand up, if not in a court of law, at least at a BHA enquiry.'

'And how are we goin' to do that?'

'I don't know yet, but I'm working on it.'

Indeed, throughout my long night on guard in the kitchen, I had thought of little else.

'But if what you say is true,' Chico said, 'and he or his heavies murdered this Bremner bloke, won't the police find him out?'

'The police don't believe it was murder. They think Gary killed himself. Seems they found a suicide note, but it was not written on paper, it was typed into his phone.'

'So anyone could have done it.'

'Exactly.'

'How stupid can you get? But the police have always been far more interested in closin' cases than actually findin' out what really happened. Like those murders in Barking a few years back. Happened right close to where I live. What was his name? Stephen somethin'. Killed four young blokes with drugs. Left their bodies almost in the same place, but still the cops thought the lads had accidently overdosed themselves. They even said one of them did it on purpose, because they also found a suicide note next to his body, but that one had definitely been written by the killer. I ask you. Didn't they check the bleedin' handwriting? Port. That was it. His name was Stephen Port. Saw a TV programme about it recently. Right weird bastard, he is. And barking mad if you ask me.' He laughed at his play on words.

'So what do we do about this Valance man and his pair of goons? Do we wait here for them to come back or go lookin'?'

'Neither at the moment. Instead we go in search of more of his victims. I've already spoken to the trainer Simon Paulson and to the jockey Marcus Capes, but I'm also keen to have words with Jimmy Shilstone.'

'And who's he when he's at home?'

'He's the jockey that definitely stopped the two Paulson horses at Catterick last week, and Paulson told me that the two of them together had done it eight times in total.'

'So where do we find this Shilstone fella?' Chico asked.

'He's got rides at Ayr in Scotland today but he's booked for two more at Market Rasen tomorrow. One of them for Simon Paulson.'

'And where the hell is Market Rasen?'

'North Lincolnshire. About two and a half hours' drive away from here.'

'But, if we go all that way, will he even speak to you?'

'I doubt it. Not willingly at least. We've already had one conversation, at Catterick – that's if you could call it a conversation. I did most of the talking. He just told me quite forcibly to go forth and multiply, and kept on walking.'

'Charmin'. So what will you do?'

'I'd really like to speak to him away from a racecourse. Maybe find out where he lives.'

'So do we follow him home from the races?'

'No chance. We'd be bound to lose him.'

'What then?'

Two hours later, while Chico snoozed in an armchair, I watched the racing from Ayr on the television. I also called Simon Paulson.

'Are you fucking crazy? I can't tell you that!'

'Why not?'

I had simply asked him if the horse he had declared to run in the fourth race at Market Rasen the following day, Oscar Mike, the one to be ridden by Jimmy Shilstone, would be running on its merits, or was it to be stopped from winning.

'Because . . . because—'

'There you are,' I said, interrupting him. 'There's no reason not to tell me. So will Oscar Mike win?'

'Let's just say it's unlikely.'

'No, Simon, let's not just say that. Have you been told by Anton Valance to ensure it doesn't win, or not?'

He said nothing.

'Silence won't do, Simon. So tell me, is it being stopped?'

'Yes,' he said quietly.

'When were you told?'

'Yesterday afternoon, after the full declarations were announced.'

'How?'

'How what?'

'How were you told?'

'Valance called me.'

'And what did he say?'

'He told me that Oscar Mike wasn't to win.'

'Did he say why?' I asked.

'No, of course not.'

'So what did he say? What were his exact words?'

'He just said two words – Oscar Mike – and then he hung up.'

'Nothing else?'

'No. That's all he ever says. Just the name of the horse.'

He would, wouldn't he? Nothing obviously incriminating to record there.

'But I know what he means, all right.'

'And what's the phone number?' I asked.

'No idea. All it shows on my phone is "No caller ID". No one else calls me like that. That's how I know it's going to be him. Oh, God. What a mess.'

It certainly was.

'But Valance must surely call you all the time to book Jimmy to ride your horses.'

'He does, but he uses a different phone for that.'

'So what's that number?'

There was a pause while he found it on his phone, then he read it out to me and I wrote it down. It started 07, so was a mobile, hence no clue to where he lived, but it was a start in finding him – a good start.

'So does he also call Jimmy Shilstone with this mysterious "No caller ID" phone?' I asked.

'I assume so. Jimmy knows, all right. I certainly don't have to tell him.'

'Where does Jimmy live?' I asked, slipping the question into the conversation in an innocent way.

'Malton. Why?'

'I thought I might go and see him.'

'He won't like that.'

'I dare say,' I said. 'But do you have his address?'

'I'm not so sure I should be giving you that.'

'So would you rather I called my friends in the BHA Integrity Department to get it? Of course, I'll probably have to tell them why I want it, and also why you won't give it to me.'

Simon wasn't to know that I'd already tried the same tactic once before, to try and get Anton Valance's address, but without any success thanks to the damn data-protection regulations.

There was a long pause from the other end of the line. 'I don't know,' he said slowly. 'I wouldn't want to get Jimmy into any trouble.'

'Trust me, Simon. He's already in trouble – really deep trouble,' I said. 'And you are too. Can't you see that I'm trying to help you both get out of this without you losing your licences?'

If only, I thought.

21

Chico and I left for Malton at five-thirty on Sunday morning, well before it was light, having cajoled Charles into looking after Rosie, albeit against his better judgement.

'Can't you take her with you?' Charles had implored as he'd met me bleary-eyed at his front door, still wearing his pyjamas.

'No,' I'd said. 'We can't. We may not be back until very late.'

'We? Who else are you taking?'

'Chico. Chico Barnes. He's in the car. He's come to help me.'

'Ah, yes, I remember him. He's that curly-haired, crazy young man who doesn't go to bed.'

It was true. On the last occasion that we'd all been together, Charles had provided a perfectly good room containing a comfy bed for Chico to use but, instead, he had spent the whole time sleeping upright on a chair in Charles's kitchen, on watch, as he had done so again the previous night at my place.

And, for the second night, no one had come.

'Perhaps they've come to their senses,' Chico said to me in the car.

'You really think so?'

'No.'

'Exactly. Nor do I.'

Simon Paulson had eventually given me Jimmy Shilstone's address and also the gem of information that he rode out every morning for someone called Albert Frost, a Malton trainer.

I'd also asked Simon where Anton Valance lived.

'I don't know,' he'd said. 'Harrogate, maybe. I think he once mentioned to me something about going to the Turkish Baths there. Said he often needs to have a massage after his stressful mornings talking to, as he put it, "bloody trainers like you" on the telephone.'

'Where's his bank?' I'd asked.

'How the hell should I know?'

'You told me you pay his trainers' premium by bank transfer, so what's the sort code?'

'I'll have to look.'

I had waited patiently for him to log on to his online banking.

'Twenty, thirty-seven, thirteen.'

I typed the code into Google – Barclays Bank in Harrogate.

'What's the account number?'

'I surely shouldn't be giving you someone else's bank details.'

'So you'd rather I called the mobile number you gave me and tell him that you've given me his sort code but you said to ring him for the actual account number?'

'You wouldn't do that.'

'Okay. Maybe I wouldn't. But I still need it.'

'But those things are private.'

'No, they're not. Every time you write someone a cheque it has your sort code and account number printed along the bottom. There's nothing private in that.'

'I don't write many cheques these days.' He'd said it wistfully, as if yearning after some long-gone, simpler life.

In the end, and after much procrastinating, Simon had finally given me Valance's account number, not that it did me much good. Knowing his sort code and account number didn't give me access to anything, and certainly not how much he was raking off the trainers, or making on bets from the fixed races, that was if he had been stupid enough to use the same account for his gambling activities, which I very much doubted.

'So what's the plan?' Chico asked as we joined the M1 northbound at Leicester.

'We're on our way to Malton,' I said, 'to speak with one Jimmy Shilstone, jockey of that parish.'

'The one that you said has stopped eight of Paulson's horses?'

'Indeed, and possibly many more for other trainers. I want to catch him between him riding out for a local Malton trainer and him leaving for Market Rasen. That's assuming he does go home between the two. If not, we're in trouble, but I think he probably will, as he'd have to drive right past his house anyway.'

'What time will he leave for the races?'

'He's due to ride in the first – not one of Paulson's – and that's at two o'clock, so he'll probably aim to get there by one. According to Google Maps it takes an hour and forty minutes from Malton to Market Rasen racecourse. If I were him, I'd allow an extra half hour for traffic near the racecourse or for some other sort of hold-up. So I reckon he'll leave home between ten-thirty and eleven o'clock. But, to be on the safe side, I plan to be outside his house from nine.'

'What will you do if he won't speak to you?'

'I think he will. Especially as I intend blocking his driveway so he can't get his car out.'

'Sneaky. So where after that?'

'If we fail to speak to Jimmy this morning, we'll have to see him at the end of the day. There's no time to go to the races because we have to be in Harrogate by three o'clock.'

'What for?'

'Have you ever had a Turkish bath?'

'I doubt it. Never been to Turkey. Greece, yes, Turkey, no.'

I laughed. 'Do you even know what a Turkish bath is?'

'Obviously not takin' a normal bath in Turkey, then, or you wouldn't be askin'.'

'It's a steam bath, plus cold and hot dry rooms, and then a freezing-cold plunge pool, and there's one in Harrogate.'

'Sounds a bit bleedin' masochistic to me.' Chico turned and gave me a broad, full-teeth grin. 'But I'm game if you are. I'm not quite sure, mind, why we're goin' all the way to Harrogate just for a wash.'

'We're going there to see someone.'

The previous afternoon, after speaking to Simon Paulson, I had called the Turkish Baths in Harrogate.

'How can I help you?' said the friendly receptionist who answered.

'Hello,' I replied. 'My name is Valance, Anton Valance, and I was wondering if you could tell me when my next appointment is as I seem to have mislaid the note I made.'

'Certainly, sir. Just a moment. I'll check on the computer.'

There had been a very slight pause.

'Here we are. You're booked into our three o'clock session, tomorrow afternoon.'

'On Sunday?'

'Yes, on Sunday. And you have a fifty-minute massage with Laura at three-thirty.'

'Of course, thank you.'

Now, why did I think that Valance had made the appointment at that particular time as an alibi for what was going on eighty-five miles away in the three-thirty race at Market Rasen? Who could possibly think he had fixed a race that he wasn't even watching?

Well, me, for one.

I assumed Valance wouldn't have his two goons with him for his massage and, without his clothes on, I might catch him off guard.

I had also searched deeper into the internet for an image of him, so I knew which particular middle-aged man wrapped in a towel to accost.

Mr Valance was clearly a publicity-averse individual, and he was very hard to find. But, eventually, I discovered him in a two-year-old photo published in the *Yorkshire Post* of a group of five men standing smiling at the camera at a local charity event at Headingley Cricket Ground in Leeds. He was named as the second from the right.

I studied the photo in detail, trying to burn his image into my head. A quite portly gentleman stared back at me from the picture and I took careful note of his features, including his receding hairline, large nose and heavy jowls. After ten or fifteen minutes, I was confident that, despite him now being two years older, I would recognize him again, even without his smart white shirt and bow tie.

'So what do you want me to do while you're chattin'?' Chico asked.

'I want you to be with me and to look menacing.'

'But I'm really a pussycat.'

Yes, I thought, but one with sharp claws.

Jimmy Shilstone's driveway in Hill Street, Malton, was empty as we pulled up across the road at ten to nine.

'What do we do now?' Chico asked.

'We wait. If he's not back here by eleven-thirty, he's not coming.'

I manoeuvred down the road about thirty yards, so that we were not too obviously waiting right outside his house, but we could still see his gateway clearly.

On this occasion, we had come north in Marina's Skoda. There were times to be ostentatious and times to be covert. This was one of the latter. I was sure that if Jimmy spotted MY S1D waiting on his road, he would drive straight past, probably at high speed.

'Where's he ridin' out?' Chico asked after we had been there for forty minutes with no movement.

'In a village called Amotherby, just outside Malton. Albert Frost's yard.'

'Why don't we go and see if he's still there?'

'Because we might miss him. And I don't know what car he drives.'

We went on waiting. And waiting.

At quarter to ten, with still no sign of him, I made a series of calls to local Malton numbers.

Ten o'clock came and went, and there was still no sign of Mr Shilstone.

Then, at ten past, a silver Audi drove quickly along the road towards us and turned into his driveway. Jimmy was back.

I gave him a few minutes to get into the house, then drove the Skoda over the road and parked it in the middle of his gateway. There was nowhere near enough room on either side for him to get his Audi out.

'You stand by the car,' I said to Chico. 'I'll go and ring the doorbell.'

I leaned on the bell and didn't take my finger off it for the next two minutes, not until the door finally opened. Jimmy's hair was dripping and he was wearing only a towel round his waist. I had caught him in the shower.

'What the bloody hell . . .' he was shouting as he flung open the door, but he tailed off when he saw who it was ringing his bell.

'How the fuck did you find out where I live?'

'I find out all sorts of things, Jimmy. It's my job.'

'What do you want?'

'A chat, that's all.'

'I haven't got time for a chat, not with you, anyway.'

'Oh, I think you have.' I spoke quietly and without any threat.

'I have to get off to the races.' He looked past me to where Chico was leaning up against the front wing of the Skoda, trying to look menacing. 'And you can move that bloody car for a start.'

'I'll happily move it, but only after we've had our little chat.'

'But I have to leave in a few minutes.'

'Then we had better talk fast.'

I could see, once again, the same touch of panic in his eyes that I had first witnessed at Catterick.

'I have absolutely no intention of talking to you,' he shouted with a slight quiver in his voice. 'Because I have to go now.'

'To Market Rasen races?'

'Yes.'

I shook my head and tut-tutted. 'What a pity. It seems like you might not make it there today, after all.'

'But I have to,' he beseeched.

'And why is that?' I asked with my first touch of belligerence. 'Why do you *have* to go to Market Rasen, Jimmy? Is it to make sure that Oscar Mike doesn't win the fourth race?'

He stared at me and, just like Charles's had before, his mouth hung open in amazement.

'Like I told you, Jimmy,' I said, quieter again. 'I find out all sorts of things.'

22

'Who told you that?' Jimmy asked, finding his tongue.

'So you don't deny it?'

'Of course I do.'

'How about eight other Simon Paulson runners you rode that also didn't win when they could have done – do you deny stopping those as well?'

'Lots of horses I ride don't win. Most of them, in fact,' he said, echoing what Marcus Capes had said about jockeys having to get used to losing.

'Yes, I know, but there are eight specific losers that never had a chance, did they, Jimmy? Because you had been told not to win on them.'

'I don't know what you're talking about.'

'So what's your plan for Oscar Mike today? Start too slowly and leave him too much to do at the end, or perhaps engineer that he falls, just like you did on Night Shadow at Catterick last week? Or maybe you have some other ruse this time to ensure he doesn't win?'

'I think I've heard enough of this nonsense. It's time you left.' And he started to close the door, but I placed my right foot forward to prevent it closing fully.

'Okay, Jimmy,' I said through the narrow gap. 'If that's what you want, but I won't be moving my car any time soon. Can you run to Market Rasen in time?'

'I'll call the police.'

'And tell them what, Jimmy? That you have to get to Market Rasen races to commit a fraud? I don't think so.'

'Then I'll get a taxi.'

'Then you'd better hurry up. It's already almost half past ten and I can tell you that there are no taxis free in Malton.'

'How can you know that?'

'Because I called all the local firms and I booked the only two taxis still available, both to collect me from the station in York at eleven-thirty.'

I looked at my watch.

'They'll be on their way soon. Which means you will need to get a taxi from York or from Scarborough, and neither of those would get here in time to get you to Market Rasen for the first.'

I stared at him but he said nothing.

'So if I were you,' I went on, 'I'd call the trainer now and tell him that you're indisposed and can't ride his horse today. Maybe you won't get to ride any of them.' I paused while the enormity of his problem sunk in. 'Or else you can talk to me now and be away from here in just ten minutes.'

He opened the door wide again.

'What do you want?'

'I want to know what hold Anton Valance has over you. Only then can I help you get away from him, while also hoping to keep your jockey's licence.'

'Huh,' he said. 'Fat chance of the second, if I tell you the first.'

'Did he film you taking money for agreeing to stop one? Or maybe he lent you some money, say to buy that fancy Audi, and now he's charging you extortionate interest?'

'Neither.'

'Jimmy, you're wasting time you haven't got. Tell me, what is it?'

He still hesitated.

'Look,' I said. 'You either speak to me now or I'll make a report to the BHA about the two horses you stopped last week, and also about your plans to do it again with Oscar Mike today. Then there will be absolutely no chance of you keeping your licence. Is that what you want?'

'No,' he mumbled.

'Then speak to me.'

He sighed deeply. 'Do you promise not to tell the police?'

'The police?' I'd thought he was afraid of the BHA, not the police.

'Yes, the police. Do you promise not to tell them?'

'I promise.'

But withholding information from the police about some serious crimes is, in itself, a criminal offence.

Another sigh, and he looked up to the overcast sky as if searching for divine intervention.

'It was a girl.'

'What was?'

'Valance got me a girl,' he said. 'I went to Liverpool for the Grand National meeting – he'd booked me six rides spread over all three days. I would have preferred to drive back and forth each day to Malton but he insisted I stay over or else I'd be too tired to ride, he said, especially on Saturday with all the National traffic.

'Anyway, on the second night I was down there, he calls me and says he knows how to cheer me up after none of my rides thus far had won. Next thing I know, this girl arrives at my hotel room and says she's dead keen to be ridden by a real jockey. She ends up staying the whole night, not that we got much sleep.'

'So? Nothing criminal in that.'

Stupid, I thought, *but not criminal.*

He sighed once more. 'You don't understand. She was a real girl. Turns out she was only fifteen.'

'Ah.'

'Ah, indeed,' he said. 'Sexual activity with a child. You can get fourteen years for that.'

'But, if you honestly believed that she was older, and didn't know she was only fifteen, is it still a crime?'

'It seems that the Crown Prosecution Service always consider it's a crime if the man is more than six years older than the girl. I was twenty-three at the time, so they'd claim I should have known better or that I should have asked for proof of her age. And maybe I should have done.'

He stared up at the ceiling.

'I knew she was young, just not quite that young. She told me she was eighteen but I had my doubts, even then. Seventeen maybe, I thought, but not as young as fifteen or I wouldn't have touched her. She was certainly well developed – lovely tits – and she wasn't a virgin either, I can tell you. Not with all that knowledge. And she was keen as mustard for me to get on with it. Stripped off all her kit almost as soon as she was through the door.'

Jimmy wasn't the first man to be seduced in such a manner, and he certainly wouldn't be the last. Throughout human history, the male of the species has had a tendency to move all his brains from his head to his underpants in such circumstances.

'But Valance must have known how old she was.'

'Course he did, but he denies it.'

'But procuring a fifteen-year-old girl for sex with someone else is a far worse crime than actually having it, so Valance must be culpable as well.'

'Yeah, maybe, but it's not his face on the damn video, nor his cock.'

'What video?'

'Of the girl and me having sex.'

'How come there's a video? Did you take it?'

'Of course not. Neither did she. There was a secret camera set up in the hotel room. Filmed everything.'

It was my turn now to stare at him, dumbfounded.

'Valance must have fixed it. He assured me that, as my agent, he would take care of everything for my Liverpool trip, booking the hotel and such. All I have to do, he says, is turn up and ride. He bloody did take care of me too, stitched me up good and proper, with a full-frontal view of me riding all right.'

'How did you find out the girl was under-age?'

'I was emailed a copy of her passport. Her name was blanked out, but the photo on it was definitely of her, and it showed her date of birth clear as daylight. On that night in Liverpool, she'd been two weeks short of her sixteenth birthday.'

'Was the passport copy sent to you by Valance?'

'I didn't think so at the time. The email address it came from wasn't his and I thought it must be from the girl or her pimp or something, and they were going to blackmail me. But now I believe it must have been Valance that fixed it all. He certainly knew about it later.'

'But how would he get a copy of her passport?'

'God knows. Perhaps he's her father.'

I thought it very unlikely that a man like Valance would use his own family in such a sordid manner, but who knew what lengths some people will go to in the pursuit of illicit gains.

'When did you get this email?'

'The following July. Came with the video attached. Looked like some cheap porn movie. I was terrified my girlfriend would see it. She hadn't wanted me to stay down at Liverpool in the first place.'

'Is she still your girlfriend?'

'She certainly is,' he said gloomily. 'I'd been planning to ask her to marry me but . . . how can I now?'

'Where is she?' I asked, looking past his bare shoulders into the house.

'Not here, thank God, not with you turning up. She's staying with her mother in Cleethorpes for the weekend.'

So Valance had a double stranglehold over Jimmy – not only having had sex with a minor, but also sleeping around when in a steady relationship. He only had to send the passport and the video to either the police or his girlfriend to totally destroy his life.

No wonder Jimmy had done what Valance demanded of him.

At eleven o'clock I called the two local taxi companies and cancelled my bookings to be collected from York station, telling them that I was so very sorry but I had missed my train.

Five minutes later, Jimmy Shilstone left home for Market Rasen races. It was a little after he would have liked, but he would still be in time for his ride in the first, provided there were no major hold-ups on the Humber Bridge.

Before he left we had continued our little chat and it had lasted somewhat longer than the ten minutes I had promised, and we had moved into his kitchen.

After the arrival of that damning email in July, Jimmy had heard nothing for a month. Letting him sweat, I thought. Then Valance had approached him in the car park at Beverley races and given him a print-out copy of the girl's passport.

'I was absolutely shitting myself. I thought someone must have sent the passport information to him and he was about to blow everything wide open with a police investigation. But he just told me quietly that my secret was safe with him, provided, of course, that I did as I was told. Only later did I finally work out that it had to have been him who had set the whole thing up in the first place.'

'And how many times has he told you to stop a horse?' I asked.

'God knows. Too many. Maybe twenty or thirty.'

I took that to mean at least thirty.

'So not just for Simon Paulson?'

'No. For several trainers.'

'Was Gary Bremner one of those?'

'I don't think so. Right bloody shame about him.'

'Yes,' I agreed. But a right bloody shame was only the half of it.

'How do you find out which horses you have to stop?'

'He calls me on a different phone to the usual and just says the name of a horse. That's all, but I know what it means.'

Exactly the same as for Simon Paulson.

'And do all the trainers know that their horses aren't going to win?'

'I don't know. I don't exactly ask them, now do I? But Paulson obviously knew. That was made clear to me last week at Catterick with Night Shadow. He wanted out of that one due to your snooping.'

'But the trainers must realize you don't win when you could have?'

'I'm pretty good at stopping them. I've had no trouble with the stewards.'

He wasn't that good, I thought, *because I'd spotted it.* But, there again, I'd known where to look.

'But it must be very damaging to your career.'

'Too bloody right it is. Up until this year I was thinking I might go places, possibly down south to a lucrative stable, maybe even to Lambourn, but word is getting around this season that Jimmy Shilstone has lost his touch. I've heard it on the jockey grapevine. Keeps mistiming his runs, they say, and he fails to win when he should. But what can I do?'

'Well,' I'd said. 'The first thing you do is try your best on Oscar Mike this afternoon. Win if you can.'

He had stared at me. 'Are you fucking crazy? Valance will shop me to the cops in a heartbeat.'

'No, he won't. Trust me. He's invested far too much time and effort getting you into the predicament in which you now find yourself. He's not going to undo all that just because you win once when he's told you not to. Sure, he'll probably be very angry, and he might even threaten you with exposure, but he won't do it.'

'How can you be so sure?'

'I just am. And it might just bring him out of his cosy safe shell so that he becomes more open to attack. I intend to nail Mr Anton Valance and free you from his tyranny, but I'll need your help to do it.'

He didn't seem at all keen. Quite the reverse, in fact. And I fervently hoped I was right about Valance not sending the video to the police if Shilstone won on Oscar Mike. Or to the girlfriend, for that matter.

'Think about it, Jimmy. You can't spend the rest of your career dancing at the end of his puppet strings. He's never going to go away unless you and I do something about it.'

'But I still have a career of sorts. And it's better than being locked up in a cell twenty-three hours a day for the next fourteen years. Do you have the slightest idea what happens to sex offenders in prison?'

Actually, I did.

I'd once been falsely accused of child sex abuse and I was all too aware of the aggressive attitude towards the wellbeing of kiddie fiddlers, as the police privately called them.

Taking down Anton Valance and, at the same time, keeping young Jimmy Shilstone out of jail might prove a tad more difficult than I had thought.

23

Anton Valance had put on quite a few pounds since the *Yorkshire Post* had snapped him at the charity event two years previously. But I still recognized him immediately. Just to be sure, I'd had another quick look at a printout of the newspaper photograph and had also given it to Chico to look at on the journey from Malton to Harrogate.

I was already lying on a daybed in the long waiting gallery outside the treatment rooms at the Turkish Baths when Valance arrived. I was wearing a newly purchased pair of swim shorts and I had two white towels – both issued at reception – one placed over my head in the manner of a boxer and the other covering my left forearm. Valance was similarly attired, with one of his white towels doing its best to stretch around his ample waist, while the other was in his hand.

He sat down some distance away from me on another daybed and I kept my head down, ensuring that my eyes did not make contact with his. I might not have known what he looked like prior to studying the newspaper image, but I was quite sure he would have recognized me, especially if he'd been able to see the zigzag join on my arm between the old and the new.

After a few minutes, one of the staff, a young woman in a white tunic, came into the gallery and shouted for Mr Valance. Laura, the masseuse, I assumed.

With some considerable difficulty, he heaved himself to his feet off the low bed and followed Laura into one of the treatment rooms for his fifty-minute massage.

Poor girl, I thought, *having to massage all that flab.*

Chico then came into view, also with a white towel wrapped round his waist. He briefly put up a thumb, then made a zero sign with his thumb and forefinger before disappearing again.

Good, I thought. There was no one else here with Valance. He had arrived alone. He had obviously gone straight into the magnificently restored Victorian changing room and, from there, directly to the treatment area. Perhaps he would stay for a steam bath afterwards, and to use the other facilities, or maybe he would simply get dressed again and go straight home.

But I was ready for both eventualities.

The Turkish Baths in Harrogate are something of an anachronism. From the outside, the building looks more like a dour, grey, north-country mausoleum. You even have to enter through a somewhat underwhelming basement entrance more akin to that of a crypt than of a pleasure palace. But once you step inside, you are transported from thoughts of death to the delights of Oriental life, with multiple Moorish arches and multi-coloured glazed tiled walls in geometric eastern patterns. Rich walnut-coloured wooden furniture abounds and the floors are laid with sparkling blue, red and yellow terrazzo mosaics, while exotic golden lanterns hang from the roof. There are Islamic-inspired arabesques painted on the ceilings to delight the eye, interspersed by extravagant hexagonal multi-paned skylights.

Overall, it feels like you have been whisked away, as if by a magic carpet, from a drab Yorkshire afternoon to some Middle Eastern timeless paradise.

Only an ornate wooden screen surmounted by an impressive white-faced circular clock gives any indication of the passage of the hours as one moves from the Frigidarium, the cool room, to the Tepidarium, and then to the Caldarium. For the fearless, there is a final step to the Laconium, the very hottest room kept at 75 degrees Celsius, before an invigorating immersion into the icy plunge pool – all of it designed to cleanse both the body and the spirit.

But, on this day, I wasn't there to sample such Turkish delights. Instead I remained where I was, sitting on the daybed outside the treatment rooms, full of my own eastern promise, waiting in anticipation for Anton Valance to appear from his massage.

While I waited, I removed my mobile phone from my swim-shorts pocket and checked the recent results on the *Racing Post* app. Oscar Mike had finished second in the three-thirty at Market Rasen, beaten by just half a length.

Maybe Jimmy had been doing his best to win after all and the horse hadn't been quite good enough, or perhaps he had lost his nerve and made sure he didn't, but only by a small margin so as not to attract the attention of the stewards. Only time, and another little chat, would tell.

Slightly disappointed, I looked up a few other things on the internet and then put my phone back in my pocket. I then went on waiting.

Laura, the masseuse, appeared first, bang on the fifty-minute mark and, soon after, Valance emerged looking suitably relaxed.

It almost seemed a shame, I thought, *that I hoped to recreate in him all the stress that the massage had just taken away, and more.*

At first he seemed undecided but quickly opted for a session in the steam room, a small fully tiled area directly off the changing room. I followed him through the glass door and sat down next to him on the blue-tiled bench seat. I still had the towel over my head and I also had my left forearm covered. Fortunately, except for the two of us, the place was empty.

He said nothing and nor did I, just the merest of grunts between us to act as both a welcome and also a warning that speaking was not wanted or required.

Too bad, I thought.

However, we sat side by side in silence for a minute or two as the steam billowed around us.

Then the door opened and someone else came in, a man of about fifty. More grunts. The newcomer sat down on the far side of Valance, closed his eyes and put his head back, flattening his dark curly hair against the tile wall.

'Now then, Mr Anton Valance,' I said quietly but distinctly straight into his left ear from about two inches away, while at the same time taking the towel off my head. 'I met two friends of yours in the car park at Catterick Racecourse. They gave me a message about pissing off back south and not coming back. Do you want to hear my reply?'

He turned his head towards me and remained remarkably calm.

'Sid 'Alley, I presume.' With his Yorkshire accent, he had dropped the H.

'One and the same.'

He glanced down to my left arm, also now removed from under its towel. Would I ever get used to that? Probably not. But at least he was now looking at a real living hand rather than a plastic-and-steel doppelganger, not that I would have ever brought those delicate electronics into such a humid atmosphere as this.

'So do you want to hear it or not?' I asked again.

'I 'ave absolutely no idea what you're talkin' about, Mr 'Alley.' He began to stand up. 'If you'll excuse me, I 'ave to go now.'

The man beyond him also stood up. He went over and leaned against the inward-opening door. He grinned at me.

'My friend, Chico, here, is a black belt at judo,' I said. 'I assure you, he's very good. Unless you want yourself thrown over his shoulder onto this rather hard-looking floor, Mr Valance, I suggest you sit down again.'

For the first time he looked slightly concerned. And he sat down.

'There, that's much better,' I said.

Chico remained leaning on the door, holding it shut. We didn't want any interruptions.

'Now,' I said with some menace. 'I have a message for you too, Anton. If you ever send your two friends to see me again at my house, or anywhere else for that matter, I will lay everything I know before the police and the racing authorities. Do you understand?'

He just waved a dismissive hand.

'I don't know what you're talkin' about.'

'In that case,' I said. 'Let me tell you.'

I felt uneasy about telling him the facts I already knew, but I had to give him something substantial for him to realize that I had enough to cause him significant trouble, otherwise he would simply ignore my warning to keep his goons away from me and my family. But, equally, I was wary of placing him in a position where he felt that his only option was to cut and run, turning in Marcus Capes to the BHA and sending the video of Jimmy Shilstone's sex antics off to both the police and his girlfriend.

A subtle middle path was what was clearly needed.

'Let us talk about Gary Bremner,' I said.

'What about 'im? Terrible business.'

'Yes, indeed. Terrible,' I agreed. 'Not only did someone burn down his stable yard but they also murdered him.'

'I 'eard that the fire was an accident due to a careless cigarette being dropped in his 'ay store, and I think you'll find that the police are treating 'is death as suicide. Apparently, 'e left a note.'

'Let's discuss that suicide note, shall we? It was not written out with pen and paper but typed into his iPhone.'

'So I believe.'

'Are you aware that you cannot type anything into an iPhone wearing gloves? The keys don't work on pressure – there has to be an electrical contact between the fingers and the conductive touch-screen surface. Fingers that will leave fingerprints – and maybe even some DNA from the person's sweat.' I paused. 'Will they be your prints, Anton, on Gary Bremner's iPhone? Or your DNA? Or maybe some from one of your henchmen? Do you really think they won't give you up if they get charged with his murder? They as good as told me at Catterick that it was you who had sent them.'

There was a slight tightening of the skin around his eyes. I now had his full attention. But I wasn't finished with him yet.

'Did you know that Gary Bremner called me nine days ago?'

Valance stared at me and there was a hardly perceptible shake of his head.

'He was worried that someone might try and kill his horses. He told me all about your little trainers' premium ruse and the threats you made to him because he wouldn't pay up. I even drove to Middleham to see him. That was last Sunday, a week ago today, the day after the fire and the day before he was found dead. He didn't talk to me about suicide then – quite the reverse – he was determined to nail the bastard who had burned his stables and killed his best horse, and he also told me the name of the bastard responsible. It was your name, Mr Anton Bastard Valance. So what have you got to say for yourself?'

He said nothing. He just went on glaring at me and I wondered what was going on in his brain behind those staring eyes.

He finally cleared his throat. 'I'm sure I don't know what you're talkin' about. Anyway, anythin' that you may claim Gary Bremner said to you is irrelevant. I've been told it would just be 'earsay and would be inadmissible in court.'

'You clearly don't know your hearsay law very well, do you, Anton? I thought the same as you, but I've since checked. It may have been the case before, but the Criminal Justice Act of 2003 provides for certain conditions when hearsay evidence can be considered by the courts, especially if the original witness is unable to give it in person, such as because he's been murdered.'

And I only knew that because I had looked it up on the internet as I was waiting for him to emerge from his massage.

I changed tack.

'Do you gamble much, Anton? On the horses?'

'I 'ave the occasional flutter.'

'With a regular bookmaker? Or perhaps you do it online, maybe on an exchange such as Betfair? Do you have your own online account or do you use one in someone else's name?'

'That's none of your fuckin' business.'

'Oh, yes, I think it is my business, especially if you are defrauding other users of the exchange. Have they not worked it out yet?'

'Worked out what?'

'That you are laying horses that you know for certain won't win, something which is, by the way, explicitly against the Rules of Racing if the horse is ridden by a jockey you represent, and the penalty is disqualification from racing for up to ten years.'

I was taking a bit of a punt myself at this point. I had no actual evidence that he was betting against, or laying, the dead-cert losers, but I reckoned he wouldn't have been able to resist having just a small earner on an exchange every time he had arranged one to lose, even if it wasn't his main killing.

'You're talkin' nonsense,' he said, but a distinct shallowing of his breath and a slight tremor in his right foot indicated that I had hit the bullseye.

'Am I? Well in that case I'm sure you won't mind if I ask Betfair to check their records for certain races.'

'Which races?' He was, at last, getting a bit flustered.

'Two at Catterick last Tuesday for a start. Plantagenet King and Night Shadow. Both started favourite and both failed to win. Did you lay them both to lose, Anton? The betting exchange records will show it conclusively.'

He went on staring at me for quite a long time, maybe ten or fifteen seconds, while the cogs in his brain turned over.

'What do you want?' he asked finally.

'I want you and your goons to leave me and my family alone. And if anything happens to me, like my sudden death or if there is an unexplained fire at my house, then I have instructed my solicitor to refute any suggestions of suicide and to give the package he holds for me to the relevant authorities. The package contains everything I know about your dubious activities and names you specifically as the chief suspect.'

'Is that all you want?' he asked.

'That's all for now.'

But I'd be back. He could certainly bet on that as a sure thing.

24

'Was that what you wanted?' Chico asked after Valance had scuttled away out of the steam and back to the changing room.

'Not really.' I removed my iPhone from my shorts pocket and switched off the recording. 'He never said anything remotely incriminating. Nothing that could be of any use as evidence. That's if this thing is still working after all this heat and damp.' I wiped some moisture off the screen and put the phone back in my pocket.

'How about you?' I asked. 'Everything go okay?'

'Piece of cake. Couldn't have been easier.' He handed me the Skoda key, now missing the small, flat, circular *NeverLoseIt* tag from the centre of the attached key ring. 'Didn't even have to force his locker. I just pushed the tag through a convenient tiny tear in the linin' of his overcoat, which he'd helpfully left hangin' on a peg next to it. He's very unlikely ever to find it.'

I didn't ask if Chico had caused the convenient tiny tear in the lining himself. I didn't care, but I would have to buy Marina a replacement tag.

'Good. Then we can just let him go. No need to follow. We'll find out where he's gone later.'

'Is it true?' Chico said. 'That stuff about you givin' a package to your solicitor?'

I smiled at him. 'No, but he's not to know that, and maybe it would be a good idea to do that anyway.' Not that I had a friendly solicitor to ask.

We gave Valance another five minutes or so before Chico and I went into the changing room. There was no sign of him.

'Right,' I said. 'Let's get going.'

We changed into our outdoor clothes and went back to the Skoda. I still looked both ways to make sure that Valance's goons weren't waiting for me. Would my warning to leave me alone actually work or would it make him more determined not to, as it would have done for me?

'So what now?' Chico asked when we were back in the car.

'First, let's find out where Valance has gone.'

'His home, I expect.'

'I hope so. I've been trying unsuccessfully to find out where he lives.'

I switched my phone from my own ID to Marina's, turned on the *NeverLoseIt* app and selected her tag. Immediately the screen showed a map with the position of it indicated by a small blue circle. The circle was on the move, towards the south-east.

As we watched, the little blue dot doubled back twice, and also went three times completely round The Prince of Wales Roundabout on the A61.

'He's trying to make sure he's not being followed,' I said with a laugh.

I gave the phone to Chico to hold, while I drove.

After negotiating the one-way system in the town centre, we also took the A61 southeast.

'He's stopped,' Chico said.

Finding him was even easier than I thought. The app even gave us audible directions.

'Turn left onto Hookstone Road,' said a disembodied female voice from my phone.

I did as I was told.

'In two hundred yards, turn left into Oatlands Drive.'

I did that too.

'In eighty yards, turn left into Park Edge.'

I turned left once more.

'Your *NeverLoseIt* is one hundred yards on your left side.'

I drove down Park Edge, a quiet suburban cul-de-sac of very expensive and stylish residences.

'You have arrived,' said the voice, and the app changed to show the tag was just twelve yards away, with a big arrow pointing to the left.

I didn't stop the Skoda but drove on slowly past.

Half hidden behind a tall hedge, and with high, elaborate, wrought-iron gates firmly shut across the driveway, was a large house, more like a mansion, with two swanky cars just visible on the gravel in front of the double-width front door. And there was an intercom system on the wall next to the gate.

'Blimey,' Chico said, with his big eyes wide. 'He must be doing bleedin' well.'

Yes, I thought, *but how many other people is he bleedin' dry to afford it?*

'Okay,' said Chico. 'So we know where he lives. What now?'

I turned the car round in the turning circle at the end of the road.

'Use my phone to take some pictures of his house.'

Chico clambered through into the back seat and snapped away as I again drove slowly past. But Park Edge was one of those places where unfamiliar cars driving by at slow speed, with the occupants staring out of the windows taking photographs, would quickly get reported to the police, so we didn't linger any longer than necessary.

However, I pulled into a garage forecourt just down the road.

I took my phone back from Chico and used the app to remotely switch off the *NeverLoseIt* tag. I didn't want it beeping and giving away its position, as it would certainly do when it realized it was tracking somebody else.

I changed the phone back to my own ID before scrolling through the photos Chico had taken of Valance's house.

'Well done,' I said. 'They're great.'

'What are you going to do with them?' he asked.

'I thought I might send one of them to Valance's mobile number with the caption: *If you burn down my house, I'll burn yours down too.*'

'Is that wise? Especially from your own phone.'

'Probably not. But I want him to realize that I now know where he lives. I might just send a picture of his house without the caption. He'll have to work out what it means.'

'And what is that exactly?' Chico asked.

'Mutually assured destruction. MAD. The deterrent formula that had mostly kept the peace between the Russians and the Americans since atomic bombs were invented.'

And long may it do so, I thought.

'But won't you also be giving Valance your phone number?'

'I certainly will, but it's hardly a secret anyway. For years it was on my website so potential clients could contact me. I'm sure he would have had it already. And I don't think it's a bad thing anyway. Bit like the Red Telephone Hotline.'

'Eh?'

'The direct line between the White House in Washington and the Kremlin in Moscow. Better to talk than to fight. Less likelihood of mistakes with nervous fingers hovering over respective nuclear buttons.'

'So you think Valance will call you?'

'No. Not really. But it gives him the option to negotiate if he wants to.'

So I sent him just a picture of his house without any caption attached.

Then I filled the Skoda's tank with fuel before setting off south towards home.

Chico was snoozing as I joined the M1 south of Wetherby.

Something that Anton Valance had said was niggling somewhere in the deep recesses of my brain. And it wasn't the only thing I'd heard that had rung some alarm bells. I tried going over in my head again all that had been said but it wouldn't come. I'd have to listen again to the recording later, when I didn't have a curly-haired sleeping beauty sitting next to me.

However, his slumbers were disturbed anyway going past Leeds, as my phone rang.

'Hello,' I said, answering it on the Skoda's hands-free system.

'Sid, I've made a decision. Provided my father doesn't die before then, I'm coming home on Friday with Sassy, so she can go to Annabel's party on Saturday afternoon. I don't know whether we will stay on after, that's up to you.'

I rather thought it was up to her, but I didn't say so.

'Darling,' I said instead, 'I have Chico in the car with me and you're on speaker.'

'Oh.' She paused. 'Hello, Chico.'

'Hello, gorgeous,' he replied. 'How you doin'?'

'Not great at the moment,' she replied curtly. 'My father's not well. In fact, he's dying.'

'Yeah. Sid told me. What a bugger. Sorry.'

'Shall I call you later?' I said.

'Yes, do that. Oh, but one other thing, my phone's been telling me that someone else has been using my personal ID. It happened once last week and it did it again today.'

'That was only me. I was looking for the Skoda keys.'

'They're in my dressing-table drawer.'

'Yes, I know, I used your *NeverLoseIt* tag to find them. That's why I had to use your ID. I didn't want to bother you.'

'But it did bother me.'

'I'm sorry. But if it happens again, don't worry, it'll only be me.'

'Why will it happen again? You're not trying to spy on me, are you?'

I forced a laugh. 'No, of course not, my love. If I need to do it again, I'll call you first. How's that?'

She didn't seem much placated, and I wasn't really sure why I hadn't told her the whole truth, except that I was afraid she would be cross I had used something of hers for my investigating.

'I'll ring you later, when I get home,' I said.

She hung up and I drove on in silence, eyes fixed firmly on the road ahead. Only when we left the motorway did Chico say anything.

'Why didn't you tell me?'

'Tell you what?'

'You know perfectly well what. That you and your missus are havin' troubles.'

I looked across at him. There was no point in denying it.

'It's not the sort of thing you advertise.'

'But I'm your mate.'

I sighed.

'I think it's my new hand.'

'What about it?'

'She says she can't stand it. Claims it feels like she's being touched up by a stranger.'

He laughed. 'Don't be so bleedin' stupid. That can't be the real reason. It may be what she says but that's just a smokescreen, an excuse.'

'Are you actually trying to make me feel worse?'

'Course not. I'm just tellin' you the truth.'

Maybe I didn't want to hear the truth.

'Perhaps she's bored with me.'

'I'm not surprised,' Chico said. 'You're gettin' unexciting and ponderous in your old age. Where's the old Sid Halley who would whisk Marina off her feet and give her a good seein'-to in the garden during the afternoons?'

'We have a daughter, you know.'

'So? The kid's at school most of the day. So do it in the mornin'. Get on with it. Or do you want to end up bein' one of those borin' old farts in an ill-fittin' grey cardigan with your trousers pulled up to your tits, more interested in what's comin' on the television than the passion you can still generate in the bedroom department?'

'And who do you think you are?' I said. 'Dr Ruth? It's not as if your love life is anything to write home about. Have you heard from Ingrid, or should I say Ivan?'

'Fuck off,' he said.

I wished I could.

Chico and I spent the rest of the journey to Charles's place at Aynsford in an uneasy silence.

It gave me time to think.

Was I really boring?

I had to accept that maybe I was.

When Marina and I had first met, we had both been living in London. Indeed, I'd had a flat in Belgravia, just a stone's throw from the gardens of Buckingham Palace, and in that great fun-fair of a city there had always been places to go, new restaurants to try, cinemas and theatres by the score, to say nothing of concerts, museums, river boats on the Thames, and a whole host of other things to do, all of them just a few Tube stops away and many within easy walking distance of our bed.

After Marina had moved in with me, we had almost never spent an evening at home in the flat, and when we had, we'd certainly not been watching television – there was too much else to do, too much fun to be had either just the two of us alone in adoration, or over a convivial dinner with friends.

We had spent the weekends on adventures out of the city, staying in grand country-house hotels or in rented cottages overlooking the sea, taking walks hand in hand – her left in my right – come sun, wind or rain.

In spite of Marina working full-time at the cancer laboratory and me conducting my self-employed investigating business, we had still managed to take spontaneous holidays, flying off at a moment's notice to the Maldives or the Mediterranean, anywhere where there was warmth and sunshine to brighten our lives.

And laughing. We had always been laughing.

I suddenly realized how much our lives had changed since we had moved out of the noisy Smoke to the calmness of the countryside.

It wasn't all bad, of course.

Saskia had been born just two months after we had arrived in Nutwell and both of us had taken to parenthood with a passion, adoring our new beautiful daughter and caring for her every need, never minding the fact that it left us both too tired for anything else except staying in, watching television and going to bed early.

I suppose, as time had moved on and Saskia had grown from being a baby to a toddler, then to a little girl, and now a not-so-little girl of nine and a half, we had become rather used to our quiet country lives.

It's not that we didn't go out. We did, but only rarely, maybe once a week or so with friends such as Tim and Paula, Annabel's parents, when we might venture on foot to the village pub for supper or to Banbury for a curry.

I couldn't remember the last time we had been to the cinema, usually waiting instead for the new releases to become available as a DVD or streamed on Netflix. And, as for live performances, we hadn't even managed to get to the Royal Shakespeare or any of the other four theatres in Stratford-upon-Avon for years, and they were just a few miles away.

What had happened to us?

No wonder Marina was bored with me. I felt quite bored with me too.

But it had been her idea to move out of London in the first place. Indeed, it had been more than an idea, more like an ultimatum – move out or lose her. She had longed for the peace and quiet of the countryside, and she had particularly loved it when we had stayed for weekends with Charles.

That's why we had bought a place near to him.

Except, of course, we never stayed with Charles now because he lived so close. On the occasions we all had dinner together at Aynsford, we would drive home afterwards, usually quite early in order to put Saskia to bed.

So, had moving out of London been the wrong thing to do?

FELIX FRANCIS

And had it also been wrong for us to have had a child?

The jury may still be out on the first question but the answer to the second was a definitive *no*. It certainly hadn't been the wrong thing. Saskia had provided us both with immeasurable happiness, as she still did. My deepest regret was that we hadn't had more children, but it hadn't been from lack of trying.

Marina had completed course after course of fertility treatments, but all to no avail. The doctors couldn't understand why she wasn't becoming pregnant. They couldn't find anything wrong with either of us. Maybe it was due to stress, they said, but Marina had conceived easily in the stressful environment of SW1, while she couldn't do so again in the tranquillity of OX15.

She was still young enough to be a mother again but we had long resigned ourselves to having just the one child. Perhaps things would have been different between us now if she'd been able to have more.

I resolved to make myself more exciting, more spontaneous and more attentive. I just hoped it wasn't already too late.

25

Once again, both Charles and Rosie were delighted to see me when we drove in to Aynsford at half past eight.

'Do you want to come in?' Charles asked.

'We're both hungry,' I said. 'I'd better get back and fix us some supper.'

'I have some left-over shepherd's pie,' Charles said. 'You're welcome to have that if you like. Mrs Cross always makes a large pie so that I can eat the rest for my lunch over the next few days. She only made it today, instead of a Sunday roast.'

'So Mrs Cross has finished her grandmotherly duties?'

'Indeed. Grateful to be back too, I think. She complained that those two young grandsons of hers totally wore her out.' He laughed. 'So, do you want the pie or not? It only needs to be put back in the Aga for twenty minutes.'

I looked across at Chico. He nodded.

'Okay, that would be lovely, as long as we're not depriving you of your lunches for the rest of the week.'

'Mrs Cross can always make me another one tomorrow.'

The three of us, plus Rosie, went into his kitchen.

'Good to see you again, Admiral,' Chico said.

'Ah, yes, thank you. Good to see you too.'

The excellent-looking shepherd's pie was sitting on the kitchen table.

'I'd have put it in the fridge before I went to bed,' Charles said in unnecessary explanation. 'Once it had cooled completely.' Instead, he now put it back in the oven and set a timer for twenty minutes.

'I always use this thing now,' he said, holding up the clockwork timer. 'I've recently been putting things in the Aga and forgetting about them, only to find them completely black and carbonized several days later. Must be my old age.'

I don't know about that. Both Marina and I had often done the same in our Aga, usually with stuffing or sausages.

While we waited for the pie to reheat, Charles fetched three tumblers and a bottle of fine Scotch from his dining room.

'Don't suppose you have any beer?' Chico asked as Charles poured the amber spirit into the second glass.

'Beer?'

'Any beer will do. I'd much rather have that than drink your whisky.'

Charles gave him a look of incredulity that anyone could prefer a beer to his ten-year-old single malt but, nevertheless, he waved a hand towards the large fridge in the corner. 'I think there's some in there, but it might be out of date.'

Chico found two bottles of lager hiding behind some salad dressings on one of the lower shelves in the fridge door.

'Left over from someone's visit, I think,' said Charles. 'Can't remember who. How about you, Sid?'

'I'm very happy with one of these,' I said, picking up one of the tumblers. 'Thank you, Charles.'

Twenty-five years of drinking whisky with my ex-father-in-law had given me a discerning taste for fine Scotch.

We sat at the kitchen table waiting for the twenty-minute timer to ring, Charles and I drinking from the finest Waterford cut glass, while Chico drank his lager direct from the bottle.

'You don't happen to have a tape recorder, do you, Charles?' I asked.

'What for?'

'I'd like you to tape me saying something. I know I've already told you some of the things I've found out but I think it would be better to get my voice recorded as I say it, just in case there's a problem.'

Anton Valance's reference to hearsay not being admissible in a criminal court had worried me somewhat, especially as, if anything happened to me, Charles would not only have to recount to the police and the racing authority what I had said to him, but much of that was also what other people had said to me. Hearsay of hearsay. Very dubious. At least with my voice directly recorded it would be one degree less removed.

'I can do even better than that,' he said. 'I have a video camera somewhere.'

'Perfect. Let's do it after we've eaten.'

On cue, the timer went off.

Chico and I tucked in to the excellent shepherd's pie while

249

Charles went off to search in his office for the video camera. Soon he returned triumphant, having not only found the camera but also some blank tapes, the mains lead and a tripod.

He set it all up on one side of the kitchen table, with the camera pointed across at me on the other.

'Right,' he said, standing back from the tripod. 'I'd better just check it's working.'

He pushed the record button and took a short video of me finishing my pie, saying how good it was and thanking Mrs Cross. Then he played it back on the small screen attached to the side of the camera. All worked perfectly, in spite of my voice sounding rather metallic from the in-built tiny speaker.

Charles pushed the record button again and gave me a thumbs-up.

I looked straight into the camera lens.

'My name is Sid Halley,' I said. 'And I am making this recording of my own free will with no coercion or financial inducement. There are two witnesses here present, Admiral Charles Roland, Royal Navy, retired, and Mr Chico Barnes.'

I waved for them to come round the table to stand in the shot behind me.

'We are in the kitchen of Admiral Roland's house in Aynsford, Oxfordshire.' Next, I gave the time and date before waving the two witnesses back to their seats.

'I wish to make this recording regarding information that has come into my possession over the past nine days.'

I covered everything I could remember in strict chronological order, right from that first telephone call from Gary Bremner asking for my help and telling me how frightened he was of the threats made to kill his horses.

I went through how I had been to see him at Pinker's Pond the day after the destruction of his stables, and my first discussion with Simon Paulson on the same afternoon about the trainers' premiums. And I spoke about the final call I had received from Gary that evening, naming Anton Valance as the bastard he blamed for the fire and how he had intended, far from killing himself, to nail the culprit responsible.

I spoke to the camera about me going back to Middleham on Tuesday morning and shouting from the top of the Swine Cross. And about being taken to see a detective in Gary Bremner's garden, and of then finding a yellow piece of paper with a telephone number under my windscreen wiper, and the subsequent warning about Valance not being a very nice person.

I talked about how I had spent that afternoon at Catterick races and how I was convinced that Jimmy Shilstone and Simon Paulson had conspired to ensure Plantagenet King and Night Shadow both lost races they could have won, and how I had then been attacked by two balaclava-wearing thugs in the racecourse car park.

I described how I had been to see Marcus Capes and how he had told me that, at a time when he'd been desperate for cash to pay his rent, he had foolishly accepted two hundred pounds to stop a horse that he knew had no chance anyway, payment of which had been secretly filmed by Valance, who was now using the video for blackmail.

I recounted the whole sorry story of Simon Paulson's wife

leaving him and then him getting into financial difficulties because no one was sending out the invoices to the owners. And how Valance had taken advantage of that situation by lending him £60,000 at such high interest rates that he had little chance of ever paying it back, and how he, Paulson, had then been thrown a financial lifeline to reduce the loan – all he had to do was ensure that another no-hoper didn't win. Of course it didn't, but Valance now had the leverage to blackmail Paulson into losing other races.

I described how I had disturbed two men, also in balaclavas, who had turned up at my own home, and of how the local police had found a container of petrol in my garden.

And finally, I spoke into the camera describing the events of today, my visit to Jimmy Shilstone, and then the confrontation with Anton Valance himself at the Harrogate Turkish Baths.

I finished by saying that, in the event of anything happening to me, Admiral Roland had my authority, indeed my instruction, to lay this video before both the police and the racing authorities.

I nodded at Charles and he stopped the recording. It had taken the best part of an hour.

'Bloody hell,' he said. 'Why don't you give that to the police right now and get this man Valance arrested?'

'Because he won't be. Everything is supposition and hearsay. Sure, the police and the BHA might investigate, but you can bet your life that nothing will stick on Valance. The only ones warned off or arrested would be his victims.'

'But at least it might stop what's going on.'

'Maybe, maybe not. He'd probably just find other jockeys and trainers to blackmail. Like Gary Bremner said to me, I want to nail the bastard, good and proper. I just have to find a way to breach his defences.'

'Or go around them,' Charles said. 'Do to him what the Germans did to France in 1940.'

'What was that? Invade?'

'During the 1930s, the French built a huge defensive wall on their eastern border. The Maginot Line. Originally designed to reach all the way from the Mediterranean to the Channel, it was never finished in the north due to complaints from the Belgians, who were allies of the French.'

'What has this got to do with Anton Valance?' I asked.

'Wait and see,' Charles said, clearly slightly irritated by my interruption. 'Anyway, when Hitler ordered the invasion of France in mid-May 1940, the German troops simply went north into Belgium before turning west into France, outflanking the Maginot Line altogether.'

'I still can't see what this has to do with defeating Anton Valance.'

'They also did something else. The French were so convinced that the Germans couldn't possibly attack with their tanks through the dense Ardennes Forest that they didn't even bother to defend that part of their border with Belgium, but that's exactly where the Germans came through, simply carving new roads through the trees for their tanks to use. Just four weeks later, Paris had fallen and the Nazis were goose-stepping down the Champs Élysées.'

'So?'

'What I'm saying is you need to outflank Valance's defences and then catch him off-guard by doing something that he thinks is totally impossible.'

'And what, pray, is that?' I asked.

'I don't know,' said Charles. 'That's for you to work out.'

Oh, thanks, I thought.

Chico and I took Rosie home from Aynsford to Nutwell just before midnight.

As we turned into my driveway, I was relieved to see that my house was still standing and not a smouldering wreck, but nevertheless I let Rosie out of the Skoda first and she wandered off towards the back door, while Chico and I remained standing on the gravel next to the car.

In a minute or two, Rosie came back as if to find out why we were taking so long. There had been no barking and no growling at any furtive visitors lurking in the undergrowth.

But Chico still spent the night sitting up in the kitchen with Charles's shotgun close to hand, while I went to bed and lay awake for hours, trying once more to remember what it was that had rung the alarm bells in my head, and also trying to think of something I could do that Anton Valance would believe was totally impossible.

26

'You didn't call me back,' Marina said indignantly when she woke me with a call at six-thirty on Monday morning.

Oh, God! So I hadn't. With everything else going on last evening, I'd completely forgotten.

'I am so sorry, my darling. Chico and I spent the evening with Charles at Aynsford and it was too late to call you when we got back here.'

'You could have at least sent me a text. I was worried about you. You might have been in a car crash or something.'

Worrying about me was good, I thought. But if she was really that concerned, she could have always called me again last night, and she hadn't – not so good.

'How is Charles?' she asked.

'He's fine. But I think he's missing you and Saskia.'

'But we've only been gone a week.'

'Ten days,' I corrected.

There was a pause from the other end.

'Do you want to be right or do you want to be happy?'

I laughed. It was a piece of advice we had first heard given to the groom at the wedding of one of Marina's work colleagues, as the panacea for a successful marriage – a line that Marina and I had often repeated to each other since.

'Happy,' I said, still smiling.

'Right then,' she said.

It had been a good moment – a very good moment.

'How's your father?'

'Not much change. But he's a fighter, that's for sure. He even sat up in bed and ate something yesterday, first time in two days. I thought he'd completely given up on life but it seems he hasn't.'

'How will your mum cope with him when you come home on Friday?' I asked, very much hoping that she wasn't about to change her plans.

'I've finally got the local health service here to provide a home carer to come in twice a day. It's only fair. After all, Mamma and Pa still have to pay their health insurance. They'll be fine for a few days without me.'

The Dutch health system had always been a bit of an enigma to me, with its strange combination of state funding and private insurance premiums paying for exclusively privately run hospitals, but the population seemed happy with the result, with much shorter waiting times than is usual under the fully state-managed, vast monolithic system of the NHS here in the UK.

'Is Elmo still there?' I asked.

'He leaves tomorrow morning. He's said his goodbyes.'

'It must be very hard for him being so far away.'

'It's hard also for Mamma and Pa. Both their children live abroad.'

'At least you're closer than New York.'

'Maybe, but it still takes the best part of a day to get here. It's not as if I'm just down the road if Mamma needs me.'

She was suddenly sounding very morose.

I, meanwhile, thought it was time to change the direction of this call.

'Let me know which flight you and Sassy will be on,' I said. 'I'll meet you at the airport.'

'Okay. That would be nice. Thank you.'

There was a moment of silence between us as if neither of us knew what to say next.

'I've been thinking,' I said finally.

'So have I,' she replied.

'Okay. You go first,' I said, desperately dreading what she might say.

'Things have got to be different in the future,' she said. 'I can't really put my finger on why, but I haven't been very happy these last six months or so, in fact I've been downright miserable.'

'Is it your job?'

'No,' she answered straight away. 'My job is my escape. It's when I'm at home that I'm miserable. At times, I dread coming home on Thursday evenings, even though I am desperate to see Sassy.'

That doesn't say much for me, I thought.

'What is it that makes you so miserable?' I asked. 'Is it me?'

She sighed. 'I don't know if it's you or not, Sid. It's just that

I feel trapped somehow – trapped as if in a river backwater that goes nowhere. I need more from my life.'

'More than me, you mean?'

'Yes . . . No . . . Oh, I don't know. I worship you, Sid – I always have – but there are occasions when you irritate me, even make me angry. Like when you've had too much whisky with Charles, and then you ignore me when we go to bed, just rolling over and going to sleep without as much as a "good night". You become a different person when you've drunk too much.

'And I don't say anything to you at the time because it would make you angry and we would row, and I hate that even more. And I know you hate it too. Both of us are confrontation-averse when it comes to things between us, so we always keep quiet about each other's gripes – you know we do – but it means they just fester and get worse, when we should be talking them through and resolving the problem.'

Wow! That was quite a thing to put on a chap before seven o'clock in the morning.

'Why didn't you speak to me?' I said. 'Rather than packing your bags and leaving?'

'I couldn't. I don't know why, but I just couldn't. Sam and I had talked it through and, at the time, leaving seemed the only way out.'

'Sam?'

'Samantha, the colleague I lodge with in London. We seemed to have talked about nothing else for weeks.'

But still she hadn't spoken to me about it.

'And now?' I asked.

'Now, I'm more confused than ever. Since I've been here, I've been trying to sort everything out in my head. The truth is, I think that leaving you has made me even more miserable.'

'You think?'

'My emotions are so mixed up here at the moment, what with Pa dying, I don't know anything for certain, except I do know that I'm missing you.'

She was crying.

'I need you,' she sniffed. 'I need you to hold me and tell me that everything will be all right – except it won't be, because Pa will still die.'

I was now almost in tears too.

'Marina, my darling, I'll come over there today.'

'No,' she said sharply. 'Don't do that. I'll be home on Friday and we'll talk over the weekend.'

'Are you sure? I could easily be there by this afternoon.'

'Quite sure. There is a degree of stability for Sassy here at the moment, what with Pa not getting any worse over the last few days, and I think the last thing she needs right now is to see her parents arguing or being in tears together. Friday will be soon enough.'

'Okay,' I said. 'If that's what you want.'

'It's not what I want,' she said, again quite sharply. 'I'm just being practical. Look, I have to go now as the home carer has just arrived. Call me later – and don't forget!'

She hung up before I even had a chance to say "I love you", let alone tell her what *I* had been thinking – about us perhaps moving back towards London, maybe not right back into the very centre, but into the suburbs, close enough for her to be able to commute to the cancer labs at Lincoln's Inn each morning, and yet still be home to Sassy and me every evening at a decent hour. Somewhere from where we could easily access the pleasures and delights of the big city without the need for expensive hotels and overnight babysitters.

I believed that the three nights a week spent away from me in London with this Samantha woman, sampling again the exciting nightlife that Marina and I had once enjoyed together, had turned her head, to say nothing of the way the two of them had clearly worked themselves into an anti-Sid frenzy.

Perhaps the last ten days Marina had spent in Holland, away from Sam's influence, had, ironically, been to my advantage.

I sat on the side of my bed for quite some time, holding my phone in my hand, going over and over what she had said. Was it good news for our marriage? Or bad? Perhaps only time, and the coming weekend, would tell.

Chico was snoozing in Marina's comfy kitchen armchair when I went downstairs for some coffee.

'All quiet?' I asked him, as he opened one eye.

'As a church mouse. Not so much as a squeak.'

'Good. I hope my little intervention may have frightened them off.'

'Let's hope so, but I wouldn't bank on it,' Chico said philosophically. 'So what's the plan for today? More wanderin' around in towels?'

'Not if I can help it,' I replied, but I had little or no idea what else to do. My overnight thinking had produced absolutely no results – nothing, nada, zilch – just a tired boy, who'd had insufficient sleep. I yawned.

'But I want to listen again to the recording we made in the steam room yesterday. There was something Valance said that I want to hear again.'

'What?'

'If I knew that, I wouldn't have to listen to it again. But I know there's something in it that's not quite right.'

I set my phone up to play the recording while I made the coffee, and it was the bit when Valance was talking about hearsay that had me reaching for the replay button.

'. . . anythin' that you may claim Gary Bremner said to you is irrelevant. I've been told it would just be 'earsay and would be inadmissible in court.'

I've been told . . .

Those were the exact words he had used.

Who had told him? His wife? His lawyer?

Surely not. So who?

Then the alarm bells went off, this time loud and clear in my head.

I remembered the something else that had been niggling away in my brain since the previous afternoon. It was the words Simon Paulson had used when he'd told me about calling Valance to tell him that Night Shadow would be running on his merits in the fifth race at Catterick. Simon's exact words to me had been: *Claimed they had too much invested on the race and I would be liable for their losses if Night Shadow won.*

They and *their*. Not *he* and *his*.

And Gary Bremner may have given me only a single name, that of Anton Valance, but he had always referred to the 'bastards' who had burned down his stable yard. Bastards – in the plural. I had thought that he must have meant Valance's two goons, but maybe he hadn't.

Was Valance not working alone, but with someone else?

And, if so, who was it?

'Penny for your thoughts?' Chico said as I stood there with my coffee cup raised halfway to my mouth.

'There are two of them,' I said. 'Maybe even more.'

'Two of who?'

'Valance has an accomplice.'

'Who?'

'I don't know. But we have to find out. That's how we can outflank his defences.'

'And how is that, exactly?'

'By setting them against each other. And we also have to do the impossible.'

'What's that?'

'Find out who this accomplice is, then defeat them both, and do it all by Friday.'

27

At nine-thirty, I received a call from Marcus Capes.

'Valance just rang me,' he said. 'He told me I was not to win on my ride this afternoon at Hexham.'

'What's the name of the horse?'

'Meeru. Five-year-old gelding trained by Mr Kline. It runs in the first, a two-mile handicap hurdle, at one o'clock.'

'Does it have a chance?'

'A good chance, I'd say. He's filled out really well in the last couple of months and I won on him last time out at Wetherby.'

I looked up the race on the *Racing Post* website. There were eight declared runners for the Class 3 contest and the website predicted that Meeru would probably start as favourite at about three-to-one.

'What do you plan to do?' I asked him.

'I don't know. Now I've told you, I suppose I should try and win it, otherwise you'll simply tell the stewards I wasn't trying.'

'I won't do that,' I assured him, 'but, yes, you should try and win if you can.'

'But Valance will surely then send the incriminating video to the BHA.'

Just like Jimmy Shilstone, Marcus was terrified of both consequences, of winning and of not winning: heads you lose, tails he wins – there were no alternatives.

'He won't,' I said decisively to Marcus, in just the same way I'd said it to Jimmy. 'He's invested too much in getting you under his control to just toss it away because you defy him once. He may be angry but he won't send the video.'

'How can you be so sure?'

I couldn't be, but I wasn't going to tell him that.

'Trust me,' I said. 'Win if you can.'

'Oh, God! I don't know.'

'Does Mr Kline know the horse isn't to win?'

'What do you mean?' Marcus asked.

'What I mean is, has Valance also got some hold over Noel Kline?'

'How would I know?'

'Well, find out. See what Kline says to you in terms of instructions for the race. If he knows that you know that the horse isn't to win, the instructions will probably be quite vague, as he'll also know you won't be following them. Then let me know the answer, preferably before the race is run.'

I remembered back to when I had asked Charles to play the part of an integrity officer to find out the name of the mystery caller. He'd not only found out Marcus's name and address but also some other little gems of information, such as the fact that he was trying his best to save up to buy a second-hand car to make getting to the races easier.

'How are you getting to Hexham?' I asked.

'Mr Kline is taking me. We leave in about fifteen minutes.'

'Discuss the race tactics during the journey and call me again when you get to the racecourse, before you're required to switch off your phone.'

'Okay.' He said it slowly, as if not quite sure. Maybe he was having second thoughts about having called me in the first place.

'Look, Marcus,' I said. 'I need to flush this man out into the open and you winning the race today is the best way. Yes, sure, he'll be angry, but not so angry that he will waste the future opportunities that you give him. When he contacts you, just say the horse was too good and you couldn't help but win without it being too obvious. But, and this is the most important bit, try and record what he says to you, either over the phone or in person. If you can't get an actual recording of him speaking, write down exactly, word for word, what he says to you, just as soon as you can. Do you understand?'

'I'll try.'

'Yes, Marcus, you try – you try very hard. I'm trying to save your career and I need you to step up and help me. Got it?'

'Yeah, I got it. I have to go now and get down to the gaffer's house or I'll be late.'

Marcus hung up and I remained sitting at the kitchen table wondering if he would have the nerve to defy Valance's instruction.

Hexham was at least four and a half hours' drive from Nutwell so there was no chance of me getting there in time to provide him with any last-minute moral support as he walked to the parade ring to board Meeru just before one o'clock.

I would just have to wait and watch the race on the television. On past form, Valance wouldn't even be doing that. However, I somehow doubted that he'd be back at the Harrogate Turkish Baths having another massage, not after his experiences of yesterday, but I was sure he would be elsewhere rather than at Hexham races, providing himself with a suitable alibi – after all, that's what the word alibi means in Latin: 'elsewhere'.

'Who was that on the phone?' Chico asked from the comfy armchair, without moving anything other than his lips.

'I thought you were sleeping,' I said.

'I was. But I always sleep with one eye, and one ear, wide open. You know that.'

I certainly did. He'd once thrown me over his shoulder onto the hall carpet at Aynsford when he'd mistaken me for an intruder. I had carelessly padded my way downstairs in bare feet in the dark while he'd been snoozing on guard in the kitchen. How he'd heard me coming then, I still didn't know. But I suppose I should be grateful.

'That was a young jockey on the phone called Marcus Capes, the one who left his number under my windscreen wiper in Middleham. He said that Anton Valance had just called him and told him to lose on a horse called Meeru in the one o'clock race at Hexham this afternoon.'

'And will he?'

'Quite likely. I told him to win if he can but that doesn't mean he will. All the others will be trying to win too.'

'So are we off to this Hexham place?'

I shook my head. 'Too far. It's right up in Northumberland.

Almost in Scotland. We'd never get there in time. Anyway, I'm more interested in knowing where Valance is going.'

'Well, we can find that out, can't we? Provided he takes his overcoat with him.'

Yes, I thought, we could, but beforehand I'd need to switch back on the *NeverLoseIt* tag and that would involve changing my phone's personal ID once again from mine to Marina's, something that would also show up on her phone.

I could hardly tell her that I was still looking for the Skoda keys, now could I?

As I was pondering this dilemma, my phone rang and it was her once more.

'Hello, my love,' I said, answering it with concern. 'Is everything all right?'

'Yes, fine,' she said. 'I thought I'd better tell you that I've just booked us on the British Airways flight from Amsterdam to Heathrow on Friday afternoon. It gets in at five to six London time, Terminal Five. The earlier one is fully booked already. Is that okay?'

'Yes, my darling. Perfect. I'll be there.'

'Good. I'll see you then.'

'Oh, Marina,' I said quickly. 'Just before you go, I might need to use your phone ID again. Is that all right?'

'You can't have lost the Skoda keys again.'

'No, I haven't.' I would have to tell her. 'I am actually using your tracking tag to follow someone's movements.'

There was a long pause from her end.

'Whose movements?' she asked.

'Someone over here. I need to know where he goes so Chico slipped the tag into his coat. Not the key ring, just the tag.'

There was another long pause.

'Don't worry,' I said. 'I'll get you another one.'

'It's not the damn tag that I'm worried about.' She sighed audibly. 'Charles always says that I couldn't change you so I shouldn't even try. You are what you are. That's what he said to me very early on, when you and I first got together. Do you remember that time we went to Aynsford after someone had punched me in the face? That's when he said it to me. Take him or leave him, he said, but just the way he is – and I took you then, and eventually I took you as my lawful wedded husband, so I shouldn't really complain.'

Another pause.

'So is that all right then?' I asked again into the silence. 'About using your phone ID?'

'I suppose so. Just don't tell me what you're doing, I don't want to know.'

'Okay, thanks,' I said. 'And I'll definitely be at Heathrow to meet you on Friday, I promise.'

'That's if I haven't changed my mind by then.'

She hung up.

Take me or leave me, just the way I am.

But Marina *had* changed me, dramatically. After my first marriage to Jenny, Charles's daughter, had ended in such acrimony and spite, I had firmly decided never again to get romantically involved with a woman, let alone pledge my troth to one.

I had been afraid that, as had happened with Jenny, pain

and despair would quickly follow any love and excitement, so I believed it was best not to be in love in the first place. But Marina had broken through my determination to live a henceforth bachelor life, indeed she had swept away my resolve not to fall in love again with her first spine-tingling kiss on my lips.

But, in fact, had I been right all along? Were pain and despair about to replace, once again, the love and excitement of the past twelve years?

But Marina had changed me in other ways, too. The most intense change was in her allowing me to become a father. To watch the fruit of my loins be born into this world, then grow from being a helpless crying baby into a true human individual with all the emotions, strengths and weaknesses that we all possess, and for me to have helped mould that individual into the loving, caring person that Saskia had become, was a joy beyond measure.

So, whatever might happen between Marina and myself in the future, Saskia would always be a huge part of both of us and, as such, the last ten years would never be viewed by me as the wasteland of recrimination and regret that my years with Jenny now were.

'So did she say yes?' Chico asked, bringing me back from my daydreaming to the present.

'Yes,' I said. 'She did.'

'Good, well get on and do it then. Let's see where he is.'

'There's no hurry. Valance may be a villain but he is also, primarily, a jockeys' agent, so he will have been on the phone at home since early this morning talking to the trainers, and even some of the owners, trying to sort out which of their entries will actually be declared to run.'

I looked up at the kitchen clock. It was just gone ten o'clock.

'The declarations for tomorrow's jump races and Wednesday's flat were only published a couple of minutes ago, and every declared runner must have a jockey booked for it by one o'clock today. Right now, he'll be busy calling his jockeys and the trainers again, concluding things and getting the jockeys properly booked in on the Racing Admin website. So we know where he is without using the tag.

'Anyway, if I leave the tag switched on for too long and it moves about only in sync with someone else's phone, it has an inbuilt way of realising that and it will put a message up on that phone to warn the owner that they're being tracked. It will also start making a noise to alert them where it is. That's why we must be patient, and only use it in very short bursts.'

'You seem to know a lot about it.'

'I read a news report on the internet about these tracking tags. Seems that some people were complaining that they were being stalked using them.'

'And they are exactly right,' Chico said. 'We're stalking Mr bleedin' Valance with one, all right, just like a Highland stag.'

'I didn't realize you were into deer hunting,' I said.

'Worked on an estate one school summer holiday, didn't I? Way up in Scotland as a ghillie's mate. Years ago now. Toughest work I've ever done, draggin' dead stags down off the hills. But the sooner we get Valance into our crosshairs and pull the bleedin' trigger, the better.'

If only it were so simple.

As expected, Meeru started the first race at Hexham as the betting favourite, and his starting price was even shorter than had been predicted, at just nine-to-four.

Marcus Capes had called me again at five past twelve.

'The gaffer doesn't know about the stop.'

'Are you sure?'

'Absolutely. He reckons that, with a victory here today, we should step Meeru up a class, perhaps two classes, maybe even go for the Swinton Handicap at Haydock next month, that's a Class One. And the gaffer says that I could ride him there too. He's really excited by the prospect and so am I. The Swinton Handicap has a purse of over a hundred grand. That means big money for me if I won it.'

'So you're going to win today if you can?'

'Dead right, I am.'

I remembered back to when I'd first started out in my own racing career and how excited I had been at the prospect of riding a really good horse such as Meeru. There was no feeling like it. I just hoped Marcus's enthusiasm to win would last until the actual running of the race and he wouldn't have had, by then, second thoughts, or third, fourth or fifth thoughts, or even thoughts of pulling up or purposely falling off.

At ten minutes to one, Chico and I went into the sitting room and tuned the TV to the correct racing channel for Hexham.

'Shall we see where Mr Valance is?' I said.

'Good idea.'

I switched my phone's ID to Marina's and turned on the tag. Immediately the map with the small blue circle appeared.

'Where is he, then?' Chico asked.

I spread my fingers on the screen to expand the details.

'The tag is in the Crown Plaza Hotel in Harrogate, probably hanging in the cloakroom while Valance is having lunch with a friend.'

'Shame it doesn't tell us who the friend is,' Chico said.

'No doubt it will be someone who can safely vouch for his exact whereabouts at precisely one o'clock.'

I remotely switched the tag off again.

'We'll try again later. Now let's watch the race.'

Meeru was among the eight runners that jumped off from the two-mile start as the starter dropped his flag, bang on time.

Hexham is an undulating oval track of about a mile and a half round, so the start was near the end of the back straight.

With only a circuit and a bit to race, and a mere eight flights of hurdles to negotiate, the initial pace was strong. Marcus settled Meeru in just behind the leading pair as the field made the stiff climb up towards the home straight and another flight, before passing the winning post for the first time at a good, fast gallop.

After two more flights in the straight, they swung left-handed and downhill. Over the three hurdles in the back straight, Meeru began to show his class, stepping up the pace and taking the lead as the horses went into the dip before turning for home and up the steep rise to the final flight and the finish.

There were good reasons why the racecourse bookmakers had made Meeru the short-priced favourite. Not only did he have the winning form from his last race at Wetherby, but the handicapper had been unusually generous in only asking him to carry ten-stone-eight. With Marcus's five-pound allowance as a novice rider, that weight was brought down to ten-stone-three, when the top-weighted horse was carrying a stone and a half more.

As a result, Meeru made easy weather of the hill, sweeping up into the straight with a lead of five lengths from the nearest of those struggling behind.

Just the final flight of hurdles to negotiate.

I held my breath.

Would Marcus make a hash of it and tumble off onto the bright-green spring grass? Or would he go on and win, setting himself up with a date in the Swinton Handicap at Haydock next month . . . that was provided, of course, that he hadn't lost his jockey's licence by then?

Meeru literally flew over the last, flattening his back in the manner of a true potential champion, and he galloped untroubled along the run-in to win, easing up, by ten lengths. Probably by too much for Noel Kline, I thought. The handicapper would not be so generous again.

'Well,' said Chico, clapping his hands and with a huge grin on his face, 'That should have put the cat among the pigeons.'

28

Chico and I continued to watch the afternoon's racing from Hexham, interspersed by other races from further south at Ludlow.

But it was the television images of Marcus Capes as he was led in to the winner's enclosure after Meeru's victory that would long remain in my memory.

The poor boy clearly didn't know whether to be ecstatically happy or downright miserable, and his facial expression seemed to flip-flop between the two extremes. But, in both cases, there were deep worry lines across his forehead, and with good reason. He had defied his blackmailer and was now terrified of the consequences.

Now we just had to wait for the fallout to begin.

At three o'clock, Chico went upstairs to lie on a bed and get some proper sleep, while I remotely switched the tracker tag back on to see where Valance had got to.

He was back at home – or, at least, his overcoat was.

I switched it off again.

He would know by now that Meeru had won, and I tried to imagine what his reaction would be. Disbelief probably, that young Marcus Capes could have ever defied him, and anger that he had. Perhaps, by now, he had watched a replay of the race and seen what a textbook ride the jockey had given the horse, without a single hint that he wasn't in the race to win it.

I smiled at the thought, but I was wary too, and not just for Marcus, but for me as well. Would Valance see this reversal as my doing? Sticking my nose into other aspects of his villainy rather than just into the death of Gary Bremner?

I had purposely not mentioned any of the names Simon Paulson, Jimmy Shilstone or Marcus Capes to Valance during our brief sojourn in the steam room. I had not wanted to alert him to the fact that I knew how he had corrupted them for fear of retaliation against them, or against me.

But, if I'd been him, I would have thought it highly suspicious that, on the very next day after I had warned him not to come near my house or my family, one of his other little projects had backfired. Indeed, I had been quite surprised that he had gone ahead with the fix so soon after the Turkish baths episode.

He must have thought he was safe.

Did he still?

I called Clive Beale.

'Hi, Sid,' he said, clearly on a hands-free system. 'I'm just leaving Ludlow. How can I help?'

'Did you speak to Timothy McKeen about last Tuesday?'

'You bet your life I did. Got hold of him on Wednesday morning, the little shit.'

'What reason did he give for not turning up?'

'Said his car broke down on the way to Catterick and he couldn't call me because his phone was out of battery.'

'And you believed him?'

'Not really, but what else could I do? I told him he'd never ride for me again.'

'Did you hear anything else about it?'

'Yes, I did. His agent called me Wednesday evening. He started off by apologising but then he kept spouting some nonsense about these things sometimes happen and that it was not really anyone's fault. Bloody idiot. He didn't exactly say so in so many words, but he implied that it wouldn't happen again, just as long as, in future, I paid his premium. I told him to get lost and to never call me again. I got the impression he found that quite funny and he warned me that all agents would soon be doing it and then I'd find myself without any jockeys prepared to ride my horses. God, I was so angry.'

'Did you report the conversation to the BHA?'

'No, of course not. Waste of time. It would be just my word against his. It wasn't as if I had a recording of it or anything.'

'Make one if he calls you again.'

He laughed but it wasn't out of amusement. 'Yeah, maybe I'll do that. Let's hope he never does.'

Yes, I thought, *and let's hope he never offers to lend you any money either.* But I didn't say it.

*

When I checked again at five o'clock, the little blue circle was on the move northwards on the A61 towards Ripon – and Ripon was on the route from Harrogate to Middleham.

I called Marcus Capes.

'Hello,' he said.

'Hi, Marcus, it's Sid. Are you still in the car with Noel Kline on the way back from Hexham?'

'Yes,' he said.

'When will you be getting home?'

'Soon, I think. We left before the last. We're almost there.'

'Okay,' I said. 'Just listen to me. Don't talk or react.'

'Fine,' he said.

'I think Anton Valance may be on his way to see you.'

I could hear a slight groan from the other end.

'Now listen, Marcus. That's a good thing. If he wanted to simply turn in the video to the BHA, he wouldn't bother to come and see you, now would he?'

'I suppose not.'

'Well, then. You're safe, but there's something I need you to do.'

I told him what it was.

'Okay,' he said. 'I'll try.' He sounded afraid.

'Don't worry,' I said, trying to be encouraging. 'Everything will be all right. And well done today. Great win.'

'Yeah, it was, wasn't it?'

'Yes, really good. And one more thing. Best not to mention anything about what I've just said to Mr Kline. Ask him to drop you at home first as you have things to do. Tell him this call is from your girlfriend and she's coming over to help you celebrate your win, or something like that, and you need to clean your place up before she gets there.'

As if his room could be made any cleaner.

'Okay, love,' he said loud and clear. 'Will do. That sounds lovely. I'll see you in a little while then.'

He hung up and I wondered if he would go through with it.

The little blue dot was well past Ripon now, on the A6108 and still moving fast towards Middleham. I just hoped that Marcus arrived there first.

I remotely switched the tag off and then waited, making myself sit still and watch as the second hand of the kitchen clock moved round and round the face, counting out the complete circuits it made.

The internet news report had stated the *NeverLoseIt* tags were programmed to automatically alert any person it was secretly tracking by showing a message on their phone and also beeping, but only after anything between eight and twenty-four hours had elapsed. I didn't know whether that was in total or continuously, or only when switched on, but I was taking no chances.

After ten very long minutes, I switched it on again.

I watched intently as the little blue dot moved quickly into Middleham before stopping in the marketplace. Then it started moving again, much more slowly this time, down the Leyburn Road towards number 42.

I called Marcus and he answered straight away. He'd been waiting for my call.

'Are you back?' I asked.

'Yes, got in about five minutes ago.'

'Valance is right outside your door already. Get everything in position while Doris lets him in.'

'Doris has gone out to a WI meeting. I'm here on my own.'

I clearly heard his doorbell ringing in the background.

'I've got to go,' he said.

'Good luck, Marcus,' I called out, but he had already hung up.

I stared at the little blue dot, spreading two fingers wide on the screen to expand the view. The dot moved slowly into the house as the doorbell was answered, and I could imagine Marcus leading Valance up the stairs and across the landing to his over-tidy bedsit.

I switched the tag off again and sat there, hoping nothing would go wrong.

Chico came into the kitchen rubbing sleep from his eyes. He stood by the sink, his back to me, looking out through the window at the uniformly grey overcast sky.

'What time is it?' he asked.

'Six o'clock,' I replied, glancing up at the kitchen clock.

'Mornin' or evenin'?'

I laughed. 'Evening.'

'Thank God for that. I feared I'd been asleep all night.' He turned round and yawned. 'Anythin' happenin'?'

'Valance has gone to see Marcus Capes,' I said.

That woke Chico up properly.

'Has he indeed. How do you know?'

'I used the tracker tag to follow him right to Marcus's front door, and then actually into the building. Pity it doesn't also transmit what it hears. Since then I've been waiting for Marcus to call me.' I looked up at the clock for the umpteenth time – five past six. 'He should have called by now. I can't imagine that Valance would have been there longer than he needed to be.'

I remotely switched the tag on again. The blue dot was no longer in Leyburn Street. Indeed, it was no longer in Middleham but about two miles away in the village of East Witton, and it was stationary.

'Bugger,' I said with feeling. 'He must have taken Marcus with him, to talk to him in his car.'

'Is that a problem?'

'A big problem. Marcus must have been rumbled.'

'Rumbled?'

'Yes. I had convinced Marcus to make a recording of their conversation by hiding his phone somewhere in his room. Even to make a video of it if he could. Perhaps Valance found the phone.' I stared at the blue dot and drummed my fingers on the kitchen table in frustration. 'Or maybe Valance didn't find it but he's just being ultra-cautious.' I drummed my fingers some more. 'And I don't dare call Marcus just in case his phone is switched on and Valance is still with him.'

'Is secretly recordin' a conversation with someone in your own home legal?' Chico asked.

'I think so. It's certainly more legal than secretly tracking them with a *NeverLoseIt* tag. I suppose it depends on what you use the recording for. If you publish without consent, it might be a breach of privacy. But journalists do it all the time. They sometimes get into trouble, mind, unless they can prove it's in the public interest.'

'Do you think this case would be in the public interest?' Chico asked.

Before I had a chance to answer him, my phone rang.

It was Marcus. I put him on speaker so Chico could hear.

'Oh my God. Oh my God,' he said breathlessly. 'That was awful. I've never been so bloody frightened in all my life.'

And that, I thought, was quite a statement from a steeplechase jockey.

'What happened?'

'He pushed his way in as soon as I opened the front door. Almost dragged me up the stairs to my room, he was so angry.'

So much for me imagining Marcus leading Valance up the stairs.

'Then what?'

'He demanded to see my phone! God, I was bricking it.'

'So what did you do?'

'I patted my trouser pockets and looked round my room, as if I was looking for it. Then I told him I must have left it in Mr Kline's car. He then called it! Thank God you told me to put it on airplane mode. Anyway, when he couldn't hear it ringing or even vibrating, he seemed happy it wasn't here.'

'And where was it, in fact?'

'I put it in my teapot on the shelf over the sink in my kitchenette. The phone stuck up over the rim of the pot and I put the lid on top of it, so that just the camera lens was visible. Luckily both my phone and the teapot are white but, nevertheless, I could clearly see that little black unblinking eye of the camera lens staring at me all the time. I was terrified Valance would see it too. It seemed so obvious to me, but he never did. As you told me, I started the video before I went down to open the front door. Good job I did too. I'd have never had a chance otherwise.'

'Did it work?' I asked.

'Did it work?' He laughed. 'I should get a bloody Oscar. When I was sure he'd finally gone and I'd double-checked twice that the front door was locked, I went up and spent some time looking at it. It's great, even if the sound is a bit muffled. Must be because it was in the teapot. But you can still hear what is said if you put the volume up to maximum.'

'Wonderful,' I said. 'Well done. I know I'll see the video later but tell me now, what did he say?'

'He was really angry, not that he raised his voice or anything, nothing the neighbours would hear, nor even Doris if she'd been downstairs.

'He said what the hell did I think I was doing winning when he had specifically told me not to. Just like you said, I told him that Meeru was just too good and it would have been too obvious to the stewards if I'd stopped him, but Valance said I should have found a way, even suggested I could have fallen off during the run-in. Bloody stupid man.

'Anyway, he told me he'd lost a packet of money because I'd won and I would have to pay it all back to him. Says he's going to up the percentage of my fees I pay to him until I do. It's not fair. And he told me not to even think about trying to change agents or he would have to send the video to the BHA. I ask you, those were his exact words – he would *have* to send it.

'I tell you, if he bloody does, the one I've just made of him will be following it pretty sharpish.'

'Did he say anything else?'

'Yes, he said that I now owed him and next time I'd better do as I was told. He said that if I received a call from an unknown number and I heard just the name of a horse that I was due to ride, then it meant that I was not to win on it, and did I understand? I played dumb and said I didn't, so he explained it all again, twice, until I finally agreed that I now understood what he was on about. Good, he'd said, and I would be hearing from him soon. Then he left.'

'Marcus, well done, you've done a fantastic job.'

'So what do you want me to do with the video?' he asked slowly. 'It's still not great from my point of view. I admit again on it that I sort of stopped that first one so . . . you won't just send it to the BHA, now, will you?'

'No, Marcus, I won't.' Although I'm not sure he was totally convinced that I wouldn't. 'How long was Valance with you?'

'About twenty-five minutes.'

'How long is the video?'

There was a pause while he looked.

'Thirty-one minutes.'

'In that case the file will be much too big to send by email or WhatsApp. I'll come up to Middleham tomorrow and we can transfer it by AirDrop. In the meantime, don't lose your phone, and just to be safe, don't answer any calls on it from Anton Valance, not this evening, anyway.'

'Okay,' he said. 'I'll sleep with it under my pillow.'

He hung up and, as he did so, my phone screen automatically changed back to the NeverLoseIt map, and I realized that I had left the tag on.

I went to switch it off but had a quick check of it first.

The little blue dot was still stationary and in the same spot.

I wondered what Valance found so interesting in East Witton.

29

After another quiet night in Nutwell, Chico and I left for Middleham at half past seven on Tuesday morning, together with Rosie.

I had tried once again to convince Charles to have her but he had point-blank refused.

'Sorry, no,' he'd said when I called him at ten to seven on Monday evening. 'I'm in London for the annual Royal Naval retired admirals' dinner tonight at The Rag.'

'The Rag?'

'The Army and Navy Club. In St James's. It's always been known as The Rag for some reason that I can't now remember. Anyway, I'm here now and I'm staying over after the dinner, so I won't be at Aynsford in the morning.'

'Can't Mrs Cross look after her?'

'No,' he said firmly. 'She can't. She's having her day off tomorrow.'

So Rosie came with Chico and me in the Skoda, her head stuck firmly out of the rear window for as long as I could stand the noise, which was until we joined the northbound M1.

Meanwhile, and in spite of the wind noise, Chico slept soundly in the passenger seat. I looked across at him and smiled. I felt so much safer at home with him on guard all night, so I shouldn't begrudge him sleeping now.

'So what's the order of the day?' he asked, waking with a yawn as we sped past Leeds.

'Middleham first, to get a download of Marcus's video. He should have finished riding out for Noel Kline by the time we get there, and he has no race rides today, I checked. Then I don't know. But I do want to make sure that the video is safe. That's the main reason for us going.'

'But you have other reasons too?'

I had remotely switched on the tag for two more quick updates during the previous evening. At eight o'clock the blue dot had shown that Valance was still in East Witton, but two hours later he was back at home in Park Edge, Harrogate.

'Yes, one or two,' I said. 'But you'll have to wait and see what they are.'

I drove on and made it to Middleham in good time, by ten past eleven.

'Nice place,' Chico said as I parked the Skoda in the marketplace.

I had been here so much recently that I had forgotten it was Chico's first visit.

'Have a wander round,' I said. 'Take Rosie with you on her lead, while I go and see Marcus. There are poo-bags down there, in the passenger-door pocket.' I pointed. He gave me a sideways look that made me feel that Chico didn't *do* poo-bags. 'It's a fifty-pound fine round here for dog fouling. I've seen a sign somewhere.'

'Tell me,' he said. 'Who's in charge, me or the dog?'

'You, obviously.'

'Why obviously?'

'Well, for one thing, you're the one holding her on the lead, rather than the other way round. She can't let go, while you can. And, trust me, Rosie wouldn't have to pay the fine, you would. I think that definitely makes *you* the one in charge.'

'So,' he said slowly, 'if I'm the one in charge, the boss as it were, why does it have to be *me* that picks up *her* shit?'

I laughed. 'Because it just does.'

Before getting out of the car, I did one more quick check of the tag – still in Harrogate. I also called Marcus.

'Are you back from morning exercise?'

'Just got out of the shower.'

'Good. I'll be there in two minutes. Best to have the door open so I'm not seen waiting outside.'

'Okay. I'll be ready.'

I walked down the Leyburn Road and straight into the open front door of number 42. Marcus was waiting for me at the bottom of the stairs.

The transfer of the video took less than a minute. We connected our phones by Bluetooth. He opened the file and then touched the share button – share by AirDrop – and I accepted it. Dead easy.

I checked that it had transferred properly by playing a bit of it and then scrolling to the end and noticing the 31-minute total length.

'Great. Thanks, Marcus.' I put my phone away carefully in my pocket.

'What should I do now?' he asked. His hands were shaking.

'Carry on just as normal. When I've checked that I've got everything, you can then delete the video in case Valance turns up again and looks through your phone.'

'What if he calls and tells me to stop one, or even to not turn up?'

'When's your next booked ride?'

'Tomorrow, at Sedgefield. This time I'm riding one for Mr Kline, Jahaz Bar, in the second, the three-mile conditional jockeys' chase.'

'Does it have a good chance?'

'Maybe. It's won before but I wasn't riding it then.'

I wondered if Valance would try again so soon. Quite possibly, just to test him.

'Phone me if Valance calls you and we'll decide what to do.'

'Okay.' The poor boy looked sick with worry.

'Keep calm, Marcus. I'm on your side.'

I wasn't sure he believed me.

There was no sign of either Chico or Rosie when I got back to the car, so I stood beside it in the watery sunshine.

The Swine Cross at the top of the town, from where, just a week ago today, I had shouted at the riders going out to morning exercise on the moors, is not the only medieval cross in Middleham.

288

There is another one in the marketplace itself, a simple iron cross inserted into the top of a six-foot-high stone shaft, which is itself mounted on four square steps of diminishing sizes, all of them heavily worn by the passage of much time and many footfalls.

Before the widespread availability of paper and the teaching of reading and writing to the masses in England during the eighteenth and nineteenth centuries, these crosses acted not only as sites of public proclamation, but also as places where market sales and purchases were concluded with just a handshake rather than any written contract, as if swearing the deal in the sight of God's cross made the transaction binding on both parties.

Perhaps I should get Valance here to swear a few binding deals with a handshake, not that I really had any desire to touch him.

Chico returned, holding Rosie on her lead in his right hand, and two full tied-up poo-bags in his left.

'What do I do with these bleedin' things now?' he asked.

'Put them in the bin provided,' I said, pointing at a square black box attached to a pole nearby.

He pulled a face and deposited the said items in the bin, but at arm's length.

I laughed. 'Anyone would think you'd had a privileged upbringing.'

But I knew perfectly well that he had spent all his childhood either in violent children's homes or, occasionally, with foster parents, mostly the former. He had once told me that he was mercilessly bullied as a youngster by the older boys in the homes, probably because of his curly hair and smallish stature. It was why he'd taught himself judo, learning the throws from black-and-white photos in an old dog-eared training manual he'd found, in order to fight back against the bullies.

I'd always thought it strange that the word judo, in its native Japanese, means *gentle way*, when it seemed far from gentle to be thrown over someone's shoulder onto the hard ground.

'I clearly didn't have such a privileged upbringin' as old Dick the Shit by the looks of it,' Chico said.

'Dick the Shit?'

'Richard the Turd. Have you seen the size of his castle round the corner? Ruined now, mind, but it must have been quite a sight in its heyday.'

'I know. I've been in there.'

'Bit bleedin' creepy, though, if you ask me. I wonder how many of Dick's enemies came to a grisly end in there.' Chico made a chopping action to his neck with his open hand.

'He definitely had form,' I said. 'He almost certainly murdered his own two nephews – the Princes in the Tower – to become king in the first place. But he, himself, also came to a grizzly end. He'd only been on the throne for two years when, at just thirty-two, he had the back of his skull hacked off by a Lancastrian sword at Bosworth. He was the last King of England to die in battle and he ended up being buried beneath a car park in Leicester.'

'But surely they didn't have cars back then?'

Good point, I thought.

'Come on, let's get into this particular car,' I said. 'There's a video to watch and I don't want to be seen doing it here.'

I drove out of town on the Coverham Lane and again pulled

off the road next to Pinker's Pond, the exact same spot where I had previously met Gary Bremner.

'Right,' I said. 'Let's see what he got.'

We watched the video all the way through, all thirty-one minutes, and it was just as Marcus had described it, only better. Sure, the voices had been somewhat muffled by the teapot and, even with the volume turned up to maximum, I still couldn't catch every word, but to make up for that there were crisp, sharply focused images of Valance in full colour, first telling Marcus off for having won when he'd been told not to, and then, as a true bonus, describing how Valance would in future give the details of other horses he wanted stopped from winning.

And thanks to Marcus's shammed lack of understanding, we even got to see and hear that part from Valance three times.

I clapped my hands with satisfaction. We had him.

But how could we use it without also incriminating the young conditional jockey?

'I'll have one too, if you like,' said Chico, 'just to be on the safe side.'

'Okay. Good idea.' And I used AirDrop to transfer another copy of the video to Chico's phone.

Once we had checked that both the new copies were as good as the original, I called Marcus and told him he was safe to delete his.

'No way,' he said. 'I'm going to keep this little baby. I reckon I could use it to my advantage.'

'Don't show it to Valance,' I warned him urgently. 'Or even tell him about it.'

'Why not?' he replied. 'I've been thinking about it ever since you left. If he knows I've got this, I can simply tell him that if he posts the video he has of me onto social media or sends a copy to the BHA, this one will follow on straight away afterwards, and with bloody bells on. It might keep him off my back.'

'Now, Marcus, listen,' I said with as much gravitas as I could muster. 'It's a very dangerous game you're playing. Remember what happened to Gary Bremner?'

'He killed himself.'

'But I don't believe it was suicide. Don't you remember what you said to me in our first phone call about Gary Bremner maybe also thinking he was quite able to look after himself?'

'I didn't mean nothing by it.'

'Well, I'm sure Valance actually murdered Bremner because he was threatening to go to the BHA. So, if I were you, Marcus, I'd be very careful indeed before I made threats of any sort to Mr Anton Valance.'

'Murder? Fucking hell.' I could hear his voice quivering at the other end.

'Like I told you, just carry on as normal,' I said. 'And call me immediately if he tells you to stop a horse, but don't, under any circumstances, call him. Do you understand?'

'Bloody right, I do.'

I hung up and sat there thinking about what must be going on in his head.

'Poor kid,' I said to Chico. 'Talk about being trussed up and ready for the oven. He doesn't know what to do.'

'Do you?'

'Not yet, but I'm working on it.'

'So, are we goin' home now?' Chico asked.

'In a while,' I replied. 'First, I'm going to let Rosie out for a run.'

What simple joys she has, I thought, as I watched her, nose to the ground, chasing scents of rabbits back and forth through the long grass close to Pinker's Pond, with no worries about evil men trying to make an illicit buck or even of loved ones leaving home, bored with life as it was.

Dogs would never leave their owners or their family just as long as they were fed and watered.

I wondered why people couldn't be more like dogs. Dogs just loved being at home, always welcoming you back at the door with wagging tails and a happy demeanour, and they were never judgemental simply because you'd been away longer than you said you'd be or had rolled home rather the worse for drink.

A loving pat on the head and a tasty treat would solve all their problems in an instant. And no accusations would ever be stored up in their memories, ready to be recalled and reissued with fervour at a later date.

'Come on, Rosie,' I shouted, curtailing her fun. 'Time to go.'

She came bounding across to me and nuzzled up to my leg for a moment before jumping into the Skoda and curling up into a ball on the back seat, ready for a snooze.

Yes, indeed, I thought, why couldn't people be more like dogs?

'So where to now?' Chico asked as I climbed into the driver's seat.

'East Witton.'

30

'Quaint,' Chico said as I drove into East Witton, two miles south-east of Middleham.

The western end of the village had all the hallmarks of once being estate-owned, with two neat lines of identical grey-stone cottages built down either side of a long, wide village green. Several of the cottages, those on the north side of the green, had white-painted picket fences enclosing small front gardens of smart lawns and neat flowerbeds full of early-budding roses.

As Chico had said, it was quaint.

'So, what are we lookin' for?' he asked.

'This is where Valance spent a couple of hours after his visit to Marcus Capes in Middleham last night. I was wondering why.'

'Perhaps he was havin' supper in the pub,' Chico said as we drove past the Blue Lion Inn.

'If so, the dot on the map would have been in the pub, or perhaps in the pub car park, that's if he'd left his overcoat in his car. But it wasn't. It had clearly been down here near the old chapel.'

I drove slowly past the chapel for a second time, looking intently at the properties on either side, some of them somewhat larger than the rest of the cottages.

But, just like where Valance lived in Park Edge in Harrogate, this was net-curtain-twitching territory, where every unrecognized car, especially one moving slowly with the occupants staring out of the side windows, would soon be clocked by someone from the local Neighbourhood Watch.

'I wonder how we could find out who lives in these houses,' I said. 'But I'm not very keen on simply knocking on their front doors and asking them who they are. If one of them turns out to be Valance's son or daughter, or even just a friend of his, it would be sure to get back to him that we'd been here snooping around.'

'We could always ask at the village post office,' Chico said, pointing ahead.

I drove past it. OPEN 9AM TO 1PM, MONDAY TO WEDNESDAY, said a notice in the window. True, it was only Tuesday, but it was already well past one o'clock.

'How about the pub?' Chico said. 'Publicans always know their locals' business.'

'You might be right,' I said. 'But, in my experience, people from round here keep what they know to themselves, rather than telling anything to strangers, especially strangers from 'daan saaf' like you and me. Trust me, folks from these parts are different, totally different. It's almost as if they believe they live in a separate country from the rest of England – the Independent Republic of Yorkshire.'

He laughed, but I knew I was right. Most Yorkshiremen would close ranks behind any other Yorkshireman, even if they suspected he was doing something wrong.

But we tried nevertheless, although not at the pub.

Chico spotted a woman in a tweed coat walking a black Labrador on the village green, so, while I kept driving on out of the village, he jumped out of the Skoda and took Rosie with him.

'Fellow dog owners,' he said with a smile. 'An even stronger bond than that of Yorkshire. Come back for me in twenty minutes.'

'Useless,' Chico said, getting back into the Skoda when I returned twenty minutes later. 'Silly old bat doesn't even know what day of the week it is.'

'What did she say?' I asked.

'I asked her if she knew the names of the people who live in the houses near the chapel. She then said, quite seriously, that the Prime Minister lives in one of them. I pointed out that the Prime Minister lives in London, at 10 Downing Street, but she said that was a lie because he definitely lived here. She even told me she'd met him. Stupid old woman. Totally bleedin' senile, if you ask me. Didn't even know what year it is when I asked her. Kept sayin' we should be gettin' ready for war with some bloke called Kaiser or somethin'.'

'The Kaiser?'

'That's what she said, straight up. And why hadn't we given women the vote yet? Even accused me of being one of the Liberal Party scum who deserved to swing at the end of a rope.' He threw his hand up in frustration. 'Trust me to choose the village nutter to talk to. And to top it all, her bleedin' dog tried to bite my ankles.'

I made an effort not to laugh, but without success.

'You can bleedin' shut up for a start,' Chico said crossly at me. 'I'm tellin' you, that crazy woman is livin' in the past. Even her dog was called Gladstone.'

With no one else visible walking their dog, and with me being reluctant to ask questions at the Blue Lion Inn in case word spread among the locals that two strangers had been asking for names of the village residents, we set off back south.

We had what we'd come for – Marcus's video – now safely stored on my phone, and also on Chico's for good measure.

Even if I hadn't yet worked out what to do with it.

'So, tell me,' Chico said when we were travelling south on the motorway, 'does it feel the same as the other one?'

He was looking at my left hand on the steering wheel.

'No, not quite. The sensations are there all right, but they are rather dulled, as if I'm wearing a rubber glove. But it's a lot better now than when it was first done. Initially, I couldn't feel anything even though I could move the fingers very slightly from day one.'

I remembered how the area of sensation had gradually worked its way from my wrist, through my palm and finally up to the fingers. There were still some bits of skin I couldn't feel but the doctors had said that even those should come back eventually.

'I was told it would take some time for my brain to relearn the meaning of the signals it receives from the reattached nerves, especially as I didn't have a hand there at all for so long.'

'Amazin' really,' Chico said. 'Makes you wonder what they'll transplant next. Heads, maybe. If your body packs up, just get a new one.'

'But someone would have to die to provide the body,' I pointed out. 'And transplanting heads does seem a bit extreme. Even my surgeon, Harry the Hands, can't reattach a severed spinal column. Not yet, anyway.'

I had a thought about something else, but then, suddenly, a truck pulled out right in front of me to overtake another and I had to brake sharply to avoid a collision.

The fleeting thought had snapped into my head but, just as quickly, it had slipped out again as I concentrated on the road. What the hell was it?

I drove on, thinking hard as Chico went back to sleep, but the thought wouldn't come back again, not all the way home.

'We have to find a way of finishing this,' I said to Chico as I turned into my driveway in Nutwell. 'Marina is due back here on Friday and I don't want her and Saskia mixed up in it.'

'Well, how are we goin' to do that?'

'I think it may soon be time when I have to use the Red Telephone Hotline.'

We let Rosie out of the car first. She trotted happily over to the back door and seemed totally unconcerned about any possible unwanted visitors waiting in the bushes.

We had stopped briefly at a local Indian takeaway and I now carried our curries into the kitchen, placing the bag on the lid of the Aga hotplates to keep warm while I gave Rosie her supper.

'I see,' Chico said in mock complaint. 'That's not fair. Not only do I have to pick up her shit, but she also gets to eat her dinner before me.'

'Trust me,' I said, leaning down and stroking Rosie's back as she munched away at her biscuits. 'This dog probably saved my life last week, so if she wants to eat first, second or even third, that's fine by me.'

'That's only because you're a bleedin' softie,' Chico said, laughing.

Was I a bleedin' softie?

No, I bleedin' wasn't. Not when it came to Anton Valance. And it was high time I proved it.

I sat bolt upright in bed.

It was still pitch-black outside, but something had definitely woken me.

I touched the clock on my bedside table. It briefly lit up. Two-fifteen.

I lay very still in the dark, listening.

Nothing – nothing other than my pounding heart.

As silently as I could, I got up, put on my dressing gown and went to my bedroom door, opening it very slowly.

'Chico,' I whispered over the banister into the hallway beneath. 'Are you there?'

No reply.

I padded down the stairs in bare feet.

'Chico,' I whispered again.

I heard a chair move on the kitchen floor.

'Sid, is that you?' Chico said.

'Yes. Something woke me.'

'I've heard nothin'. I'll go and check.'

I waited in the hallway while Chico went outside.

'Nothin' there,' he said, coming back in through the kitchen door. 'All quiet. Not a peep from Rosie either.'

'Okay, thanks,' I said. 'It must have been a dream.'

I went back upstairs to my room feeling somewhat foolish, and climbed into bed. But I lay awake in the dark for some time, listening for any strange noises and wondering what it was that had woken me.

I must have drifted off but, suddenly, I was awake again and, this time, I knew why. The thought that had fleeted in and out of my brain in the car on the motorway had finally returned – and, this time, it stuck.

I looked again at my clock – two-fifty.

I didn't want the thought to evaporate again so I wrote down 'Harry the Hands for Prime Minister' on the notepad beside my bed as a reminder, then went soundly back to sleep for the rest of the night.

I went downstairs at six-thirty, again wearing my dressing gown, to find Chico fast asleep in the kitchen armchair.

'Call yourself a bodyguard?' I said, gently kicking his foot.

He opened one eye. 'I knew it was you,' he said.

'Liar.'

I made myself a cup of instant coffee, then sat at the kitchen table and opened my laptop.

There were eight new emails in my inbox – two were bills, one was from my accountant about changes in rates for the new tax year, one was an invitation to a past-champion jockeys' lunch at Cheltenham the following month. The other four were all spam.

I deleted the spam, accepted the invitation and decided that the bills could wait for another day.

Next I logged onto the internet and removed the notepad from my dressing-gown pocket: 'Harry the Hands for Prime Minister'.

Not that I really wanted my hand-transplant surgeon to go into politics.

I googled British prime ministers.

Then I looked up a certain name in the *Thoroughbred Business Guide*, but it didn't appear. Not surprising, really. No one was obliged to have their details included in the guide. Anton Valance's name didn't appear there either.

Next I called Simon Paulson.

'Can't you bloody leave me alone?' he said. 'First lot goes out in twenty minutes and I'm busy.'

'I only need one thing,' I said quickly, before he had a chance to hang up.

'What thing?'

I told him.

'Why do you need that?'

'I just do? It's no skin off your nose, but I could ask the BHA Integrity Department if you'd rather. However, they will probably also want to know why I want it and I might end up telling them about your little arrangement with Anton Valance.'

'Bastard,' he said with feeling. But he told me what I wanted, and it was just as I had expected.

I disconnected.

'Okay,' I said to Chico. 'I think I may have worked out who is Valance's accomplice. And it pains me to say this, but it's all thanks to you – you and the Kaiser.'

31

After breakfast, Chico and I took Rosie over to Aynsford.

Reluctantly, Charles had agreed to look after her again, even though he didn't particularly like it.

'But come in for a cup of coffee before you go,' he'd said. 'I hope it might make the dog settle better than when you just drop her off at my front door.'

So we did that, and I took Rosie's usual bed along with me so she would feel more comfortable, placing it in Charles's kitchen next to his Aga in the same manner as it was at home.

'Did you have a good dinner?' I asked.

'Excellent,' he said. 'The only trouble is that most of the admirals I served with have now fallen off the perch. Only young chaps these days, some of whom didn't join the service until long after I had retired. But it was fun nevertheless, and it was good to spend a night in London. I even walked up to Jermyn Street yesterday morning and bought myself some new shirts.'

He poured coffee into three mugs and carried them over to the table.

'So who is this Kaiser chappie?' Chico asked him.

'The Kaiser?' Charles said.

'Sherlock Holmes, here, says he's helpin' us.'

'That isn't quite what I said.'

'Kaiser Wilhelm II?' Charles asked.

I nodded.

Charles stared first at me, then at Chico, who looked back at him with an expectant expression. 'Sid said you would know him.'

'He was the last German Emperor. *Kaiser* is the German word for emperor. It was he who started the First World War.'

'I thought it was because someone was assassinated,' I said.

Charles nodded. 'That's what the history books will tell you. Archduke Franz Ferdinand, heir to the Austro-Hungarian Empire. He was shot dead during a visit to Sarajevo, causing the Austrians to declare war on Serbia. That caused the whole international diplomatic house of cards to collapse due to various military alliances, but it was the Kaiser who really wanted the war, and he made sure it happened.

'When he became German emperor on the death of his father in the 1880s, he sacked all the politicians and assumed total control, building a huge army and a massive navy in order to threaten all his neighbours. He was absolutely itching for a war. Dreadful man. He also wore an appallingly stupid moustache.'

That was clearly, in Charles's eyes, almost as damning as having caused a world war. After all, moustaches on their own are not permitted in the Royal Navy – British sailors either have to be clean-shaven or have a full set: a moustache together with a beard.

'But I suppose we should be grateful,' he said.

'Grateful? Why?'

'Grateful that he wasn't also the King of England.'

'You mean because Germany lost the war?'

'Oh, no. Long before that. Back in 1901. Kaiser Wilhelm's mother was Princess Victoria, Queen Victoria's eldest child. If the succession rules for British monarchs had been then as they have recently been changed to, stopping male preference in favour of the first-born of either sex, then she would have become Queen Victoria II when her mother died, instead of her younger brother becoming King Edward VII, and then Wilhelm would have become King of England six months later when she also died. It's quite scary really when you think about it. We would never have had Queen Elizabeth II or the House of Windsor.'

'But what has this got to do with us?' Chico asked, clearly confused.

'Nothing,' I said, standing up. 'Thanks for the history lesson, Charles, but Chico and I have to get going. We'll pick Rosie up later. I've left some dog biscuits for her supper in case we're late.'

Charles didn't look at all happy at the prospect that we might be late.

We went north in the MY S1D Discovery, not least because I felt that I had already put enough miles on Marina's Skoda.

All this driving up and down the country reminded me of the

years I had spent as a jockey. Back in those days, I'd put seventy thousand miles a year or more on my car's clock, riding perhaps at Newton Abbot in south Devon on one day, at Doncaster or Haydock in the North the next, and maybe at Fontwell or Plumpton races way down close to the Sussex coast the day after. And so on, six or even seven days a week, most weeks of the year.

'So, where to this time?' Chico asked.

'We're off to see the prime minister,' I said. And hence he was all the more confused when I joined the northbound M1 at Leicester.

'What happened to using the Red Telephone Hotline?' he asked.

'That's a last resort. Only to be used when we absolutely have to.'

'Don't we absolutely have to already?'

'Not quite.'

As we were passing Nottingham, my non-red black telephone rang. I answered it using the Discovery's hands-free system. The call was from a breathless Marcus Capes.

'Valance just called and told me to lose on Jahaz Bar.'

'And will you?' I asked.

'I told him I wouldn't. I said I would ride Jahaz Bar to win and that, in future, every horse I ride will be trying its best to win.'

'And what did he say to that?'

'He asked me if I was sure. Because he said he would post the video he has of me counting his bloody money on social media and send a copy to the BHA unless I did what he told me.'

'And what did you say?'

'Look, I'm sorry, Sid, but I told him if he did that, I would send the video I took of him on Monday evening in my room to the BHA as well.'

So much for my dire warnings, I thought.

'And I also told him that it wasn't any good him doing something to me to stop me, because I've already told Sid Halley about the video I'd made.'

Oh, great, I thought, *thanks a lot.*

Marcus had just massively raised the stakes in this dangerous poker game. But who would blink first?

I turned the Discovery into the free public car park at Sedgefield Racecourse at a quarter past twelve.

'I didn't realize the prime minister liked racin',' Chico said with a grin.

'Didn't you know that Tony Blair was the local MP here for over twenty years?'

'Please don't tell me we've come all the way up here just to see Tony Blair.'

'No,' I said, laughing. 'We haven't.'

Surprisingly, this was my first ever visit to Sedgefield racecourse, having never ridden here as a jockey. County Durham had always seemed so far away from my then home in Berkshire, but that was silly, really, as I rode several times in Scotland, including twice at Perth, which is nearly 200 miles further north than Sedgefield.

We were quite early as the first race wasn't until two o'clock, so I parked the Discovery in the largely empty car park, as close as I could to the main entrance to the enclosures, rather than tucking it away in a dark corner where thugs in balaclavas might be waiting for us when we came out later.

Chico and I went in through the turnstiles, buying racecourse-entry tickets that included not only a complimentary racecard but also some traditional fish and chips, complete with mushy peas and curry sauce, from the on-site fish-and-chip shop.

We sat on a wooden bench in front of the grandstand, eating our fish lunch in the warm early April sunshine, which had replaced the heavy overnight rain.

'So, are we here to give Marcus Capes some moral support?' Chico asked between mouthfuls.

'Partly, but we were always coming here anyway, even before his phone call.'

'To see the prime minister?'

'Exactly so,' I replied with a smile.

I sat and perused the racecard.

As expected, Jahaz Bar was listed among the seven runners for the second race with Marcus Capes riding, but there was another horse that I was also interested in: Ricardian, a declared runner in the fifth race, a two-and-a-half-mile handicap hurdle for four-year-olds and older. He was trained by Simon Paulson and was due to be ridden by Jimmy Shilstone.

According to the printed probable starting prices, both horses were expected to start as their race favourite, but would they both be trying to win? That was the big question.

As the time for the first race neared, the place began to fill up, even though that was a relative term.

Sedgefield in April was not like Cheltenham for the annual racing festival, which had taken place the previous month. Then crowds in excess of seventy thousand had flocked to Prestbury Park to witness the very cream of British and Irish steeplechasers battle it out in a series of Class 1 championship races, some with purses well in excess of half a million pounds.

Here at Sedgefield today, there were seven scheduled races. Three of those were Class 4 and the other four Class 5, with the biggest prize of eight grand going to the winner of the fourth, while most of the others were worth less than six. And the attendance reflected the lesser standard of the racing, with fewer than a thousand souls actually paying to get in.

In footballing terms, while Cheltenham and Aintree racecourses were certainly in the Premier League, Sedgefield, as far as size of crowds go, was probably in the fourth tier or even lower. Not that the racing itself would be any less competitive, with plenty of runners here today vying for the moderate spoils.

Just before one o'clock, with still over an hour to go before the first race I positioned myself close to the entrance to watch the arrivals, while Chico nonchalantly leaned against a wall some distance away to my left, so that it was not too obvious that we were there together.

The first persons of interest to appear were Noel Kline and Marcus Capes walking in side by side, deep in conversation.

Marcus saw me almost as soon as I spotted him and there was a small but distinct falter in his step, but he quickly recovered. I gave him a small thumbs-up sign with my right hand and he fractionally nodded in my direction, before turning to his left towards the weighing room and the jockeys' changing rooms.

Jimmy Shilstone was next to arrive and he was far more concerned by my presence.

'Is Ricardian a good bet?' I asked him as he walked past me.

'Go away,' he said. 'I can't be seen talking to you.'

'Why not? Is an ex-jockey giving a current one some advice so bad?'

'You know why. I wish I'd never told you anything.'

'Okay, Jimmy,' I said. 'I'll leave you alone, but only if you tell me to back Ricardian to win – and mean it.'

'He'll be doing his best as far as I'm concerned.'

'Good lad,' I said. 'Does everyone else also think that?'

He gave me a look that included that slight touch of panic I had first seen at Catterick. So, no, everyone else didn't think that.

'Do your best to win,' I said, but I wasn't sure he was listening as he also hurried off towards the sanctuary of the weighing room.

And still I waited.

A few more people arrived who I recognized, mostly trainers and a few jockeys who had made the journey up from the South, but none of them were the person I was waiting for.

With just twenty minutes to go before the first race was due to start, Simon Paulson hurried in. I knew from the racecard that, in addition to Ricardian in the fifth, he had another runner in the second and he was cutting things rather fine.

I let him go. He was not the man I was waiting for either.

Just when I was beginning to think that my prey wasn't coming to the races at Sedgefield today after all, he appeared in his camel-coloured overcoat and battered trilby. But he wasn't alone. He had a woman and a young boy with him.

That could make things awkward.

'Didn't he come?' Chico asked when I finally waved him over to me.

'Yes, he did. But he's not alone.'

'So?'

'I was hoping to corner him as he arrived but that was not possible.'

'So what do we do now?'

'We bide our time and watch the racing.'

32

Jahaz Bar didn't win the second race but it was due to no fault of Marcus Capes. And, in an ironic twist, the race was actually won by Simon Paulson's runner, even though it had no right to the triumph.

Jahaz Bar had shadowed the long-time frontrunner throughout and, coming to the last fence, Marcus moved him almost upsides of the leader, ready to strike for glory. The horse in third was half a furlong adrift, and the remaining four runners were completely out of sight and pulling up, after the fast-run three miles in testing ground had sapped all their stamina.

But it was the tiredness of the leader that was to prove decisive.

As he jumped the last, he twisted to his right in midair, pitched nose-down on landing and fell forward right into Jahaz Bar's path, causing both horses to crash to the turf. The third horse, which had itself almost pulled up, now staggered over the last and trotted the final hundred yards to the line for a totally undeserved victory.

Meanwhile, I kept my eyes on the carnage at the last fence and was relieved to see both horses and riders quickly rise to their feet. Being 'brought-down' when in a winning position was a dreadful way to lose a race, but it happens and had probably happened to every jockey at some stage or another. It certainly had to me.

'Come on,' I said to Chico. 'Let's go down and watch the winner come in.'

We went down from our lofty position in the grandstand and I leaned on the rail of the unsaddling enclosure while Chico stood some way off to my right.

The victor was led into the space reserved for the winner by Simon Paulson, and he had a rather embarrassed expression on his face.

I, meanwhile, wondered if the plan all along had been for the horse to lose and, short of joining the other two on the floor at the last fence, he'd had no choice but to win. But maybe I was being uncharitable.

'That was a bit of luck, Simon,' I shouted across to him.

He looked back at me with the same air of panic as I'd seen in Jimmy Shilstone's eyes earlier. 'What the hell are you doing here?'

'Enjoying a day's racing,' I replied. 'Is there anything wrong in that?'

He didn't reply as he busied himself trying to put a rug over the steaming body of his horse, but his body language spoke volumes. 'Hold him still, can't you?' he snapped at the unfortunate stable lad, as the horse shied away from the rug. Simon Paulson was clearly unnerved by my presence.

As well he might be.

He glanced back at me and then his eyes moved to my left and, if anything, his look of panic intensified.

I nonchalantly stood up straight, looked at my racecard and turned to my left. Standing just a yard or so away from me was the man I was interested in, together with the woman and the boy. All three of them were watching Simon.

'Hello, Harry,' I said. 'Was that one of yours?'

The man turned slowly and looked at me. He did his best to keep his face unmoved, but a touch of the colour in his cheeks drained away ever so slightly and I thought I could spot a slight glistening of sweat breaking out on his forehead. But maybe I was imagining it.

'Hello?' he said in a slight questioning tone as if he couldn't remember where he had met me before. But he knew me, all right.

'Sid Halley,' I said, playing the game.

'Oh, yes, of course.' He turned and looked as the horse was led away, back to the racecourse stables. 'No, not one of mine this time, but I like to support my trainer.' He waved a hand towards Simon Paulson. 'A good win, but a fortunate one in the circumstances.'

'Yes, indeed,' I said. 'Very fortunate.' I looked at his companions.

'Ah, yes, sorry. Sid, can I introduce my daughter, Carrie.' We nodded at each other. 'And also my grandson, Henry. He's named after me.'

'Henry Payne,' the boy said with a big wide smile. 'I want to be a jockey when I'm older.'

'He'll be too tall,' his mother said. 'Shooting up like a beanstalk.'

Henry pulled a face.

'Mr Halley here was a jockey,' his grandfather said. 'A champion jockey.' So now he'd proved he knew who I was.

Young Henry's eyes widened in excitement. 'Wow.'

'And how old are you, Henry Payne?' I asked him.

'Eleven.'

'And do you ride?'

He nodded. 'A bit. Grandad bought me a pony three years ago.'

I looked at his grandfather. 'And is the boy any good?'

'He's brilliant. His pony is only a Shetland called Blackjack, but he also rides his mother's horse and he makes that jump like a stag.'

'Then good luck, young man. But remember one thing, always strive hard to win. Winning is everything. Never be satisfied with anything less.'

'I won't,' he promised.

Together, the four of us stood and watched the race presentation, Simon Paulson collecting the small glass-vase trophy on behalf of the absent owner.

I went to move away but, in true Columbo style, I turned back to ask a final question. 'So, Harry, should I back your horse Ricardian in the fifth race?'

He stared at me. 'That's entirely up to you.'

'But will it win?' I asked. I stared back, deep into his eyes, for several seconds, until he finally looked away. I was certain he knew exactly what I meant, and he knew I knew too. But there was also something else in his expression – an assurance that he was in total control of the situation.

'We hope he'll win. Don't we, Henry?' He tousled his grandson's floppy light-brown hair.

Henry Payne looked up at his grandfather with his large grey-blue eyes in loving admiration. 'We certainly do, Grandad.'

'And what does Anton say?' I asked him. 'Does he think Ricardian will win today?'

This time, he was shocked. I could tell by a slight tightening of the skin on his face but, otherwise, his cool control won through.

'Anton who?' he asked calmly.

'Anton Valance.'

He looked up as if thinking. 'I don't think I've ever heard of him.'

'That's strange,' I said. 'Considering he spent two hours in your house on Monday evening. You know, the big house next to the old chapel in East Witton.' I smiled at him but he didn't smile back. His cool control was beginning to crumble.

'I think this conversation is over,' he said.

And, with that, Henry – *call me Harry* – Asquith ushered his family away, back towards the owners and trainers' hospitality suite in the Roflow Stand.

'So what happened to the prime minister?' Chico asked as he finally joined me.

I laughed. 'I was just talking to him. Didn't you see?'

Chico looked first to his left, then to his right, in fact all around him.

'You're havin' a laugh,' he said, settling his eyes back on my face.

'Can you remember what the crazy woman in East Witton said to you yesterday?'

'About the Kaiser?'

'Yes, but what else?'

'That women should get the vote.'

'Yes. And?'

'That the prime minister lives in the big house next to the chapel.'

'Exactly. The house where Anton Valance parked his car outside for two hours on Monday evening. And who was the prime minister at the outbreak of the First World War?'

Chico shrugged his shoulders. 'No idea, mate. Not the bloke you've just been talkin' to, that's for sure. He ain't old enough.'

I laughed again. 'If it were him, he'd be a hundred and seventy by now. No, but his name is the same. Henry Asquith. The prime minister was actually Herbert Henry Asquith, but he was known by his family as Henry.'

'How the bleedin' hell do you know that?' Chico asked.

'Because I looked him up on the internet this morning. It's funny how the brain works. You were talking to me about my new hand as I was driving home yesterday afternoon. Because of that, I thought about Harry the Hands, my transplant surgeon. Word association and all that. I knew I'd met someone else called Harry recently and spent ages trying to remember who. Suddenly, in the middle of last night, the brain engaged and *bingo!* Henry – *call me Harry* – Asquith. I met him at Catterick races eight days ago.

'And the crazy lady, living a hundred years in the past, had met him and she must think he really is the prime minister. I checked Asquith's address with Simon Paulson this morning and, sure enough, it's the big house next to the chapel in East Witton.'

'So is he Valance's accomplice?'

'He might be, although I have a sneaking suspicion that it is, in fact, the other way round.'

I stood by the rail of the parade ring watching as Ricardian was led round prior to the fifth race.

Standing on the grass in the centre of the ring were the owners and trainers of the seven runners, including Harry Asquith, his daughter, his grandson and Simon Paulson, the three adults in conversation, while young Henry concentrated on watching the horses.

Jimmy Shilstone soon joined them and Henry stared up at the red-and-blue-clad figure in total adulation.

A bell was rung and the seven jockeys moved over to their respective horses and were tossed up onto the saddles by the trainers.

As Jimmy rode past me, adjusting his stirrup leathers, I called out to him.

'Good luck.'

He stared down from his lofty position with that panicky look back in his eyes.

'Do your best,' I said. And he nodded, just ever so slightly.

The horses made their way out onto the racecourse and I watched as the Asquith party plus Simon Paulson went up into the space on the grandstand reserved for owners and trainers. Chico joined me in another section of the stand to watch the race.

As expected, Ricardian was the clear leader in the betting market, with most bookmakers showing a price for him of five-to-two on their brightly lit boards, with the next best at four-to-one.

The start for the two-and-a-half-mile handicap hurdle was in front of the stands and the horses would have to complete two full circuits of the rectangular course, jumping five hurdles on each one.

The starter dropped his flag as the horses moved towards him, and they were off. There was no hanging back at the rear for the red-and-blue colours on this occasion, and Jimmy settled Ricardian in about fifth place as the horses galloped away from us towards the first flight of hurdles.

Over the next three hurdles, the field remained closely bunched and the pace was sensible, with no one wanting to overexert themselves too soon. As they swung sharply left-handed into the home straight for the first time, Ricardian appeared to be travelling well in fourth place and the crowd gave them all a cheer as they passed the winning post with still a full circuit to go.

Down the back for the second time, the pace quickened and some of the outsiders began to lose touch with the leading pack. Sedgefield is an undulating track and the constant ups and downs can unbalance even the best of horses. As the leading group of five, including Ricardian, turned for home, some of the others were already pulling up.

The finishing straight is initially downhill, but then with a steep incline in the final half a furlong up to the line. Ricardian made the most of the downhill section, closing up and jumping the second-last flight of hurdles in third place. Jimmy then switched him to the stand-side rail where he found firmer ground, and he passed the second horse as they ran towards the last, before producing a mighty leap at the final hurdle, overtaking the leader in the air, before running up the hill to win easily by three lengths.

Jimmy Shilstone had just provided a masterclass in how to ride the perfect waiting race, and he and Ricardian were duly cheered into the unsaddling enclosure by the crowd, many of whom had clearly backed the favourite to win.

Waiting for them there were Harry Asquith and his family, together with Simon Paulson. Little Henry was almost jumping up and down with excitement, but I wasn't sure whether his elation at Ricardian's victory was shared by his grandfather, who remained somewhat tight-lipped. Simon Paulson, in contrast, seemed neither content nor disappointed by the victory.

Jimmy slid down off the horse's back and undid the girths. But he wasn't smiling as he removed his saddle and he walked off towards the weighing room to weigh in without looking back. Neither the owner nor the trainer appeared to say anything to him – no word of congratulation on a well-ridden race, nor any terse reprimand for winning when he shouldn't have.

No doubt, the second of those would come later, in private.

I had positioned myself close to the rail, close enough to call out.

'Well done, Henry,' I shouted across to the boy. 'What a great victory.'

He came bounding over to me before his grandfather could stop him.

'Wasn't it brilliant?' young Henry said with another wide smile. 'And Grandad says that I'm the one going to be presented with the trophy.'

He was understandably excited by the prospect, but his excitement was premature.

Over the public address system came the familiar three-tone signal indicating that there was to be a stewards' enquiry.

'Uh-oh,' I said. 'There could be a problem.'

'What problem?' asked young Henry.

'That sound means there's going to be a stewards' enquiry,' I said, and it was quickly confirmed over the loudspeakers with a warning that all betting slips should be retained.

'What's it for?' Henry asked me.

'I don't know,' I said. 'Everything appeared to be in order to me.'

Simon Paulson hurried out of the unsaddling enclosure towards the weighing room building, with the Stewards' Room within.

'Looks a bit sus to me,' Henry said.

'Sus?'

'Suspicious.'

It certainly is, I thought.

The first three horses past the post were led away while their connections stood around waiting for the outcome.

Eventually, the three-tone signal was again played over the speakers and everyone went quiet to listen.

'Here is the result of the stewards' enquiry,' came the announcement. 'Ricardian, first past the post, has been disqualified following an objection from the Clerk of the Scales, after the jockey weighed in two pounds lighter than he weighed out.'

There was a collective groan from all those who had previously cheered Ricardian home, their 'winning' betting slips having suddenly become totally worthless. And young Henry Payne was also distraught and close to tears.

I, meanwhile, thought it was even more *sus*, as young Henry would have said.

I watched as Harry Asquith led his family out of the unsaddling enclosure, empty-handed, back to the owners and trainers' suite.

Chico came and joined me.

'What was all that about?' he asked.

'I'm not totally sure, but I suspect that Simon Paulson made sure Ricardian couldn't win even if Jimmy wanted him to.'

'How?'

'According to the racecard, the horse should have carried ten stone, thirteen pounds, and that was what would have been weighed out. But Jimmy must have only weighed in at ten-stone-eleven. And the allowable leeway is only a pound light, not two.'

'But how could that happen?'

'Paulson may have removed some lead from the weight cloth, or maybe he didn't put the weight cloth on the horse at all. It happens occasionally by accident but, in this case, I reckon it was intentional.'

'But won't he be in trouble?'

'He certainly will. He'll be fined by the BHA, but maybe that will be less trouble for him than he'd be in with Valance if the horse had won.'

'Unbelievable.'

It certainly was, and a major fraud on the betting public.

33

I collared Jimmy Shilstone as he was leaving the racecourse after the sixth race.

'So what happened?' I asked.

'That bloody man Paulson didn't put the fucking pads on the horse when he saddled it. Left them in the corner of the saddling box. Claims he forgot them.'

'Pads?'

'Non-slip pads. Two of them. Weigh a pound each. They're designed to stop the saddle slipping – not that mine ever has. Because of the number cloth covering everything up, I didn't notice they were missing until after the race.' He rolled his eyes. 'Bloody idiot.'

'Was it an accident or did he do it on purpose?' I asked.

Jimmy shrugged. 'No idea. Either way, it cost him a fifteen-hundred-quid fine from the stewards, to say nothing of his share of the winner's purse.'

But I was certain Simon Paulson *had* done it on purpose. A

£1,500 fine from the stewards, plus the loss of the winning trainer's share of the meagre purse, was probably a lot less than Valance would have added to his outstanding loan if the horse had actually won.

'How about you?' I asked. 'Did you get fined as well?'

'Not bloody likely,' Jimmy replied. 'Why would I? It wasn't my fault. But I don't get my share now either.'

'Did you tell Paulson beforehand that you would be doing your best to win?'

'Too bloody right I did. I told him that I was fed up riding good horses to lose. It makes me appear a fool. Like at Catterick last week.'

I remembered back to what had been shouted at him by a disgruntled racegoer when he'd purposely lost on Plantagenet King.

You're a disgrace, Shilstone. Call yourself a jockey? My old grandmother could have ridden better than that.

Those sort of comments hurt, especially when he was more than capable of showing everyone how good a jockey he could be if he was really trying, as he had done so today on Ricardian.

'Keep the faith,' I said. 'And tell me what Valance says to you next.'

'What's the fucking point? I'll end up in prison anyway.'

'The point is, Jimmy,' I said, catching hold of his shoulder as he tried to walk away, 'I'm the only hope you've got, and you'd better believe it. I could report Valance to the BHA tomorrow for all I care about him. But I'm trying to save your career and your freedom, and don't you forget it.'

'Why?'

It was a good question.

Why was I so intent on keeping Jimmy out of prison and saving Marcus Capes's jockey licence? Why didn't I just do what Charles had said I should and send everything I had found to Toby Jing in the BHA Integrity Department, and be done with it?

Maybe enough dirt would stick on Valance and Asquith to get them banned from the sport, but for how long? Or maybe it wouldn't even come to that. And Jimmy, Marcus and Simon would meanwhile take the fall for their deviousness, to say nothing of what had already happened to poor Gary Bremner.

And then Valance and Asquith would be free to start all over again, terrorising and blackmailing new jockeys and different trainers to do their dirty work.

'Because I care,' I said.

And I did care. I'd been there once myself, orphaned at sixteen, suddenly alone in a grown-up world, trying my best to make an impression in horse racing. Maybe I'd just been lucky, back then, that I'd not come to the attention of people like Valance and Asquith.

But what was my aim now?

I suppose I had some crazy notion that I could broker a deal, to de-escalate the situation, and to muster sufficient evidence against Valance and Asquith such that they couldn't use what they had against Marcus and Jimmy, or even continue their little schemes. But first I needed to convince them that I had enough of my own intercontinental ballistic missiles aimed at them, such that they daren't ever fire theirs for fear of retaliation and mutual annihilation.

It was the whole basis of peace by deterrence, but would it work better here than it had in the Falkland Islands?

And did I yet have enough evidence?

Maybe I had against Anton Valance with the video that Marcus had made, but so far I had precious little, or even nothing, on Harry Asquith other than anecdotal suspicion and the slight tightening of the skin on his face, which no one else but me had seen.

I reckoned I still needed to do a little more digging before negotiations could begin.

Chico and I set off south after the last race.

I had tried to catch up again with Harry Asquith but he had not emerged without both his daughter and grandson in tow, and only then to move swiftly from the owners and trainers' hospitality suite to the car park, and then away at speed.

As Chico and I were bypassing Darlington on the motorway, I received a call from Marcus Capes. I answered on the hands-free system.

'Yes, Marcus. How can I help?'

'Can you come and see me?'

'When?'

'Right now.'

'Why?'

'Because I have another recording of Mr Valance. He called me just now, after I got back from Sedgefield, to tell me I was a very lucky boy that Jahaz Bar was brought down at the last. Otherwise, I'd have been in real trouble. I managed to record it. So come and get it.'

I looked across at Chico and he shrugged his shoulders, as if he was happy to do so.

'Okay,' I said to Marcus. 'We'll be there in about forty minutes.'

We detoured off the motorway just south of Catterick and made our way across country towards Middleham. There was a bit of a fair going on at the top of the marketplace, with a children's roundabout and several stalls of games, so I parked down the bottom, outside the Black Bull Inn.

I called Marcus to tell him I'd be there in about two minutes and, like last time, to have the door open ready.

'You stay here,' I said to Chico. 'I'll only be two ticks.'

I walked up past the fair and down Leyburn Road, but something was ringing an alarm bell in my head.

As I walked, I changed the ID of my phone to Marina's and remotely switched on the *NeverLoseIt* tag. The little blue dot on the map was reassuringly in Harrogate. I switched it off again and returned my phone to my own ID.

But the alarm bell went on ringing.

What was it that Marcus had said?

I have another recording of Mr Valance.

Mr Valance. Not just Valance, but *Mr* Valance.

I called him again.

'Marcus,' I said. 'Are you on your own? Is Valance there with you?'

'No, of course not.'

I wasn't convinced. All the little blue dot had shown me was that Valance's overcoat was in Harrogate. But the weather today had been rather mild, so maybe he didn't need his heavy coat.

I stopped about twenty yards from Marcus's door.

'Tell you what, Marcus,' I said into my phone. 'I have a new plan. Walk up to the marketplace and I'll meet you there.'

'But I can't be seen talking to you in public.'

'Is your landlady at home?'

'No. She plays whist on Wednesdays in Leyburn. Please come.'

There was something in the tone of his voice that had me even more worried. He was being too insistent.

'No, Marcus,' I said. 'Either you come up to the marketplace or you can send me the recording online.'

'But you must come,' he said, sounding almost desperate.

'No, I mustn't. And, for anyone else currently listening in to this conversation, I'm not about to walk into your trap. Perhaps you would like to call me yourself on your own phone, and then I will choose where and when we are to meet. If I'm wrong, Marcus, and you actually are on your own, I will see you in the marketplace, again alone, in five minutes. Either that, or I'm going home.'

Just up from number 42, on the opposite side of Leyburn Road, was a high stone wall with a gated entrance into a stableyard. The two large wooden gates were wide open. I went through the gateway and hid behind one of the gates, but in a position from which I could clearly see the front door of number 42 through the narrow hinge gap.

I waited but Marcus did not emerge in the five minutes I had given him. However, I stayed put, waiting to see who would emerge.

I called Chico.

'Everything all right?' he asked, answering at the first ring.

'Fine, but I might be a little while. Stay right where you are and keep your phone handy.'

'Okay. Will do.'

I put my phone onto silent mode.

I was always keen for Marina to call me, but not right now.

A good fifteen minutes after I had last spoken to Marcus, the front door of number 42 opened and a man's head appeared, looking up and down the road. It wasn't a head I recognized.

The head withdrew and, after a few seconds, three men came out and turned up towards the marketplace. I recognized one of them straight away as Anton Valance and I had a pretty good idea who the other two were as well. Judging by their heights and builds, they were the two I had met twice before, but this time they were without their balaclavas. One of the two had a tattered old golf bag slung over his shoulder, but I didn't think for a moment that he was looking for a game.

I held my breath and used my phone to video the three men as they seemed to be coming directly towards where I was hiding. But they passed by the gateway on the road not ten feet away from me, and I captured them all in glorious technicolour, their faces brightly lit by the last glimmers of the evening sunshine.

When I was sure they were out of hearing range, I called Chico again.

'Yep?' he said.

'Three men are walking up from here towards the marketplace. One of them is Valance, but he's not wearing his overcoat. He's in a blue jacket and one of the others has a golf bag over his shoulder. Try and see where they go.'

I hung up.

I looked back at number 42. In their haste to get out, the three had left the front door wide open.

I dialled Marcus's number but there was no reply.

I stepped out from my hiding place and went gingerly to the edge of the road. I looked up towards the marketplace. There was no sign of the three men, so I went across the road and shouted through the open front door.

'Marcus.' No reply. So I shouted again. 'Marcus, are you there?' Still no reply.

I checked once more that the three men were out of sight and not coming back, then I stepped inside, went quickly up the stairs, and straight into Marcus's bedsit.

At least he was alive.

He was on his knees beside the bed and he was groaning.

I looked around his room.

Last time I'd been here, it had been in pristine order with everything in its proper place. But not today, not any more. The place was a complete mess, with broken crockery and smashed glass all over the floor and the bed, along with what looked like the contents of all his food packets and tins. Corn flakes mixed with sugar, instant coffee, baked beans and some indistinguishable brown stuff had all been ground into the erstwhile spotless carpet, and someone had squeezed tomato ketchup all over Marcus's bed in long thin lines.

'You okay?' I asked from over his shoulder.

331

'No,' he said, without turning or looking up. 'I think they've broken my bloody collarbone. Why didn't you come?'

'Because, Marcus, then we would have both ended up just like you are now. Or even worse.'

'He said he only wanted to check your mobile phone.'

'And you believed him?'

He gestured with his head towards his kitchenette.

Lying on the worktop by the sink were the remains of his own phone, totally shattered beyond any hope of repair.

'He was after the video I made of him on Monday.'

'Did he watch any of it?' I asked.

'Only a few minutes at the beginning. He wanted to know where I had hidden the phone. I told him it had been in the teapot. He went over and took the teapot down from the shelf and stamped on it but it didn't break, and he also hurt his foot trying. That made me laugh, but that was a big mistake because he got angry and told the other two to smash the whole place up. Then he took the SIM card out of my phone before getting one of his men to hit the rest of it with a wooden bat they'd brought with them in a golf bag. Used all his strength, too. Hit it over and over. About six or seven times.'

Looking at the tangled mass of what was left of the phone, I wasn't surprised. Valance had clearly been trying to remove any trace of the video. That's why he'd wanted to check my phone. But little did he know that Chico also had a copy of it.

Perhaps it would be wise to make a few more copies. Maybe I'd even lodge one with Charles or with a solicitor.

'Then they hit me with the same bloody bat,' Marcus said.

'One of those brutes held my left arm out and the other one hit me really hard on the collarbone. I heard it snap. How could anyone do that?'

I thought back to my encounters with the same two men, first in the Catterick racecourse car park and then in my own garden. I'd clearly got away quite lightly.

'And did Valance just stand by and watch while the other two did all this?' I waved my hand at the lines of ketchup on his bed.

'Stand by and watch? Don't make me laugh. He bloody directed it. He told them exactly what to do. He kept saying, very calmly, that it was a real shame they had to smash the place up and hurt me, but it was my own fault. He said that if I'd done what I was told, I'd have been left alone. He also told me that, because I had twice disregarded his instructions, he had to do something to me that I'd remember, so that, in future, I would know what to expect if I defied him again.'

'And will you?' I asked.

'Will I what?'

'Defy him again?'

He looked up at me, wincing slightly from the pain in his shoulder.

'Too bloody right I will.'

I smiled at him. He was clearly a boy after my own heart.

34

I decided to wait with Marcus in his room until Chico called. The last thing I wanted to do was walk straight into the three I had seen leaving here or, worse still, call Chico's phone when he was secretly watching them.

I managed to get Marcus up off the floor, and he sat on the arm of his armchair while I fashioned a towel into a makeshift sling. He grimaced as I ran my finger along the skin above the bone and I could feel the break move due to the pressure I applied. As far as I could tell, the bone seemed to be lined up in the correct place with the broken ends touching, but he would probably need an X-ray in hospital to confirm it.

I had broken my collarbones on several occasions during my own riding career – three times on one side and two on the other. It was a common injury for jockeys, mostly as a result of one instinctively putting out a hand when falling from a horse. Unless it was a very serious break, say with bits of the bone sticking out through the skin, there was not much the medics would do except put your arm in a sling and wait for nature to do its stuff.

While Marcus sat there feeling sorry for himself, I did my best to pick up some of the smashed glass and crockery from the floor.

'Doris is going to be livid about her carpet,' he said. 'And God knows what Mr Kline will say when he finds out I can't ride.'

'Tell him that you hadn't realized anything was wrong after your fall from Jahaz Bar until you got home, and your shoulder started hurting.'

Broken bones were an occupational hazard for steeplechase jockeys and both they and the trainers they rode for just had to get used to them. However, none of them expected to have their collarbone broken by a baseball bat while standing in their bedroom.

Accepted medical advice was that a broken collarbone would take about six weeks to mend plus another six weeks to get back to full strength, but I'd known of several jockeys who had raced again within three weeks of a break. In fact, thinking back, I'd been one of them.

And there were plenty of verified accounts, from the days before mandatory medical checks were introduced after every racing fall, of hardy jump jockeys riding with the ends of a broken collarbone grinding together, rather than lose a ride on a well-fancied horse in a big race.

'Look on the bright side,' I said to Marcus with a smile. 'At least you won't have Valance telling you to lose a race for a while.'

He tried to smile back.

'Perhaps I'll go home for bit, but things are not great between my parents at the moment. Ever since Dad left the army, he's been rather lost with no real direction in his life. He and Mum have begun arguing all the time, mostly over how much he drinks now.'

Marcus sighed and I felt sorry for him.

Chico finally called me.

'Did you see them?' I asked.

'You bet. Followed all three of them to start with but then they separated. The two goons got in a car and drove off – don't worry, I took a photo of the car and I got the reg – and then Valance walked on through the town to the ruined castle. I followed him and, guess what? Your chum turns up – the one from the races this afternoon. Bleedin' nearly catches me too, as I'm hidin' from Valance behind a car right next to where he parks.'

'He's hardly my chum,' I complained. 'So then what happened?'

'Suffice to say that you are not flavour of the month with either of them. They had a right barney, right there and then, over how you knew that Valance had been at Asquith's house in East Witton on Monday. Asquith accused Valance of being bleedin' careless.'

My plan to outflank their defences by setting them against each other seemed to be bearing some fruit.

'So where are they now?' I asked.

'They went into the castle. It was already shut for the day but Asquith brought the key to the gate with him. They're now in a wooden buildin' just inside the castle entrance. It looks like a ticket office or somethin'.'

'So where are you?' I asked.

'I'm standin' right next to the wooden building. Round the back, away from the door.'

'Be careful they can't hear you.'

He laughed. 'No chance of that. They're still goin' at it hammer and tongs inside. I've put my ear to the wood. I can't actually hear all the words but there's no doubt they are arguin' about somethin', and I think it's about Marcus Capes. I'm sure I heard his name shouted at least twice.'

It may not have actually been due to Anton Valance's carelessness that I found out about his trip to East Witton, but breaking Marcus's collarbone had been extremely careless of him. He should have realized that it would be counter-productive, making Marcus more determined to defy him, not less so. Maybe Asquith realized that, and hence it was another source of friction between the two of them. I hoped so, anyway.

But it had also raised the poker stakes another notch or two.

'How about you?' Chico asked.

'I'm with Marcus. They beat him up quite badly, and also smashed up his place. But I'm going to come and join you now.'

'Yeah, okay, but keep your phone handy in case they come out. I'll text you if they do.'

'Great. See you in a bit.'

I hung up and turned to Marcus. 'How are you feeling?'

'Sore.'

'You're bound to be sore. Think of it as just the result of a fall in a race.'

He looked across at me. 'But this is different. All racing falls are accidental. This was done on purpose. Somehow it makes it worse.'

It certainly did.

'Will you be all right here on your own for a bit or is there someone else I could call to come round? I need to go and do something.'

'I'll be fine.'

'You will need to go and have an X-ray on that shoulder to check everything's in its proper place. Where's the nearest hospital?'

'There's one at Northallerton. The Friarage Hospital. I went there last year when I got kicked on the knee by a three-year-old.'

'Where's Northallerton?'

'Twenty miles east of here. But it's quite small. There's a bigger one in Darlington, but it's further away.'

I'd driven past Darlington only an hour or so ago on the way south from Sedgefield racecourse, and I didn't want to have to go back that way as it was in the opposite direction to my home.

'You'll have to get a taxi.'

'How?' he asked, pointing at the remains of his phone.

'Does Doris have a landline?'

'She won't want me using that.'

'But this is an emergency,' I said.

'Even so,' he said, shaking his head. 'She told me that the only time I could use her phone was if she needed an ambulance or if the house was burning down. I tell you, she's as tight as an Irish navvy on St Paddy's Day. That's why she isn't going to like all this mess.'

'It could be worse,' I said. 'At least there's no blood on the carpet.'

'Not this time,' he said forlornly.

'Okay,' I said, 'you wait here. I'll be back, and I'll sort you out a taxi then. I haven't got the time right now.'

He wasn't happy to be left alone but he hadn't much choice, other than to walk somewhere else.

I rushed down the stairs, almost tripped over Tiddles lying asleep on the bottom step, and then hurried up the hill towards the marketplace, past the families at the fair and on to the castle beyond.

I slowed down as I approached and kept close to the low stone wall that ran alongside the road in front. The sun had now dipped towards the horizon and the castle ruins towered above me, dark and sinister against the brightness of the western sky.

There had been no warning text from Chico that either Valance or Asquith was on the move, but, even so, I was very wary as I crept across the wooden drawbridge over the dry moat and then in through the dark, arched castle entrance.

As Chico had said, there was a modern brown wooden building just inside the gatehouse. Attached to it was an English Heritage sign indicating that a ticket needed to be purchased before exploring the ruins, but I decided to skip that on this occasion.

The wooden structure was actually L-shaped. The near end had a row of big windows and appeared to be a gift shop. The interior of this section was in darkness, but there was a sliver of light showing under the door of the far-end segment, and I could hear raised voices from within.

Treading carefully and silently I made my way round the back to find Chico.

'It went a bit quiet for a while,' he whispered. 'But they're both still in there and they've started arguin' again. So what do we do?'

'Are you sure that the other two goons are not with them?'

I didn't fancy taking on four of them but just two were manageable, especially if the two were Valance and Asquith. Chico and I had seen all too clearly at the Turkish Baths in Harrogate that Valance was considerably overweight, obese even, and very unfit, while Asquith must be in his mid-seventies, if not older.

'A hundred per cent certain. I watched them drive away.'

'I wonder where they went. I don't really want them coming back.'

'Why not?' Chico asked in a whisper.

'Because I think that the time for using the Red Telephone Hotline has passed. This situation needs to be concluded face to face.'

'What do you mean?'

'Just watch. But you stay here as backup.'

And, with that, I walked round from behind the building, opened the door, and went in.

Asquith and Valance instantly stopped shouting at each other, and both stared at me.

This section of the building was used as a storeroom of stock for the gift shop and for some outdoor tables and chairs. The two men were at the far end close to the back wall, but I stopped just inside the door, some six or eight feet away from them.

'Good evening, gentlemen,' I said into the sudden silence. 'I think it is high time the three of us had a little talk.'

'What about?' Valance snapped angrily. 'I 'ave absolutely no intention of ever speaking or listening to you. Go away.'

I could tell that Asquith was irritated. I wasn't sure if it was with my arrival or because of Valance's point-blank refusal to negotiate.

'Let us hear what the man has to say,' Asquith said slowly.

Valance clearly didn't like it but he kept quiet. The pecking order between the two had become apparent, with, as I had suggested to Chico, Asquith as top man and Valance as the accomplice.

'It is time for your fun and games to cease.'

'Fun and games?' Asquith asked in a sarcastic tone.

'You know exactly what I mean. Messing around with the results of horse races and defrauding the public.'

'And how are we supposed to be doing that?' Asquith asked, all innocently.

'You know perfectly well. By blackmail and extortion of jockeys and trainers, and then breaking their bones when they don't do as you tell them.'

'I think you must be mistaken,' Asquith said. 'I have no knowledge of any of that. How about you, Anton? Do you know what he's on about?'

'No idea at all,' Valance replied, but he didn't sound as convincing as his boss.

This summit meeting was not going quite as I had planned. But I wasn't finished yet.

'Funny that,' I said, not laughing. 'I have been outside listening to you two arguing for the past half an hour, so I know you're lying.' I held up my phone towards Asquith. 'I have it all recorded, all that stuff about how angry you are that Anton here led me to your house in East Witton and what a mistake he's made in breaking Marcus Capes's collarbone.'

He wasn't to know that I hadn't actually been able to record anything intelligible from outside, but I was recording what was said now.

I turned towards Valance. 'And that was, indeed, a big mistake, Anton. Marcus will never do what you say now, and if you publish the video you have of him, he'll do the same with the one he has of you.'

'But 'e 'asn't got it any more,' Anton replied triumphantly. 'I destroyed 'is phone.'

I looked at Asquith, who obviously couldn't believe what he'd just heard.

I turned to Valance. 'Do you really think the video of you on Marcus's phone was the only copy? I have another one on here.' I held up my phone again. 'So let's start this little conversation again, shall we?'

I looked from one to the other, but they said nothing.

'Now where was I? Oh, yes. This game you are playing with fixing race results will cease forthwith.'

Asquith cleared his throat.

'Hypothetically, if what you are saying is true, then what would we get in return?'

I stared at him. It was like a vandal asking what he would get in return if he stopped painting graffiti on trains or bridges.

'Nothing,' I said. 'Other than my word that what I have will not make its way to the authorities.'

'It doesn't seem like a very good deal.'

'I wouldn't say that,' I replied. 'If you do nothing, then I will do nothing. That seems perfectly fair to me. Mind you, I'll be watching you closely and checking. And the alternative is that I go to both the racing authorities and the police to lay before them everything I have. I assure you, even if it may not be enough to get you two sent to prison, I have more than enough to get you banned from being a registered racehorse owner, and Anton here would definitely lose his licence to be a jockeys' agent. Remember, the BHA only needs to be satisfied on the balance of probabilities to act.'

'And what assurances would we get that you wouldn't go to the BHA anyway?' Valance asked.

'No assurances,' I said. 'That is a chance you will have to take.'

'That doesn't seem very attractive to me.'

'Tough,' I said. 'That's all you're getting. In fact, you have no choice whatsoever in the matter.'

'Oh, I think we do,' Asquith said softly.

I switched my gaze from Valance to him and my heart missed a beat.

In poker terms, Harry Asquith had just gone all-in.

In his gloved right hand he held a pistol and it was pointed straight at me.

35

I forced myself to smile at him.

'Come on,' I said, trying to keep my voice calm. 'What are you going to do? Kill me?'

'That certainly has its attractions,' Asquith responded. 'But first I want your mobile phone.'

I didn't move.

Was he holding a winning hand, or was he bluffing?

'Is it even loaded?' I asked. 'Or is it a non-firing replica?'

He glanced down at the gun. 'I assure you it's very real and it is fully loaded. A Mark IV Webley service revolver. A genuine British army officer's sidearm. It belonged to my great-grandfather during the Boer War and has been handed down to me through the generations, along with the ammunition. They may be old but, trust me, they still work. Chambered at .455 inches, this little baby could take your head clean off your shoulders.'

He sounded a bit like Clint Eastwood's character in the film *Dirty Harry* – an appropriate title under the circumstances.

'Give me your phone.'

I had once before underestimated someone with a gun and had walked straight into a .38 slug. The resulting damage to my small intestines had left me at death's door for several days and consuming only liquefied food for months. I didn't like to imagine what a .455 would do.

Hence, I threw my phone across onto the floor in front of him. I didn't worry about breaking it – I was certain he would do that himself anyway – and I didn't fancy getting too close to the dark circle at the business end of the Webley's short stubby barrel.

At least that was in my favour. I knew that all handguns were notoriously inaccurate, especially those with short barrels such as the one facing me, and the old adage about them not being able to hit a barn door at ten paces had not been coined without good reason.

'Now what?' I said, doing my best to keep any fear out of my tone. 'Shall I go?'

'Not so fast. What do you suggest, Anton?'

'Shoot 'im, 'Arry,' Valance said in a matter-of-fact way, just as if he was suggesting that Asquith should step on a spider.

'That really wouldn't be a very clever move,' I said as calmly as I could with my heart pumping fast. 'As I told Anton in the Turkish Baths in Harrogate, I have lodged everything I have on you both with my solicitor, to be handed to the police in the event of anything happening to me. And there's no way a corpse turning up with a .455 slug embedded in it would be considered by the police to be a suicide, even if you do type a fake suicide note into my phone, as you did with Gary Bremner.'

'Don't listen to 'im,' Valance said. 'If you let 'im go, 'e'll go straight to the police. Kill 'im now. I'll get the boys back to help clear up.' He tapped his phone twice and then lifted it to his ear.

For some reason I looked down at the wooden floor and my mind began to wander.

'Do you have any idea how difficult it will be to get my blood out from the gaps between these floorboards? Forensics will have a field day.' I snapped my brain back into the awful reality, and looked up at Asquith. 'Several people know where I am. If you shoot me, I promise that you will be arrested within hours and you will spend the rest of your life behind bars. Is that what you want?'

The gun still didn't waver one millimetre.

'And is that what you want young Henry Payne to live with as he grows up? That his beloved grandfather, after whom he was named, turned out to be a cold-blooded murderer? Do you think he'll ever come to see you in prison?'

He didn't react and I was beginning to fear that I wasn't getting through to him at all. All I could see in his eyes was his absolute conviction that getting rid of me would also rid him of all his problems rather than simply creating many more new ones, and whatever I said wasn't going to make any difference.

On my immediate right was a stack of four large cardboard boxes, each about eighteen inches high, with MARYLEBONE CERAMICS, FRAGILE CONTENTS printed large on the sides. Slowly I slid my transplanted left hand between the stack and the wall.

Just as I could tell that Asquith's mental cogs were all lining up to produce a conclusive thumbs-down for my future existence,

I pulled the whole stack of boxes forward towards him and Valance, and to hell with the fragile contents. At the same time I ducked down low and dived for the door.

The gun indeed worked, and it was definitely loaded.

Asquith fired it, and the noise of such a large-calibre weapon being discharged within the confined space of the building was incredible. Not that I cared much about that. I was just grateful that the bullet had missed me, and I wasn't hanging around to give him another shot.

I flung the door open and went through it like the proverbial bat out of hell, running hard for some cover in among the dark castle ruins.

God knows what Chico made of it all but, wherever he was, I hoped he was keeping his head down. He must have heard the gun go off and perhaps, with luck, he had already called in reinforcements in the form of the North Yorkshire Police armed-response unit. I just hoped they might get here before the return of 'the boys'.

I ran down the north side of the central keep and into the deep shadows beyond before stopping to catch my breath and listen out for any pursuers.

The daylight was now fading fast and the only sounds I could hear were the multiple sharp 'kya' calls of the jackdaws, eerily echoing, as they flew back to roost high up on the castle walls.

I knew from my previous visit that there were many places to hide out, not least in the cubicles of the western latrine tower. But those had only one entrance/exit and I didn't much fancy being cornered in one by Asquith with his mark four Webley.

Hence, I kept on the move through the ruins down the western side, trying to work out what Asquith and Valance might do next.

I soon found out.

Just as my eyes were beginning to adjust to the deepening darkness, my night-vision was destroyed by a dazzling high-intensity torch beam that caught me unawares in the open space of the apron between the keep and the outer ranges of the south-west corner.

There was a shout and a second torch beam appeared from where I had just come from, down the western side.

Casting any remaining caution he might have had to the wind, Asquith loosed off another shot at me. For an instant, I thought that he had missed me again, but my right hand suddenly started hurting as if it had been stung by a large hornet.

I ran fast for the opening into the bottom floor of the keep, jumping through the space into the former state kitchens and nearly tripping straight into one of the wells in the floor.

Once inside, I reached down with my new transplanted left hand and was amazed that I could actually feel the warmth of flowing blood. The bullet had just clipped the fleshy part of my palm, beneath my little finger. It was sore but not life-threatening.

So now where?

I tried desperately to remember the castle layout from my brief visit in the daylight the previous week. I did not want to get trapped and, as Asquith had arrived with a key to the gate, he would almost certainly know the castle layout better than I did.

Maybe I should have run straight to the castle exit when I escaped from the wooden building, but that would have given

Asquith a clear shot at me. Now, getting well away from here alive had become my main priority.

My right hand started hurting like hell but it seemed still to be working okay, even if I was dripping my lifeblood onto the earth beneath my feet. But it wouldn't kill me and it was the least of my worries for the moment.

I could recall from my previous visit that the north, west and south outer walls were intact at ground level, meaning there was no way out except either through the main gatehouse in the north-east corner or through the missing sections of the east wall, and that would involve crossing the dry moat and scaling the boundary wall beyond. And all in the dark, with a bad and bleeding right hand and a transplanted left one.

It seemed to me that I had only two choices – either to get out through the main gate or to survive long enough in here for Chico to summon the cavalry to come and save me.

But there was also the problem of 'the boys'.

I thought that I could remain ahead of Valance and Asquith among the dark castle ruins, although the torches certainly didn't help my cause, but against four I'd have absolutely no chance.

Chico had said that he had seen 'the boys' drive away, but where to?

It had been no more than twenty to twenty-five minutes between them leaving and Valance calling them to return. Had they been driving away all that time or had they stopped only a mile or so down the road? At best, I had only twenty minutes or so before they would be back, and then this deadly game of hide-and-seek would quickly reach a finale – and I would be the loser.

But my immediate prime concern was to keep out of the torch beams.

I decided against going up.

There were two staircases to the upper levels – the stone spiral in the south-east-corner tower of the keep and a modern straight wooden structure that now stood on the site of the original external entrance staircase on the east side.

Two staircases and two assailants didn't seem like a very good bet to me. They would simply need to take one stairway each and move up together, leaving me no way out, and those parts of the upper levels that hadn't already collapsed were very small with precious little space to hide.

I felt I could easily overpower Valance, if only I knew which one was him, but I had no wish to rush at one of the torches only to find another .455 slug coming rapidly in the opposite direction.

The two of them still seemed to be moving around outside the keep. I could tell by the light from their torches that shone through the opening in the walls, which had once held leaded-glass windows.

Originally, for added security, there had been no entrances to the keep on the ground floor, access only being into the first floor via the external staircase, but, over the years, several holes had been punched through the ten-feet-thick walls. It was only a matter of time before Asquith and Valance came through them, and there was nowhere in there for me to hide either.

I needed to get out of the keep, and fast.

Down the centre there was a dividing wall and I went through an opening in this wall from the old kitchens to what had once been a large vaulted cellar.

In the southern wall of the cellar were two ways out, one with a modern wooden raised walkway to help visitors gain access over the uneven stones underfoot and the other an almost circular hole beneath what had once been a window. This second one was smaller but still easily big enough for me to get through if I crouched.

I could hear Asquith and Valance talking outside without being able to actually hear the words but, presently, I could tell from their torches that one of them had moved round to enter the keep on the western side while the other seemed to be coming directly towards me.

But which of them was which?

The torchlight coming into the keep got brighter and then I could hear footfalls on the wooden walkway.

I inched myself up and silently crept through the circular hole, moving my body outside at the same instant that the person holding the torch moved in, using the thick wall between us as cover.

Now where?

I continued anticlockwise, feeling my way in the dark up the eastern side, past the ruined chapel. It was the route back towards the wooden building and the castle exit beyond.

I could hear Asquith shouting for Valance from within the keep.

'Anton, where are you?' he shouted. 'Have you seen him?'

There was no reply.

I was inching my way silently towards the castle exit, alongside the new wooden stairway, when, quite suddenly, a torch came on not six feet in front of me and it was shining straight into my eyes.

Bugger!

36

I decided to rush it, just hoping it was Valance with only a torch and not Asquith also with his gun.

But, as I bunched my muscles for the attack, with my heart rate rising to near two hundred beats a minute, the light pointed suddenly upwards showing me the face of the man holding it, and he was grinning.

'Hiya, Sid,' Chico whispered. 'Need any help?'

I could have kissed him.

'How did you get the torch?' I whispered back.

He switched it off. 'It's the one Valance had.'

'So where's Valance now?'

'Shall we just say that he's indisposed. Nursing a nasty headache, I shouldn't wonder.'

'But where is he?'

'Somewhere over on the other side. He walked right down past where I was hidin', but with his torch shinin' onto the big building in the middle. So I simply gave him a gentle tap on the head with a rock. He went out cold.'

'Where on earth did you find a rock?'

'I prized it off a crumblin' castle wall.'

'You can't do that,' I said in a mocking tone. 'This is a Grade One listed building.'

'Tough,' Chico said. 'My need was greater.'

'Will Valance wake up?'

'Not for a bit, I hope. It wasn't that gentle a tap I gave him. In fact, it was bleedin' hard.'

'Even so, he might.'

'What else could I do? I didn't exactly have a pair of handcuffs in my bleedin' pocket, now, did I?'

I smiled in the darkness at his turn of phrase.

'You do know that Asquith has a gun?' I said.

'Tell me about it. Had my ear right up against the wood when he let it off. Nearly bleedin' deafened me. And I thought you were a goner.'

'So did I. But now what? Did you call the cops?'

'Certainly did.'

'So why aren't they here?'

It felt as if I'd been hunted through these ruins for hours, but it was probably only about five or ten minutes since I'd escaped from the storeroom in the wooden building.

'I think I made the mistake of tellin' them there's a man shootin' off a bleedin' gun. To hurry them up, like, but that backfired. They said that they would then have to wait to get their firearms team out. I just hope they're not comin' all the way from London.'

So did I.

Suddenly there was more angry shouting from inside the keep. 'Anton, where the hell are you? I need you here.'

'He'll soon realize that Valance isn't coming,' I said. 'What do you think he'll do then?'

'God knows,' Chico replied. 'The man's totally unhinged.'

'I completely agree. That's why I think it's time to get out of here and leave him to the police firearms team.'

'No way,' Chico said adamantly. 'Me and you need to nail this bastard ourselves – right here and right now.'

He sounded just like Gary Bremner on that first Sunday I'd come north to Middleham to see him – and look what had happened to him.

'How exactly do you think we can do that?' I asked. 'And before the two goons come back. Valance called them.'

'All the more reason to finish it now,' Chico said. 'I don't want to leave here and run straight into them on the way out. You distract Asquith and I'll do the rest.'

Fine, but I didn't fancy distracting him by giving him the chance of loosing off another shot at me. Third time, I might not be so lucky.

'Give me the torch then.'

I took it in my left hand as my right was beginning to not work properly. I grimaced and sighed.

'Are you all right?' Chico whispered.

'Not really,' I whispered back. 'I've been shot.'

'My God! Where?'

'In the hand. But I'll survive.'

'Which hand?'

'The old one.'

'Is that good or bad?'

'Good, I suppose. At least, it will heal. The other one might not have.'

'You okay to go on?'

'Yeah, I'm fine, but is this really a sensible idea to go after Asquith just on our own?'

'No, of course it's not sensible,' Chico said with a whispered laugh. 'But when have we ever done anythin' that is sensible? It was you that walked away from me and straight into that wooden buildin' in the first place, remember? Was that sensible?'

Probably not, and I wouldn't have done it if I'd known that Asquith had a loaded gun in his pocket.

'Okay,' I whispered, 'what's the plan?'

''Arry, over 'ere, quick – 'e's ere and 'e's been shot.'

Had I sounded enough like Anton Valance with his Yorkshire dropped aitches? I very much 'oped so – my continued existence might depend on it.

'Yes!' Asquith exclaimed triumphantly. 'I thought I'd hit him. There's blood here on the ground in the keep.'

Too right, there was. My blood.

I was standing over in the north-western corner of the castle, a remaining arch partially hiding me from the place where I thought Asquith would emerge from the keep, and I was also pointing the torch that way so that he wouldn't be able to see me beyond its glare.

He came out as I had expected, even with a swagger in his step and the gun down by his side, coming directly towards me across the grass.

'Is he still alive?' he asked as he walked. 'And turn that bloody torch off, Anton. I can't see a damn thing.'

I didn't switch the torch off. I didn't even move it one inch.

Only when he was getting quite close did he realize that something wasn't right. His right arm, and the gun, started to come up but, by then, I could see a shadowy figure moving quickly behind him.

Chico hit him with his rock but in the final moment, just before impact, Asquith obviously sensed or heard something and half turned, so that the rock caught him on the shoulder rather than on his head as we had planned.

For a man in his mid-seventies, Asquith was surprisingly strong and nimble.

Chico jumped on his back and grabbed him round his neck while I ran over to help.

I hit Asquith in the face with the torch but my strike didn't have enough power to stop the gun coming up towards me.

I had to grab it but, by now, my injured right hand was in complete spasm and totally useless.

I had no other choice.

I dropped the torch, still switched on, and closed the fingers of my transplanted left hand round the stubby barrel of the Webley and used all the strength I could muster to force the gun's aim away from me.

Asquith pulled the trigger.

The bullet missed me by no more than a couple of inches,

FELIX FRANCIS

struck the castle ruins and ricocheted off into the night with an impressive zinging sound.

The gun had jumped due to the recoil and some of the propellant gases escaped through the tiny gap between the revolving cylinder and the barrel, scorching my fingers, but still I didn't let go, pushing it further away to my left. But I could feel that I was beginning to lose this battle, not least because Asquith had now dropped his own torch and was trying to get hold of the revolver with his left hand as well as his right.

'For God's sake, Chico,' I shouted, 'do something.'

'I'm bleedin' tryin',' he shouted back at me.

In the light from the dropped torches, I watched as Chico grabbed at Asquith's face, sticking his fingers into his eyes.

'Get off me!' Asquith shouted.

'Then drop the gun,' I shouted back at him.

He didn't drop it, but he was now back holding it one-handed, as he tried to prize Chico's fingers out of his eyes with the other.

In the far distance I thought I could hear a police siren. *Come on, you cops,* I thought, *hurry up. We need you.*

I was beginning to lose strength in my left hand. I could feel it beginning to shake with the effort but still I wouldn't let go of the barrel. To do so was to die and I wasn't yet ready for that.

In this moment of great peril, I thought of Marina and Saskia. How would they manage if I died here? Somehow, it gave me extra strength.

I placed my right forearm against my left wrist to help push the gun barrel further to the side, away from my body.

Asquith fired the Webley again and, once more, the escaping

gases burned my fingers, but that was the only damage it did to me, and that wouldn't kill me.

I thought way back to the politically incorrect days of my childhood in South Wales, when my classmates and I had endlessly played games of 'cowboys and Indians' in the woods behind our street. I'd always been a cowboy with my shiny toy revolver, and it had had a lever on the side to open it, so that I could load it with endless rolls of pink paper caps.

Did this gun also have a lever to open it?

While not easing up on the sideways pressure I was applying to the barrel, I felt around for a lever, imagining it would be where the thumb would rest for a right-handed person holding the grip.

I found a protrusion and pushed it down.

Amazingly, the revolver opened, the barrel and cylinder hinging down from the hammer and the grip, and, for an added bonus, the Webley patented automatic extraction system emptied the cylinder of both the four empty cases and the two remaining live rounds, dropping them all onto the grass at my feet.

'Gun safe,' I shouted, letting go of it. But did Asquith have more ammunition in his pocket? Indeed, he seemed to be reaching for some with his left hand.

Chico let go of Asquith's face and jumped down from his back, but he was far from finished with him. With the threat of being shot having receded, at least for the time being, Chico was able to move round in front of Asquith and employ some of his more conventional Japanese fighting skills.

In spite of Asquith being some six inches taller than Chico, or maybe because of it, Chico was able to turn his back into Asquith, take the taller man's right arm over his own right shoulder and, by first bending his knees and then sharply straightening them, toss the older man clean over his head in a full somersault, slamming him hard down onto the turf in a classic judo throw.

The sharp impact of his back with the ground audibly drove the air from Asquith's lungs. I stepped over to him and trod on his right wrist, pinning it to the floor. I leaned down to remove the Webley from his hand but still he resisted. So I moved my foot slightly and trod hard on the pistol grip itself, jamming his thumb underneath.

He cried out in agony, but I didn't care. If anything, I trod on it even harder, applying all my weight through the ball of my foot.

'Let go of the gun and I'll remove my foot,' I said down to him.

He looked up at me and nodded ever so slightly.

Without removing my foot completely, I eased the pressure somewhat and again leaned down to take the gun with my left hand.

This time he did not resist.

I held the gun only by the barrel. Even if Asquith had only handled the gun with his gloves on, I didn't want to put my prints, or rather those of my transplant donor, on the grip for the police to find.

'What now?' Chico asked.

I could definitely now hear approaching sirens. They were closer but still some distance off.

'We watch out in case the hired help turns up. Where's Valance?'

'Over there,' Chico said, pointing off to the side.

I stuffed the Webley into my coat pocket and picked up one of the torches.

'You watch him,' I said, shining the torch straight at Asquith, who was still lying face-up on the ground. 'If he moves at all, smack him on the head with your rock. And don't worry about killing him. We'll just claim it was self-defence.'

Chico grinned at me, which was more than could be said for Asquith's reaction.

I walked over to where Chico had indicated and found Anton Valance behind one of the small ruined walls. He was still unconscious and was lying on his left side with his right leg pulled forward, as if Chico had placed him in the recovery position.

I'm not sure I'd have bothered.

He was still breathing, the air rasping in his throat, but I could see in the torchlight that some blood had oozed out of his right ear, a sure sign of major damage done within, quite likely a fractured skull. Chico must have hit him harder than I'd thought.

I felt in his jacket pocket for his mobile phone. I was sure I had seen him use fingerprint recognition to switch it on when he had called 'the boys' in the wooden building.

I lifted his right hand and placed his thumb on the 'home' button.

Try again, read the screen. Next, I used his right index finger and, as if by magic, the phone came alive.

I checked the list of calls made. The most recent was the one I was interested in.

Placing the phone on the ground and using the forefinger of my left hand, I typed in a short text and sent it to the same number: *No longer needed. Go home.*

I wouldn't have been able to do that with a plastic hand, I thought. There would have been no conductivity between it and the touch-screen.

While I had Valance's phone unlocked, I also took the opportunity to select all his stored videos and delete them.

I had no real expectation that the videos of Marcus counting the money or Jimmy having sex with the girl in Liverpool weren't also stored somewhere else or that simply deleting them from the phone's video library would mean they weren't somehow still retrievable from the depths of its memory, but at least they wouldn't be the first things the police would see.

I put the phone in my coat pocket along with the Webley, and went back to where Chico was standing over Asquith, the large piece of stone from the castle wall now in his hands as if he was willing the older man to move.

'Valance needs an ambulance,' I said. 'I think you may have fractured his skull. Not that I care much. Have you got your phone? They took mine.'

To Asquith's relief, Chico put the heavy stone down and then removed a mobile phone from his trouser pocket. He went to pass it to me.

'Dial 999 for me, will you. I don't think I can hold it and dial at the same time.'

In fact, I was beginning to feel decidedly unwell – very sweaty, yet strangely cold at the same time. It was a feeling I had become quite used to during my time as a jockey, after a racing fall. It was the body's natural reaction to trauma.

'Perhaps you need an ambulance as well,' Chico said.

I think he was probably right.

'Emergency, which service?' asked the operator.

'Ambulance,' I said.

There were a few clicks and a female voice came on the line. 'Is the patient breathing?'

'Yes,' I said, 'but with difficulty. I think he may have a fractured skull.'

'Did he fall?' she asked.

'Something like that. Please hurry.'

She asked me for my name and also my location. I told her both.

'An ambulance is on its way. Please stay on the line.'

But I decided not to, and disconnected.

Asquith suddenly sat up straight.

'Give me the gun,' he said.

'You must be bleedin' jokin',' Chico replied. 'We're not giving you anythin', mate, other than an extremely long stretch in the slammer.'

'Please give me the gun,' he pleaded. 'And a single bullet.'

We all knew what he wanted to do.

I looked across at Chico, and he shrugged his shoulders.

But, after what had happened to Gary Bremner, I'd already looked up the law on suicide. It states that a person who aids or abets the suicide of another may be subject to imprisonment for up to fourteen years.

And who was to say he wouldn't shoot me with his single round instead.

'Not a chance, Harry,' I said.

37

The first police to arrive were not those we had heard in the distance coming by road.

One minute, all was quiet in the castle, and the next there was a cacophony of sound as a police helicopter suddenly appeared overhead, its brilliant searchlight illuminating the ground around us as if it was in full sunlight.

'Stay right where you are,' came an order from above.

We stayed right where we were.

Finally, lighting up the high walls, I could see a mass of blue flashing lights as the road posse arrived.

'Now come on out with your hands up,' said the voice from above.

Hands up? He'd be lucky. My right arm hung limply down at my side, now totally useless.

'Come on, Harry,' Chico said, giving him a kick on the ankle. 'You've got a date with some handcuffs.'

Asquith clambered reluctantly to his feet.

'And don't try anythin',' Chico said, pushing Asquith ahead of him. 'Or you'll be back on the ground again in a flash, and I won't be so bleedin' gentle next time, neither.'

We left Valance lying where he was. He was definitely a customer for the paramedics, or even the undertakers.

The remaining three of us walked down the northern side of the castle keep and through the gatehouse, now brightly lit up not only by the searchlight from above but also by several floodlights positioned on the outside.

'Put your hands up,' shouted someone through a megaphone when they saw us appear.

Asquith and Chico put theirs up and I lifted my left, while holding my right away from my body so that they could see it was empty. I was slightly disturbed to notice that Asquith's hands were now bare. He had somehow disposed of his brown leather gloves.

'Come forward over the drawbridge,' the megaphone instructed, 'then lie down, face down on the grass with your hands out in front of your heads.'

We did as asked, although I was not sure I would be able to get up again on my own.

Several shadowy figures dressed all in black approached us, their metallic machine guns glistening in the lights.

Asquith didn't hold back.

'Officers,' he shouted loudly at them, 'thank God you are here. I have been kidnapped and attacked by these two men.' Then he pointed at me. 'Watch out for that one. He's got a gun in his coat pocket.'

Mention of a gun galvanized the police into even greater action. I suddenly had three or four of them standing over me, pointing their own weapons down at me from just a few inches away.

'You are under arrest on suspicion of offences contrary to the 1968 Firearms Act,' one of them said formally. 'You do not have to say anything. But it may harm your defence if you do not mention when questioned something which you later rely on in court. Anything you do say may be given in evidence.'

Another of them grabbed my hands and roughly bent them round behind my back, securing them one above the other in stiff, painful handcuffs. The pain in my right hand was excruciating.

'It's not me you should be arresting,' I shouted at them angrily. 'It was he who shot me. Look at my right hand.'

They didn't seem to take any notice but, in fact, they handcuffed all three of us. Meanwhile, one of the other officers knelt on my back and searched through my pockets, finding first Valance's mobile phone and then the Webley revolver, which caused much excitement. Both the phone and the gun were placed carefully into an evidence plastic bag and carried away.

But Asquith wasn't finished yet.

'There's a friend of mine still lying somewhere in the castle,' he shouted. 'He's had his skull crushed by this one.' He jerked his head towards Chico. 'They are both murderers.'

'It's all right, sir,' one of the policeman said to him. 'You are now perfectly safe. We have both of them in custody.'

'Then get me out of these damn handcuffs,' Asquith demanded loudly. 'I'm the victim here, not the criminal. I have to tell you that I am a personal friend of the Chief Constable.'

I was lifted to my feet by two large policemen, one holding firmly on to each arm.

'Please don't listen to that man,' I said urgently to the one on my left. 'I don't care if he's a personal friend of the Pope, the Dalai Lama and the Archbishop of Canterbury, he's still lying. Check him for gunshot residue. Whatever he says, he is definitely the baddy here. He shot me. I only had the gun in my pocket because I managed to take it from him.'

I'm not sure if he believed me or not, probably not, but he spoke to the other officers nevertheless, and they didn't remove Asquith's handcuffs.

I turned again to the policeman on my left. 'But he was right about one thing. There is another man in the castle and he desperately needs some medical attention. I have already called for an ambulance.' I told him where to find Valance but he seemed reluctant to pass on the information.

'We have to wait here,' he said. 'Until we get the all-clear to go in from the chopper.'

'But why?' I said. 'Other than the injured man, there's no one else in there.'

'And why should I believe you?' he replied cynically, taking a firmer grip on my arm.

'Because I'm telling you the truth.'

He laughed. 'I'd be a rich man if I had a fiver for every time I've been told that by some lying villain.'

But did I really care about Valance? I suppose it might make things easier for us now if he lived, rather than if he died, but I wouldn't cry about it either way.

Several more police vehicles arrived, plus the ambulance I had called, all with a plethora of more flashing blue lights.

Quite a crowd of locals, alerted by the sound of the hovering helicopter, had turned out to watch the action, although the police were trying to get them to move further back by unrolling blue-and-white tape everywhere.

Standing among the onlookers, I could clearly see Simon Paulson, who'd only had to step outside his front door. Goodness knows what he was thinking as he watched both Harry Asquith and me being frogmarched away with our wrists firmly cuffed behind our backs and a burly policeman holding on to each of our arms.

My pair took me down the sloping path, out through the little gate at the bottom, before escorting me along the road to a police car.

'Hold on a minute,' I said. 'I need the ambulance.'

'Why?' one of them asked.

'As I've been trying to tell you, I've been shot.'

'Where?'

'In the right hand.'

Without letting go of my arms, they both leaned round my back to have a close look at my hand.

'It won't kill you,' one of them said unsympathetically. 'Get in the car. You can see the medic at the police station.'

'Please,' I said with a considerable degree of pleading. 'Please move the handcuffs round in front of my body. My hand really hurts and I really don't want to have to sit on it.'

For a moment, I thought they weren't going to, but then one of the policemen unlocked the handcuffs and moved my hands round in front of my body before securing them again with my right hand on top and my left underneath.

'No funny business, mind,' he said.

'No funny business,' I agreed. 'Thank you.'

I climbed into the back seat of the car, and in the glow from its interior light, I had my first real look at the damage. The bullet had just caught the fleshy part of my palm beneath my little finger. There was a lot of dried blood around the wound, and some of it was still oozing out, but, overall, I'd been very lucky that the bullet had missed all the bones. Just an inch or two further over and the .455 slug could have easily taken my hand off completely.

I went hot and cold at the thought of it.

As Oscar Wilde's Lady Bracknell might have said: *'To lose one hand, Mr Halley, may be regarded as a misfortune; to lose both looks like carelessness.'*

One of the policemen climbed into the back next to me, while the other one drove.

'Where are we going?' I asked as we sped past my Discovery, still parked in the town marketplace.

'North Yorkshire Police HQ. In Northallerton.'

Northallerton.

What had I recently heard about Northallerton?

I remembered. That was where the Friarage Hospital is.

'Stop the car,' I suddenly said loudly.

'Why?' asked the driver over his shoulder.

'There's another victim. Back in Leyburn Road. He also needs to go to hospital.'

The driver didn't stop but he slowed slightly.

'Who is it?' he asked.

I told them about Marcus Capes and his broken collarbone, and that he was waiting in his bedsitting room for me to arrange his journey to hospital. I didn't go into all the details of how his collarbone had become broken. There would be plenty of time for that later.

The car didn't stop but the policeman next to me used his personal radio to pass on a message that a second ambulance was needed to go to 42 Leyburn Road, Middleham.

Satisfied that I had done everything I could, I leaned my head back against the headrest and watched through the window as the lights went by. Everything would surely get sorted out just as soon as I arrived at the police headquarters.

Wouldn't it?

The most frustrating thing about being locked in a police cell is that you have no idea of what is going on elsewhere; no knowledge of what lies are being told by others and no control over if and when you can tell someone what really happened, whether or not they would believe you anyway.

When I arrived at the North Yorkshire Police Headquarters in Northallerton, I was taken into their custody suite still in handcuffs, and made to stand in front of the custody sergeant's desk.

'Reason for arrest,' he asked.

The policeman on my right answered him. 'Being found in possession of a firearm in contravention of Section 5 of the Firearms Act 1968.'

The custody sergeant tapped the information into his computer and then he looked up at me. 'I am authorising your detention under Section 37 of the Police and Criminal Evidence Act 1984. Do you have anything to say?'

'Yes, I do,' I replied. 'I only had the gun in my pocket because I had just taken it away from the man who had used it to shoot me.' I held up my right hand as best I could in the cuffs. 'It is Harry Asquith you should be charging not me.'

'You are not being charged,' the custody sergeant replied cuttingly. 'You are only being detained for interview. You can explain everything to the interviewing officer in due course. In the meantime, I will arrange for your hand to be seen by the FME.'

'FME?' I asked.

'The Forensic Medical Examiner.'

They emptied my pockets.

My wallet, a tube of mints and my reading glasses, together with my belt and my wristwatch, were placed in a plastic tray for safe keeping. They then gave me a full pat-down search. Only when they were satisfied that I wasn't concealing any other weapons did they finally remove the handcuffs.

Next, I was photographed and fingerprinted, both my old fingers and the new ones, and then a cotton swab was scraped along the inside of my cheek to obtain a DNA profile. I didn't bother to explain to them that the DNA of my left hand would be totally different. Finally I had both hands swabbed for gunshot residue, of which I knew there would worryingly be plenty.

When all was complete, I was taken back to the desk.

'Right, put him in cell seven,' the custody sergeant said to my escort,

'Hold on a minute,' I complained. 'Don't I have the right to make a phone call?'

'No, you don't,' said the sergeant, 'but you do have the right to have one person informed that you are here.'

I asked him to inform Admiral Roland, and I gave him Charles's number. The sergeant dialled it straight away on the phone on his desk.

'And please tell him that I won't be coming back tonight to collect my dog and that, if my wife calls him, just to tell her that I've lost my phone.'

The custody sergeant raised his eyebrows a tad at that last comment, but he passed the message on to Charles nevertheless. Then he listened for a moment. 'The admiral has asked whether you want him to organize a solicitor.'

I didn't really believe I needed a solicitor because I hadn't done anything wrong. But, so far, nothing else had quite panned out as I had expected. *Better to have and not need*, I thought, *than to need and not have* – just like those pesky nuclear weapons.

'That would be great,' I said, and that message was passed on as well.

'Right,' said the sergeant, putting down his phone. 'Cell seven.'

'Where are the others?' I asked.

'Never you mind.'

And so I had been marched off unceremoniously down the corridor to cell number seven, thrust inside, and then the cell door had been slammed shut behind me with a great metallic clang.

It was no wonder that Chico had referred to prison as 'the slammer'.

If the noise was designed to intimidate the inmate, it was working.

38

After a while, maybe half an hour or so of me staring blankly at the sickly cream cell walls – I had no way of telling the actual duration – the cell door was opened again and a young woman came in. Sadly, she also brought with her one of the burly male constables, who stood on guard by the open door.

'I'm Dr Grossi,' the young woman said with a slightly detectable Italian accent. 'I've come to look at your hand.'

And about time too, I thought, but I refrained from saying so. I needed to be on good terms with this medic if she was going to stitch me up.

However, she only had to take one look before telling her chaperone that I needed to go to hospital for treatment. He, in turn, put his head out of the door and shouted some instructions down the corridor. He then returned and resumed his position on guard by the door.

'I tried to tell the custody sergeant that it was bad,' I said. 'But he wouldn't listen.'

'The damage is worse than I can repair here. You need to be seen by a plastic surgeon.'

I laughed.

'What's so funny?'

'I used to have a plastic hand.'

She looked somewhat confused so I asked her to roll up my left sleeve, revealing the ugly zigzag join on my forearm.

'The transplant was three years ago,' I said.

Dr Grossi became suddenly far more interested in my left hand than in my damaged right.

She asked me all the usual questions about how well it could feel and how strong was the grip, but then she asked something that was far more erudite.

'Does your soul inhabit your new hand yet?'

I looked at her. 'I'm not sure I know what you mean by that.'

'Do you think of it as being you? Or is it still somebody else, only attached to you?'

I thought back to what Chico had said just eleven days ago when I'd collected him from Banbury station: *You're walking around with some dead geezer's hand sewn onto your arm.* I'd told him at the time that the hand had become totally a part of me and that I didn't even think about it as being different, but that wasn't actually true.

Even when I had been fingerprinted, only an hour previously, I had looked at it as an alien being and wouldn't have been much surprised to see it wander off on its own, like Thing from the *Addams Family* movies.

'That's a very good question,' I said. 'And I'm still working on the answer.'

'I have been doing some research,' the doctor said. 'Asking transplant patients how they view their new organ, and the psychology of accepting that it is now fully part of them. Of course, it's much easier to accept for those who can't see what has been transplanted, like those receiving a new kidney or even a replacement heart. And the problems are most profound for those few people who've been given a new face. Do they become the person they now see each morning in the bathroom mirror or do they remain the person behind the mask?'

'And what's the answer?'

Now she laughed. 'There is no simple answer. Everyone is different, but I do know that those who accept a transplant as being part of them entirely do much better in the long run, at least psychologically.'

I could have easily chatted to Dr Grossi for very much longer, but she turned towards the door to go.

'I will arrange for you to go to hospital to have that wound repaired.'

'Thank you,' I said. 'Could you also arrange for me to be given some immunosuppressant drugs? I have none of my usual ones with me and I can already feel my transplant beginning to itch.'

She smiled at me. 'It's not your *transplant*, Mr Halley, it's your hand.'

It took two hours for a plastic surgeon at the Friarage Hospital to repair the damage to my right hand, all of it done under local anaesthetic with a surgically masked policeman watching every move from the far corner of the operating theatre – probably there to ensure that I didn't conceal a scalpel about my person.

When it was all over, I ended up with my repaired right hand being strapped to my upper-left chest.

'It needs to stay like that for at least the next week,' said the surgeon. 'Keeping it elevated should prevent any excessive swelling of the tissues.'

So I was, once more, single-handed, albeit, this time, on the other side.

I was then taken from the hospital back to the custody suite at police headquarters and, if I thought everything would have been sorted out by then, I was much mistaken.

'Cell seven,' said the custody sergeant to my escort as we arrived.

'When do I get to be interviewed?' I asked.

'All in good time,' he said. 'We are authorized to keep you here until nine o'clock tomorrow evening.'

'But I want to speak to a senior officer now.'

'All in good time,' the sergeant said, again unhelpfully. 'Cell seven.'

And so I ended up staring at the same sickly cream cell walls, wondering what pack of lies Harry Asquith was spinning to his chum the Chief Constable, and fearing that I might never get out of here, and certainly not in time to pick up Marina and Saskia from Heathrow at five to six on Friday afternoon.

I was finally interviewed at eleven o'clock on Thursday morning after a long, difficult, sleepless night in cell seven.

As the local anaesthetic had gradually worn off, my right hand had started throbbing mercilessly and my left hand had continued to itch because the hospital had been unable to provide my usual cocktail of all six immunosuppressant medications.

To take my mind off the pain, I had spent most of the hours thinking about what Dr Grossi had said.

How could I expect Marina to accept my new hand as a fully integrated part of me if, deep down, I didn't accept it myself?

In the glow from the ever-on light in the cell ceiling, I had found myself looking closely at this incomer, studying it, and, eventually, I started talking to it.

'So, do you want to be part of me?' I asked it. 'Or would you rather be rotting underground in a box, along with the rest of your former owner?'

Unsurprisingly, the hand didn't answer me directly, and I felt rather foolish. But the die had been cast.

My left hand and I communicated back and forth together for the rest of the night, me asking it question after question and it, point-blank, refusing to answer any of them out loud. But, in fact, it did answer them all in its own way.

It never shied away from my inquisition, never once hid from reality.

I studied the surface of my new *manus* in fine detail, noting every blemish, every crease, every wrinkle. I flexed the fingers straight and then curled them into a fist, and I rotated the thumb, marvelling at how the skin so readily stretched and relaxed. I also noticed a tiny white scar at the base of the wrist and wondered how it had come about.

By the time the small, high-up cell window turned from dark to light with the coming of the dawn, my hand and I were far better acquainted than we had ever been, with a much stronger mental bond, at least on my side.

A while later, the door of the cell was opened and a young uniformed policeman brought in a cup of tea and a toasted bacon sandwich for my breakfast.

'Thanks,' I said. 'What's the time?'

'Seven o'clock,' he replied.

There seemed no point in asking him anything else. I would simply have to wait.

'I've put tomato ketchup in the sandwich,' he said. 'I hope that's okay.'

'Lovely.'

He went out and slammed the door shut again.

I drank the tea and ate the sandwich, the tomato ketchup oozing out of the sides as I bit into it. I stopped eating and stared at the escaped droplets of bright-red sauce and, for the first time in the three years since I'd received them, I licked my left fingers clean.

It was a moment of true awakening and it almost had me in tears.

'Mr Halley, we would like you to unlock your mobile phone.'

I was sitting at a table in a brightly lit interview room with two plain-clothes detective constables sitting opposite, one of whom had just spoken.

They had already dealt with the usual introductions for the audio and video recordings, and I had been cautioned once again.

On my side of the table, next to me, was a solicitor, Geoffrey Swaby from Leeds, the one organized by Charles.

Geoffrey and I had met briefly before the interview had started. He advised me to say nothing and reply 'no comment' to every question asked, other than to give my name.

'But that makes me look guilty.'

'It's still the best policy.'

I didn't agree, not in this particular case,

I looked down at the mobile phone the policeman had put in front of me.

'That's not my phone,' I said.

Geoffrey Swaby coughed, but I ignored him.

'It was the phone found in your coat pocket when you were arrested,' said one of the detectives in a rather condescending tone.

'As may be,' I said. 'But that one belongs to Anton Valance. I took it from him last night. He is the man who was injured in Middleham Castle. It can be unlocked by using the index fingerprint of his right hand.'

The two detectives looked at each other and then back at me.

'So where is your phone?'

'Last time I saw it, it was lying on the floor of the storeroom in the wooden building inside the castle entrance.'

One of the detectives stood up and went out of the room.

After a minute or two he returned and placed a second phone on the table in front of me.

'Is that one yours?' he asked.

Geoffrey Swaby touched my leg under the table and fractionally shook his head.

'It looks like mine,' I said, again ignoring him.

I noticed that the phone's screen now had a crack right across the middle, probably caused by me having thrown it across the storeroom towards where Asquith had been standing with his gun.

'Please unlock the phone,' the detective asked.

I leaned forward and touched it. It immediately lit up with my home page of a photo of Marina and Saskia that I had taken the previous Christmas. I was relieved to see that its trip across the storeroom didn't appear to have broken anything other than the screen.

I entered my four-digit unlocking code.

The detective leaned forward to take the phone back but I snatched it up.

'Mr Halley,' he said, angrily. 'Give me the phone.'

'In a minute,' I replied. 'I want you to listen to something first.'

The two detectives weren't happy but I ignored them and pressed 'play' on the voice memo page, also turning up the volume.

'Good evening, gentlemen.' My voice emanated from the phone's speaker in a rather high metallic tone. 'I think it is high time the three of us had a little talk.'

I put the phone back down on the table, as the ten-minute-long recording of the conversation between Asquith, Valance and myself in the storeroom played back.

Everything was there, including Harry Asquith's voice proudly describing the mark four Webley revolver as his great-grandfather's Boer War officer's sidearm and how a .455 bullet fired from it would take my head clean off my shoulders, right up to the point when I had pulled over the stack of boxes with a crash and Asquith had fired the first shot. There was even a small bonus exchange between the two of them, occurring after I had escaped out of the door.

'What do we do now?' Valance had asked.

'First we find him and then we kill him,' Asquith had said quite clearly. 'Get the torches.'

The two could be heard leaving the storeroom, and then all went quiet.

In the silence, I leaned forward and switched off the playback.

The audio file on my phone seemed to change everything. Suddenly, the police couldn't be more helpful, even if they weren't being exactly apologetic.

The two detectives halted the interview and they both went out of the room taking my phone with them, as they left me alone with Geoffrey Swaby, the solicitor.

'Well, that's a first,' he said. 'Looks like you don't need me after all.'

He put his leather-covered notebook back into his briefcase.

'I'm sorry that you've made a wasted journey,' I said.

'Don't be. I wouldn't have missed that for the world.' He laughed. 'Did you see the look on their faces when that last bit played? Absolutely priceless.'

After about fifteen minutes the pair of detectives returned and I was taken back to be presented in front of the custody sergeant – a different one from the previous evening – to be de-arrested.

'What does de-arrested actually mean?' I asked.

'In the light of new evidence emerging,' the sergeant explained, 'there are no grounds for having made the original arrest, so you are now being de-arrested. It is as if the original arrest did not occur.'

'But it did occur,' I pointed out. 'So are you now admitting you made a mistake?'

'Given the circumstances known at the time, the arrest was a reasonable course of action.'

There was no hope that he would ever admit that they had been somewhat hasty.

'How about Mr Barnes?' I asked. 'Has he been de-arrested too?'

'You will have to discuss that with the SIO in the case.'

'SIO?'

'The Senior Investigating Officer.'

'And who is that?' I asked patiently.

'Detective Chief Inspector Williams. He's waiting to speak to you.'

This could be interesting, I thought. He was the man I had spoken with in Gary Bremner's garden, the one who had explicitly told me to leave all the investigating to the police. Hence, I wasn't particularly looking forward to seeing him again, and I don't think he was particularly pleased to see me either.

I was taken to another interview room in Northallerton Police HQ.

The chief inspector had one of the detectives from the previous interview sitting beside him and he informed me that the interview was being recorded.

Recordings are good, I thought.

'What were you doing in Middleham Castle in the first place?' the chief inspector asked as his opening gambit.

'I was there investigating something,' I replied.

'What?'

'The death of Gary Bremner.'

DCI Williams snorted slightly. 'I thought I had told you to leave the investigation of Mr Bremner's death to the police.'

'I know, but you think it was a suicide while I believe he was murdered. So we are starting from different places. Did you even check his phone for fingerprints?'

He clearly didn't like being asked if he'd done his job.

'We did, and there were no fingerprints found on the phone.'

'Not even Gary's?' I asked.

'None at all,' he replied.

'But surely that is highly suspicious in itself. Why would Gary bother to wipe it clean after typing in a suicide note? How about DNA?'

'There was also no DNA present on the phone.'

I just sat there looking at him.

'Okay, Mr Halley,' he said eventually. 'Tell me what you have found out.'

'All right,' I said. 'But tell me about the others first. Where is Chico Barnes?'

'Mr Barnes has been arrested on suspicion of causing grievous bodily harm.'

At least that told me that Valance was still alive.

'And will he now be de-arrested?' I asked.

'That may depend on what you tell me.'

'And how about Harry Asquith? Is he under arrest?'

'He is helping us with our enquiries.'

I laughed. 'And what does that mean exactly?'

He smiled. 'He is trying to explain how his family has kept possession of a Boer War officer's sidearm for more than the past hundred and twenty years.'

'So you now know that it is definitely his?'

'Oh, yes. It seems that Mr Asquith has not been very discreet to his family about his ownership of the weapon. He told his wife that he was allowed to have it because it was an antique firearm manufactured before 1919.'

'And was he allowed to have it?'

'Not without a firearms certificate, which he hasn't got.'

'He tried to kill me with it.'

'Yes. Tell me about that.'

I went through the details of all that had happened in the castle – my escape from the storeroom, the manhunt through the ruins and the way that Chico and I had turned the tables from hunted to hunters. I stressed that Chico had only used appropriate force to neutralize Valance.

'And why, exactly, were you in that storeroom in the first place?'

What did I say? I would have to give him some details.

'I thought I was going there simply to have a chat to Asquith and Valance about certain things in horse racing. I have my suspicions that they have been trying to manipulate some of the results.'

He would have known that from listening to the recording, but he seemed far less interested in the details of any race fixing than in the violent goings-on, both in the castle and at number 42 Leyburn Road.

'Tell me about Marcus Capes,' said the chief inspector.

'What about him?'

'How is he involved in this?'

'He's a young conditional jockey who Valance has attempted to blackmail into losing races.'

'So why did he need to go to hospital?'

'Because he wouldn't do what they told him to, so Valance broke his collarbone with a baseball bat, or rather his two goons did.'

'Goons?'

I explained how Valance had two hired musclemen to do his dirty work. I also told him about the two occasions I had come across them, at Catterick races and at my home, and that he could check with Thames Valley Police about the second.

'Chico Barnes has a picture of their car, including the registration number. He watched them leave Middleham before we went to the castle. And their phone number is in Valance's phone.'

He wrote it all down.

'Thank you, Mr Halley. Is there anything else you would like to tell me?'

'I don't think so,' I said.

Jimmy Shilstone and Simon Paulson would have to take their chances.

39

On Friday afternoon I was at Heathrow in good time to collect Marina and Saskia, in fact I was ridiculously early, and for no other reason than waiting at home was not an option. I had also given myself a huge leeway just in case of a breakdown, a puncture, a hold-up due to bad Friday-afternoon traffic on the M25, or any other unforeseen mishap.

Hence, I arrived at London airport well before their flight had even taken off from Amsterdam. But I didn't care, I was so excited, but also maybe a touch frightened. How would Marina react? Would she greet me warmly and lovingly, or in the same rather distant manner with which she had left me exactly two weeks ago – two weeks in which much had happened to both of us?

I parked the Discovery in the short-term car park and then waited in the café in the International Arrivals hall of Terminal 5, drinking coffee and thinking back to events over the past forty-eight hours.

Chico hadn't been de-arrested, as I'd hoped, but he had been released under investigation. The police were clearly hedging their bets over whether he had used appropriate or excessive force in fracturing Anton Valance's skull. Much depended, it appeared, on when, or even if, he would ever regain consciousness.

It seems that, on Wednesday evening, after the helicopter had finally given the all-clear for paramedics to enter the castle, Valance had been taken by ambulance to the large hospital in Darlington, where they had a neurosurgical department, while Marcus had gone in another one to the smaller Friarage for his collarbone x-ray.

Valance's two goons had been traced from Chico's photograph of the registration number of their car and they, too, were now helping the police with their enquiries concerning the breaking of Marcus's collarbone and several other matters, not least the fact that automatic number-plate recognition cameras had shown their car in Middleham marketplace not only on the night of the fire at Gary Bremner's stable yard, but also on the day his body had been discovered hanging from a tree.

For the umpteenth time I checked the arrivals board.

British Airways flight number 433 from Amsterdam, scheduled to arrive at 17.55, was described as being ON TIME. But, as I looked at it, it changed from reading ON TIME to EXPECTED 17.52.

I knew from experience that a change from ON TIME to EXPECTED meant that the flight had now taken off from Schiphol Airport in Amsterdam and was on its way south-west, on the short hop over the North Sea. And it would be arriving three minutes early.

My excitement level, and also my fear and trepidation, rose a notch or two.

Chico and I had finally left the police headquarters in Northallerton at about three-thirty on Thursday afternoon. We were taken back to Middleham in a police car to collect my Discovery, this time with me sitting in the front seat.

Before then, we had both been asked, once more, to go through everything we could remember concerning the events of Wednesday afternoon and evening, and one of the detective constables had written it all down.

The statement had then been typed up and presented for our signatures.

'Sorry,' I'd said. 'I can't. I'm right-handed.'

The constable had looked at my right hand and arm, still strapped to my chest.

'Then you'll have to sign it with your left hand.'

I'd had a few practices on a spare sheet of paper until it had looked less like the squiggles of a three-year-old, and I could just about discern the words 'Sid' and 'Halley' among the scribble.

And signing wasn't the only thing I had to do left-handed – in fact, I'd had to do everything left-handed – and it made me appreciate my new hand more than ever.

By the end of Thursday, I was really beginning to understand what Dr Grossi had been on about. Whereas it had taken the best part of three years for movement and sensation to creep slowly up through my hand and into my fingers, within the previous twenty-four hours I felt my soul had galloped up my forearm to encompass my very fingertips, and it had made me chuckle.

'What are you bleedin' laughin' about?' Chico said to me as I drove the Discovery, left-handed, out of Middleham, thankful for it being an automatic. 'You're all right, Jack. They let you off, but I'm technically still under arrest.'

'I'm sure you won't be for long,' I said confidently. 'After all, they did let you go. If they really thought you'd done something wrong, they'd have surely kept you in and put you up before a magistrate.'

'It's funny, really,' he said. 'I don't know whether I want Valance to die or not. After what you told me about him tellin' Asquith to kill you, it don't make any difference to me either way.'

'But it might make things easier for you if he recovers. Inquests can be fraught with danger.'

As I'd driven southwards, I had remembered back to the inquest into the fiery death of the Irish terrorist and the extremely hard time I'd been given in the witness box by a barrister acting for his widow, even though it had been he who had been trying to kill my family and me in the first place. Fortunately, the coroner had seen right through the smokescreen the lawyer had been trying to lay down and had concluded that the death was due to the unintended outcome of the deceased's own actions.

I ordered myself another cup of coffee from the airport café and checked again that the arrival board still said EXPECTED 17.52.

Just half an hour to go now, I thought. I could imagine Marina and Saskia sitting side by side on the aircraft and I just hoped they were both as excited about the prospect of being reunited with me as I was with them.

Chico and I hadn't arrived back at Aynsford to collect Rosie until after eight o'clock on Thursday evening due to heavy traffic around Leeds on the M1, by which time Charles had clearly had quite enough of dog-sitting. He hadn't even invited us in for a whisky, merely handing over his charge with her bed at the front door.

'I wouldn't mind if she just lay down and slept. It's all this going outside and then immediately wanting to come back in again that I can't stand.'

'You won't have to look after her again,' I'd promised. 'At least, not for a while.'

'I was worried when I received that call yesterday from the police that I might be keeping your dog for good.' He had laughed nervously. 'So, is everything now sorted?'

'Yes, all sorted. The bad guys have been neutralized and racing is saved.' I laughed, perhaps at the release of tension I felt. 'Maybe I'll tell you all about it over the weekend, but I must get back home now and tidy up. Marina is coming back tomorrow.'

'Yes, I know. She called me this morning when she couldn't get hold of you last night.'

'What did you tell her?' I'd asked with concern.

Charles had just moved his thumb and forefinger across his lips as if zipping them shut. Then he'd gone back into his house and closed the door, no doubt to pour himself a stiff single malt.

Perhaps I would have liked one too.

At twenty to six, the airport arrivals board suddenly changed to EXPECTED 17.57, so instead of getting here three minutes early, the Amsterdam flight was now due to arrive two minutes late.

Quite unreasonably, I felt cheated out of five minutes of my life.

Chico and I had spent the night in Nutwell, this time with

Chico sleeping soundly, properly tucked up in a comfy bed rather than sitting on guard in the kitchen with Charles's shotgun.

I, meanwhile, had spent much of a second consecutive night lying awake. Somehow, the shock of being shot at, and hit, had driven up my adrenaline level to such a peak that sleep wouldn't come no matter how many sheep I tried to count. And the continued throbbing in my right hand didn't help either.

At least my left hand had settled down after a proper dose of my immunosuppressants but, as always, there was a fine balance to be found: how to take enough of the drugs to stop my body attacking the alien tissue on my left while leaving enough natural resistance to fight off any infection in my damaged right. Only the next few days would determine if I had the balance right.

I always think that International Arrivals halls at airports are such happy places, with far-flung friends and relations reuniting after long periods apart.

I watched as a family of two parents and three small children were greeted excitedly by grandparents, while a young couple embraced passionately, the man lifting his newly arrived girlfriend off her feet and swinging her around in unbridled joy.

As 17.57 got closer and closer, I dreamed of such a reunion with Marina, constantly worrying that the reality might be frosty, even hostile.

Time seemed to almost stand still as I counted out the seconds, urging the digital clock on the arrivals board to click over the minutes.

The expected arrival time came and went and still the board didn't change.

Had something gone wrong? Had the flight been diverted, or maybe worse? Had it ploughed into the ground short of the runway?

Finally, at 18.02, the EXPECTED 17.57 changed to LANDED 18.00.

I breathed a huge sigh of relief and laughed at myself for being so dramatic.

Of course everything was all right. Marina and Saskia were here, safely on the ground at Heathrow.

Earlier, I had taken Chico to Banbury, for him to catch a train back to London.

'Why don't you wait and see Marina?'

'Thanks, but no thanks. You two need to sort this out between yourselves. You don't want me hangin' about, clutterin' up the place and sayin' somethin' bleedin' stupid.'

I wasn't sure I agreed with him. Just as with my dealings with Valance and Asquith, I thought I might need some reinforcements, but perhaps he was right after all.

'Anyway,' Chico had said, 'I've arranged to see Ingrid again tonight.'

I had looked across at him, but he'd just stared ahead at the road, saying nothing more.

LANDED 18.00 changed to ARRIVED 18.07, which I knew meant the aircraft was now parked at the gate.

I could imagine Marina and Saskia standing up from their seats, collecting their coats and stuff, and waiting to disembark, just a few yards away from where I was sitting, on the other side of the building.

My fear and trepidation levels began to outstrip the excitement.

I forced myself to calm down.

Detective Chief Inspector Williams had given me a business card with his personal mobile phone number, and I had called him at lunchtime, before I had departed for the airport.

'How goes it?' I'd asked him.

'Pretty well,' he'd replied. 'Asquith has been charged with several firearms offences and we've been given more time to question him concerning wounding with intent and attempted murder.'

'So he's still in custody?'

'Oh, yes. And, if the Crown Prosecution Service give the go-ahead to charge him with the other things, as I think they will, he'll probably be remanded to prison.'

'Probably?'

'He would only be granted bail if a judge at the Crown Court is satisfied that he is not at risk of causing physical or mental harm to himself or anyone else and, after what you told me about him wanting to kill himself prior to his arrest, that is most unlikely.'

'How about the goons?' I'd asked.

He'd laughed. 'You mean the Sefton brothers. I threatened them both with a charge of murder over Gary Bremner's death. They weren't to know that we didn't have any forensic evidence. In fact, we had no evidence at all other than some circumstantial ANPR records. But they're singing like canaries, blaming Valance for everything in an attempt to save their own skins.' He'd laughed again. 'So much for honour among thieves.'

'So will they be charged with Gary's murder?'

'Unlikely, I'd say. I reckon the CPS will say we don't have enough.

We might just get a grievous bodily harm charge through for Marcus Capes's collarbone, but even that's not certain. It's just his word against theirs, and it seems that Capes also told his employer it was due to him falling off a horse.'

That might have been my fault, I thought.

'How about Valance?'

'Still in hospital. He had more surgery yesterday evening to relieve the pressure on his brain. He's expected to survive but none of the doctors will commit on how well he might be in the long run.'

'Has he been arrested?'

'Not yet, but he will be if he recovers enough.'

'What about Chico Barnes? He's still technically under arrest.'

'It will be up to the CPS to decide if he's charged, but we're not pushing for it.'

The board changed from ARRIVED 18.07 TO BAGGAGE IN HALL.

I stared at the wall right in front of me with INTERNATIONAL ARRIVALS written on it in huge black letters. Marina would be just the other side of that wall, collecting her checked suitcase from the carousel.

My heart rate climbed and I couldn't stay still. It was just like the feeling I had experienced in the minutes before leaving the weighing room to go out and ride in the Grand National – a combination of excitement and nerves, mixed together with a hefty dose of fear.

I went over and stood next to the chrome rail so I wouldn't miss them.

There are two exits from the Terminal 5 baggage hall, one at each end, and I must have looked like a manic tennis fan at Wimbledon, with my head continually switching from one side to the other as if following the ball, checking each exit every few seconds with eagerness and anticipation.

As people came past me, pushing their laden luggage trolleys, I tried in vain to read their baggage labels to see if they had arrived on the Amsterdam flight.

And then, quite suddenly, Marina and Saskia were in sight, coming out of the left-hand exit among a large gaggle of other passengers.

I ducked under the chrome rail and went forward to meet them, my heart in my mouth.

It was Sassy who saw me first and she ran forward, giving me a tight hug around my waist. But I kept my eyes fixed on Marina, trying to read her body language.

She smiled at me and I could see that there were tears in her eyes.

She gave me a hug and I winced. She pulled back.

'What have you done to yourself?' she asked with concern.

'Nothing much. It's just a scratch,' I said, playing it down. 'I just have to have my right hand strapped to my chest for the next week to prevent any swelling.'

She looked worried. 'But how can you drive?'

I smiled at her. 'I have another hand, remember. I use that.'

We went outside and took the lift up to the car park. I put the ticket into the payment machine and paid the parking charge.

'I would offer to drive,' Marina said. 'But I had a couple of glasses of champagne at Schiphol and another on the flight.'

I wondered if it had been, appropriately, for Dutch courage.

'It's okay,' I said. 'I'll be fine. I'm used to it by now. I drove all the way home from Yorkshire left-handed yesterday afternoon.'

She looked across at me, but remained silent as I unlocked the Discovery and lifted her suitcase, left-handed, into the boot.

'I spoke to Charles yesterday morning,' she said when we were all safely strapped in, with Saskia on her booster seat in the back, and I had backed out of the parking space.

'I know,' I replied. 'He told me.'

'Oh.' She seemed surprised. 'What did he say?'

'Only that you'd called him. He wouldn't tell me what you'd said.'

Marina sighed slightly. 'I didn't really say much. In fact, he did most of the talking.'

I glanced across at her but she was now determinedly looking straight forward through the windscreen as we exited the car park.

Only when we had left the airport and were already on the M25 did I speak again.

'How is your dad doing today?' I asked.

Marina didn't answer immediately but briefly glanced back at Saskia sitting behind me.

'She's asleep.'

Sassy had always slept easily in the car. Indeed, as a baby, we had often had to take her out for a drive as the only way to get her to go to sleep.

'He was a little better this morning but . . . It's still only a matter of time. His heart is packing up.'

I glanced over to her and there were more tears in her eyes.

'I'm so sorry.'

I drove on in silence again as we joined the M40 westbound towards home.

As we passed High Wycombe, Marina turned in her seat to face me.

'Charles told me all about what you have been doing.'

'It's finished,' I said quickly. 'It's done and dusted.'

'But only until the next time someone asks for your help to sort out some wrongdoing in racing.'

It was now my time to stare resolutely out through the windscreen. She was right. I couldn't change my spots.

I drove through the Chiltern Hills cutting at Stokenchurch and on across the Thames Valley towards Oxford before the motorway turned north towards Banbury.

'I've missed you,' Marina said.

I went on staring directly forward.

'And I've missed not being there when you needed me. If only to look after Rosie.'

It broke the tension and I laughed.

'So Charles told you about that too.'

'Where is she now?'

'I left her at home. I thought about bringing her with me but Heathrow don't allow dogs in the terminals, except guide dogs, and I didn't want to leave her in the car park. I fed her early before I left. I also told her that you and Sassy were coming home, and she was very excited about that.'

Maybe more excited than me.

I drove on again in silence for a while, past the Bicester junction and on towards the motorway exit to home.

'I love you, Sid Halley,' Marina said, quietly but distinctly.

Now there were tears in my eyes. I blinked them away to see the road.

'I love you more, Marina Halley . . . so much more,' I said. 'And things can be different. I think we should move nearer to London so you can come home every night. And we can also go to the theatre and do the other stuff you love. I've already been looking at some houses on estate-agent websites.'

'Maybe,' she said.

Then she did something that had me in pieces.

She reached across and stroked the back of my left hand on the steering wheel.

'I'll just have to learn to love this as much as I love the rest of you.'

I couldn't speak and the tears were rolling down my cheeks. She moved her hand and wiped them away for me with her fingers.

I was so overcome and distracted that I drove straight past the exit for Banbury.

Marina looked back over her shoulder.

'Surely we were meant to get off there,' she said, as I sped onwards.

'Do you want to be right, or do you want to be happy?'

She threw back her head and laughed out loud.

'I want to be happy.'

EPILOGUE

Six weeks later, Marina was back in Fryslân, and Saskia and I were there with her.

She had been back and forth several times to assist her mother, each visit causing her much stress and grief. Meanwhile, Saskia had stayed at home with me to go back to school for the Summer term.

It had been the morning before Marina had been due to come home for Sassy's half-term holiday that she had called me to say that the inevitable had finally occurred, that her father's ailing heart had finally beat its last, and he had died peacefully in his sleep.

She had been quite calm about it.

'I know it's very sad,' she said. 'But I have been hoping for weeks now that, one day, he simply wouldn't wake up, and now that has happened. Mamma has been sleeping in the spare room and she went in to him at eight o'clock with some tea, but he'd already gone.'

'How is she taking it?' I asked.

'Pretty well, I think. Over the weeks, we have all got used to the fact that he would go sometime soon. Him too. He told me yesterday that he'd had enough and was tired. Mamma's been keeping herself busy since she found him, putting up white sheets over all the windows. It's a custom round here to ward off evil spirits.'

'I'll book a flight over for Sassy and me.'

'Do you think it's wise to bring Saskia? She could go to stay with Charles. I'm sure he wouldn't mind.'

'I think she should come with me. It's going to be difficult for her either way, but she needs to be with us at a time like this.'

So I had booked two seats on the British Airways flight from Heathrow to Amsterdam for later that afternoon.

Charles had stepped up to the plate and had called, offering to look after Rosie while we were away.

'It might be for quite a few days,' I said to him. 'Are you sure?'

'Quite sure,' he said. 'I've arranged for my neighbour's son to take her for a long walk every day to try and tire her out.'

So, Saskia and I had driven to Heathrow via Aynsford to deliver Rosie and her bed, along with enough of her food for a whole week. Charles had given Sassy a big hug and said how sorry he was that Opa had died.

'He isn't dead, Grandpa. He's just gone to Heaven. Like Tilly.'

The flight had been uneventful and I had booked a rental car at Schiphol.

Saskia had slept most of the hour-and-a-half drive from the airport to Fryslân, while I thought about what had happened during the last six weeks.

Anton Valance had finally recovered consciousness but was far from right due to having had a massive bleed on his brain.

'It's like he's had a really bad stroke,' Detective Chief Inspector Williams had said to me on the phone. 'And there's no guarantee he will ever be well enough to be charged with any crime.'

Henry – *call me Harry* – Asquith, meanwhile, had been charged, both with wounding with intent and with attempted murder, and he had been remanded in custody, awaiting trial.

I wondered what young Henry Payne made of that.

'How about Chico?' I'd asked the DCI.

'It's not official yet but I understand that no further action will be taken against Mr Barnes.'

Chico had been delighted to hear it when I'd called him.

On the second Saturday in May, I had taken Saskia with me to Haydock Park races and we watched together from the grandstands as Marcus Capes rode a perfect race on Meeru to win the Swinton Handicap Hurdle by half a length.

Being young and healthy, his collarbone had healed very quickly but, even so, he had only been passed fit to ride on the morning of the race.

But it had been worth the long journey north just to see him accompany Meeru into the place reserved for the winner, this time with a carefree and unambiguous broad grin on his face.

The week before, Marcus had come with me to see Toby Jing of the BHA Integrity Department in London, to help me lay some of the facts of Asquith's and Valance's race-fixing plan before the authority.

No further copies of Valance's video of Marcus counting money had surfaced so we had decided to gloss over those particular details. However, we did emphasize that Valance had broken Marcus's collarbone because he, Marcus, hadn't been prepared to lose to Asquith's orders.

I think that Toby had probably been aware that we knew more than we were saying but, short of him applying the thumbscrews, we weren't telling. But we still gave him enough to ensure that, whatever happened to future recovery or criminal trials, both Asquith and Valance would be declared unfit to be licensed under BHA regulations as an owner or a jockeys' agent, or as anything else for that matter.

'Have you heard of any trainers being asked to pay a premium to jockeys' agents?' I had asked Toby casually, as I stood up to leave.

'I've heard a few rumours.'

'And what is the BHA doing about it?'

'The financial arrangements between a jockey and his or her agent are not the concern of the Authority.'

'Even if pre-booked jockeys are being threatened by the agent into not turning up to ride a horse because the trainer won't pay the premium?'

He had looked up at me sharply. 'Have you any evidence of that?'

I did have evidence, but I was wary of giving it to him. If I knew the BHA, and I did, they would go after the jockeys first, rather than the agents.

'Nothing concrete,' I'd said vaguely. 'But perhaps the Authority should issue a notice to all jockeys' agents reminding them that, in order to keep their licences, there is a requirement for them to be considered as a fit and proper person, and that would be inconsistent with them extorting money from trainers.'

He had nodded. 'I'll discuss it with the chairman.'

It was the best I could hope for.

I had purposely not mentioned anything to Toby about Jimmy Shilstone's or Simon Paulson's involvement in any wrongdoing.

Jimmy, meanwhile, hadn't exactly helped the situation by having had a sudden attack of a guilty conscience. He had turned himself in to the police for having had sex with a minor, only for them to find out from the Passport Office that Valance had doctored the copy of the girl's passport, changing the 1 at the end of her birth year to a 4.

The girl had been telling the truth. She had, indeed, been eighteen.

As there had been no complaint, and no crime, the police had simply told Jimmy to go away and stop wasting their time. I hadn't heard what his girlfriend had said, that's if she had even known.

Between her trips to Fryslân, Marina and I had discussed our future.

We had even been to look at two houses for sale in Gerrards Cross – close enough to London for an easy commute but not so close that they were prohibitively expensive – but both of us had slightly baulked at the prospect of moving somewhere that felt so urban and constrictive after the expansive green spaces of Nutwell village and West Oxfordshire.

'We'll just have to make it work,' Marina had said. 'I will commute each day from Banbury, if that's the only solution.'

I wasn't sure if it was the *only* solution, but I felt it was a much better plan than her spending half of each week staying with Samantha, with her constantly encouraging Marina to leave Sid.

Dutch law states that the funeral must be held between 36 hours and five days after a death.

In our case it was four days.

Elmo came again from New York and we all gathered at the crematorium in Groningen, not far from Marina's parents' house.

'Mamma would have preferred him to be buried,' Marina said to me as we arrived. 'But there's so little room in the Netherlands that you have to lease a cemetery plot, and then only for twenty years. After that, the council dig up your remains and reuse the space.'

Practical, I thought, *but not very reassuring for the family.*

The funeral service was brief, mostly in Dutch but also with parts of it in English, for Saskia's and my benefit. At the end, the mourners were invited back to the house for some traditional fare of coffee and cake. And then there were tears from us all as we departed the chapel to the strains of 'Time to Say Goodbye' sung by Andrea Bocelli and Sarah Brightman.

Saskia went out first, between her grandmother and uncle, while Marina and I followed behind them, walking hand in hand – her right in my left.